D1575934

PSALM AT JOURNEY'S END

FARRAR STRAUS GIROUX

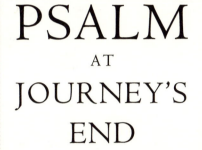

PSALM

AT

JOURNEY'S
END

ERIK FOSNES

HANSEN

TRANSLATED BY JOAN TATE

FARRAR, STRAUS AND GIROUX

New York

Translation copyright © 1996 by Joan Tate
All rights reserved
Originally published in Norwegian under the title *Salme ved reisens slutt*,
copyright © 1990 by J. W. Cappelens Forlag a•s
Printed in the United States of America
Published simultaneously in Canada by HarperCollins*CanadaLtd*
Designed by Fritz Metsch
First edition, 1996

LIBRARY OF CONGRESS CATALOGING-IN-PUBLICATION DATA
Hansen, Erik Fosnes.
[Salme ved reisens slutt. English]
Psalm at journey's end / Erik Fosnes Hansen ; translated by Joan
Tate.
p. cm.
I. Tate, Joan. II. Title.
PT8951.18.A569S25 1996   839.8'2374—dc20   96-33811   CIP

A te Katerina, perché ci sei

CONTENTS

Harfenspieler

Wer nie sein Brot mit Tränen aß,
Wer nie die kummervollen Nächte
Auf seinem Bette weinend saß,
Der kennt euch nicht, ihr himmlischen Mächte.

Ihr führt ins Leben uns hinein,
Ihr laßt den Armen schuldig werden,
Dann überlaßt ihr ihn der Pein:
Denn alle Schuld rächt sich auf Erden.
—J. W. GOETHE

Harp Player

He who has never eaten his bread with tears,
he who has never, through nights of anguish,
sat weeping on his bed—such a man does not
know you, you heavenly Powers.

You lead us into life, and by your will,
poor wretches, we fall into sin,
and then are delivered over to suffering:
for on earth there is retribution for every guilt.

PSALM AT JOURNEY'S END

SHIP'S BAND ON BOARD

RMS *TITANIC*

April 10–15, 1912

Jason Coward—bandmaster . . . . London
Alexander Byezhnikov—first violin . . . . St. Petersburg
James Reel—viola . . . . Dublin
Georges Donner—cello . . . . Paris
David Bleiernstern—second violin . . . . Vienna
Petronius Witt—double bass . . . . Rome
"Spot" Hauptmann—piano . . . . Unknown

The centuries flow on, a slow river of resonances and images.
Faces and cities pass by.
Some images are whole and clear, others dissolve as if in mist.
Every era has its images and its sounds.

There are times echoing of hymns, of notes rising
beneath stone vaultings, but also sounds of iron,
of fiery cries or mumbling that is quiet weeping. Slowly,
they glide on, a river of ice floes.

And you cannot catch them.
They are almost secret images of dreams; lost
icons from alien days and faces painted in old
colors. All eras have their images, and their sounds.

It is like a poem that has been forgotten.

And he said, Let me go, for the day breaketh.
And he said, I will not let thee go,
except thou bless me.

—GENESIS 32:26

———◆◆❈◆◆———

H E walked out through the front door and into the morning.

There's something special, he thought, about walking through these quiet morning streets, alone, in farewell, in transit, always in transit. It is still early. You can still hear the echo of your own footsteps on the pavement. The sun is not yet up.

The street slopes down toward the Thames. You have a small suitcase in your hand and a violin case under your arm. Everything. And walking is easy. As you turn the corner, you will see the sky in the east.

He walked. All around him were buildings; they were light at daybreak, transparent, almost hovering, the dawn light on the road between the rows of houses, blue as it can be only in April, impossible to catch, like an unknown interval. Not many people were out that early, a few stray birds, a street vendor or two with their carts, some early-morning walkers, himself. Footsteps on stone. Faces as transparent as the city in this light. My face is like that, too, he thought.

He had soon reached the corner.

He knew: Today I have gotten up and left the boardinghouse. The sheets had been damp and grubby. Just another lodging, another bed you'll never sleep in again. Ahead of you lies everything that you do not know. It has been like that for a long time. There have been many mornings and quiet streets like this, for many seasons, walking through cities, seeing the way people live, their clothes and bedding dried by the night, hanging there waiting on lines. They are asleep behind the windows, the children, the women, the men. If you make an effort you can almost hear them breathing. You know. But you do not understand. It's not yours. That has never been for you. That

7

used to make you angry or afraid, making you say terrible things or run away. It is no longer like that. You see nothing but your own enigma; that just makes you sad and happy.

He stood still for a moment: It is like a mirror.

Then he turned the corner. There was the Thames, colorless and calm, thin mist drifting in the middle, the sky full of that secretive blue light, but red in the east. He stopped on the corner to look. This was his river. He had grown up by the Thames and knew its colors, sounds, and smells. He knew: It is good to have been a child by a great river.

The sun rose. He put down his suitcase and violin and watched everything slowly changing, contours sharpening and deepening, the river acquiring colors.

He looked at the redness for a while.

⚜

"It should be a little to the right below the sun."

His father's voice.

"Will it be long?" That is his own voice, light, curious, a very long time ago, when he was ten. It all seems far, far away, and yet now it is coming closer.

"Only another five minutes." His father looks at his watch. What did it say? It was the venerable gold watch his father always wore, with its lid and monogram, and it was always right.

"What's the time?" His own voice again.

"Five forty-seven and a half." Yes. So the time is right. His father peers at his watch. Then he puts the smoked-glass disk in the slot at the top lens of the telescope, so he can look straight into the sun without harming his eyes. It is a summer morning out on a meadow, a smell of grass and clover, the birds just beginning to sing. He and his father, and the dog, have taken two hours to get there, to see the transit of Venus. The sun is still reddish, but coming up fast now.

"There we are. Now you can look and get it in focus." With awkward hands, which have nevertheless learned what they have to do and will soon be able to do this on their own, with chilly white child-hands, he focuses on the sun, turning the knobs and adjusting the telescope into the right position. Then he peers into the eyepiece, focuses, and adjusts. His father looks at his watch. It is right.

"Five forty-eight and forty-five seconds. Can you see anything, Jason?" Jason looks. The disk of the sun, brownish-golden through the smoked glass, seems to fill his whole field of vision, and it takes a few seconds to get used to it, but then he sees little flickering hairlines and some small brown spots on the sun.

"Father! I can see sunspots. And porminences!"

"*Pro*minences."

"Yes!"

"May I look?"

"Yes!"

His father looks, then makes way for Jason again. He takes out his watch, his doctor's watch.

"It should be there soon. In one minute, thirty-five seconds. Watch carefully now. Down at the bottom, on the right. She'll be quite different from the sunspots."

As he stands there, the adult Jason sees this picture inside him, distant, close—as if through a telescope—he knows his father's watch was right. That had been the only really right time.

"Only a second or two more now."

The sun is already beginning to glide across the lens, rising and moving up and away, away from the horizon.

"It needs adjusting, Papa."

"We can wait until the planet is in front of the sun. You ought to be able to see it now."

The sun is like a fiery brazier in all that blackness, and there, yes, there it is, in the right-hand corner, a round spot creeping across the surface of the sun, quite clearly a small sphere, perfectly circular, and no sunspot.

"I can see it now!" That light voice. The fragrance of the meadow.

"Are you sure? Let me look and I'll adjust it at the same time." His father focuses, then exclaims: "Ah, there it is." Jason can hardly stand still. This is his first transit of Venus. They have been waiting through weeks of cloudy weather, nervously, anxiously—the transit of Venus is a rare sight, as his father says. What if the clouds don't lift on Sunday? But the clouds had vanished the evening before. His father adjusts the telescope so that Jason can see again. The planet has already gone a good way across the surface of the sun and will soon pass the center.

"Rare sight," exclaims Jason gently, and his father laughs loudly.

It is soon over. Soon Venus has passed. They trudge along a country road full of muddy puddles to the inn where they are to have breakfast, his father carrying the telescope, Jason the stand. It is heavy, so they walk slowly.

The rumble of his father's voice:

". . . and because of the parallax, two observers will have slightly different results, so the distance to Venus can be calculated with the aid of trigonometry. But not only that. According to Kepler's Law, as soon as the distance between earth and Venus is known, the distance between all the other planets can be calculated. You see, the square of the circulation time is proportional to the power of three of the average distance to . . ."

It was like a song.

They meet two other amateur astronomers at the inn, and the conversation flows over eggs, toast, marmalade, and tea. Jason catches just fragments. One of the strangers is so enthusiastic, bits of egg and tea get caught in his beard.

"Today she has crept across the sun, the Goddess of Love."

Tea and crumbs land on the tablecloth.

"And how clear she was!"

"And next time?" Jason interjects. The strangers hum and haw slightly.

"There won't be a next time," his father says. "At least not for any of us sitting here."

Jason does not understand.

"But in the year 2004. She'll come back to the sun then. In a hundred and twenty years' time."

Jason turns cold at the thought. He would no longer exist then. He looks down at his hands. For a brief moment the world seems to be standing still—didn't the planets stop moving for a second? But then his father looks at his watch and it's time to catch the train.

❧

All this has stayed inside Jason. He sees it distantly, as if through celestial voids. A second. One second of the right time.

꙳

Jason straightened up. It was still crimson sunrise . . . The red light. But he didn't want to think about that now. Not that red light. So he picked up his violin and suitcase and started walking on down the street. Don't think about the rest now. Do you remember the transit of Venus? He remembered it.

꙳

Yes, but there is more. Those chilly evenings spent in that south-facing window, winter evenings of sparkling clusters of stars in the sky, the dizzy gasp inside him over the chasm between Milky Way and snow. There, on the windowsill, Jason made friends with all the planets. They had placed the telescope on the floor in front of the window, pointing out into the night.

"There, in the Twins, you can see Saturn. If the sky is clear tonight, we'll be able to see its ring." When Saturn had risen to a height just above the chimneys of the house across the street, the air was clear enough for the ring to be visible. What had been an obscure shimmering spot in the lens before was now a clear, round dot, and that dot was inside a ring. The light was even and yellow, the ring like a bridge encircling Saturn.

"It looks lonely," whispered Jason, as if afraid of disturbing the planet.

"It's a very distant planet." His father's voice was also low. "Its distance from earth is calculated at its most distant point as over a billion miles." That little gasp came inside Jason again, a small dizziness at space, incomprehensible, the void. He would often dream he was sailing through emptiness, the stars and planets all around him, and he always woke with that little gasp trembling inside him.

"And the ring, what's it made of?"

"It's really two rings. But our instrument isn't good enough to tell them apart. If the light from the planet is analyzed, it's possible to find out what the surface consists of. The surface of Saturn probably consists of poisonous gases, ammonia, methane. But it's beautiful."

"The rings. What about the rings?"

"Ice, probably."

"Ice."

There were more planets. Mercury—the companion, as his father called it. Jason became very fond of speedy little Mercury, but it was often difficult to spot it. Then there was Venus, the Morning and Evening Star, sometimes like a small clear silvery crescent moon in the telescope.

Then there is scarlet Mars, which looks like a jewel. Mars becomes Jason's real favorite among the planets, and for six whole months he follows it every evening and records its orbit on his chart.

And then—beautiful great Jupiter, with its red spot, which looks just like an eye and makes Jason shiver.

"That red eye," his father says calmly, "could be a large island floating around on the surface. Maybe an island, maybe a storm— enormous, savage, raging and raging through the centuries."

Then the moon—the earth's moon—which seems to be a stranger when seen through the telescope, it comes so close and is so large. The landscape he can see on the moon is familiar, but alien all the same. The light is yellowish-white and bluish-white, very strong. It takes a great effort to watch the moon for any length of time. His father says that happens to almost everyone; it's called lunar dizziness, a well-known phenomenon among astronomers. He explains about high and low tide, something they know well from the Thames only a few streets away. Together they would go down and record the times of the tides and combine them with the movements and phases of the moon. The spring tides are particularly interesting. That is when there is flooding.

But the strangest thing about the moon is its effect on the human mind. His father is a doctor and knows that such things exist. It is called lunacy.

🙰

On the front door of the house hung the brass plate, which was polished every week: JOHN M. COWARD, MD.

Jason's father divided his time between his work at the Mission Hospital in Whitechapel, where he was an epidemiologist, and his private practice at home, a few streets away from the Royal Mint. He kept all his instruments, wall charts, and books in his surgery. He also had a large skeleton in the corner and a locked glass cupboard in which the medicines were stored.

When his father was not seeing a patient but was working, Jason was often allowed to come down and sit with him, on the condition that he was quiet. It had been like that since he was very small. His father used to give him a book, preferably one of the large leather-bound volumes with colored plates in which he could see inside the body through an opening in the stomach. They were amazing, colorful drawings, and the cut-up people showed no sign of the opening in their stomachs hurting. On the contrary, the people were upright, with no clothes on, yes, but with their eyes open and staring straight at you, taking no notice of the fact that you could see their liver. The liver was purple. Jason thought it exciting and could sit for ages just looking at the pictures. When he was older and had started school and could read, he also tried to stumble his way through the captions, but they were mostly in Latin, and the English in between was also difficult. So gradually his father came and sat with him more and more to explain what he was seeing on the plates.

There was another book up in their living room which Jason often looked at—but that book was different. That was the big illustrated Bible full of engravings. His mother used to read to him out of it. He gradually got to know all the pictures, the gloomy cave where Sarah was buried, the terrible end of the Leviathan, the victory over the Philistines.

And the pictures of the Deluge, the water rising and rising and all those terrified naked people climbing trees and rocks to escape the waves. The ark in the background, black and closed. The people don't see it. And then, the next picture, where the water has risen to the highest peak—"and the waters prevailed exceedingly upon the earth; and all the high hills, that were under the whole heaven, were covered. Fifteen cubits upward did the waters prevail; and the mountains were covered." In the picture was a tigress, wild with anguish, sitting on top of a rock with her cub in her jaws. A father is pushing his drowning child up onto the rock—another little boy is already there, frightened by the water, already giving up, exhausted. The water will go on rising, inexorably, and it looks almost as if he is longing for it to do so.

"And the rain was upon the earth forty days and forty nights."

In the next engraving, the water has gone down, bodies are lying everywhere, and the stench of rotting damp must be hideous. The ark stands on a mountain peak, the sun shining behind it, and there is a rainbow.

Jason asks his mother. But she doesn't say whether God is evil. Instead, she reads to him that Noah made burned offerings to the Lord, and that pleased Him. Noah and the Lord made a pact, a pact for all eternity: never again would God allow man to perish. As a sign of this, God put the rainbow in the sky. And there it is to this very day.

The illustrated Bible was almost as beautiful as the anatomy books, and somehow they reminded Jason of each other. The illustrations remained with him all his life.

His father was tall, his hair brown and brushed back, and he had side-whiskers. When he was working, he wore round spectacles. He soon discovered that Jason had a natural bent for science and he made sure to find specimens, books, and charts they could look at together. When Jason was just nine, his father had the idea of getting a tele-scope. In his youth, Dr. Coward had been very interested in astron-omy, and this was something both he and Jason would enjoy. But it would be expensive; his income was not among the largest, and after initiating Jason into his plan, he also had to get his wife's permission. That happened one Sunday at afternoon tea.

"Alice," his father said. "You remember how interested I used to be in astronomy when we first met?"

Jason pricked up his ears. Now it was coming.

"Yes," said his mother, smiling. "You constantly went around with a chart of the heavens in your inside pocket. The other young men always had a pocket edition of Shelley."

"That must have been very—um—romantic?"

"In some ways, yes," she said. "But they weren't very good at reading him. Goodness, how bored I was with Shelley. While you, on the other hand, with that chart of stars of yours . . ."

"Hm, hm, hm." His father smiled broadly. "But I don't think I ever told you what started my interest in astronomy, did I?"

"No, you didn't." Jason was convinced his mother could see they were plotting something.

"It was when I witnessed an attack of star-madness."

"Really, star-madness?"

"In Crick the watchmaker."

Dr. Coward came from fairly modest circumstances and during his schooldays was in lodgings for a while with a watchmaker's family.

"Was it as long ago as that?"

"Yes, I'll tell you about it. One evening when I was in the living room after Mrs. Crick had already served my evening meal, Crick came home, very agitated and red in the face. 'My dear James,' his wife said. 'Have you been to one of those lectures again?' Crick used to go to popular scientific lectures and they could make him wildly enthusiastic. But this particular evening he was quite unusually exalted and breathing heavily.

" 'Yes,' he cried. 'I've been to Dr. Bird's lecture on the solar system. It was quite . . . quite . . .' and then it came, his favorite expression '. . . quite extra-ordinary!' He always pronounced it like that. Then he began to expound on what he had heard about planets and moons, and as he went on, his excitement grew, and finally he cried, 'I know no better way of illustrating this than by using a *mop*!' At which he seized Mrs. Crick's mop standing in a bucket of water by the door, dipped it in thoroughly, then held it up to the ceiling and started whirling it round and round so that water flew in all directions out of it.

" 'This!' he roared. 'This mop is the sun! And the spiral movements of the water are the movements of the planets around the sun. We're witnessing the creation of the solar system!' "

"And his wife—what did she say?"

"She was very worried, of course. Partly because of the furniture, and partly because of her husband, whose face had turned quite purple on behalf of popular science, but he just said in a trembling voice, 'If that Dr. Bird can do it, why can't *I*?' That was how it began."

"And how did it end?"

"Well, Crick was a simple man with no proper education, and as I had had a bit more schooling, I had to help him. The watchmaker spent more and more of his time on this new passion of his—astronomy. He thought about nothing else—and to keep my room I had to look into the matter. In the end he gave up his shop and sacrificed himself to the stars. I don't know how many times I helped him lug his telescope all the way out to Greenwich. At first, he used to go there to be close to the 'Heart of Astronomy,' as he called the observatory. Then he gradually started accepting money to allow others to look through his telescope, on the principle of a-penny-a-peek, and so managed to scrape up a living. That was when I started looking around for somewhere else to live. He gave a lecture to the amateur astronomical society and kept saying *consternations* instead of *constellations*. That didn't go over very well. The members of the society were somewhat 'consternated' and kept shouting '*Hear, hear!*' But he was not deterred. He went on educating himself and in the end actually did rather well out of his lectures to laymen. He even wrote a little book. By then I had long since left his house, but I kept up my interest in astronomy, oddly enough."

"That first lecture—it must have been very forceful?"

"I would like to have been there myself. He seemed to have been exposed to some kind of charismatic conversion. But this whole story tells you—if only in a superficial way—nothing but that science *inspires*."

Jason's mother laughed.

"What about his wife?" she asked.

"She got angina."

It was quiet for a moment.

"Well," said his mother, "what is it you want?"

"Alice, I promise you I'll never twirl mops around the living room."

"Yes?"

"Yes, I promise. It's just that I was thinking of buying a telescope. Largely for Jason, of course."

"Of course."

"I think it will be good for him."

"I'm sure it will, John."

"There's nothing so disciplined and educational as making exact scientific observations. With an exact instrument."

"And how much will it cost?"

His father said nothing.

Then his mother said, "Go outside for a moment, Jason."

Jason looked at his father.

"Do as your mother tells you."

⚜

Outside in the pantry he can hear his parents' voices piecemeal and in waves coming from inside the living room. He realizes they have come to the critical moment and a decision is now being made.

". . . not for anything . . . the house . . . decorating . . . science . . . science! . . . but a lot? . . . everything indicates that . . . the boy's development . . . and his homework? . . . the increasing importance of science in the years to . . . fresh air . . . conditions . . ."

The voices at last fade away. Then he hears them laughing and he knows there will be a telescope. A moment later the door opens and his father is standing there, smiling all over his face.

"Your mother's gone quite mad," he says. His mother's voice from inside: "Oh, John!"

"You're to have a telescope. *And* a violin."

"Violin?"

"That's the condition, you see." His father squats so that he is face-to-face with Jason. "And I think she's right," he adds. "She thinks there've been quite enough specimens and wall charts as it is. So if we're to have a telescope as well, then you have to practice hard at the violin for an hour every day. Do you see?"

Jason nods.

❧

Jason continues to stand still. He can see himself reflected in the shop window right in front of him, tall and sturdy, his suit slightly too small under his overcoat. Chestnut-brown hair, blue eyes, his violin case under his arm. Not the same instrument as in those days, but a violin he acquired later, in his early twenties. It has been renovated since then, of course, for it has experienced a great deal.

He sees himself as he was then, a fairly tall boy with red hair and large eyes. During the right time, everything had been different. Jason thinks he has a memory of his own laughter from those times, a trickling light—where is it now, that laughter?

He had enjoyed playing the violin, but the telescope had been more exciting.

From where he was standing, he could see the cupola on St. Paul's, a faint flesh color now, in the sunrise.

But he didn't want to think about the other things now.

❧

Is God evil?

❧

Jason smiles slightly at that childish question as he stands there.

It is only a shadow of a smile, almost kindly.

⚜

The great epidemics came in the winter, the slums groaning under them, trembling with them, the anguish visible in the cracked gray windowpanes. The rain falls on the streets and disease sets in in the basements and cramped, overcrowded rooms, diphtheria coming as surely as the tides. Typhus, too. In the daytime, people huddle, preoccupied, in the streets, and in the evenings there's singing in the pubs as usual. But every evening his father comes home late, his face streaked white with fatigue. Outside, it is raining or foggy, always rain or fog. He talks quietly to his wife, his voice deeper than usual, apparently far down his throat. He talks, curtly and staccato, about the *conditions*. The *conditions* will soon be such that they are unendurable, he says. Today, before he left for home, he had again compiled some statistics. They were worse than ever. Hadn't he just been—with the rest of the committee—to a nine-room house in Spitalfields where sixty-three people were sharing nine beds? *Sixty-three*, I tell you! The walls infested, the drains in ruins, everything in ruins. Doesn't he remember the summer of '58, when Westminster Bridge could not be crossed without a damp handkerchief pressed against your mouth and nose against the stench, the river green and slimy, the tide only swilling the filth back and forth. And the rats. The whole of London crawling with rats; occasionally they even came up through the drains of Buckingham Palace.

Jason has seen them himself, billowing gray clumps of horror in a back yard, or sometimes darting through the streets in broad daylight. His scalp and his underarms prickle when he thinks about them.

"All we need now," says his father, "is cholera. We're just waiting for the first case. The homeless live in the latrines in some places—because that's the only roof they have over their heads. We pray to God and compile statistics. Thousands of people in London live on what they scavenge off the streets. Some specialize and crawl into sewer outlets in the Thames to rake the mud for scrap metal or anything they can sell. Only half of all the children go to school.

"We're worried about the drinking water. Even the water from the public stands should be boiled. We can thank God at least it's raining."

Jason sits there feeling slightly ashamed, looking down at his home-work. He would like to ask his father when they can transfer the sketches of the orbit of Mars onto the new chart, but he knows now he cannot. His father is too tired, and Jason can't help feeling disap-pointed. His father is battling with a many-headed monster, a Hydra he and all his committees will never be able to conquer, and why does he do it, when he knows he can't win? Jason is ashamed.

"Shall I get you a brandy?" his mother says. His father nods absently.

"We went to another house today, too," he says, his voice seeping out of him like black smoke. "One room. Irish family. Six children, four of them girls, the oldest thirteen. The two youngest have diph-theria. There was one bed in the room, a table, and some straw in the corner. There was nothing to be done for the youngest—it died while we were there. And the mother was showing signs of scurvy."

"Here," says his mother. "This is for you." She hands him the glass.

"The three older ones—two girls and a boy—work in the match factory. You should have *seen* their hands. You almost wished the daughters went on the streets. Then they'd at least learn to wash."

"John!"

His mother glances at Jason, who looks down at his books.

"There are seven thousand prostitutes in London, the police say. Lies. There are eighty, perhaps ninety thousand. But they do at least wash."

"John . . ."

"We should do what they do in Paris. The doctors there supervise licensed brothels. Check twice a month. The other day there was a girl—well, she was in extremis. She didn't want a priest. God was an obscure concept to her. What kind of thoughts could she have on such things when she didn't even know her surname? But she said, I think I can tell right from wrong. And it's wrong, what I've done. It's wrong. School? No. No family she knew of or could remember. She was brought up in one of those institutions, or whatever you can call those illegal dens which train children to—" He senses his wife is looking at him. "She was going to die," he said, "and she would have to do so without religion or being able to read. But she lay there, her eyes all questions. It was wrong, what I did, she said. She held on to my arm to the very last moment."

Dr. Coward finished his drink, and Jason's mother immediately poured out another. Two were usually enough as long as cholera wasn't looming. Both she and Jason knew what these evenings could be like. He might tell them about the last awful days of abdominal typhus, whole wards of children choking, nurses running to and fro with bowls of steaming water, and scraping out mucus. And he told them—sometimes—about the *stadium algidum* of cholera, the spasms and leaden-gray faces.

He could be like that when he came home, his voice seeping out of him for an hour or maybe two, Jason and his mother saying little. But they knew he valued having the two of them there. Then he would lie back in his chair, exhausted, but his face its ordinary hue and his voice again back to normal.

What keeps him going? Jason thinks. What happens when he takes those statistics to the Public Health and to all those committees he sits on?

Jason thinks about Mars with shame—his father has been telling him about Kepler's discoveries, and the study of Mars' orbit plays an important part here.

His father empties his second glass.

What keeps him going?

"You can't emphasize enough the insignificance of the individual human being."

It is early one Sunday morning.

"The individual means nothing, but what he contributes means *something*."

Jason listens in silence, not sure he understands.

His mother puts her hat on. They are off to church.

The rain has stopped for the moment, but instead the fog has descended as the family walks through the streets. At a distance, with the curiosity and disgust of a sheltered child, Jason sees the street girls, and small boys with arms and legs as thin as the matches they sell. He sees the cripple with a face sooty black with filth. He sees the street musician and his boy; they are carrying small harps and both have cheerful red ribbons wound around their leggings. But all the faces are washed out, merging into the fog.

"The individual is just a piece, nothing but a small stone in a huge mosaic. And that mosaic is the floor of the future."

If only it would snow, Jason thinks. How long will this go on—fog and rain, rain and fog? If only the snow would come soon.

"The most beautiful pattern, what is most wonderful and true in that mosaic is science. In laboratories, anatomy rooms, and observatories, stone is laid upon stone for the progress of mankind. It is long, slow, and laborious work. But it will take us forward. And the individual, the one who takes part in that work, he means no more than precisely what he does; his life and soul mean nothing—he's like a novice in the temple. He bears offerings to the altar, humbly and selflessly. That's all. No more. If he does it with sorrow or joy, that has nothing to do with the *continuity*."

Jason glances up at his father a little anxiously. His father's face is too pale; he is clearly still tired.

"This century has brought us steam, electricity, and gas. Work that used to require toil and tedious drudgery can now be done fifty or a hundred times faster. One day, taming nature will give us so much power that with the help of science we can seriously begin to talk about the welfare of the masses. The culture of the masses, the century of the masses."

"The culture of the masses," says his mother. "Do you really think everyone will ever be able to benefit from—"

"It must be so!" exclaims his father. "It's inevitable. That's the way we're going. Education today is for a minority. But one day we'll have got so far that technology and science will bring light, light and enlightenment for . . ."

Jason cautiously takes his father's arm. His father looks down at him and for a moment seems far away, but then he smiles, almost as usual.

"Tomorrow," he says. "Tomorrow we'll go to a shop I know of where they sell exotic creatures. There we'll buy some larvae eggs. The larvae of silkworms. In a month the larvae will spin cocoons, and the thread they spin will be silk, pure silk."

"Silk . . ." says Jason in a low voice.

"We'll put some of the cocoons in boiling water so the worm dies and doesn't break through the cocoon and spoil the thread. Then the thread can be reeled up."

His father looks strangely relieved as he says this.

The church is full. His parents pray, and Jason sees his father clenching his fists so the knuckles turn white.

But the next day the hospital registered the first case of cholera and the silkworms had to wait.

※

Jason picked up his suitcase and violin and walked on down the street.

Give me that time back, he thought. Give me the right time back. The time when everything seemed to be all permanence, eternity. That time in which individual action, every human being—myself, too—was all eternity and meaning.

Give it back to me.

Then he shook off his thoughts and crossed Southwark Bridge. Gradually the streets had begun to fill up. The pleasant feeling of lightness and opportunity had gone, and he could no longer hear his own footsteps. Instead, there was a faint, sour, hollow feeling in his stomach.

You haven't eaten, he thought. You have plenty of time. You don't have to be at the station for a long time. You must get some food before going on to Waterloo.

The same morning
London, Waterloo Station, 7:05

———————◆◆◆◆◆———————

IMPERCEPTIBLY, the great glass roof of the station was trembling slightly above the noise of people and trains. Way up there, pigeons fluttered from girder to girder, quite unaffected by the throng on the station floor. Myriads of square glass panes in the roof slowly turned white as daylight increased and poured in.

David was leaning against a pillar on the station floor, a young man, almost a boy, and clearly also rather green in the ways of the world. His thick curly black hair seemed far too strong and wild for him; his features were fine and translucent, his shoulders narrow, the impression of youth reinforced by his clothes. They were a bit too neat, his best suit, ready-made and obviously chosen for him by his mother. His hat was under his arm and his luggage between his feet, a violin case and a suitcase. He kept yawning and thinking, If he doesn't come soon, I'll faint on the spot.

When David closed his eyes, he seemed to be inside a large bell of ringing sounds, with railway smells all around him, coal, smoke, oil, and tar. But this morning it was as if he was smelling them for the very first time—they seemed strong and unfamiliar and blended in with all those sounds.

David was feeling slightly nauseous. He could hear the newspaper boys shouting, but could not understand a word. The shouts became a monotonous, puzzling lament, and just because he couldn't understand but knew they must mean something, they seemed to him full of new and dangerous allusions, the semi-sentences going beyond his understanding and worrying him. His anxiety settled as a sharp twinge in the pit of his stomach.

This was his first visit to England, strictly speaking, his first trip abroad, but he had never imagined it would be so different. Now he discovered that it was like arriving on a foreign star. Even ordinary things like trees and houses had something different about them, as if reality had been slightly distorted. Colors were different, the light different. He noticed that he sensed things more intensely than usual; impressions were hammered into him.

It had been like this since his first evening in London, three days earlier. David thought back on it with horror. He had been stopped in a narrow street by a small man in a battered bowler who had talked to him, talking and talking as he held out a flat box with something in it. Was he selling something? Did he want to give him something? It had been impossible to understand what he was saying, and David had not known how to get rid of him. The man's face, voice, and mouth were obtrusively clear. In the box were some shapeless black lumps, and the little man seized one and held it up to David's face. It smelled rank and, uneasy, David tried to slip away. But the man stuck to him, talking on and on, following him and the whole time waving one of those things. Finally David had no way out except to run away like any thief, his violin and suitcase under his arms.

Later that same evening he was stopped by a thin young girl with bare, almost blue arms in the cool April air. She also wanted something from him, but this time David understood what. He hurried away from her and her large gray eyes. "Please, sir," she kept mumbling behind him. "Please." So he had left her. At the shabby boardinghouse—or should he say lodging house?—he had found he had understood nothing except the price. It was a wretched, bug-ridden place, all kinds of activities going on all night in the next room. He had slept badly and was now regretting more and more that he had had this idea at all. What am I doing here? he thought. Why in heaven's name did I ever think of coming here? When he considered his reason for coming and what he was now actually about to do, it struck him he must be deranged. The whole point of it all, the original incentive, suddenly seemed distant and meaningless compared to the unpleasantness and anxiety it had brought with it. There was nothing to stop him running away, leaping onto the first train to Dover and making his way across the Continent to home. He had seriously contemplated flight that same morning at breakfast in the lodging house—when he had found a *nail* clipping in his watery, half-cooked helping of scrambled eggs. David was not particularly worldly, so he took the nail clipping as a bad omen. What had stopped him was that he had hardly any money left and didn't think it would be enough for the long journey back to Vienna. He had also given his word, even signed a contract. But the most important reason why he was standing here now and would carry out his intentions was this: What would it be like to return home with his tail between his legs? That would be both shameful and embarrassing, even unbearable, after the farewell he had taken of the city of his birth, and he did not have the courage to eat such humble pie. Besides, he thought you should complete what you set out to do. That's how you grow. Anything else would be cowardly, and he was not *that* cowardly.

So David chose that for which he had sufficient courage, but he was not sure whether it was really courage. He was certainly feeling miserable at this moment. Had it been his choice, or had it been a confidence trick, what happened to him the other day in that small agency in Whitechapel High Street?

The office was on the second floor and his courage had ebbed with every flight of stairs. He stopped outside the door and hesitated. The firm's name on the frosted glass of the door was in such beautiful lettering, it inspired confidence: MESSRS BLACK & BLACK. For a moment he thought of turning back, but then he heard someone coming up the stairs, and seized with a kind of panic, he tapped cautiously on the glass with his fingernail.

"Come in!" barked a voice. David squeezed through the crack in the door.

A small, sleek-looking man in shirtsleeves was sitting writing at a desk. He did not look up as David meekly approached the desk and stood in front of him. All David could hear was the scratching of the man's pen and all he could see was the man's glossy, pomaded head.

"Yes?" said the man without looking up. "What can I do for you?"

David cleared his throat.

"Well . . ." he began, his English deserting him, nor had he thought up a good opening remark.

"Yes?" said the man, looking up, his wide silk tie red with a sparkling stone in it—the stone seemed to be winking at David.

"You want a job, I suppose," said the man with no further formalities. He looked David over briefly and did not appear to be particularly impressed. "We have no jobs," he went on. "I'm sorry, old chap." He looked down at his papers again. Disconcerted, David stood rooted to the spot. Was that all? Yes, the audience was quite clearly over, the sparkling ruby prince behind the desk was a wise man from the East who could read his thoughts, already knew the content of David's appeal, and had rejected it with no further waste of time.

The man wrote a few words, then looked up again, this time with a more ominous expression.

"Well . . ." he began, but then he was interrupted as an elderly white-haired man sailed into the room from a neighboring office, a paper in his hand.

"Damn it, John," the white-haired man rumbled. "It's that White Star ship again. Never known such a muddle and mess before. We damned well shouldn't have anything to do with these fiddlers."

"What is it now?" said the man behind the desk.

"Remember how we searched heaven and earth at three days' notice to find a new bass player for them—when the first one lost his wife, d'you remember?"

"Yes."

"Well now, first we find this bass player for them—never mind if he wasn't exactly what Coward wanted, but all the same—in *three* days. Yes, well, would you believe it, their second violin, that Smith or whatever his name is, that spoiled little Paganini—he's gone and got *appendicitis*! *Today!* Devil take the lot of them. I thought Coward had been on so many trips he could find good players, not candidates for the operating table! He can't see beyond his nose, damn him!"

The pomaded gentleman looked up at his superior with a mildly despairing expression.

"The ship sails on the tenth," he said. "Today's the eighth. Can't do it."

"No," said the white-haired man. "Can't do it. But we'll have to try."

The man behind the desk looked at David.

"Are you still here?" he said. "Isn't it time you left?"

Abashed, David turned and headed for the door.

"One moment, young man," the old man said sharply. "Isn't that a violin you've got under your arm?"

David looked down at his violin case, almost in surprise.

"Yes," he said stupidly.

The two men exchanged looks.

"Well, can you *play* it?" the old man said.

That was how David came to be hired. A violinist on the ferry between Calais and Dover had first given him the idea when they'd fallen into conversation and he had given David Black & Black's address.

"You'll get four pounds a month," said the younger Black, smiling in a friendly, very friendly way. David hastily calculated in his head what that meant in kronen.

"You can take over Smith's uniform. It should be all right. He has no use for it with or without his appendix."

"See this score?" David looked at it. It said *White Star Music* on the cover and was horribly thick.

"Practice like hell," said the younger man. "You have to know as much as possible by heart."

"Four pounds sterling per month, as I said," said the old man. "But you must keep the uniform in order yourself. We're taking you on provisionally, do you understand? Provisionally."

"*One* trip to start with. Let's sign you up."

They produced papers.

⚜

So David was now standing there, waiting, and he was not feeling particularly confident.

What am I doing in this city, anyway, he thought. To him, the worst thing about London was not the dirt or the visible wretchedness that was so much more glaring than at home. The worst thing was that he couldn't make out what people were *saying*—at least not in the streets or in the shops. He could read all the signs, but the spoken language might as well be Mesopotamian. He had arrived in Baghdad. The English Herr Schulze had impressed on him at school back in Vienna's thirteenth Bezirk bore little resemblance to the sounds he heard here.

David opened his eyes. A newsboy was standing a few steps from him, hollow-cheeked and pale, making all those *ai, oh* sounds and a number of clattering *k*s. Then a man with an umbrella stopped by the newsboy, apparently interested in what was being shouted so incomprehensibly. They stood there for a moment, exchanging difficult British coins, but no words. Then the man with the umbrella merged into the stream of people and the boy went on shouting.

David leaned his head wearily against the pillar. He could make out what was *said*, what was *sung*, but not what it all *meant*. It frightened him. Steam whistles, thousands of footsteps. Guards shouting, newsboys intoning. Fragments of conversations like squalls in the air.

David fell asleep on his feet.

❧

Jason Coward looked doubtfully at the sleeping boy.

Good God, he thought, that's not him! It can't be! He's too young. He stared into the pale face.

Damn it, Jason thought. What have they sent us?

He cleared his throat a few times, but the boy did not move.

Maybe it's not he, he thought with a mixture of anxiety and hope. Maybe he's just a schoolboy going to visit his grandmother. But he knew it was the right person; his appearance matched the foreign-sounding name he had been given. Jason tapped the sleeper's shoulder.

The boy woke with a start and looked up at Jason, anxiety in his eyes.

That's it, thought Jason. Run away from home. Damn and blast it!

While the boy was pulling himself together, Jason said, "Excuse me—good morning—would you by any chance be"—he started rummaging in his pocket— "be . . ." hoping the other man would say his name. It was difficult holding on to his violin case while searching for the piece of paper. The boy looked wide-eyed at him, then understood.

"Yes," he said in broken English. "My name is Bleiernstern. David Bleiernstern." At that moment Jason found the piece of paper. The name matched.

"I'm Jason Coward," said Jason, holding out his hand. "I'm the bandmaster."

"Pleased to meet you," said the black-haired boy. Jason looked him up and down.

"German, are you?"

"Austrian. From Wien. Vienna."

"I see."

"But I *can* play the violin."

"Hm? Yes, of course, when you . . ." Jason stopped. "How old are you?"

"Twenty-two," said David, looking Jason straight in the eye.

"Don't lie to me," said Jason, smiling faintly. "I'm your boss. Remember that. Anyhow, I have no choice. The train to Southampton leaves in fifteen minutes."

"Yes," said David, looking down. "Eighteen, Mr. Coward."

"I see."

"But I *can* play the violin."

"It's really rather more important that you aren't seasick."

"Wie, bitte?"

"Sea-sick. Do you get sea-sick?"

Then David understood.

"I don't know," he said, smiling for the first time, a pleasant smile.

"You can't throw up into your violin case while you're playing," said Jason. "The passengers don't like it."

David turned serious again. Amazing that Germans never seemed to understand irony, thought Jason.

"I shall not be seasick," David assured him.

"And I hope you sight-read well."

"Yes."

"Your first job, is it?"

"Yes."

"No previous engagements?"

David shook his head.

"Good. Have you got your passport?" With some embarrassment, David fished a paper out of his inside pocket and handed it to Jason, an elaborate document with Kaiserlich-Königlich all over it. "Hm," said Jason, handing it back. "I don't think you'll need that. I'll say you're twenty-one."

"Will they not let me go otherwise?"

"The ship needs a full band. Do you have any money?"

"Only a little."

"Well, you don't need any until we land in New York."

29

David looked inquiringly at him, and his gaze was quite open this time. Jason felt oddly touched by it.

"You must always do as I say," he said brusquely. "And always what the officers tell you."

"Yes," said David, nodding.

"Good. Shall we be off?" As David didn't understand, Jason jerked his head in the direction of the trains.

"*Gehen*," he said. David smiled again and they moved off.

As they passed the newspaper boys, David spoke again. "What are they shouting?"

"The coal strike is over and the miners have gone back to work," said Jason.

"Oh," said David, a bit disappointed.

"It means the ship'll have enough coal to sail."

The great clock up under the roof said twenty past seven. At the barrier, Jason took out tickets for them both, and when the ticket collector had clipped them, they went along the platform to where the special boat train for second class and steerage passengers left for pier number 44 in Southampton, departure 7:30 p.m. The engine had steam up and passengers were being urged to board the train.

Jason strode rapidly down the platform past crowds of emigrants and passengers and a mass of luggage trolleys, David just behind him. David was now almost incapable of anything except watching his own feet. That fearful weariness had overcome him again and he was longing to sit down, perhaps to sleep.

Jason opened a compartment door and they got in. Instrument cases and suitcases were piled on top of each other, on the luggage rack above, and on all the empty seats. Three men were already seated there, all talking, the air blue with tobacco smoke. David could just make out an older man with a thin, yellowing goatee, a small dark man with pince-nez, and another man with a short blond beard and bright eyes. Those eyes bored into David the moment he appeared in the compartment doorway. The other two faces seemed more benevolent.

"Is there room for us here?" said Jason, although he had already closed the door behind them. "Well now," he said, clearing his throat.

30

"Gentlemen, this is our new second violin, David—wait a minute . . ."

"Bleiernstern," said David, glancing nervously at the three faces. The older man with the goatee seemed to be humming to himself, and he was looking up at David with amused, slightly blurred eyes. The small dark man with the pince-nez also had a friendly glint in his eyes, but the fair man was not smiling. He again fixed his eyes on David and was staring at him.

Then he turned to Jason and pointed at David with the stem of his pipe.

"He's too young, Jason," he said.

"Come come, Alex," growled Jason quietly.

"May the whole of Black & Black roast in hell!" the fair man said, shaking his pipe. "Look at him! Hardly dry behind the ears."

"That's not his fault."

"It'll work out, you'll see," said the small dark man with the pince-nez, turning to Alex, then blinking kindly at David.

David stared shamefacedly down at the floor. Alex spluttered to himself for a moment or two, then abruptly got up.

"Excuse me," he said; then he stepped out onto the platform and into the next compartment, where the other musicians were sitting.

Jason closed the door behind him.

"Um," he said, slightly bothered. "Hm. David, this is—um . . ." Jason waved a hand at the goatee, who was still smiling just as if he had not really followed what had been going on. "This is our double bass player, Petronius Witt."

The bass player held out a slightly droopy hand. It struck David that something was not quite right about the old man.

"Giovanni Petronio Vitellotesta," the goatee said solemnly in a cracked voice. "Or, in English, Petronius Witt. Hee-hee."

He shook David's hand, his eyes blurring even more, but then he withdrew his hand as if he had burned it. He gazed at it as if offended, then held it up to examine it closely. But the next moment he was peering kindly up at David again. "Hee-hee," he said, then fell silent.

The dark man with the pince-nez held out his hand.

"Petronius is Italian, as you see," he said meaningfully. "Don't take any notice of Alex, who just went out. That is just the way he is. I'm Spot."

"Pleased to meet you, Mr. Spot," said David.

31

"No, no. Not Mr. Spot. Not mister anything. Just Spot," said Spot, with no further explanation of his peculiar name. At that moment the train started moving and David and Jason shifted cases and flopped down onto the empty seats.

"Well now," exclaimed Jason. "We're off to America."

"Hee-hee," said Petronius. Spot said nothing, just smiled distantly behind his pince-nez.

⚘

Jason leaned back in his seat and closed his eyes.

After a while he dozed off, and a closed space seemed to surround him as he sat alone with himself, the voices of the others only just audible in the distance.

The thoughts of that morning came back to him, but different now, softer.

The wheels go round, he thought. Can you hear the sound of the tracks, the thunder of metal against metal? Can you hear that you're on your way, departing, always departing? The thunder of metal against metal.

Can you hear the music?

He is practicing on the violin—his mother plays the violin well herself, and she is helping him. He has just started on Handel's *Largo*, the long, even strokes difficult to make pure. Excitement overcomes them both—she shows him, moving her face and hands close to show him the holds, pointing at the notes. When his mother is excited, her hair loosens, strand after strand slipping out of her hairnet and falling around her head, the strands like silk. When she moves they float in all directions. She has brown hair, a brown skirt, brown eyes. She is teaching him to play, not so much the technique—his violin teacher looks after that—but she is teaching him that you have to be excited, that the blood has to rise to your cheeks when you play. What is most important is *not* that it is perfect. Jason thinks he must have played the *Largo* really badly that time—he is still no virtuoso—but it depends on the excitement and the warmth in his cheeks. That's what his mother has taught him.

His father had said it was good for a scientist to take an interest in music on the side. He himself had never had time. Things are to be better for Jason than they were for him. Everything is always to be

better and more for Jason. Also something like music—even if only
as a sideline, a hobby.

Yes. But here he is, a musician on a ship going to America. His
band plays light music, Strauss, Suppé, Lehár before dinner. Things
deteriorate after dinner, *The Ragtime Revue*, *The Chocolate Soldier*, and
"The Teddy Bears' Picnic." That kind of thing. *The Tales of Hoffmann*
and Sullivan's *Mikado*.

He doesn't really understand this, is incapable of seeing the connection between the images he has deep down inside him and the
fact that he is sitting here in a compartment on a train, leader of six
other musicians of highly varying quality and background. He knows
some of them from previous trips, others not at all.

That is all part of the puzzle.

The others, Jason thinks, friends, colleagues—they are probably
also sitting there with images inside them, swirls of impressions, small
shreds gathered over the years. There are threads and tracks that have
drawn them here. As there are in me.

I never ask colleagues about their backgrounds or motives. They
have to keep those to themselves; then I, too, can have mine in peace.
But what do they dream about when they're asleep? When they sit
like that with their eyes closed, as I am now, what do they see? What
do they hear? Perhaps it is unimportant. Perhaps that's why I never
ask. Never have asked.

I stopped asking a long time ago.

⚜

Jason sees the telescope when it at long last arrives at the house after
an eternity of waiting and theoretical preparations. He remembers his
father finding all kinds of books which they looked at together so they
would have the right foundation when they began actual observations.

"Observations" . . . just the word. It tasted of journeys, of discoveries, of reality. The real thing.

Then at last the telescope came, a good instrument, its lenses from
Chance's in Birmingham, Swiss armature, precision work. It was black,
with a stand of solid hard oak. The screws were of polished steel, the
axes and balances gleaming black.

They had gone through the apparatus very thoroughly beforehand
and Jason knew the specifications by heart: refractor, three and a half

inches, with a theoretical resolution factor of two seconds of an arc. Observations could begin!

The violin had come a few months earlier, the golden-red child's violin, a beautiful shape.

By the time the telescope came, he could play a pure scale.

One evening Jason came back from an errand after school. His father had asked him to buy four extra violin strings. The two of them were to carry out an experiment. Again one of those words. Like "observation," "refractor," "its resolution," "seconds of an arc," secret words to begin with, magical words gradually acquiring meaning. And now another such word: "experiment." Jason does have some idea of what an experiment is, but he imagines it has something to do with test tubes, phosphorus and sulphur, fire and water. When his father said at breakfast that they were to perform an *experiment* that evening, before bedtime, after homework—Jason couldn't understand why he had been asked to buy four extra violin strings. Violin strings? He is beginning to build up some kind of relationship with those strings; he knows the four small strings over the fingerboard are the keys to the multitude of notes. But the experiment? He buys the strings, and when he is there in the shop and the old man behind the counter hands him the tissue-paper bag, the strings seem to have been given back all that was unknown and mysterious about them before he had begun playing the violin.

After he has done his homework, Jason goes with his father to the surgery, where the experiment is to take place. His father lights just one lamp, and in the yellow gaslight they sit down at the desk. There is a board on the desk. For a moment Jason is disappointed. Phosphorus, sulphur, he thinks. But then his father stretches the strings between nails on the board and jams wedges under them so that they can resound freely. And there, in the faint light, Jason hears for the first time that the planets have notes.

For after the delicate notes from the taut strings have shown how the repeated halving of string lengths produces intervals, and after his father has shown him why this is so, and that this comes from the increased speeds of the oscillations—he shows him how the geometrical basis of certain sequences of notes are repeated in the speeds of the *planets* according to Kepler's law. Jason gradually grasps what his father is getting at—both the notes and the geometry they can be converted into are simply expressions of other, strange conditions. In its elliptical orbit, Saturn describes in speed variation the leap from G to B, in other words, a great third; Mercury is a much longer leap, all of ten notes, while Jupiter writes a small third.

"That," says his father, "is what Kepler thought, that the orbits of the planets, like the notes, expressed harmonies in the universe. The music of the spheres."

He smiles slightly.

"Well now, if there really is music of the spheres, it's not the music of oscillations in the air but a quite different and tremendous force in the cosmos. A music of pure force of gravity, of mathematics, of . . . Whether it's like that in reality is another matter. But the idea is beautiful. What remains after all Kepler's work are his three laws of the planets. They were the first real natural laws, and they came about while he was working on finding harmonies in the universe."

Jason never tires of listening to the strings. Astronomy and violin music seem to merge together that evening. They sit in the circle of light and move the wedges beneath the strings, listening, tuning, referring to the books in which his father has found his material; listening again.

"The Greeks already thought the planets gave off music," says his father. "As seen from the earth, the planets pass in bow-like movements through the Zodiac. The ancient Greeks thought this was some kind of divine dance. And as all movement creates vibrations, sounds, and notes, they also thought the planets produced sounds—music, because they were dancing. Music that no human being could hear because the whole universe was filled with these great notes, and human beings had always heard them from when they lay in their mother's womb and got used to them. Just as you get used to the beating of your heart. That's how Aristotle explained it all. Pythagoras is said have been the last to have the divine gift of sensing that music. Then Kepler discovered there was also a kind of note relation in the new solar system, although the sun is in the middle and the orbits of the planets are no longer perfect circles but ellipses."

Jason has almost stopped listening. He looks at the strings and back at his father. It is late. They are tired. But first, just once more, Jason must hear it really is like that, that the planets, his friends of late-night hours, really do have voices.

His father turns out the lamp and they go to bed.

❧

"Have you been to America before, young fiddler?" asked Petronius, glancing furtively hither and thither, up at the luggage rack, out of the window.

"N-no," said David, looking with some confusion at this restless old man. "Have you?"

"New York's very fine," said Petronius. "Very fine. You can't make anything out. They have such tall buildings."

David understood less and less about this odd Italian. Petronius seemed small inside his clothes and his cuffs were frayed.

Jason was obviously asleep, leaning back in his seat. Spot was staring out the window with a patient, veiled look, and as they came out into the light, David could see quite clearly the gray streaks in the dark hair brushed back and to one side. He could also see the wrinkles around those eyes, partly hidden by the pince-nez. It was difficult to estimate Spot's age. Petronius could be in his mid-sixties, Jason in his mid-thirties, but Spot . . . Spot was well dressed with waistcoat and watch chain, rather like a teacher, a handsome middle-class school-master, but there was something peculiar about his eyes, as if they were hiding something, a delicate, quiet anxiety—and David remembered seeing eyes like that before, back home in Vienna, in the kind of café you were not supposed to patronize.

"We are going on the largest ship in the world," said Petronius, pulling at his wispy beard. "Biggest in the world. So big it can't sink."

David stared at him; then Spot intervened.

"It's true," he said, smiling ironically. "They really do say the ship can't sink. There's been a lot in the papers about it."

"Yes?"

"The ship's got a number of transverse watertight bulkheads, fourteen or fifteen, I think, and they're constructed so if there's an emergency, the captain on the bridge can close the doors between bulkheads by pressing an electric button. The doors slam shut in the bowels of the ship. So we won't get our feet wet."

"Ah, electricity, electricity," exclaimed Petronius enthusiastically. "I find it really moving."

"It would be a great improvement if only they could now invent an electric captain," said Spot solemnly.

"Yes, you're right, you're quite right," said the old man. "But do you think that's possible? An electric captain?"

"Of course. Who would never navigate wrongly. And electric musicians. Who would never *play* wrongly," said Spot, looking sternly at Petronius.

"Thank the Lord my time on earth will soon be over," said Petronius, shuddering, then after a pause adding: "Do you think I might have possibilities as an electric musician?"

He said it without a trace of irony. In an almost desperate attempt to put an end to this absurd conversation, David said abruptly: "I've been on a proper ship only once before. On the ferry between Dover and Calais. I mean, Calais and Dover."

"Oh, Calais to Dover," said Spot rather acidly. "We're going on the biggest ship in the world. It can carry over three thousand passengers." He fell silent and again started staring out the window.

"Do you understand Italian, young fiddler?" asked Petronius hopefully.

"Very little, I fear."

"Oh well. But do you ever go to the little theater? The little one?"

David did his best to look polite and obliging. Perhaps it was difficulties with language that made everything this old man said sound so peculiar.

"I like the theater," he said.

"Yes!" said Petronius, opening his eyes wide. "It's true the little theater is the most beautiful, is it not?"

"The little theater?" David said.

"Yes! The only real theater! The purest! The most truthful! With the most beautiful little actresses, who can dance in the air." As he spoke, great tears came into his eyes. "Oh, the little theater. And all those little spectators." David looked anxiously around for help, but Jason was sound asleep in his seat and Spot was staring steadily out the window in a state of elevated calm.

"I'm really pleased to hear," Petronius went on, "that *you*, too, young man, *you*, too . . . The ancient Chinese knew how to appreciate . . . or the Arabs . . . everywhere they had the most sumptuous, the most artistic . . . but in our day—in our day . . . so I'm doubly pleased that you, young man, *you* also are a lover, a connoisseur of the marionette theater. I knew it. I could see in your face you were a cultured man!"

David began to see what this was all about, but he was given no chance to say anything, as Petronius launched into a long discourse on the history of the marionette theater from ancient days to the modern era, the words gushing out of him like water from a fountain, in abrupt phrases and unclear sentences. David could understand only about half of it, but he politely made an attempt to follow. Then fatigue overcame him, particularly when, as his enthusiasm increased, Petronius also kept reverting more and more to his native tongue.

"*Si, mio giovane musicante taciturno,*" he said. "My silent young fiddler. *Mi sembri una piccola bambola.* A little puppet man. That's what you look like. *Una marionetta!* But everyone looks like a tiny little puppet." David tried to indicate that he didn't understand, but the fountain became a cascade, a geyser. "*Sì! Perché ti devo confessare un segreto!* A secret. I will tell you a *segreto.* And that is that in *realtà le marionette sono uomini . . . e gli uomini sono marionette.* Do you understand? In reality *we* are the marionettes and the marionettes are human beings. This is a *rivoluzione nella metafisica!*" he cried ecstatically. "And no one knows it. Only me . . ." He suddenly started whispering, moving closer to David and staring into his eyes, his own eyes glowing. "And perhaps God. *Forse Dio.* If He now is not a human being —hee-hee . . ."

It had gradually dawned on David that this man was quite mad. Frightened, not knowing what to do, he stared at Petronius, now disintegrating before his very eyes. Another wave of words came and swept him away with it.

"And painted with shellac!" shouted Petronius. "Yes, it's the *teatro di marionette.* We're moved by strings and we speak with other people's voices. *E chi conduce i fili?* Who pulls the strings? *Chi parla?* Who . . . who speaks? Have you ever *thought* about that?" The last question came on a triumphant note.

Jason had been woken by all the noise. He sat up, rapidly surveyed the situation, and without the slightest change of expression, he interrupted the bass player.

"Petronius. Shut up now. I want to sleep. I'm certain David wants to sleep, too. He's sure to be tired. You can talk to him another time. Keep quiet now."

Petronius calmed down immediately and looked at his own hands. They were trembling slightly, and he clasped them together, staring at them all the time as if the flow of words were continuing inside him but didn't dare come across his lips, which just went on moving. David was painfully touched. He looked across at Jason.

"Get some sleep now," said Jason kindly. "We have to play later on today." Then he added, "You'll get used to it. But get some sleep now."

Obediently, David curled up on his seat and closed his eyes. He wanted nothing but to sleep, to escape from this cramped compartment and these not very pleasant men who were suddenly his colleagues. Again the question ran through his mind: What am I doing here?

He was soon asleep.

The compartment was quiet: Petronius in his corner, his hands clasped and his eyes moist; Spot as unmoving as a sphinx by the window; David and Jason asleep.

Now that they had left the city, it was lighter outside; the gentle landscape of southern England glided by. The train ran through Winchester, the sky full of shimmering pure April light. They hadn't seen that in London. This light was to follow them all through their journey.

The same day
Pier 44, Ocean Terminal, Southampton, 9:25

—————◆◆◆◆————

THERE she was. They had been able to see her from the compartment window as the train ran slowly through the harbor area and out to the terminal. She lay there like a great black-and-white supernatural creature. Passengers were boarding, cargo was being loaded, and up on the decks people could be seen moving like termites on the great body of the ship, the morning sun making the metal and glass glint and tremble with light.

When he saw the ship through the train window, David realized what an exaggeration it had been to say he had ever been on a ship when he had mentioned the Calais to Dover ferry—a miserable barge in comparison with this great sea serpent, all set for its journey across the ocean. They could just see the great curved stern from the window and the lettering glowing yellow against the black background:

TITANIC
Liverpool

Her name was right. The very sight of her vast shape—the cranes, the masts, the wires, and four enormous funnels—made David feel almost faint. The ship had a wonderful supernatural unity that made him think of music, of Bach, of sequences of notes extending and growing together into one vast structure. The other men were also looking at the new ship with some curiosity, but they had seen so many ships, they were soon much more occupied with their luggage and instrument cases.

The train stopped. They got out, and the other three musicians emerged from the next compartment into the seething chaos all around them. They soon started making their way through the terminal building and out the other side, where they broke away from the stream of passengers and set course astern toward the crew's gangway.

At close quarters, the slim organic impression dissolved into iron plates, each plate as large as a fully grown man and fixed with countless thick solid rivets. Along the side of the ship, the sight of it vanished into an infinity of those plates—the plates that together were this ship.

David thought Bach had now been combined with Wagner and this was *Die Walküre* and *Götterdämmerung*, the greatest steamship in the world. Grayish-black smoke rising out of three of the four stacks was being wafted away across the bay by the west wind.

The seven musicians went up the gangway and on board; Jason exchanged papers and lists with a ruddy-complexioned man in uniform. Then they were guided through an endless series of corridors and stairs down into the interior of the ship. Everything smelled new, of paint and oil; lights were still missing here and there, and the corridors were crowded with crew and passengers drifting back and forth, trying to find their way in this impossible labyrinth. Black stokers, white galley boys, emigrants and their large families, fragments of conversations and cries in English, German, Scandinavian, and Gaelic. They got lost several times and had to turn back, but at last the man in uniform clapped his hand to his forehead and exclaimed, "Here we are! Christ, it's hard to find your way around down here." His face was now an even deeper red beneath his white cap as he wiped the sweat off his forehead, as if he had been walking along miles of corridors and stairs since early morning.

"My name's McElroy," he said, fiddling with a bunch of keys, then adding with some pride, "I'm the purser on this tub—ha-ha."

He opened a door.

"This cabin's yours," said the purser to the musicians. "Next to the potato washer."

The cabin was simple and bare, four bunks along each long wall, a small table and some wooden chairs by one short wall, above the table a small porthole, a little light now cautiously trickling through it.

"It still smells a bit of paint in here," said the purser. "There's a cupboard for your instruments behind that door, and the washroom is on the left down the corridor. Any questions?"

"I understand we're already to play at lunch?" said Jason.

"First class have lunch as soon as we get to Calshot Castle, and you're to play in the lounge on D-deck before they sit down. You've got a corner by the piano." He thought for a moment. "To go up to D-deck, you follow a long corridor running to the fore until you get to a door on the right marked STAIRS. That's for crew only. You go through there; then you come to the first-class Grand Staircase. Go up the Grand Staircase to a deck, and that's where the lounge is. Be rather *discreet* as you go up those stairs, won't you. Always stick together, eh?"

"Of course, of course," said Jason courteously.

"I'll tell you how to get to the Palm Court later on. You play there at teatime and in the mornings. If you have any problems, ask me or the crew. The seamen, I mean, the real crew. You'll have all your meals with them."

"Excellent," said Jason.

"I must go now. I've other things to do." The purser hurried out, but then stopped in the doorway for a moment.

"Now, be good lads, won't you. No drinking, right? No running after girls."

"We'll be good lads," Jason assured him.

"I've sailed with musicians before."

"You can trust us as you trust your own children, Mr. McElroy, sir."

"I was afraid you might say something like that."

The door closed behind him.

"Nice chap," said Spot sourly. He had already commandeered a lower bunk for himself and was sitting on it, hat on lap, regarding the company with an expression of exquisite weariness. Practical matters were agreed on and arranged between the musicians. Jason and Alex unpacked, while David introduced himself properly to the two musicians from the other compartment, Jim and Georges. Jim was a rosy, smiling man who laughed at David and called him shipmate. Georges was more reserved and smelled so strongly of toilet water it almost drowned the smell of paint in the cabin.

Petronius, old and hunched, sat on his instrument case, which looked far too big for such a small man.

⚜

"This piano hasn't been tuned," said Spot. "God Almighty!" He struck a few chords.

Spot and David were in the far corner of the lounge, where the orchestra was placed, partially concealed by two palm trees. As it was only just after ten and the ship was not due to sail until exactly midday, Jason had let his musicians go and take a look at the ship and otherwise do whatever was necessary. Spot had announced he wanted to inspect his instrument, and for some reason decided he wanted David as his assistant. Jason raised no objections.

Ascending out of those dismal, paint-smelling depths was like going to heaven: knee-deep carpets everywhere, small mahogany tables with chairs grouped around them, leather winged chairs, chandeliers, glass mosaics inlaid in walls paneled in honey-golden oak and exquisitely carved. Lights had been installed between panes, creating a strange atmosphere of summer sunlight coming from outside. It could have been the entrance hall of a large Viennese café or a fashionable spa hotel. "This is what life at sea is like," said Spot dryly, noticing David's amazed eyes. Not even elevators were missing: small cabinets paneled in fine woods with mirrors and brass fittings, quietly bobbing up and down from deck to deck. Then there was also the magnificent staircase David and Spot had used, swirling in gracious curves from level to level.

The initial batch of first-class passengers to come on board appeared to be hovering around in the lounge, elegant gentlemen in straw boaters and striped trousers, lovely girls in sporty skirts and pert caps, venerable older ladies in those voluminous skirts reminiscent of draped buffet tables as they slowly and dignifiedly bobbed past, clearly laden with silver and other valuables. There were also a few solemn, formally clad men with that slightly lonely look a million pounds can give their owners. Otherwise, smart bellhops, stewards, and reception clerks were standing around in a kind of absentminded presence, glazed expressions of great dignity on their faces. In reality they were following the assembled company's movements with meticulous attention, but gave the impression of being members of a Trappist priesthood deeply absorbed in prayer for the digestions of the passengers, darting up at the slightest sign of anyone requiring anything.

David could never have imagined that such a ship existed, and even Spot seemed to approve as he put his hat and gloves on the grand piano with a satisfied expression and sat down on the stool. David noticed how well Spot fitted in—he could have been taken for a passenger. Spot had attracted the attention of one of the genies standing nearby, and in a flash he materialized by the piano, oozing a desire to be of service. What did the gentleman require? That was when Spot pronounced the piano out of tune. The steward lost some of his enthusiasm when he realized he was only talking to the ship's pianist. His expression told them he had had a difficult day.

"Never in my whole life—not even at sea—have I known a worse piano," Spot declared, his pince-nez glinting. "And I have known many."

"It was tuned when it arrived," protested the steward. "No one has touched it since then. It can't be *that* . . ."

"*That* bad?" said Spot. "Really? Oh really. Just listen. Just *listen* to this, then, my man!" He thumped out the first chords of the "Merry Widow Waltz." "It sounds just like an Indonesian *gamelan orchestra*!"

The steward listened attentively, clearly unfamiliar with this musical possibility.

"I simply *cannot* play on this," said Spot.

David was also listening carefully. Perhaps the piano *was* a trifle poor in the bass.

"I think it sounds quite passable," said the steward, shrugging his shoulders. This was all that was needed at the end of an otherwise exhausting morning, not only on departure day, but also on a maiden voyage when things were not yet really running smoothly.

The steward looked as if he would rather leave and let the grand piano be a grand piano, but Spot would not let him go.

"Passable!" he said. "Passable. So you think it's passable. I'll have you know this piano has been standing in a draft without any proper covering. Do you think *that's* passable, by any chance? Get us a piano tuner."

"Impossible."

"Here and now."

"Can't be done. We're leaving soon."

"I absolutely demand it."

"Listen," said the steward, changing tune somewhat. "Can't you fix it yourself? I've seen you people doing that kind of thing for yourselves."

Spot appeared to have been waiting for just this cue. With an expression of taking all the sufferings of the world upon his shoulders, he threw up his hands.

"Always having to do everything oneself. Absolutely everything. Well, well. Oh well. We'll do it. But you'll have to get us a half bottle of whiskey."

"I beg your pardon!" The steward's glazed expression had now returned, and his left eyebrow shot up.

"Half a bottle," persisted Spot. "It needn't be your very best." The steward's expression told them he was not going to be blackmailed.

"Please," said Spot, smiling. "Please fetch a half bottle. If you can't find a piano tuner, you must be able to find some whiskey. That ought to lie within your field of competence." The other man looked as if he would like to tell Spot something, but he swallowed his words. Now glassy-eyed in the extreme, he looked at Spot and David, his nostrils quivering.

"Right. You can have two glasses. Get it done before too many passengers arrive. The final rush will be at half past eleven. I can't have you hanging around here all morning." At that he vanished.

Spot glanced out the window, his eyes darkening as if he were ashamed, but when he looked back at David again, he smiled ironically. David looked down. He was worried. What had Jason said? Always do what the officers say. And what had the purser said? No fooling around. No drinking. Be *discreet*, he'd said. Yet Jason had not hesitated to let them come up here—on the stairs Spot had turned around and said to David, "Now we'll have a bit of fun, young man"—just that. David glanced anxiously around.

"You must never do anything like that," said the pianist. "But it's nicer up here than down in that cabin by the potato washer."

The two whiskeys arrived and work began. Spot had tuning fork, wedges, and tape in a case in an inner pocket, and a small tuning hammer was fastened under the lid of the piano.

David didn't really know what to do with his whiskey, but Spot simply drank it as well, without asking, working in silence with David looking on. Spot had an incredible technique and his ear was so fine-tuned, David was astonished as Spot caught the slightest nuances and quivers David could hardly hear. Spot seemed to be in mysterious personal relation to all the notes, as if the accurate frequency of oscillation of every one was engraved on his mind by nature and their internal relation in the tempered piano was something he could grasp with his hands. To tune a grand piano is a difficult, lengthy, and precise task, but to Spot it seemed like a game. He had unusually beautiful hands, long, lean, and muscular, moving swiftly and lithely over the keys and strings like graceful animals.

An hour later, the job was done and Spot had managed to extract two more whiskeys from the steward.

"Serves him right," Spot mumbled as the steward came back with the whiskeys.

"Who?" said David.

"The purser. I can't stand petty officers. They love deciding what musicians can and can't do. Believe you me, my boy, life is full of petty officers."

Then he bent over the piano again.

David looked at him inquiringly, but Spot said nothing more. David again felt despondent over his own situation. Here he was, an eternity away from home, with a taciturn pianist, and was supposed to be helping him tune a piano, while he had obviously been brought along only to conjure up another whiskey.

Spot was working. Behind the mask of irony was a thoughtfulness, something wary, something David couldn't make out, a little of it just visible as he worked. David sensed he might grow in stature in the other man's eyes if he made an extreme effort to please him, so it was with some satisfaction he was able to show Spot that he also had a passable ear. Spot kept striking chords, occasionally asking David's opinion, and David was able to nod back or make a sign indicating the bass note was too high. In that way, they slowly started conversing, a conversation in gestures and looks, Spot taking swigs of whiskey in between.

Finally Spot settled down on the stool and, leaning forward, started playing a Chopin nocturne. He played the piece right through without even looking at David, and David listened. Spot's playing was pure, clear, and perfectly lucid, no cheating. David played the piano sufficiently well himself to be able to judge another musician's work and he stood there listening to the way this entertainer was playing Chopin as if in a concert hall. He looked searchingly at Spot—his face pale and unhealthy-looking, lined and with dark shadows, nose thin and prominent, and his eyes, those eyes he had noticed on the train—while he was playing, Spot kept them half-closed, the anxiety in them turned into the man himself. They were listening eyes.

A hint of something resembling trust had arisen between the two of them, and David was certain that it was not just for the whiskey Spot had wanted him along. But when he stopped playing and turned to David again, his gaze was still half turned inward. David said involuntarily, "Very beautiful."

Spot grimaced.

"What's beautiful?" he said with an air of disappointment. "You mustn't say things like that. *Unbegreiflich scheint die Nachtigall,*" he went on in perfect high German, his face closed again. He got up, gathered his tuning instruments, his eyes no longer listening, and without a word left the piano and David and headed out of the lounge. For a few moments David sat there, at a loss.

A ship about to depart is a confusing world, chaotic, a ring dance of minor and major items to be done at the very last moment. People boarding a large liner shortly before departure would perhaps not be aware of the many preparations, but they would notice the special mood, a hectic, electric atmosphere rather like stage fright. Seamen shouting to each other, a tenseness in their voices, their movements animated, a frenzied air about them—a thousand minor duties to be completed before casting off.

David followed Spot, knowing nothing about the ship, what it had cost in human and technical effort to build and make seaworthy, but he soon lagged behind the pianist and gradually became lost in stairways and corridors. He sensed some of the tense, feverish atmosphere prevailing on board, but did not know where it came from.

He knew nothing about the Swedish gymnast Lindström at that very moment getting the gymnasium ready to receive passengers—a squash court, rowing machines, electric horses and camels (imported from Wiesbaden), punching bags, weight-lifting equipment, and Turkish baths at their disposal. The shipbuilders at the Harland & Wolff Belfast shipyard had even found space for a small swimming pool. In boundless good health, white flannels, and chalked gymnast's shoes, Lindström was now testing all those mechanical wonders for himself, the whole time twirling his mustache and humming a manly Swedish folksong.

In the kitchens, galley boys were hectically peeling thousands of potatoes and washing asparagus, while stokers in the bowels of the ship, almost down by the keel, were trying to clear their way to a smoldering fire in coal bunker number 5, which might cause some unpleasantness if they didn't get it under control. Astern, the engineers were polishing, tending, and coddling their engines and the enormous boilers, the miraculous turbine engine, and two piston-driven steam engines that drove the three propellers.

At that very moment, Captain Clarke, the representative of the emigration authorities, had just finished his final inspection of the ship's cabins, supply of drinking water, bunkering facilities, and sanitary conditions, and was now filling out his certificate for clearance, without which no passenger ship was allowed to leave any British harbor. The ship's doctor and several other officers had undertaken the inspection of the crew and were now writing their final report. The most dependable and experienced seamen Southampton could provide had signed on, and the most meticulous and conscientious officers were in charge of it all—just as the best engineers and technicians had made the ship seaworthy. One of these men was Thomas Andrews, managing director at Harland & Wolff, nephew of Lord Pirrie, the head of the firm, who was unable to be there owing to illness. Andrews had gone on board to supervise the ship's maiden voyage—"my child," as he called her. Andrews was a ruddy, slender little man and he had created this miracle of a ship, this Titan. With genuine passion, he was now supervising her first days. He had been on his feet from early morning until late at night for the last few days, making sure everything was according to specifications and jotting down ideas for improvements. With his own eyes, he had seen to the final details of the furnishings, noting that the armchairs in the starboard Café Parisien should be painted green, that the hat pegs on the walls of the cabins were hideous—fastened with too many screws—and what had become of the missing ten swabs out of the seventy-two ordered? You could never be quite sure, never check too often that everything was all right, whether the electric gates in the watertight bulkheads worked or the lifeboat davits were in order. Lightbulbs were missing in one of the first-class Louis XVI–style staterooms and there was no chamber pot in one of the Empire staterooms. Andrews put the lightbulbs in himself and personally put the pot in its place, just to be on the safe side.

J. Bruce Ismay, director of the White Star Line and owner of the *Titanic*, was at that moment coming on board with his wife and three children. He was proud, even overwhelmed, to be able ostentatiously to show them the ship. He had seen her many a time before, of course, but all the same—all the same, he had looked up at the mighty hull with enthusiasm as the family had got out of their Daimler down on the quay and set off up the gangway. Forty-six thousand three hundred and twenty-nine tons, he thought with satisfaction. He and his family were bowed on board. His wife and children were to be given a guided tour, while Ismay himself was to travel on her maiden voyage. His luggage was taken to his suite, numbers B52, 54, and 56.

Sparks and his assistant, John Phillips and Harold Bride, the two telegraph operators, were in the Marconi wireless room, two melancholy young men surrounded by an aura of wireless mystique. They were now trying out the technical equipment for the last time, shifting a small coil, but otherwise finding everything in order.

The headwaiter in the *à la carte* restaurant, an elegant man called Signor Luigi Gatti, had been seconded from the famous family restaurants of Gatti's Adelphi and Gatti's Strand, together with chef, sous chefs, waiters, and cellar man. He was surveying his domain, straightening the odd crooked table napkin or knife, sliding his hand down a bottle of wine to test its temperature with almost erotic delight, tasting a truffle, adjusting his bow tie—as all great artists are, he was very, very nervous.

Captain Edward John Smith, the ship's captain, in his dark gold-braided uniform, was on the bridge, leaning over one of the three shiny brass engine-room telegraphs, receiving a report from Chief Officer Henry Wilde. RMS *Titanic* was at that moment declared fully manned and ready to sail. Second Officer Lightoller had carried out his last inspection of the ship's cargo and declared it securely stowed. In the depths of the ship's dark holds were goods and merchandise worth over £80,000, all thoroughly stamped and registered. The Lustig Brothers of New York had imported four crates of boaters, while Wright & Graham of Boston were to receive 437 chests of tea. F. B. Wandegrift & Co. were to enliven the youth of America with sixty-three crates of the best French champagne. G. W. Sheldon was sending a case of surgical instruments and a box of golf balls (both intended for the surgeons' fraternity), American Express added even more crates of boaters, as well as hundreds of other consignments, including two casks of quicksilver and for some reason a barrel of soil. For unfathomable reasons, the First National Bank of Chicago was to receive 300 boxes of shelled walnuts, while W. E. Carter was to have a whole motorcar, partially dismantled and carefully lashed. There were also crates of refrigerators from Anderson Refrigeration Machinery Company, sacks of capers, bundles of dried fish, Bruyère pipes, pâté de foie gras and anchovies, ostrich feathers, rabbit fur, gutta-percha, and an expensive edition of *The Rubaiyat of Omar Khayyam.* All of this, but all of it, was on Lightoller's list and safely stowed. Captain Smith listened to his conscientious officers with satisfaction, then walked slowly across the mahogany bridge over to the window. He remained there, gazing out.

Captain Smith was a broad, strapping man in his sixties, with white hair and beard and deep-set blue eyes. His appearance was magnificent, even awe-inspiring, but he was unobtrusive and calm and seldom raised his voice.

He was looking ahead. He had sailed the North Atlantic run for many years and was the White Star Line's oldest and most experienced captain, a lengthy series of faultless, almost uneventful crossings behind him. He recognized both the maritime as well as the social role of a captain, and to him the captain's function seemed to be constantly changing. In the minds of both passengers and crew, the role of captain seemed to have become increasingly symbolic, more and more that of the ship's monarch, a constitutional monarch with limited functions, with the right of veto and also with official entertainment duties, the ship's symbol of power and dominion. With so many skilled officers and on such a safe ship, he thus had a simple assignment. He relied entirely on his subordinates, so never needed to raise his voice, and indeed had almost forgotten what it might say. But he took his assignment seriously and he did not simply approve his officers' reports.

This was to be his last trip. He had actually been about to join the ranks of the retired when Ismay wanted to bestow on him the honor of captaining this new flagship of the fleet on her maiden voyage— in honor, Ismay had said to Captain Smith, of your past service.

He knew it was the last time he would be on the bridge accepting his officers' reports. He knew the gold braid endowed him with power on this trip—then no more. His young wife, Eleanor, was waiting for him at home with their little boy, scarcely a year old. So this time he took longer than usual. He pondered over the reports, listening carefully as he was told that lifeboat drills and inspections had gone according to plan and that everything was shipshape. He was looking ahead.

Lightoller now gave the captain the long list of first-class passengers, with the latest additions and deletions, which would soon be sent to the ship's printing shop to be duplicated and distributed among the passengers, so they would know with whom they were on board ship. Captain Smith examined the names as every good British host does before giving a party, rapidly deciding with whom he had to have supper and in what order—the role of a steamship captain is not least one of official entertainment. He registered Guggenheims and Astors on the list, noted that the Vanderbilts had canceled, and found to his horror that Sir Cosmo and Lady Duff Gordon were on board. He couldn't stand them—well, the party had to go on.

Seven thousand heads of cabbage, he thought (not meaning the passengers), two and three-quarter tons of tomatoes (some of the head steward's figures had fastened in his mind), 36,000 oranges, 75,000 pounds of fresh meat, 20,000 dozen fresh eggs, 40 tons of potatoes, 7,500 bottles of wine, 35,000 bottles of beer and mineral water, 850 assorted bottles of spirits, and 8,000 Havana cigars—they should all guarantee the party's success. The head steward had been extremely busy.

Captain Smith turned to his subordinates, and the aura of royal sanction was actually tangible as the old commander looked sternly at them.

"Carry on," he said.

His first and second officers saluted.

Well, that is the ship. A black stoker shouts something obscene to his mates through the racket down in the underworld, and white smiles shine in all that darkness. Two stewardesses dreamily roll their eyes as they talk about their recent adventures ashore (he's a *bank clerk*, Laura, just imagine!). A bellboy receives a whole dollar as a tip from the newly married John Jacob Astor, who has come on board with his bride—the bellboy simply stands there goggling at the multimillionaire. The crowd in the lounge thickens and in a cabin next to the potato washer two musicians are looking over their uniforms. A button needs sewing on and trousers need to be shortened. The orchestra's assignment is to entertain the passengers, playing before and after dinner, giving concerts in the evenings and promenade concerts in the mornings, plus playing for services on Sundays. To manage all that, the orchestra has to divide up into groups, each with its set of uniforms—one shift in white jackets for the promenade trio, blue jackets with green lapels for the evening serenades. All the uniforms have golden harps on their lapels, just as on all the White Star ships. Jim and Alex are the two down in the cabin shortening trouser legs.

Ahead of them is a new and strenuous crossing, a new ship, a new cramped existence in a small cabin. They are discussing their pay, which has actually been reduced by a whole pound since Black & Black took over the agency for the North Atlantic. They are no longer formally regarded as members of the crew but as second-class passengers, which is insane, but it makes it easier for the shipowners to do as they like with them.

Alex is furious, wishing Black & Black a dismal future. Jim, the gentle, rosy North Countryman, is more controlled. But both of them need that extra pound at the moment.

The peak of ridiculousness is that the musicians—now that they are "passengers"—must be able to produce the $50 demanded by the immigration regulations, in order to be allowed to go ashore in New York.

They are sitting there, sewing away, cursing and swearing. That is also the ship.

Jason Coward, their leader, is up on deck.

⚜

Out in the wind on an aft deck, Jason was on his own, the air ruffling his hair as he gazed across the harbor up into the narrow little streets of Southampton, where there were families, children—homes.

He liked doing this just before sailing, gazing at the city he was leaving, his own riddle again, his own great why. It filled him with peace.

Jason could really have chosen any number of professions, but circumstances had led to him to become a ship's musician, and he was not unhappy about that. He had not counted how many ships he had been on over the years, or how many crossings he had made. Things were always on the move. There were always new ships and people. The bandsmen came and went. He had played with some of them for many years, while others he saw on only one trip before they went down the gangway and disappeared into the harbor streets Jason could see from there. Perhaps a house was waiting for them, a house containing childish voices, voices that would say loudly to anyone who cared to listen in the street that father was back home. Or perhaps all that was waiting for them was a miserable room in a boardinghouse. They came and went, the musicians. Jason never even raised an eyebrow about that nowadays. Everything changes. Only he himself and his golden-brown violin were always the same.

Jason had been in transit for a long time. He knew the ships and the seas. He knew the secrets of his trade and that it was quite different being a musician at sea from being a musician ashore—for instance, just a simple matter of having to avoid certain forms of music when the sea was rough. Who could know beforehand that old ladies threw up at *The Tales of Hoffmann* if the winds were high? Who could guess that? Traveling man, man at sea, is a remarkable phenomenon. Life had taught Jason that. He himself was a traveler to such an extent that like all Plimsoll lines, he was limited by the permitted displacement of various seasons and conditions, so he was also classified and defined by the many varying circumstances. The lowest displacement line on all hulls is WNA—Winter North Atlantic, and Jason was prepared for the North Atlantic winter, for the dismal atmosphere that could overcome passengers when the ship sailed into fog just west of the Grand Banks—then he had to choose cheerful but not *too* lively music. He knew the storms and the winds, the sigh of the gray foaming sea, the iron cold that arose when the ships entered a field of icebergs—the North Pole sending its cold ambassadors far to the south, even in the summer. He knew the shifts of the winds with the course of the sun, the long, indolent afternoons when the waves slackened in the months of June and July, so the music he chose had to be not too demanding. He had seen passengers of all sorts, healthy and sick, friendly and angry—and he had learned his trade bit by bit. Once on the *Lusitania* he had played "Yankee Doodle" in honor of an American senator traveling first class to England. Who could have imagined that the man was a Southerner and could not stand being reminded of anything north of the Mason-Dixon Line? The purser's anger when the meal was over and the very real threat of having to use his violin case as a means of transport home was among the items Jason bore with him in his heart. He knew how difficult officers could be and what an amazing and capricious race musicians are. He knew about the squabbling that always arose with seven or eight men in one small cabin. The same sorrows always afflicted members of the orchestra: homesickness, drink, the clap. Money troubles and depressed outbursts about not having done anything better in life than to accompany seasick people in three-quarter time. Jason was used to dealing with them. But on the trip ahead of them, the composition was perhaps particularly unfortunate.

This new boy—David—it had been pure chance they had got hold of him at all at two days' notice. They ought to consider themselves lucky and not behave as Alex had on the train. Alex was an old friend of Jason's, and in many ways was his second-in-command in the orchestra. Jason knew perfectly well Alex was not overjoyed to see the young musician. They had already had to renounce their original hopes for the makeup of the band and were now faced with a very uncertain hand of cards. Spot, for instance. A skillful musician, yes indeed, how skillful, but Jason was not really terribly pleased to have him, for he never knew where he was with him. And as far as Petronius was concerned . . . well. It was known among musicians on the Atlantic run that Petronius Witt's harp was a trifle out of tune, to put it mildly. Occasionally the old Italian had behaved so oddly he had been unable to work. Jason was praying to God for a calm and untroubled crossing. The job wasn't difficult, for they had to play only in first class, where things mostly ran smoothly. The weather would be good and the crossing time short. But their playing had to be faultless, no mistakes, no misbehavior. The ship was the pride of the merchant fleet, indeed, the pride of the British nation, and there would be nearly a whole congress of millionaires on board. True to his habit, Jason had checked the social columns, and both Guggenheims and Astors were to be on board, as well as Stead, the newspaper magnate, Isidor Straus and wife, the writer Futrelle, and some special envoy from Washington. Then the usual bunch of titled people, gamblers, and drifters. Jason had played for them all before, and he knew some wealthy people liked to complain to the captain about the music, perhaps just to have something to do, or perhaps to show their fellow passengers that millionaires also have an ear for music—who knows? With the orchestra he had, it was not easy to predict how the light music would go.

Jason thought with horror of the last time he had sailed with Petronius, on the *Mauretania*. One Sunday the captain had held Communion service and the band had played for the hymns. In the middle of "Amazing Grace," Petronius had started playing quick little trills —a kind of ostinato—on a theme from "Maple Leaf Rag," and only with the greatest presence of mind had Jason and Alex managed to save the situation. After that fearful scene, Alex had sworn he would never again play with Petronius. So when the double-bass player originally supposed to be on the *Titanic* trip bowed out and the agency had not been able to find any other replacement except Petronius— well, Alex had not been gentle. For a moment it had looked as if he would also back out, but Jason and Alex were old shipmates, so Alex stayed.

As leader, Jason had gradually acquired a good feeling for people —for his purposes, anyhow. When he judged a musician, the most important thing was that the man had the will to find his sea legs in more ways than just maritime. Next he had to be able to play and keep his uniform in decent shape. Finally, it was also good if he did not come out with his entire life history, the last only because that suited Jason best.

David would perhaps not have fulfilled those demands had Jason been able to choose. The boy had clearly run away from home and was now as lost as a champagne bottle in a harbor basin. God knows what this would bring with it when they were finally at sea. But the boy at least seemed honest and helpful. Spot had insisted on an assistant to help him with the piano and David had simply gone with him. It could have been worse. Alex would not have been so obliging.

Jason glanced over at Southampton again. Here and there, white washing was waving them goodbye, and the usual crowd of curious spectators had flocked to the harbor to see the ship cast off.

Jason turned around to find Alex standing beside him.

"I thought you were fixing the uniforms?"

"I didn't feel well. Thought I'd get a bit of fresh air."

Jason looked closely at him. His friend was gray in the face under the fair beard.

"And I wanted to be in on the departure," said Alex. "There's always something good about departures."

They said nothing more. For a while they stood in silence watching the last stokers coming up the gangway after their final pints, then the last mailbags being brought on board. Jason looked at his old brother-in-arms. Alex's face gradually grew less gray, but he was very quiet.

Jason had known Alex ever since one appallingly wet evening over many years ago. They had been in a pub down by the London docks, a dismal, smoke-filled place. That was in Jason's homeless period, a time it was not always pleasant to think back on.

Jason had been sitting with his violin at a table at the far end of the pub, enjoying the squalid atmosphere. At the time he was playing in pubs to earn his daily bread. He had occasionally tried to get taken on by a regular orchestra, but so far without success. But his sound was good and he could also play songs on demand, so he was well received in most establishments, where he would play for half an hour for a handful of small change. That evening Jason had already played and had sought shelter from the weather in this stinking dump. Most of the customers were drunk, squabbling, fighting, and surreptitiously pouring gin out of bottles under the table. Jason had a pint of brown ale in front of him, his fourth, and was hoping the downpour would soon end. It didn't; it simply went on and on. He had just begun to consider dashing out into it when a strange figure at the bar suddenly attracted the attention of everyone in the pub.

A tall, fairish man with a mustache and beard, blue eyes and a sturdy frame—had he been sober and better dressed he would have made a handsome figure. But he was unkempt and ragged, and also extremely drunk. He demonstrated the latter by suddenly letting out a bellow which made everyone jump, no ordinary drunken roar but a deep booming sound that filled the whole room, almost like a note, and it went on and on. He put his head back and simply roared, his eyes half-closed, bellowing until he had no breath left in him. Then he drew a deep breath, put his head back, and started all over again.

It was incredible that so much sound could be contained in one man.

The clientele were looking at the man with some benevolence. In this part of London good entertainment was sparse. The man put his head back and bellowed just once more, a long, lamenting note, like a fearful caged wild animal, and now they could see that he was shutting his eyes tightly as if in pain and there was something running down his cheeks.

"It's the Russian," Jason heard a voice say at the next table. "He gets like that every time he wants to go home. It happens every week when he's put together enough money to get drunk."

Jason looked at the Russian, and it was true: the ragged man had a violin case between his feet, black and shabby. He bellowed again, but this time it became a long-drawn-out howl.

"He'll stop soon," the voice said again. "He usually gives up when they want to throw him out." The innkeeper sized the Russian up. Then it came.

Innkeeper: "Now look here, mate . . ."
Russian: "Ooooooooooooo . . ."
Innkeeper: "We can't have no howling like that here."
Russian: "Aaaaaaaoooooooo . . ."
Innkeeper: "We just can't, you must see that."
Russian: "Oooooooooouuuuuu!"
Innkeeper: "You can't stay if you goes on howling like that."
Russian (with renewed force): "Aahhhrk! Aooooooo . . ."
Other voices (to the innkeeper): "He can't hear you." "He can't speak proper English." "Not when he's drunk." "And he's drunk." "Throw him out!"
Innkeeper: "Give us a hand, then, men."
Russian: "Ghrrrr! Grrraaaoooo!"

Two or three men got up to help the host, but the moment they got hold of the howler, he seemed to wake up. He let out a number of drunken sounds, probably mostly Russian, and with tears spurting, he started resisting.

Jason stayed where he was, watching. He felt sorry for the Russian, who was weeping and homesick. That was enough for Jason, and in addition, the Russian had a violin case. That kindled something in Jason—he normally ignored the fights and the misery down here in the slums. He got up abruptly without really knowing what he was doing, went over to the exit, and put his own violin case just outside the door. Maybe he was also somewhat under the influence himself after four beers. He noticed to his astonishment that he was angry, yes, raging, filled with red-hot fury, a great injured rage on behalf of the Russian welling up inside him. If a Russian wanted to howl with homesickness, he should be allowed to. Enough! What did it matter to the innkeeper if a Russian howled. Hadn't he paid his way.

With a roar Jason threw himself at the four men grappling with the Russian. Hell and damnation, he thought. Take this!

It was a fine fight. Jason was big and strong, and even if he was not particularly used to fighting, he had a devilish trick: He grabbed his opponents, grasped them by the seat of their pants, and heaved them aside as if they were sacks of corn. The sacks screamed as they flew through the air and grew quite still as they crashed to the floor. After a few moments, five or six men were in dry dock and the Russian seemed to have luck on his side now that Jason had joined in the fray. He fought, was hit; he spat blood and cursed. More customers joined in the battle, most of them on the host's side, but some of them for Jason and the Russian. Then glasses started shattering. The Russian grabbed his violin case and slammed it down on the host's head, but the host came back with a vengeance and the Russian was given a taste of his own violin case. Meanwhile, Jason was on the receiving end of most of the assaults and was slowly being pressed back against the wall. That was fatal. Four or five men grabbed his arms and legs and, while he bit and struggled as best he could, he was dragged over to the door and thrown out. The Russian followed a moment later; the innkeeper had dealt with him personally. As he sailed out onto the pavement, the Russian let out a new howl. It was his last.

In the few seconds he had been lying on the muddy street, Jason had realized there might possibly be what they call judicial aftermath. So by the time the Russian came flying out, Jason had already grabbed his violin case and was ready for immediate departure. He grabbed the other man's wrist, hauled him to his feet, and they rushed off through the dark and the rain, slipping and sliding on the dirty cobblestones and running on. They had to get away before a certain man in a helmet and with a truncheon appeared. Behind them they could hear shouts and curses.

After a while they stopped in an alleyway. The two men looked at each other. The Russian, who had become relatively sober from the fight and the cold, turned his light eyes, one of them already swelling, on Jason and smiled.

"My friend!" he cried, dribbling blood.

Jason had also collected himself by now and was beginning to feel idiotic. Idiotic and battered. Why on earth had he wanted to be a hero on behalf of a drunken Russian?

"My friend!" the Russian said again, this time embracing Jason, repeating, My friend, my friend, over and over again, until Jason had had enough.

"Goodbye," said Jason, holding out his hand. "They shouldn't have attacked you like that." Best to be off before it all became ridiculous. But the Russian didn't understand.

"I," he said, pointing at himself, "I Alex. Alexander Byezhnikov. You—*moy drug*. My friend. Yes. You."

The Russian smiled, his face dripping with rain; then a whole stream of Russian poured out. Jason remembered something.

"Your violin," he said. "The violin. You've left it behind. There." He pointed in the direction they had come from. Alex understood and grinned.

"Ah," he said. Then he began to laugh, slapping his knees, laughing long and happily.

"No," he said, still laughing. "Come!" He dragged Jason with him along several more streets, laughing all the time, then finally stopped outside a shop. A pawnbroker's.

"Violin *there*," he said, pointing at the shop. "And there," pointing in the other direction, "there in pub, only *case* in pub." He laughed loudly again. He had cheated them properly. Jason had to laugh with him. "I," began Alex hesitantly, "I drinked up violin in pub. Violin *there*." He pointed at the shop again.

"I see," said Jason, making a sign that he wished to go on.

"*There!*" said Alex again, very earnestly, his long forefinger directed at the pawnbroker's.

"I understand," said Jason.

"No—no!" said Alex. "You—my friend. *Moy drug!*"

"My name's Jason," said Jason uneasily.

"Yes! My friend Jason. My friend Jason. My violin—*there*. Very cheap price." He fished out a pawn ticket. Violin. Eight shillings. Not much, just about what Jason had in his pocket.

"Jason!" said Alex. "Friend! Play violin like me! My violin *there*."

Jason sighed. Slowly it dawned on him that he had been stupid to get involved in the fight for this stranger. The Russian knew you could not say no to a friend. Jason resignedly took out the money, went into the pawnbroker's, and redeemed the violin. Outside, he handed it to Alex, who carefully tucked it inside his overcoat.

"There you go," said Jason, wanting to leave and cursing that he had been so easily fooled. God, he could be conned into anything.

But Alex held on to him, thumping him on the back and apparently about to start weeping again.

"Ha-ha!" he cried. "Hah! See." He hauled a shabby purse out of a pocket, counted out eight shillings, and handed them to Jason. He laughed again.

"*There*, in pub . . ." He thumped Jason's shoulder. "I not have time to pay!"

⚘

That had been the beginning, and it was a friendship that lasted. Jason had to smile when he thought about it. It turned out to be impossible to get rid of this incredible Russian. He hung on, insisting on playing together with Jason, and despite everything, since two men have greater musical opportunities than one, from then on they took to playing together in pubs and on the streets, Jason first part, Alex second. The day came when Jason found he missed the Russian when he didn't appear. A kind of free companionship had arisen, simple and without words—wordless because, to start with, Alex didn't speak much English, but as he gradually learned, it had not depended on words. There was something else at the root of their friendship, perhaps the fight, perhaps because they were both homeless in the great city. The friendship lasted despite the differences between them.

Neither of them had ever told the other much about himself. Jason knew nothing about Alex except that he had been in London for four months before that rough-and-tumble evening in the pub down at the docks. Nor had Jason said anything about himself except that he was a student and things had gone downhill for him. Why and how was of no interest to the other man.

After a while they got work with an orchestra in a music hall, then they played Palm Court music in a hotel, and in 1908 the Cunard Line hired them.

They had been at sea ever since. Playing on ships was respectable regular work and fairly well paid, even if the pay had been reduced by a whole pound in the last six months.

Jason looked at Alex as he leaned over the railing, his chest pressed against it. He's not himself, Jason thought. On recent crossings Alex had been cross and very irritable over minor matters. Jason wondered whether one of his attacks of homesickness was on the way. The Russian used to get them in the spring or early summer. But it wasn't that, either. There was a melancholy in his expression as he stared out over the city, his eyes sunken, his nose and cheekbones apparently protruding, as if his skin were stretched tight over his skull.

What is he thinking about? Jason asked himself. Is he thinking what I'm thinking as I stand looking over the city we're leaving? Does he also see the laundry waving goodbye? Or are his thoughts in his own language and is he seeing cities and people I have never seen? Is he thinking about what no one else can see, images, voices from childhood, those quiet evenings before life took over? I have never asked him, would never be able to ask him.

The steam whistle let out three hoots, three deep triple notes which echoed over the shore.

Mooring ropes were cast off and hawsers hauled on board. Three small tugs, tough as giants, slowly started towing the ship out into the shipping lane.

Departure. The pilot was on the bridge with the captain; the crowd by the terminal building waved, the promenade decks were dark with people fluttering scarves and handkerchiefs, shouting jubilantly.

Jason and Alex stood there as before, neither waving nor shouting.

After the *Titanic* had been towed down into the shipping lane and turned around ninety degrees by the tugboats so the long trip down-river could start, something happened, an event quite clearly visible from the afterdeck. A row of steamers was lined up along the channel, delayed by the coal strike, and as the *Titanic* passed the slender hull of SS *New York*, the *New York* starting moving like a ghost ship. The swell the *Titanic* had set in motion created great suction and counter-suction in the cramped harbor basin, and the crack from the thick manila hawser snapping could be heard on the afterdeck where Jason and Alex were standing. The *New York* came sliding swiftly out from the shore, prow first, like a gigantic lance heading straight for the *Titanic*. Passengers retreated fearfully away from the railings as a buzz of panic spread on board. The *New York* had no steam up and could not be steered. A few hectic seconds followed; then one of the tug-boats, the little *Vulcan*, which had already let the *Titanic* go, headed for the unmanageable ship to try to get a hawser aboard her, suc-ceeding on the second attempt. She was still sliding toward the *Ti-tanic*. The manila hawser shrieked as the *Vulcan* hauled away at the *New York* with all its might. With frighteningly little clearance—barely five feet—a collision was avoided. The little *Vulcan* slowly but surely hauled the *New York* back toward shore again.

The people on the decks of the *Titanic* collected their wits, and the cheering broke out once again.

The *Titanic* was still while the *New York* was being tied up, and extra moorings were attached to the other ships along the channel so that the same thing would not happen again at the next attempt. Thanks to the alertness on board the tugboat, an accident had been prevented that could have stopped the whole crossing, and at worst could have claimed lives.

Instead, they were now delayed by an hour.

Jason and Alex spat in the sea to counteract the bad omen and then went below.

As the *Titanic* slowly made her way down the channel and out into open water, everything went well. The bugle signal for lunch was given and passengers started heading for the dining rooms.

In first class, in the lobby of the magnificent restaurant, the or-chestra was already seated, elegantly dressed, and, under the leader-ship of bandmaster Jason Coward, playing cheerful tunes in farewell to England. As the ship glided past the Isle of Wight, the passengers crowded to the tables, elated after such an exciting morning.

JASON'S STORY

The same day

In the English Channel, on the way to Cherbourg, 17:10

— ◆—◆◆◆—◆ —

As soon as Jason came up on deck, tired after having played half the afternoon, he was faced with the sunset, the scarlet sphere in the west just above the horizon. The sky was quite clear, like a sheet of glass polished clean by the wind.

Some of the emigrants had begun singing on the afterdeck. One man had produced his accordion and was playing a jig. A crowd soon gathered around him, happy, almost crazed now that the journey had at last begun. Jason could never understand the joy they felt. He could see that what was happening was something magical to them, something unfathomably beautiful, terrible, and great. They were leaving Europe, leaving home, and commending themselves to the journey. They sailed in limbo between one home and another—a home they knew nothing about. Many would never see the old continent again. Jason knew New York sufficiently well to realize what they would encounter there.

Jason felt a kind of monotonous meaninglessness about it all. He did not understand the joy flushing their faces, or the shadows of pain flitting across as the refrain accentuated a particularly beautiful feature of the Cornish hills, or wherever they came from. He was outside both, both the longing for the new and the longing for the old home.

Or was it that he didn't *want* to understand?

He was filled with that brilliant light—there it was again, again overcoming him. The sun itself was heavy and sated, coloring the sea. The singing and laughter from the emigrants became a tinkling sound, bouncing like a ball up to the skies and across the surface of the sea. Then it came to him, all over again, his thoughts that morning, his thoughts of *that other* morning. The crimson sunlight—do you remember it? Do you remember the morning when the sun poured in on you like a river of malice? The voices from the afterdeck become part of the memory, of the image vibrating inside you, of the morning when the right times came to an end.

❧

It was a late September day. Through the high leaded windows, the sunlight spread over the oak paneling and floor of the ancient hall of his boarding school. Everything was bathed in this sunlight; the darkness up in the beams was like lumps of congealed blood.

Loud voices of boys echoed from the corridors, a group of them occasionally passing through the hall, chattering eagerly, laughing, on their way to a class. This was the oldest part of the school, heraldic shields and portraits of admirals above the paneling and two suits of armor over by one double door, two lances by the other.

A fairly tall red-haired boy was standing facing the windows, his face buried in his hands, not moving, as if outside the space around him. He did not notice the comings and goings in the hall.

All he could see was that crimson sunlight. He could see it through the fingers over his eyes. He could see it was no longer ordinary light but something else much more powerful, something that hurt. It went right into him.

Everything else was nothing but a distant accompaniment, an undertone. A cold chill rose from the stone floor; a chilling softness pulled him down. I'm going to fall, he thought. I want to fall. But he didn't, for the light held him and would not let him go.

A piece of paper protruded from the top pocket of his blazer, and that had also turned red.

Jason is standing on that stone floor, weeping.

Always, he would weep for that morning. That light would continue to dawn in him; that day would never begin. He would remember the letter, remember the headmaster's stiff phrases before letting him off lessons for the rest of the day. He would remember a Jason who was no longer himself but another Jason, the old Jason, thanking the headmaster politely and leaving his study, then disappearing.

He got no farther than the hall before the tears came. That was when he saw the crimson light pouring in through the Gothic windows. He doesn't know how long he has stood there quite motionless. He is fifteen. But he is ageless.

✧

Three years earlier, his father had applied for a post as regimental medical officer in India, near Madras. Dr. Coward was seriously over-worked and it was supposed to be good for him to get away. Inter-esting, epoch-making work was being done in his field there and he wanted to take part in it. The pay was also good, and besides, Jason was going to boarding school that year. He was sent away—much against his mother's wishes and in reality probably against his father's. Two years had gone by since his parents had left for their three-year stint. Then this morning Jason had been summoned to the headmas-ter's study after morning prayers and he thought the delayed birthday letter from his parents had come.

✧

A group of boys spot that immobile figure in the hall, exchange glances, then go nearer.

"Carrot-top," says one of them.

"Gingerknob!"

They are sharp and malicious. They exchange smiling looks as Ja-son just goes on standing there so strangely, paying no attention to them.

"Sleepwalker," says one.

"Deaf as a post," says another.

Jason really is as if deaf that morning. He doesn't come to life until one of the bigger boys plucks up courage and punches him in the back. He stumbles forward, half turns, and looks up at them, his eyes vacant.

They are in a semicircle around him. In the red light their faces seem to have a kind of veil over them, their bodies black as soot.

The boys exchange looks again. It would be an achievement, an unparalleled deed to beat someone up right there in the middle of the hall. That would enhance their reputations for years to come.

Jason didn't tattle; he had that much sense at the time.

✧

Things have not been entirely easy for Jason at school, though some boys have a worse time. But an image appears inside him, like a spark, distant and still. Something his father had once shown him when they were in the woods. He had shown Jason an anthill, the brown ants working away in it, industrious and orderly. His father had told him about its organized construction, the beautiful natural hierarchy prevailing in ant society, the whole anthill like a great organism. For a while they stood there observing the ants together. "Observing." That was his father's word. To his father the whole world was comprised of things to contemplate, each phenomenon nothing but an image of something else. But then—then his father had gone over to another anthill about a hundred yards away and fetched a small black ant on a matchstick. Now we'll make another observation, he had said. Look what happens when I put this little fellow in with the others. And Jason *observed* and saw the alien ant attacked by the resident ants the moment it landed among them. They went straight for it and bit it to death despite its stout attempts to defend itself. Then it was unceremoniously stowed away, perhaps in a storage space, or to be used for building material.

"That's because it has a strange scent," his father had said. Jason nodded. "The human body's defenses against infections are also thought to work like that. The organism, the entity, fights and rejects what does not belong to it. It reacts to it as if to an alien scent."

Jason had found out what that meant during his last three years at school—having a strange scent, as if there were something about him, and that something soon separated him out. That was clear without any doubt whatsoever to both Jason and the other boys. Perhaps part of the explanation was that he had grown up an only child, almost exclusively in the company of his parents. Perhaps it seemed strange to the other boys that Jason used adult language, many of his words taken from science, books, and experiments. Perhaps they picked on him because he played the violin and sang in the school choir, or they had found out that Jason had gone to school in the wrong part of London. But none of that, alone or together, provided him with any reasonable explanation for why it was he. There seemed to be something else, something about and inside him, behind all the rest . . . Jason didn't know.

Never tattle, his father had said, just before his parents left for India. Those were the words his father had sent with him to boarding school, and Jason had stuck to them.

He had done so once, and then not even about anything that had to do with himself but something they had done to a smaller boy by the name of Rider. He had been given a dunking one very cold winter morning, for no particular reason, as if out of pure high spirits. Rider had come down with pneumonia and there had been a huge commotion. Jason had reported the culprits without giving a thought to the consequences to himself. He had not regretted his act, not even after the long series of reprisals: his books smeared with mud, homework essays torn up, the strings of his violin cut halfway through so that they broke one after another during a school concert when he had a solo part. Jason also had a small collection of natural history objects he had found in his free time. One morning when he had forgotten to lock his study door, he found most of them ruined, birds' eggs and beetles crushed and strewn over his worktable.

Nevertheless, he did not regret what he had done. He thought he had acted rightly and wrote to tell his parents about it all, though he toned it down slightly and left out their acts of revenge. In his reply, his father had agreed. So Jason walked with his head high—until a few months went by and he came on the same Rider busy filling his inkwell with sand. He would never forget Rider's eyes as he caught him red-handed, a frightened, abject look, but with not a hint of shame. Then Jason realized that the other boys had not made him do it.

That was when Jason had hit out. He punched Rider in the face, hard, dizzy with anger and disappointment, and was beaten by the headmaster for striking a younger boy. That had been almost a year ago now. The ridicule and tormenting had been harder to bear. It also seemed as if the other boys sensed that Jason was weaker now, and they allowed themselves to do more unpleasant and bolder things than before.

Jason was looking forward to his parents' return—in just six months. He longed for every letter and wrote to them once a week. When he received a letter—his mother wrote vividly about all manner of things, large and small, and his father told him about his work and the alien countryside—Jason felt he was almost out there himself in that distant country. He could feel the heat, smell the strange pungent scents, see the emaciated cattle in the streets. He could hear the grasshoppers on the soft nights—then everything around him retreated, school, the endless games, the shouting, the torment—they all ceased to exist, and he yearned. The letters helped, and today—when he had been summoned to the headmaster—he had been expecting a birthday letter.

⚜

They surrounded him and he just stared at them. The look he gave them *was* the look of a stranger. He *was* somewhere else then. A sweet and tempting voice inside him whispered that he should just let them go ahead, just let them beat him up, so everything would be neutralized, so he would be obliterated and eliminated at their hands. It made no difference now. He almost longed for their blows. But something in him—that *something* again—resisted. He was able to feel the reality around him, his own incomprehensible existence—like great circles spreading all around—and he sensed that everything would break and he would be swallowed up and gone if he let them do it. So when the first boy raised his clenched fist to hit him, Jason put his hands up to his own face, dug his nails fiercely into his skin, and dragged his hands down his cheeks, scoring them deeply. Then he did the same thing again, this time starting farther up.

The boys stopped as if frozen, staring at him, seeing the streaks of dark blood suddenly running down Jason's cheeks and throat. In stunned silence, they saw him do it again, without a word, not a sound coming from him, his lips pressed so tightly together they turned white, his eyes narrowed to slits and behind the tears nothing but two black pupils.

Frightened, they backed away.

"What's he *doing?*" a boy whispered. Once again, Jason scored his face, feeling nothing now but the pain in his cheeks and the tears, salty, mixing with the blood. He could just see the other boys still standing around him. Who were they? Why didn't they go away? Why couldn't they leave him in peace with the sun, let him stay there alone, just looking? He did not claw at his face again, but turned back to the window, then forgot them all. The sun had risen a little farther and the light was now pouring through the window even more fiercely, straight into his face, making the scratches smart. That was good, that burning, somehow right.

Jason was sobbing now, uncontrollably.

At that moment, Saunders, the biology master and Jason's housemaster, happened to come through the double doors, a gray-bearded, absentminded man who seldom really noticed what was going on around him. But something about the little group over by the window, the motionless boys, must have startled him, because he stopped to look. He frowned, then went over to them. They didn't notice him until he spoke.

"What's going on here?"

They turned and stared at him, frightened, but Saunders knew they were not frightened of him—he was not particularly frightening, so it must be something else. He glanced fleetingly at them, noting which boys they were, the childish faces, quite soft, still so unmarked that a shock went through him every time he caught them at some devilment. Whenever he saw those faces, it always puzzled him. Saunders was a scientist, an adherent of Darwin, and he did not believe in the biblical original sin. But occasionally he thought there must be a kind of biological original sin. Something must have gone wrong with the human race when even its *children* could . . . Then Saunders noticed the figure facing the window and from his red hair recognized a boy from his own house, Jason Coward. Good at biology, too. He bit his lip and cleared his throat harshly.

"Away with you!" They hesitated for a second or two, as if paralyzed.

"*Away with you!*" he snapped. They left, slowly, and not until they were out of the hall did Saunders turn his attention to Jason, who had not moved. But then he turned around and Saunders saw the boy's cheeks glistening with blood.

He took Jason with him back to the house, where his wife bathed his cheeks and dressed them. He canceled his lessons and spent all morning talking to Jason, trying to bring him back to reality. Then he went to see the Headmaster.

Long before the sun was in its zenith, the whole school knew from the jungle telegraph that Coward—that funk with red hair—had gone mad.

⁂

But Jason was not mad. He was weeping over the letter. Jason was on the threshold of adult life, and this morning was to remain inside him for many years to come, returning to him night and day, for years and years. The letter—black writing on white paper and bathed in red light. He was to call on God to ask Him the meaning of that letter. He was to be filled with an uncontrollable, mindless rage, and that rage was to assume different forms and take him far far away from the life apparently staked out for him.

Everything changed.

Children are often said to forget easily and go on living with greater ease. They said that about Jason, too. In reality, he became another person. The event went so deeply into him that the memory of it changed his whole constitution, his whole way of life. The memory seemed almost physical.

Later he would perhaps admit to himself, to his own sound judgment, that much worse things can happen to a person. Nevertheless, that morning sliced Jason's life in two. Afterward he was another person, someone he did not know.

It was not a birthday letter but a very short, very formal statement to say that both Jason's parents, John Coward and Mrs. Alice, née Clarke, had died at their residence in Vellore, near Madras, of an unspecified disease. The department sent its deepest condolences and most respectful regards.

Dear Jason [his father wrote],

Things are much the same here. It's hot today and some of the soldiers are laid up with "Vellore tummy." Nothing much to worry about, the officers say, but I'm giving them solid quinine treatment to make sure. Everything here goes bad at the moment.

There are interesting light phenomena in the night sky, something to do with the heat, I suppose. A kind of heat lightning, but much stronger, with unusually varied shades of colour.

Your mother sends her love. She has gone off on an outing today. A certain Mrs Johnstone has involved her in evangelical work. Mrs Johnstone is a masterful elderly lady to whom the natives listen with amazing patience. I hope your mother can contribute to spreading some general health rules among the people through these activities. We had some nasty epidemics after the last monsoon, as I told you.

While we're on to religious matters, I saw an interesting cosmogony the other day in an old abandoned temple: the god Shiva clinging to the universe—the sun and all the celestial bodies—with his four arms and an indescribable, sardonic smile on his lips. He is the destroyer and the creator as far as I can make out. But I don't have time for more profound religious studies.

I hope your schoolwork is going well. Your mother and I are expecting you to do well in your exams. For your next letter I am giving you the task of writing a short account of the zebu, a species of cattle with a hump of fat over their top vertebrae. They are used a lot as draught animals here. With much love from your . . .

The following weeks were a great strain on Jason. His aunt and uncle were already his temporary guardians in his parents' absence abroad, and now some kind of permanent arrangement had to be made. Then there was the will. Colleagues and friends had arranged a memorial service for Jason's parents, who had been buried in India, and the occasion seemed suitable for a gathering to decide Jason's future.

Jason sat in the front pew with his aunt, his eyes rigid and mouth clamped shut, the long red scars still on his cheeks as he listened to all those words about Dr. Coward, this Dr. Coward who had been such an outstanding man. The name finally seemed quite alien to Jason, so alien he almost managed to forget whom they were talking about. This man, who with his indefatigable industry and strength had been an example, a model and inspiring force to his colleagues, honored, highly honored to have been allowed to meet this man, deeply shaken by his sudden death and grateful before God, now assembled here to remember this man and his wife—Jason could see from surreptitious glances that one or two of the deeply shaken colleagues were glancing at their watches. His Aunt Mabel was staring vacantly ahead with a pained expression. She was his father's sister. She and his father had grown up together in his grandfather's vicarage in a town on the river Severn, where they had played together, talked together, but Jason could see nothing of his father in her. All the circumstances and people around him seemed utterly alien. None of this was really happening to him.

He listened to the words in numb horror, finding that all those moving words, those consoling and warming words, were making not the slightest impression on him.

The gathering afterward was held in his old home and consisted of his guardians, a relative, and some friends of his parents, one of them the solicitor in charge of the family's affairs. They had to plan Jason's future and decide what should be sold to ensure means for his upbringing and education. They found the boy much more amenable and unsentimental than they had feared. Indeed, almost too amenable.

The living quarters of the house had been closed in the absence of the occupants—covers on the furniture, pictures taken down off the walls, rugs rolled up, and small articles packed away in chests and bags. The adults now held a council of war in the living room, and to ease the situation, a decanter was unearthed and sherry handed around in his mother's small, heavy glasses. Jason was in his school clothes, sitting stiffly in a chair by the piano, his cheeks scarlet. On the way from the hotel in which they were staying, Aunt Mabel had asked him if he was feverish. Now they were all there, finding it hard to start, so there was much clearing of throats and scraping of chairs.

Jason looked around the room. It seemed to him a caricature of his childhood home, only vaguely familiar, alien, no longer his.

First of all, said Mr. Scott, the solicitor, a means had to be found to best ensure Jason's future. Dr. Coward had not been wealthy; there were still some outstanding debts on the estate and the insurance was at most modest. But if they made the right dispositions with regard to the sale, and between them agreed to appoint an economical, permanent and—er—considerate guardian . . .

They all turned to look at Jason, anxiously, gravely. Jason nodded, equally gravely.

"He's taking it very bravely," Aunt Mabel said quietly. She was standing over by the window; the white lace curtains were drawn back and the autumn light gave a pale, pleasant glow to the faces in the room.

"The ground floor is already rented, and we could of course arrange to rent the whole building, to ensure a steady income. However, there are both practical and financial responsibilities involved in owning property . . . On the other hand, if the house was sold and the sum realized invested . . ."

Jason was *observing*. He was observing the room they were sitting in, and his observations told him it was fundamentally just any old room, nothing special about it at all, a living room like thousands of others. He thought about his own room upstairs. He knew it was empty, but had been up to take a look. He had vaguely recognized the bed and bedside table; it had been like looking at an old photograph of himself. The sky outside the dormer window was bright. Then he had closed the door behind him.

Uncle Ralph, his mother's cousin, coughed discreetly and looked at his watch. The solicitor was taking his time before coming to the point. Jason observed his relative looking at his watch. He was observing it all and basically understood that this was an almost everyday event, one of those things that happen in life. Honorable, industrious people suddenly finding themselves morally and personally responsible for an orphan. Something one doesn't *expect*, but gentlemen that they were, they were taking the responsibility, spending their time on it, and if they looked at their watches, they did so discreetly; that was understandable. Life goes on. All this suddenly seemed to Jason understandable to the extent that it reaffirmed his decision to put no obstacles in the way of anything or anyone. He said practically nothing during the negotiations. Jason was in reality a talkative boy, and if they had known him well, his silence would have been noticeable. Though—"in reality"? What did that mean now? What was reality now? They knew nothing about him; that was all. That was to Jason's advantage.

So when it came down to it, it was all quite painless. Dr. Coward, good old John, would certainly have wished his son—apart from personal memories—to have chosen individual pieces of furniture, pictures, and larger objects . . . perhaps some things from his father's practice . . . The solicitor was sure of that. So if Jason wished to keep anything for himself . . . There is, for instance, a wall clock here . . .

But the wall clock was soon disposed of, as were the dining-room furniture, the winged leather chairs, the china cabinet, the linen cupboard and its contents. The dignity of the assembly acquired a strained, frenzied undertone as they continued on their mission. Such an amazing number of objects—furniture and objects make a home. A home consists of objects. Jason observed—coolly. He saw that a home is a kind of dollhouse, a kind of equipped shoe box in which miniature furniture is kept, and then it is peopled with a father and a mother, a child or two, and a dog. So—a home. But some things were missing now, including their bull terrier, Ernest; Ernest, whom Jason had had before he went away to school. Ernest and his cold wet nose were horribly missing. Jason had been told that Ernest was going to a good home, but Jason knew they were lying, and he knew his father knew he knew. So, no Ernest, now gone to a good home. Nothing was left but a few objects and Jason, and Jason did his best not to disturb them. It all seemed as simple as a shoe box to him. Fewer and fewer things remained. Soon the silverware was sold, although Aunt Mabel and her husband, the vicar, had wished to redeem a few things from the estate, as did his mother's cousin Ralph—Jason had no objections. He was so compliant, Mr. Scott the solicitor asked Jason whether he understood what he was agreeing to. Perhaps Jason would, after all, like to keep some of the paintings? They could be stored— perhaps later on in life Jason would regret he had let them go so easily. No? Well, all right, then.

Jason hesitated only once, and that was when they came to the brass-bound chests and cases from the basement and suddenly a case lined with velvet was in front of him, a telescope. Lenses from Chance's in Birmingham, a two-and-a-half-inch refractor with a theoretical resolution factor of two arc seconds.

Jason turned pale when he saw it.

"Well now?" said the solicitor kindly. "A beautiful instrument. Is it yours?"

Jason looked, memories rushing through him like shooting stars.

"No," he said, looking away.

The adults exchanged looks.

"It must have belonged to Father," said Jason, pulling himself together. "I've never been particularly—interested in astronomy."

"But perhaps you might be in the future?" That was Scott again, looking searchingly at Jason with his shrewd lawyer's eyes.

"An instrument like that might bring in a lot of money," Jason said lightly.

A comforting numbing atmosphere descended. There was talk of Jason's future and what was left of Dr. Coward's medical equipment and books. Then Aunt Mabel's husband, the Reverend Chadwick, a thickset, buttoned-up man with a lilting voice, spoke. He took a practical view of things.

"I presume," he said, "that in time young Jason will take up medicine." They all nodded. Jason saw the clergyman as if through glass, at a distance that was not an insignificant part of infinity. Then he looked down at his own hands.

"Taking that fact into consideration, and the fact that—if I may say so—medical studies are both time-consuming and costly, and also that medical textbooks and instruments are expensive, then—er—to look on it in *practical* terms . . ." The Reverend Chadwick looked across at Dr. Falls, who was taking part in his capacity as a friend and colleague of the father. "Dr. Falls, perhaps you could go through—if I may say so—with a truly practical eye—all the instruments and books that must be here in the practice and in the house in general and extract both the most elementary as well as the most precious instruments and books, so that these may be kept for Jason's future vocation, so that increasingly costly and unnecessary new purchases at that point in time will not be required."

Dr. Falls nodded briefly at this pronouncement. Jason kept looking at them all, looking and looking without taking in what he was seeing. A voice, almost that of a stranger, came to him from far, far away: *Yes, I know he's married to my sister, my dear, but I can't stand those sermons of his.*

"This," said Aunt Mabel, holding up a large brown bound book. "Are you keeping this, Jason?" She sounded hopeful.

Jason glanced at the book. It was the picture Bible, his mother's illustrated Bible.

"Yes," he said. "I'll keep that to read."

His aunt tentatively stroked his head.

Dear Jason [his mother wrote],
I hope all is well with you. I am sitting here writing to you in peace and quiet in the afternoon heat. Your father can't be tempted away from his work. I am afraid he doesn't work any less hard here than he did in Whitechapel. They are now trying to isolate a microbe of some kind. He's sure to tell you about it.

Yesterday evening I experienced something I really wish you could have taken part in. It was a reddish-violet evening, with those misty mellow colours that are impossible to describe but that give the impression of eliminating all distance. Since early morning the pilgrims had been on their way down to the river; it was Dasehra, the tenth day of the festival of Durgapudja, which is celebrated for Durga, "the impassable," "the maiden from the mountains," Shiva's consort. On this day her idol and other idols are lowered into the river. I know nothing more about it. Your father had fetched me from church and we came home together,

across the market where spices, vegetables, plaited wreaths, and multi-
coloured powders and perfumes were being packed into baskets and jars.
Then a group of musicians in the middle of the square started playing.
We stood there listening for half the evening. Their music, Jason—it's
not only very strange but really impossible to describe. I have heard it
said at the mission that it is abominable and ought to be counteracted
because of its powerful heathen content. And it's true it sounds strange.
It is centred on one central note, which I am intentionally avoiding
calling the base note; it's more a kind of mid-note. Then the music is
spun round that. It is like the misty rosy dawns we get out here, appar-
ently without end or any real beginning. The little orchestra your father
and I listened to last night played so that the actual darkness began to
come alive. According to beliefs here, as far as I have understood the
Brahmin story of the creation, life began with a primaeval sound, an
Ur-note, from which everything else is resolved. It was so strange last
night walking though the streets with my soul filled with that amazing
flowing resonance . . .

Take great care of yourself and don't get cold.

With love

Yes, it is all going so smoothly. He is so amenable. Objects glide past
him. He lets them go as if they had never been his, as if he had never
been in touch with them. It all turned out as he had thought. It was
agreed the Reverend Chadwick and his wife would be his guardians,
and he would spend his school holidays at the vicarage in Devon as
before. His other relative, Cousin Ralph, worked in the City and was
unmarried, so it would not be appropriate for him to have a ward in
the house. But Mr. Scott arranges to place some money with the bro-
ker before he puts on his coat and top hat and an expression of trusted
reliability, raising his hat and leaving. Dr. Falls wishes Jason good luck
and assures him he is ready to be of assistance at any time; he will
keep in touch and if possible help with his education when the time
comes. Then he disappears just as the memory of a handclasp leaves
the hand. They depart, all of them.

Objects, objects and time all glide away from him. A house with a
brass plate on the door. A stove with a clock on the mantelpiece
above, a clock that has counted seconds of grace, seconds of childhood. A red plush couch someone has rested on, a piano which still

remembers. It is easy, easy. He is someone else now. Jason knows he is someone else. He seems to have extended himself into something new over these weeks. His schoolmasters and fellow pupils meet him with diffident looks. He does not know them. It is easy. He hurls himself over his schoolbooks, almost desperately, as if searching for something.

From now on he is homeless.

⚜

The years passed slowly, school and exams, holidays at his uncle and aunt's comfortable but rather quiet and distant home in Devon.

Jason was someone else.

In the beginning this had a strange effect on him at school. At first it was thought Jason had been thrown off balance by the tragedy, but the change in his behavior did not abate, instead grew stronger, more manifest. So fiercer measures were necessary and the cane was brought out. None of the masters found it compatible with their principles to punish a pupil who had just gone through so much, but there was soon no other way out. Jason took his punishment without a murmur, his attitude almost arrogant, considering the kind of things he had started doing. When corporal punishment turned out to be useless, letters had to be written, letters to Jason's aunt and uncle. Gradually the number of these letters increased and the contents were such that Mr. Scott eventually heard about it. Jason's behavior was increasingly giving cause for anxiety.

How to describe and explain what was happening to him? When Jason went back to school, there was a distance between him and everything else, a chilling, incomprehensible lightness that meant no one or nothing ever really reached him—a wall of glass. He quietly avoided everyone's eyes. He made himself invisible. Invisible to his masters, impervious to both praise and reprimand. Coolly, indifferently, he accepted good reports, and with a distant, almost contemptuous expression, he looked at the headmaster before the latter carried out a beating. An element of something unassailable and dangerous had crept into him. When Jason spoke in class, his eyes were dark and grave. He seldom allowed himself a smile, and any smile soon dissolved. His masters simply disapproved, detecting an outlandish, disrespectful defiance. He never *participated* in either good things or bad. What had happened to Jason was incomprehensible. *He* would now be the one to take the initiative if on some rare occasion he found it to his liking. Now it was he who planned and took the lead in some prank or vandalism. He himself seemed unclear about this new ringleader role, as if he had done nothing to bring it about and couldn't be bothered with it. The distance between him and the other boys remained just as great. They were afraid of him, anxious, because there was something *about* him, something large, indifferent, and dangerous, something looking *down* on them. He had a quiet way of asking them for things; often one look was enough for them to obey. He himself slid away and apparently found no enjoyment in the pranks he carried out.

In the course of the next year or two, Jason grew a great deal and became a large, strong youth.

To Jason himself, everything seemed simply a continuation of the same sense of having a strange scent, of something in him separating him from the others. But now it was as if that something in him had changed, had matured and hatched out and was thrashing about with dark wings, a cold distance, and a quiet, savage despair. He also discovered he enjoyed this distance from everything and everyone. He could manipulate others into doing what he wanted, and they would grovel to him. He relished the lack of effort, physical or emotional, it took to dominate them. It was easy, easy. A strong, tough rebellious streak slowly materialized in him—almost a hatred. Hatred of the school and the masters, the pupils, his uncle and aunt and their peaceful vicarage. He did not belong with them! He was homeless, and that was how it should be. That was right. But they had to notice him, feel that he was there.

He always seemed to be attacking himself to see whether the glass wall would break. But it held. Old Saunders, his biology master, grew tense when Jason suddenly got up in class and asked questions that were outside the curriculum but never irrelevant, questions drawn from his own reading, and put so unyieldingly Saunders had to scratch his beard in despair. Jason used his own cleverness as a weapon. In reality, that weapon was equally directed at himself, but no one understood that.

He was calm for long periods of time, turned in on himself, relaxing in that distance from things. But then an unease would come over him, rippling the outside surface, and he would turn to mischief again. As if numb, with almost no idea what he was doing, he would draw a mustache on one of the portraits of admirals in the hall, or seized with icy rage after a beating, he would hurl a stone through one of the leaded windows in the headmaster's study. He did things others would never even think of. He released the biology lab's collection of white mice in chapel before morning service and set off firecrackers during choir practice. Even his favorite subjects were not allowed to escape.

At the same time—at the same time, he was silent, almost dreamy. He *was* a clever pupil, accurate and industrious, and he worked hard. He played the violin with more enthusiasm than before, and a new note had come into his playing. But what was to be *done* with him . . . ?

The pranks he carried out had a perfidious and premeditated character about them; he was not always caught, but Jason's hand could be sensed behind them. It was never clear just who had cut all the branches off the rosebushes in the school garden so they never flowered that year, and no one could prove who had put horse dung in the Communion chalice early one Sunday morning.

The latter caused turmoil in the school for several weeks. All the free periods were canceled and the headmaster spent hours trying to get the culprit to confess, or to get others to testify against him. The case was finally abandoned for lack of evidence, but from that day on, a state of war was declared between the masters and Jason. There was no more talk of a rebellious pupil; instead it was a direct attack on the values this venerable school was founded on, values society itself, the Empire itself, were built on. The danger was that this kind of activity could give the school a bad name, for naturally the stories would go back to the parents during the holidays.

The other pupils were afraid of him.

But Jason seldom did anything to them. He never attacked, so to speak, an individual; his assaults were directed at loftier and larger targets; the other pupils were apparently beneath his contempt.

But there were exceptions.

For instance, that business with young Denton.

Dear Jason [his father wrote],
I happened to be talking to an old officer in the bar the other evening and he told me about the Sepoy Rebellion in 1857. Fat, purple in the

face, and trembling behind his white moustache, he told me about when he was a young subaltern and was sent to Delhi to carry out the required cleaning-up operations and acts of vengeance. He told me of events no one could comprehend, human actions beyond all good and evil, things we would normally not be able to credit. Countless gallows along the city streets, and women and children tied in front of the gun barrels before orders were given to fire.

The Denton affair happened on a Sunday a few weeks before the end of term. A cricket match was being held and the boys not taking part were in their Sunday clothes, a welter of straw boaters and whites and a mildly festive atmosphere prevailing on the cricket field. A lot of parents had come down to watch the match and there was an air of semiofficial end of term and a preview of the summer holidays. The masters were in a good mood; the match was going well for the school and also sufficiently protracted to allow the spectators to think and talk about many other major and minor matters while they were being entertained—the actual game providing diversionary spells. In between, people were strolling about. Mothers and sisters were escorted around, and a pleasant buzz of voices and laughter spread all over the school grounds.

In one corner by the rose garden a conversation had arisen, a kind of discussion, the contents of which none of the boys present considered particularly important, a fact which later made it difficult to reconstruct what really happened.

Denton was a pupil at the school in a form above Jason: tall, elegant, distinguished, scion of one of the foremost and oldest families in the country. He had grown up in a castle, and his father was not only an earl but was also in the cabinet. Young Denton was in every respect a rare bird. He had been sent there and not to the grandest public schools because he was actually academically gifted and Jason's school was known for its good academic results. Young Denton mixed easily with the other boys, did not lord it over them, and was friendly and natural. But of course it was *known* who he was and he also knew it himself, so relations to both the other boys and the masters were affected by that. Jason and Denton had no particular antagonism between them; on the contrary, Denton seemed to be one of the boys Jason got along with best. So what happened was doubly incomprehensible.

This little group of pupils had started talking, a very youthful and self-confident conversation marked by the participants as yet having no particular skills at flying, having hitherto done nothing but flap their wings. They were also in a good mood. Jason was standing on the edge of the crowd in his dark Sunday suit, listening but taking no part. They were discussing class differences in society, particularly those with no property. That was a theme of the day. None of them had the slightest idea what they were talking about, so it was no wonder a number of ill-considered things were said.

Denton was ordinarily reserved and friendly, though no less self-confident. His interests lay in quite a different direction from the subject of conversation, and the comments he made were founded on the limited experience and impressions his upbringing had provided. So when he made a few remarks suggesting that the poor in the big cities had no one but themselves to blame for their situation, and that many of them were of doubtful morals, had no education, and possessed neither initiative nor responsibility—in short, many of them were good-for-nothings who deserved their degradation, it was clear this young aristocrat drew his conclusions partly from what he had heard from his father. Just because of this, the other boys were keen to hear more, and then a dark shadow suddenly appeared between their ranks and stood facing Denton. It was Jason Coward. Jason was heard to say something to Denton in a low voice, and the latter was heard to reply with a one-syllable word . . . Then everything happened very quickly. Jason grabbed the older boy and hit him in the face and the solar plexus. Then, white-faced, his teeth clenched, he lifted his victim as high as his shoulder and flung him with all his strength face-first into a thorny rose bush. Slowly and deliberately, he walked over to the bush, seized Denton's jacket, heaved him halfway up, and was about to throw him back among the thorns when someone at last intervened and brought Jason down to the ground.

Attracted by cries of pain, people came running up: members of the staff, parents—and Lady Violet, the victim's mother.

"*Let go of me,*" snarled Jason to the four boys holding him down. "Let go! I'll get him! I'll get the bastard! Let me go."

That was how a good cricket match came to an end halfway through.

⚜

". . . and you can thank your Creator, young man, that he didn't lose his sight. Have you seen the length of those thorns?" Mr. Scott had come down from London to straighten Jason out and if possible prevent his expulsion.

"Yes," said Jason. "It's a species of wild brier, *Rosa canina*, if I remember rightly, according to Crépin's system."

"Yes, quite. Now just calm down a little, will you. I have been told your behavior here has become scandalous. In general! Neither I nor your aunt and uncle can understand what has got into you. I must say I am disappointed. What would your father have said?"

Jason looked down, but said nothing.

"I've had a talk with the headmaster. You should be pleased this happened after your exams. You've done brilliantly in them this year, the headmaster tells me. Coward is a good pupil. But expulsion is now imminent, young man. In your last year. What would John have said?"

Jason still said nothing, but let his gaze roam out the window into the high summer day, the blue sky and the great white cumulus clouds above the hills.

"What have you got against young Denton, by the way?"

"Nothing."

"Nonsense. Don't lie to me. You don't throw a fellow schoolboy, an aristocrat at that, the son of a member of Her Majesty's government, into a thorn bush for no reason whatsoever. Had he insulted you? Are you too proud to answer back?"

"He hadn't insulted me," said Jason.

"But for God's sake, it must have been *something*."

Jason mumbled something.

"What did you say?"

"Let's say it was a political matter," Jason said. "He said something about the poor deserving their poverty. I asked him to take it back and he wouldn't. So I thought I'd teach him a lesson."

Mr. Scott was quiet for a long time.

"Good God," he said finally. "I think you *mean* it." He looked closely at Jason, trying to form a picture of this sturdy seventeen-year-old in front of him, what kind of person he could have become since he had sat there that day, watching in silence as his childhood home dissolved before him.

"You've changed a lot," he said, "since I last saw you."

"No," said Jason. "Not fundamentally."

Scott appeared to understand.

"Maybe so," he said, looking Jason straight in the eye. "But listen carefully now, Jason. You're young. You're inexperienced and hotheaded. I have spoken to Denton's parents. That has cost me time and energy, but I have succeeded. They are willing to let this pass because the boy escaped injury and because no one wants a scandal. The earl simply asks that you apologize to his son. Very noble of him. The headmaster was not so easy. He wanted to expel you, Jason."

"I understand," said Jason.

"You don't look as if you mind," said Scott harshly.

"Mind? I said I understood. Why should I mind?"

The solicitor looked at Jason, and their eyes met. Those eyes, he thought, those eyes.

"I don't think you understand anything," he said wearily. "But I have spoken to the headmaster and he is willing to allow you to stay on for your last year, on *probation*, young man, on *probation*. One more minor thing and you are out on your ear. Even if it's in the middle of term. Do you understand *that*, then?"

"Yes," said Jason. "I understand."

"Please bear it in mind."

"Yes," said Jason.

"I hope you will use your holiday to think things over. I have advised your foster parents to . . ."

"My aunt and uncle," said Jason.

"I have advised them to let you use up some of your energies during the holidays. I hope you will mature over the summer."

Jason looked at him, and this time it was Scott's turn to look down.

After this conversation, Jason's rebellious attitude changed, at least outwardly. It took another direction and was no longer quite so visible.

❧

He spent the summer holidays at home at the vicarage in Devon, away from school. At home. He never really felt at home there, although his aunt and uncle were friendly enough. But they also felt he was more like a guest, a lodger, than a foster son. They never really talked to each other. He was careful to please them, rising at

cockcrow, eating his porridge, spending long sleepy Sunday mornings
in church as the Reverend Chadwick preached away in his singsong
voice. Or he spent time on his books, his natural history. He read
Darwin and he also read the illustrated Bible. He reads and reads, but
finds no answers. He listens to Chadwick's sermons, walks around the
church looking at the stained glass, looking at the beautiful little gran-
ite font and the ornamental pulpit. He finds no answers. He walks
across the moor and along the river, searching but finding nothing.
He searches through his uncle's theological books and finds nothing
there, either. Nothing, apart perhaps from a little verse, translated
from Sanskrit.

He copies it out in large, even letters onto the frontispiece of his
edition of *Origin of Species*.

> Shiva, you are without mercy
> Shiva, you are without heart
>
> Why, why did you let me be born
> wretched into this world,
> in exile from that other?
>
> Tell me, Lord,
> have you not one single
> little tree, a single little plant
> created just for me?

In the faint light of the summer night he looks at the cheap print
above the end of his bed in his room, an angel on a cloud looking
down at him. He thinks about his mother's quiet voice as she turned
the pages of the illustrated Bible, and he remembers his father's white
knuckles in church on Sundays.

He remembers his conversation with Saunders, that terrible crimson
morning when his tears would not stop. Saunders had eventually
brought him back to earth in the only way he knew how. They were
in Saunders's study, among flasks and tubes and innumerable exam-
ples of animals and plants. Saunders had not known what to do with
Jason, but he had noticed that despite his distress, the boy's eyes kept
straying to a skull lying on the desk, the skull of a saber-toothed tiger,

an unusual rarity Saunders was studying, a complete cranium, brilliantly white, lying beside the padded case.

He carefully picked up the skull and put it down in front of Jason. "Would you like to take a closer look?"

Jason fixed his eyes on the smooth, almost sculptural object. It was good to look at, and for some reason it calmed Jason down. Saunders held it up against the light so Jason could get a better view of it—the intricate, curved bone formation, the great eye sockets, the blunt nose section, and the powerful jaws. The teeth attracted Jason in particular, those two saber-like teeth arching out of the mouth in a great curve. He recognized them as incisors like his own, but grown out, and far too large. Saunders opened the jaws and pulled slightly at the saber teeth so that they became a little longer. He let Jason hold the skull for a while. It was as good to touch as it was to look at, and Jason grew considerably calmer, the very feel of these objects providing him with firm ground beneath his feet, bringing him back to earth. For a moment he sat there feeling the cool, smooth bone, feeling a kind of gratitude toward Saunders for finding him there in the hall and now sitting here not knowing how best to console him. Without thinking, Jason asked a question relevant to his subject.

"Can you show me the mid-jawbone?"

Saunders smiled with relief, took the skull, opened the huge jaw, and showed Jason how the mid-jawbone, *os intermaxillare*, was clearly interwoven with the other upper mandibles.

"Until seventy or eighty years ago," Saunders began cautiously, trying to lead Jason's thoughts away from his hurt, "it was thought humans had no intermaxillare as animals have. That was evidence, so to speak, that people did not stem from apes. All other animals, the primates, too, have. But human beings haven't. That is . . . that's what it looks like at first glance." He fetched another skull, a rodent of some kind, from a glass-fronted cupboard.

"This is a beaver," he said. The skull was surprisingly small and had two long rust-colored front teeth that could be pushed in and out of the jawbone. Saunders pointed out the most important bones and found the same ones in the skull of the saber-toothed tiger, but shaped differently. "You see," said Saunders, "there it is. The little *os intermaxillare*. But look here now." He went over to a cupboard and brought back a human skull. "Can you find it on this?"

Saunders was absorbed in it now and was pleased to have Jason there. He could not cope with tears. Bones were his territory, not emotions. Bones and specimens. Saunders was a good teacher, often made fun of because of his eternal explanations and digressions, all produced in a rapid, gravelly voice; it was as if it lay too far back in his throat. Wicked tongues maintained his intermaxillare got in the way. But he could arouse enthusiasm, because he himself was so obviously enthusiastic about his subject. Among specimens, flasks, and tubes, he looked like Dr. Faustus, with his beard and the fringe of hair at the back of his round pate, a survivor from the Age of Enlightenment. His medicine for chaos was natural history, and that suited Jason.

"Where is it in a human skull, then?" Jason was counting out the sutures in the skull but, of course, found nothing, although he knew perfectly well it was there. Then he let Saunders have the pleasure of showing him where it was hidden.

"There it is," said Saunders, tapping his forefinger inside the roof of the cranium. "*Os intermaxillare.* When that was discovered, the last scientific argument for the adherents of the biblical story of creation was demolished." He sounded almost triumphant. Saunders was considered somewhat controversial because of his constant overt attacks on Adam and Eve.

Jason had stopped crying, but the feeling of unreality and pain would not release its hold and his cheeks were still smarting; it helped, however, to hear about that bone. "A poet discovered it," said Saunders, "a German. A declared devotee of Adam and Eve, a poet who thought he was a scientist but with the decency to admit to what he had found, although it terrified him. He had found the *decisive proof.* We *are* like the primates."

Saunders put the human skull alongside that of the saber-toothed tiger and, suddenly uncertain, glanced at Jason.

Jason was looking at the bone formations on the desk, thinking how many organisms were born and die every day. Then he thought about his parents and a great coldness came over him. He did not realize it until later, but at that moment he lost God.

⚕

He is lying in bed in the little vicarage bedroom, listening to the birds singing. He has been searching and searching. Everything he has read confirms this—there is no God, nothing behind it all—and nothing *afterward*. It is a difficult thought, but at the same time joyous; a liberating thought, but a joy and a freedom beyond the threshold of pain.

Incurable homelessness! A song of the spheres portraying seconds and years. He lies there in the darkness thinking, thinking until the birds start singing outside. Then he falls asleep, a deep, dreamless repose.

Dear Jason [his father wrote],
India was the end and I barely remember it. I left it all on a very warm morning. It torments me that I held out a shorter time than your mother. But no doubt she was thinking about you and clung harder to life.

You see, I've come to Saturn. All the elements of the cosmos space are visible from here, beautifully arranged. Everything can be seen through, from the heavy saturated chaos of the clouds of gas to the crystalline formations. Combinations are made and dissolved. Here there is a bridge of ice in the heavens.

I was extremely overworked, you must remember, and I was in much worse shape than I ever let on to you or Alice. That last year in London I was plagued with pains in my left arm, which was why I found it so difficult to walk on our last trip with the telescope.

Here I am now, noting a faint, strange irritation at not being able to see the results of the last bacteria cultures we were producing in Vellore—although that was probably what finished me off, so I was able to see the results after all. I have never been cautious. I must say I miss your mother, Jason, and I am sorry if she was in pain. I am afraid I did not take enough care of my health in India, either. But what can one do when one has no God and work is the only thing that appears to provide any meaning to it all? You are old enough now for me to be able to talk to you about this, Jason. I suppose you are with my sister and her husband now, if I am not mistaken. Mabel's and my father was also a vicar, as you know, and she still has a great deal of that in her. But for me God went out of my sight on the way somewhere in all that insane and endless work for the committees. Don't think I didn't know it was meaningless all the time. But I did my best. I gave it all I had, and occasionally tried to find my way back to my faith on the way. Jason—you will soon be adult and will understand this now—I probably never really had any God at all, but just imagined one, an inherited ghost in many ways resembling my father. A kind of Admiral Lord Nelson of a God, terrifying and slightly foolish—that is the prevailing image of him, I think, and it does not take much for that to die. I never found another God. What was left? A belief in reason, in science. Contexts can be seen in science, images which speak to you and provide some understanding. Finding a place in that understanding is perhaps a meaning, I don't know. Your mother thought differently about these things. I wish she were here now, in me and around me.

I am in the elements of the universe now, just as I always was from the beginning of time. Life starts somewhere in the chaos of elements around me, protozoa, corals and bryozoans, invertebrates. Coelenterates and fungi. Organisms that are almost entirely calcium, entirely mineral. Almost. Slowly, the aeons glide past, periods of time unfathomable to anyone alive. Slowly, small worms appear, annelids and invertebrates. Trilobites and crustaceans, and in the still primaeval sea, the vertebrates appear, remaining in the depths, first as primitive agnates, eels and lampreys, then fish of various unknown and macabre kinds. In the depths and in time they sank and decayed, and nothing is left of them except an occasional impression in stones, in stones now found in deserts and on high mountain peaks. The first amphibians crawl clumsily over shores of unknown continents, plant life clings to stones and rocks, and birdless forests block the sun in uninhabited lands. Insects swirl in the air. And then, in a majestic, bloodthirsty, and mighty heave, the spinal columns of the vertebrates rise as monstrous lizards and fabulous creatures; dragons flinging their fearful bellows up to a steaming sky. The mountains shudder, innocent small furred animals tremble in their holes and dens. The monstrous lizards writhe in their convulsive strength and power; then something happens and they curl up and fall, fall in on themselves; slowly they become birds, birds as light as undreamt dreams. The searing roars become birdsong, whimpering flutes on warm nights. The poets who will listen to them are not yet born, and Mozart is still only a possibility in the sea of distant not yet created forms of life. So is a homeless young man falling asleep to the sound of birdsong. Small mammals leap through the grass. Soon he is there, a new warrior in the forest, more powerful than all others; he is naked and carrying a spear; he thinks and worships, thinks and worships through the centuries. Now he is here, he who will grasp a spear just as he will later grasp a plough, an executioner's axe, a pen.

My dear Jason, you will by now have come far enough to be able to understand my thoughts. I am on Saturn, or nowhere. Chance is engraved on all objects. Who has said we are the last creatures to rule the world? Is Man now the aim and final meaning of all things? Seen from here, Man and microbe may come to be one. So what significance does it have whether I raise a stethoscope or a sword to my neighbor? Or whether I hold up a stolen emerald or a test tube of microbes to the sun? So I was working on microbes when I had to disappear. Beloved Jason, I greet you from Saturn and wish you well. Your . . .

"Why are you dropping all those bits of paper in the river?"

A thick branch hangs far out over the water and Jason is sitting on the middle of it dropping a fine shower of white paper, torn-up letters and photographs, into the swirling current, which takes them with it.

She is standing on the bank looking up at him.

"What are you doing, Jason?" she says. "Tell me. Don't be so superior. Tell me!"

"Oh," says Jason. "Just something I want to get rid of for good." He is not looking at her.

He pulls another letter out of his pocket, glances at it, folds it four times, and slowly and precisely tears it to shreds.

"They're letters," she says gently.

"Yes, Chippewa," says Jason. "They're letters." If she asks what kind, he thinks, I'll hit her.

"And photographs," she says.

"Yes, Chippewa."

She doesn't ask any more but looks up at him with her dark searching eyes. He goes on for a while, tearing up papers and photographs and following the pieces with his eyes as they reach the water, are dispersed, and float away like petals. A few words in careful handwriting are visible, an *and*, an *I*, a *we*. Meaningless words now, dissolved into individual elements of language, atoms of language; interjections, verbs, articles. The photographs similarly—thick, brownish pieces shower down from his fingers into the water, though in contrast to the scraps of letters, they sink almost immediately. A nose, a throat, a patch of skirt. They sink into the darkness and are gone.

She is still standing on the bank looking at him, wondering.

"There," he says as the last fragments disappear. "Now they're gone." He turns to look at her and she can see he has been crying.

"Chippewa," he says. "Mary . . ." Her real name is Mary and she lives next door to the vicarage. "Mary . . ." His voice is low, almost pleading.

"Yes?"

"Don't look now," says Jason. "You mustn't see what I'm going to do now. Because . . ." He wants to say she won't understand, but she has already turned around and has her back to him.

"Like this?" she says.

"Yes," whispers Jason. Then he bends down over the water again, fumbling in his pocket for something, an object, a thing; it lies in his hand like a golden egg. He can hear it ticking even above the roar of the river. Then he throws the old watch far out into the water and it vanishes without a sound, leaving circles on the surface of the water. The river is flowing fast.

He climbs back onto the bank. She still has her back to him.

"You can turn around now," he says. "There's nothing left to see. Nothing but the river."

She turns around and he sees her peering out over the water.

"It's nice here," she says.

"Yes."

"Are you miserable?" she asks cautiously.

"No, Chippewa."

She nods briefly. For a moment it is quiet; then she smiles shyly.

"My father sometimes says you can't go out into the same river twice."

"Must be something he has read."

She looks uncertainly at him.

"Yes. It's the same river," she says.

"Yes," he says. "It's the same river. It's only water all the time. The same river. Always the same river."

✢

She had been around during the holidays ever since he first came here. Chippewa. Mary, the shopkeeper's daughter, ordinarily neat and tidy in her gray school uniform, and nevertheless what his aunt with an extreme euphemism referred to as "a healthy country girl." At first he had been wrong about her, thinking she was different from what she was. He ran away from her, just as he avoided all settled people, just as he turned away from everyone who had a *place*, a home, security.

But she was not like that. She was as wild as the birds on the moor, unpredictable as the wind and the snow; not like other children, never coming home on time from her long, lone walks, playing hooky from school because the day outside called to her. She would refuse to answer when spoken to, and she worried her parents profoundly when she came home wet and muddy from the rain, having fallen into the river, been riding a colt, climbing trees and grazing her limbs. One holiday after the death of his parents, he had noticed her following him and had called out to her: Go away, Mary. I don't want to play with you. For he thought she was like the others, and a girl as well. He thought she did not understand. But she gave him a dark look and said, Don't call me Mary, because that means bad luck. Call me Chippewa, because that's the name of a terrible murdering Red Indian tribe who scalp people.

After that they often went off together on rambles across the moor, along the river, and up into the hills. They never said much to each other, parting and meeting without words, and they never played together except running races and fighting. They were like two stray animals.

But this summer something happened.

"Did you know a storm is raging on Jupiter? It's red and looks like an eye."

It is high summer; the moor is below them and ecstatic birds chatter in the trees and brambles.

"You're strange," she says slowly. "You're the strangest person I know."

"Do you think there's life on other planets?" says Jason. "The same elements are all over the universe, so why not life?"

They have walked a long way that day, and she stretches out alongside him in the heather.

"They say in biology . . ." Jason begins, but her look stops him.

"Are those the things you go around thinking about?" she says gravely.

"They say in biology . . ." Jason says, slightly more quietly.

"Lean over this way. I'll show you something."

He leans over toward her. It is still for a long spell. She is like the birds. A storm is raging on Jupiter. She runs her hand over his head. He is seized with an amazing feeling, almost like anxiety, almost as if he were going to cry.

She presses him against her mouth. When I was little, I wanted to eat everything I saw. I wanted to eat flowers and I wanted to eat stones. Once I ate a little china ornament. It disappeared, and they wondered where it was. It was a dog. I wanted to taste everything in Dad's shop and I wanted to eat the most beautiful insects. When I was seven, I ate a flower and was poisoned. Then I stopped doing that.

He moans from above her. How strange you are. It's as if nothing can penetrate you. Give me your mouth, like this; I want to taste you, taste you all over me.

She was mad, or that's what they said in the town, a girl who would never be under control, crazy, respecting nothing—that was true, he knew that. Now it grows in them, like anxiety, like rage. The heather scratches their faces and she laughs—it's like when they fight, uninhibitedly. He can spit on her and she can bite him. She helps him undo his clothes; then she tastes him as if he were made of smooth china. They say in biology . . . Venus creeps across the sun . . . clamps herself to him, quite still now, moist and alien against his own body. Then he heaves himself up and forward—someone's calling—one of them, he doesn't know which.

Later they walk slowly up through the hills; it is getting late. They rest at one place, and she lies with her head against his throat and is no longer a savage Red Indian, just a child who has run away from home. He suddenly thinks about the shopkeeper, plump and narrow-minded, standing behind his counter looking like a sausage. The shopkeeper's daughter—it does not sound like fun.

They don't talk. He looks at her, studying her features: the disquieting, rather plain face, the untidy hair. They said she was mad and mumbled in horror about what would come of such a . . . Jason is seized with a kind of obscure need to console her, to hold her and run his hands over her hair. He does not really understand what has just happened; it could be rage, it could be wild grief. He doesn't know. But he knows what he is feeling now, and that frightens him.

She raises her head and looks at him. She is Chippewa again.

It's late, he whispers.

There's a little barn up here, she whispers.

They get up. For the first time she takes his hand and leads him, guiding him through the woods, her hand rough and warm. When they reach the barn, he knows what is happening. Now he knows. And he hears quite clearly that it is she who is calling; and perhaps it is to him she is calling, as she clutches, clutches at him.

⚜

Jason went back to school a little while later. She said goodbye to him on his last evening—otherwise their farewells have been just as brief and silent as before. She briefly holds his hand, rather awkwardly, and looks at him. That's all. He is leaving, will be away, and she is going back to her moor, alone.

Then she says something.

"Do you also think I'm crazy?"

He shakes his head. "Not really. No more than I am."

"Jason," she says, a strange note in her voice, "it's such a long way into you." Then she turns around and starts walking.

"Anyway," she says. "Anyway, I know what you threw in the river that day."

"What?"

. . .

"What, Chippewa?"

But she has disappeared into the darkness.

⚜

Christmas holidays. Snow on the ground. His aunt's agitated voice when he comes through the door: Goodness, how you've grown. I hardly recognize you each time. You'll soon grow out of . . .

Uncle Chadwick, the practical one, droning on about things: And school, young man, have you taken note of what Mr. Scott said?

Jason feels profoundly alien toward them, but finds it easier to mumble dutifully, Yes, yes, things are better. That pleases them. He can see that pleases them. And it's true, there has been nothing to remark on that autumn. But whether that is Scott's doing . . .

At church on Christmas Day he looks cautiously around at the congregation.

Then turkey and Christmas pudding.

Something does not fit, something is wrong.

By the evening he thinks he has waited long enough and can ask.

"And Chipp . . . Mary? The shopkeeper's Mary?"

There is a silence. The vicar harshly clears his throat, then gets up and goes into his study as if he had not heard.

"Oh . . ." Aunt Mabel says gently, stirring her hot punch. "Well, that was a terrible story . . ."

Jason, Jason. What is the matter with *you*, that things like this happen to you?

You are falling, falling now, falling through the distances in space, falling and waking, just as you did when you were small, but this is no dream. Outside the vicarage the snow is on the ground. You are freezing into ice, Jason. You walk across the moor alone and know it is the last time. You never want to walk there again.

"Well now, gentlemen, now that we are to take up the question of heredity and reproduction, we had better start with the rats."

University Medical Department 2; the professor cheerful and morning-brisk at the lectern.

"Everyone knows rodents reproduce themselves very rapidly, but just *how* rapidly this occurs in rats you will soon find out after I have briefly sketched for you the life cycle of the rat—its biography, if I may put it that way."

His students murmur with amusement.

"If we look at the common rat," he says, taking a rat out of a cage beside him, "there's not much about it to inspire respect. It doesn't look particularly repulsive. From its characteristics, it seems a pleasant little animal, moist nose, whiskers, peering eyes . . . Its tail is slightly unpleasant but . . ."

The students laugh.

"But this little animal is more dangerous to man and society than the largest and strongest predator. Here in England we know of two types of rat, one the black rat, *Rattus rattus*, which earlier was the common variety but which has now been overtaken by the common brown rat, *Rattus norvegicus*. This species is generally about nine inches long, light brown in color, mixed with gray, its neck and abdomen dirty white, its paws pale skin color—as is its tail, which is as long as its actual body. This rat lives almost everywhere. Along riverbanks it eats frogs, fish, and small birds, but it also takes rabbits, young pigeons, and so on when it can get at them.

"However, it can also live off a vegetarian diet and does immeasurable harm to grain crops in the fields and barns, as well as in stores of fruit and vegetables. It bites very fiercely, and the wounds heal with difficulty. Its bite is very painful because of those long, sharp, unevenly shaped teeth.

"The rat is extremely fertile. Were it not for its astonishing appetite, the number of rats would soon be out of control. For lack of other food, they eat each other, and the large male rats, which often live alone, are feared by the other rats, the worst enemies they have. They eat smaller members of their own species. That is an excellent example of the principle of the survival of the fittest, as well as of self-regulation by a species. Please take note of this.

"It is an interesting fact that skins of rats that have been eaten by other rats can be found in rat holes, and these skins are often *inverted* during the eating, in other words, inside out . . . even toes and tail."

The professor picks up an inside-out rat. His students laugh, somewhat uncertainly, at such a grotesque sight.

"The female is fertile all year round, and twelve litters in the course of a year is nothing unusual. She carries her progeny for scarcely a month and is accessible for reproduction as soon as the dear little things see the light of day. On an average, she gives birth to sixteen young in each litter, and she has been known to go on feeding them until the very moment the next lot drop out of her. She is a living spawning ground, and the male rat's urge to reproduce is almost as uncontrollable as his hunger.

"The young are sexually mature after five or six months, so if you reckon on a lifetime of four years, one pair of rats can theoretically produce issue amounting to three million in that short period of time.

"The consequences of such fertility—if allowed to continue unhindered—are obvious. We have accounts of whole villages on the plains of Spain ruined by rats, fertile fields becoming deserts, and Plyny the Elder tells of how Augustus once sent a whole Roman legion to Majorca and Minorca, where these small vermin had practically taken over the islands. They were wading in rats there and the legionaries' task was not pleasant.

"So we should be grateful for the rats' tendencies to cannibalism and civil war. The male has an astonishing thirst for the blood of his own issue, and the female knows that, so does her best to hide her young in places where the father can't get them—until they're big enough to defend themselves against him. Nonetheless, the male often finds his young wherever the female has hidden them. He often kills her, too, to get hold of them. And he eats as many as he can.

"There is a great deal more to say about these interesting animals, but that will have to suffice. As we now move on to the question of heredity, I must ask you to note the following . . ."

The university. They dissected rats and corpses, at first with uncertain hesitant movements, then with skilled indifference. To Jason, this time took on a vaguely nightmarish light, flickering and dim, the light from the gas lamps burning on dark evenings in the pathology room. In the half-light, young men in waistcoats and shirtsleeves were smoking as they folded back abdominal membranes and pleural sacs, revealing secrets no one ought to see and no one understood. Naked gray limbs lay on the slabs, all with that characteristic chilly skin, old and young, men, women, and children. At first they just lay there; then they were opened up and slowly taken apart, until finally nothing was left. That was the secret. And the smell—the sweetish smell of formaldehyde and disinfectant, mixed with the nauseous odor of decomposition—clung to his clothes, his skin, his very nostrils.

In the evenings, filled with images of the day, Jason went back to his room, an anonymous attic in a poorish part of London. He often picked up his violin the moment he got inside the door and went on playing until almost midnight, ignoring the fact that he should be reading or preparing for the next day. He never knew what he was playing, using no score, just playing everything he knew, wildly and unsystematically. Then he played what he didn't know, mindlessly, just pure notes, until someone banged furiously on the ceiling or the wall, or his landlady, Mrs. Bucklingham, came up to demand quiet. Mrs. Bucklingham was a stout, shuffling busybody. She smelled of frying and damp wool. She was always angry with one or several of her tenants, and Jason suspected her of going into his room to snoop around when he was out in the daytime. She ruled her lodging house despotically, and one wit had already renamed the place Bucklingham Palace. Whenever she came up to him, tut-tutting and shaking her fist, Jason looked at her as if she were already one of the ugly nameless bodies in the mortuary, and with a medical man's sober, somewhat cynical mind, he saw her in front of him, stripped and sliced open, the layers of white fat folded to one side while someone fingered her liver. That was Jason's revenge. He caught himself regarding the whole world in that way: his fellow students, the professors, the wash-erwomen who came and went in his street, the vegetable sellers, the animal tamers, and the countless street girls. It was all there in front of him like a bad dream, all of it, the homeless children of the slums, born into a quagmire of hopelessness, filth, and ignorance, roaming the streets munching on cabbage leaves they picked up off the ground. As soon as they were old enough, they would be victims of itchy crotches, coupling and producing issue. Toil and beg for food, man, bite your nearest and pray to God. Look at microbes in your microscope. Chat and smile. Everyone chats and smiles, chats about nothing, shouts and drinks himself silly occasionally or all the time. Then they die one fine day, old or young, they die, are tucked up into the earth with laurel wreaths or are found in the gutter and taken to the mortuary for dissection. That's what it's like. Swarming lives, with no meaning, no number.

Occasionally he could see himself quite clearly, lying there with his abdomen slit open, grinning teeth behind gray lips, white slits of eye-balls visible between rigid eyelids.

If he did not go home and take up his violin, he might go out into the abyss of the city for a night or two. There was a lot to do there. That was how Jason discovered a great deal about himself, did things he would never have imagined possible, things that filled him with a faint, wondering self-contempt.

His studies did not go well after the enthusiasm of the first term had worn off. He thought of the illustrated books of his childhood, the glass cupboards in his father's surgery, the experiments and the telescope, and what had attracted him to medicine became more and more indistinct. A sense of honor, that was true, a kind of duty to the memory of his father—he was doing what was expected of him. Also, the medical profession would provide him with a livelihood. But beyond that? What *was* it all about? What had attracted him to science and medicine? His own disposition? The fact that his father had been so good at explaining and bringing things alive? Yes, but there had to be something else. What were his own motives, his own thread through it all?

It did not occur to him until later that he was in a situation few scientists ever seriously approach with the same gravity. Science is principally driven by the sheer need for understanding, and that is enough in itself, the driving force behind much monotonous research work. It fills the weary slow days and nights in laboratories with flames, with meaning. Next comes its usefulness, the practical dividend of penetrating nature, controlling it, and modifying it. Jason was asking for something more than that, and it was presumably inappropriate to ask about your own place in that picture.

He also believed a doctor should serve people, cure them, with compassion.

Compassion. Jason had lost his God early, that was true, but now, at this time, human beings also disappeared from Jason's view of the world, and with that human qualities such as unselfishness, enthusiasm, and compassion also vanished. Things no longer had anything to say to him. The orangutan and the amoeba—they were all the same to him. Flowers in the ground or people in the wretchedness of their cities. He saw the sick and the decrepit in the hospital vainly clinging to life. He dissected rats and cut up corpses. Death was all around him. He walked through foggy streets and saw the wretched of the city, saw them eating, saw them starving, saw the heart desperately hammering through the shirtfront of a boy dragging a heavy cart behind him. He listened to lectures. He saw organisms fighting and collapsing, rattling in the wards. He studied the construction of the organs. He studied the sex of a whore he slept with, that strange flower of flesh; he was seized with loathing.

In that way he shut everything out, denying himself impressions, unable to take anything into himself.

This awful state—for he was perfectly aware of its awfulness—was something he had experienced since the incident with Chippewa. His time at the university had simply confirmed it, and it was nothing he had learned from books, nor had he ever seen it described. When he read about the early great thirst for knowledge and those creative people, he had the impression they had been obsessed by something to an unfathomable extent—an idea, a longing, a hope, something that drove them on. He saw it in a number of his fellow students, too: Christian ideas, philanthropic ideas, socialist ideas, or a straightforward simple desire for a secure position, ambitions for a career. Or both. He was not like any of them. He was an idealist with no ideals. He was empty of enthusiasm, empty of compassion. He wished for calm rest, no thought, no questions, no being. He shrieked out all his pain and suffering into the arms of a little street girl. She had been frightened and had wanted to leave him, and then he hit her. What would Chippewa have done? Perhaps she would have let him shriek, or would have shrieked back, or held on to him hard. Hold me tight!

He occasionally pulled himself together, going to socialist meetings, for instance, trying to *make* ideals appear, make himself feel compassion.

But the rhetorical fervor of the many speakers and lecturers glanced off him. He understood them, he understood their intellectual point, but not their emotion. Distant and sick, he noted their integrity and realized it stemmed from the same rationalistic attitude to life he himself had, but nonetheless was passionately inspired by compassion, a will to fight injustice. But they did not move him.

He hauled himself out of his lethargy with a violent effort of will and applied himself to the curriculum for a few weeks—then collapsed again, unable even to find the energy to open his books. For a few days it was as much as he could do to drag himself off to lectures, leaving his reproachful books on the table—an unpleasant lump came into his throat each time he looked at them.

This was when his bad dreams began; anguished, incoherent images leaving him sweating and wide-awake, images that meant nothing, but which filled him with fear all the same. A bare branch dripping with raindrops. Two quiet horses in driving mist—but beneath it all a fear, unknown and invisible. That was what his nights were like, while in the daytime he had periodic fits of rage.

Ah, but his friends! His friends Munroe and Hugo, *they* understood

him, or at least he could sit with them for hours or days, drinking,
going to pubs, thinking up pranks at the university. Munroe and Hugo
did not reject him if one evening he started smashing things or lashing
out.

At the university Jason made friends for the first time, and naturally
they were the two most hardened of the lot—Munroe and Hugo, two
hopelessly lost men who were always on the verge of being thrown
out of the halls of Aesculapius for their behavior; who stuffed their
cigar butts into the nostrils and ears of the dead when smoking in the
pathology room. Hugo, small, perfidious, and dark; Munroe, thickset,
violent, and careless. They were noisy and troublesome friends, and
Jason loved them, not least because with them he could laugh—laugh
and laugh, laughing everything off.

His two friends were always teetering on the edge of expulsion from
the university, and Jason was soon teetering with them, so no wonder
things worked out as they did. If one event had not become the
decisive factor, another would have. Jason could see perfectly well the
way things were going, but he did nothing to stop it. This inevitability
had been obvious over the course of his last year as a medical
student—stemming from his state of mind about the profession he
had chosen, to which he no longer felt drawn. He was twenty-one
and was swept along on the current of carousing and apathy, fights
and rebelliousness—inexorably drawn to a break with all the certainty
of a sleepwalker, as if led by alien forces, as inevitably as if it were
written in the stars.

⚜

The decisive event happened one evening in the pathology room,
and it began innocently enough. Together with Munroe and Hugo,
Jason had ensconced himself there with some medicinal spirits. Munroe had acquired the keys, and they secretly let themselves in after
everyone else had left. To them it seemed an unusual place for an
unusual evening.

"I can't stand this smell," mumbled Jason. "I'll never get used to
it."

"My dear chap," growled Munroe good-humoredly, "you'll soon
have something else to think about apart from the smell. Here." He
handed Jason a bottle.

Hugo fished a couple of candle stumps out of his trouser pocket and lit them. Then they sat down, a bit expectantly, passing the bottle between them as they watched the shadows flickering over the walls and ceiling.

After they had emptied the first bottle, they began the evening's program.

First they walked around from corpse to corpse, looking down at them. There were a lot there, for at the time the students were concerned with accidents and violent deaths, so the curriculum covered such causes of death and what the human body looked like afterward.

One was a man rather like Admiral Lord Nelson in appearance, but he had also landed underneath a brewer's dray, so by now he looked more like that gentleman *after* the Battle of Trafalgar.

They also examined gunshot wounds and some fairly undramatic knife wounds. Owing to a series of disciplinary matters the previous year, Hugo was repeating the course, so he had been through the material before and was able to lecture Jason and Munroe with a knowledgeable air. He also had the pleasure of demonstrating a neck after hanging and the hanged man's face with all its characteristics. Jason and Munroe followed with interest. There was also a case of poisoning, and several nasty injuries. The three of them were drinking all the time, but when they came to a fisherman, they lowered the bottle and stood in silence for a few minutes, looking down at this man who had drowned in the Thames. Jason noticed Munroe's rigid face and he could feel his own stomach churning.

"Why does he look so bloody awful?"

"Because he drowned, Jason," said Hugo matter-of-factly. "That's what they look like."

"Blown up?"

"Yes. Haven't you seen a drowned corpse before? They're the worst. The absolute worst."

"Christ!" Jason looked at the purplish, grotesquely swollen body and cautiously touched the leathery skin. "Why is it so hard?"

"I'm not quite sure. Probably a chemical reaction between the layers of fat in the tissues, so the fat changes consistency and turns hard."

Munroe interrupted, his eyes rigid.

"And how long . . . Excuse me . . ." Words failed him and he clapped his hand over his mouth and left the slab to lean over in a corner.

Jason went on staring at the drowned man and completed Munroe's question. "How long had he been in the water?"

"Difficult to say. Over a week, I should think. Maybe two. That's why he's so swollen."

Jason raised the bottle and took a gulp.

"The water penetrates the tissues by osmosis and stays there," said Hugo. "No, he doesn't look too good."

"And the face?"

"Yes. No. Christ no. Drowned . . ."

"Is it a simple death?"

"Easy, do you mean? Drowning?"

Jason took another gulp and looked questioningly at Hugo.

"Well," said Hugo. "First of all the air passages fill with water and the drowning person tries to hold his breath but can't. He breathes in deeply and respiration stops for about ninety seconds. Then some more deep breaths follow and water is drawn into the lungs; he loses consciousness, and after a few spasmodic terminal breaths, death occurs. Four or five minutes. It can be quicker because of the shock. You're conscious, or semiconscious, for the first few minutes of the process."

"Do they float up again?"

"Gradually. The characteristic floating position is with the abdomen and face down in the water, buttocks and back of the head above the surface, the limbs hanging loose."

"I see."

"But an easy death . . . Why do you ask?"

"Oh, nothing," said Jason. "Just that I heard a story once about someone who'd drowned." He stopped and reached for the bottle, drank deeply, then went on somewhat indistinctly. "Ugh, it was really rather a terrible story. As I said, really terrible. A young girl, fairly young, only a child really, drowned herself in a fast-flowing river. Quite without warning. No one had any idea she was going to do it, neither the parents nor the vicar. Or even that she could have such a thought in her head. She just walked into the river one late November day and disappeared into the swirling currents. I can see her floating, half above, half below the surface, her eyes open because she wanted to see what it was like, I suppose."

Hugo looked closely at Jason as he took another swig at the bottle.

"I wonder if it was an easy death," Jason went on. "A terrible story, that's what they said, a terrible story. I think she had loosened her hair—it was brown and must have floated out freely in the water, and she had a gray skirt on. At first they searched for her everywhere when she didn't come home, but then they began to drag the river. They found her a few days later farther downriver, caught in a tangle of branches and twigs. They carried her home in the rain. Do you think—do you think she looked like that?" Jason nodded at the swollen creature on the slab.

"No, Coward. Not very likely. Not after only a few days."

"I suppose not," said Jason quietly.

"Why . . . I mean, did she do it on purpose?"

"At first they thought she'd fallen in as she was walking along the river. But she hadn't."

"No?"

"You mean, how did they find out? Well, it's not really certain, but I suppose it must have been when they were washing her and getting her ready for the coffin. As she was lying there on a slab and they were drying her, they noticed. She was thin, sparrow-like, and it showed. She was four months along."

The air around Jason was sober and clear now, though he had begun to snivel.

"And then?"

"And then," said Jason, "they put her in the coffin and buried her."

"I mean—the father?"

"Her father was the shopkeeper," said Jason.

"The child's father."

"The child's father, the father of the child. They thought all kinds of things. Maybe some goatherd, they said. Or a traveling salesman. Or a Gypsy. Or a tinker. So many people get the blame for things like that, except the actual culprit. It was a local boy, nothing more dramatic. They ought to have realized that. Perhaps they did actually sense it. Anyhow, he told them himself when he came back from school and heard what had happened. He announced it loudly to anyone who cared to listen. Then he was thrown out of his home, right in the middle of Christmas Day. It was an extremely Christian and moral place."

"Not everyone would voluntarily own up to such a thing."

"There was a huge commotion." Jason took another gulp.

"Why do you think he told them?"

"He shouldn't have. Not to avoid the commotion, but because it was his concern, not theirs. And the dead girl's concern, inasfar as the dead can have 'concerns.' He ought to have realized no one would understand. His confessing was a pathetic gesture."

"But pathetic things can be honestly meant."

"Yes," said Jason gravely. Then he emptied the bottle and dropped it on the floor. "Hurrah!" he cried.

Hugo shushed him, then they laughed.

A few minutes later, Jason went quite wild. The other two drank to keep up with him, and then things started developing. Their evening in that dismal place became frightfully amusing and amazing, frightfully frightfully amusing, all of it foggy to Jason, an indistinct whirlpool, a wild dance of impressions and happenings, and the dance went like this:

DANCE MACABRE

First they drank a bottle
  —it was frightfully funny
Then they played with corpses
  —it was frightfully funny
They laughed at a gassed old lady
  —and had quite a bit of fun
And engraved their initials
  —scalpels are versatile tools
Then they sniffed at formaldehyde
  —and Jason was dreadfully sick
And put a toe in the keyhole
  —it fitted the hole so well
Then they exchanged a few organs
  —absurd objects on a woman
Then drank yet another bottle
  —Jason made a speech to the dead
But then came a great apparition
  —but it was only the caretaker
They danced around and around him
  —and had such frightful fun

Then came two men with helmets
—and the dance went gaily on
Then came two men with helmets
—then it was thanks for the dance.

The next day it was made known that *Coward, Jason, Hugo, Paul,* and
Munroe, Peter had been permanently suspended from the University
of London. Owing to the particularly grave nature of their offenses,
all other universities were notified of their activities and the British
Medical Association was also informed.

Raindrops run down a bare twig.
  Two colts stand in the mist.

You are walking along the river and I can see you. It is late autumn,
soon winter, fog and rain and moisture everywhere. You like this
weather. You like being soaked through. You walk along the riverbank
and look around. The sky is low and gray, the first snow soon to come.
If you like, I can hold your hand for the last bit, hold your hand as I
once did; it was rough and warm in mine. Your face is quite open as
you walk, raindrops running down it. Are you sad? Are you happy?
Such foolish words, "sad," "happy," limited adjectives covering nothing. Aren't there other states of mind for which there are no human
words, beyond an unconditional positive or negative? Walk along the
river, see the water flowing by, swollen and fierce from all that rain.
The water hides everything. Your face is quite open. If you like, I
shall hold your hand for the last bit. Your face. Your chin is pointed
and protrudes, your forehead is too high and round. You have an amazing face. Let me hold you now. Rain, rain, eternal rain. Speak to her
as she walks, tell her the horses are close together in the meadow,
heads over each other's back, protecting each other from the rain. The
laughing sound of running water, of drops falling, of whirlpools pulling; can you hear it now? I don't even think you're sorry. I think
you're walking along the river because you *want* to, because that's
what you're *like,* and I don't think you consider anything else but
what is right for you. But all the same—all the same, I wish you would

listen. Listen to the rain if you can. I would like to hold your hand.
You are not mad. I know nothing about you, and yet there's no one
I know so much about as you. Here is my hand, if you like. Don't be
afraid. I won't talk. I am calm. I imagine you thought about me. So
foolish. Consolation. I imagine myself pressing your hand a little. The
river bends here, and there is a dark branch hanging out over the
river. Your hand.

⚜

It was suffocatingly hot in his attic room. He was lying in bed and
could not wake up. Indistinct, vile images slipped through him, great
moths with brown dusty wings and slimy, bulging egg sacs landing all
around him. He seemed to see rotting human limbs, thighs, calves
. . . He forced himself to sit up and stared around the swaying room.
The bright glare from the skylight was like a question, but half-asleep,
he could find no answer. When he got up to open the window for
some air, everything turned black before his eyes. He swallowed a
few gulps of cold tea, staggered back to the bed, and flopped down
onto it.

He lay like that for a long time, not knowing what was wrong with
him, shuddering now and again; people came into the room, people
he knew far too well, but he pretended not to. Then they left. Then
he was up, trying to shave, but his hand was so unsteady he cut
himself. Maybe he was feverish. Then it was dark again.

He woke once and saw two people he did not know in the room,
two men in top hats standing in the harsh morning light, staring solemnly at him. He pretended not to see them, turning away, but they
did not disappear. Then he realized they were real.

"Don't you recognize us, Jason?"

Yes, yes. It is someone familiar.

"It's me, Mr. Scott, your solicitor. And Dr. Falls. I don't think
you've seen him since—since that little gathering."

Ah yes.

"You look wretched, my boy. Perhaps you'd take a look at him
later, Dr. Falls."

As long as he doesn't cut me up.

"I've spoken to your foster parents. About what's happened. But
they have no wish to have anything more to do with you. Not after
that episode. The girl."

What girl?

"Compensation also had to be paid to the girl's father, as you know. You'd hit him so hard, he lost his hearing. You disgraced your aunt and uncle. Why should *you* hit *him*, may I ask?"

No, it's more than I can comprehend.

"To tell the truth, he should have hit you."

He did, too, insofar as a sausage can find the strength to hit anyone. Blows.

"But I see you're ill and I won't make things worse by scolding. You are twenty-one and no longer under the protection of your aunt and uncle, or me. But I—and Dr. Falls—have talked it over, and we would like to help you. What you've done is shameful, but we still honor the memory of your father."

How delightful.

"We'll try to get you reinstated at the university, Jason. We'll stand behind you. We'll say the other two put you up to it. They have both been sent away to sea by their parents. We'll try to get you back into the university, Jason. There's not much money left, to be sure, but we're willing to endorse a loan if you see it through. Are you listening, Jason? Then answer me. Say something. You haven't even said good morning. Dr. Falls, I think you'd better take a look at him."

"Good morning," said Jason as the doctor leaned over him.

"Good morning," said the old doctor kindly. "What's the matter with you?"

"I don't want to do medicine," said Jason faintly.

"I beg your pardon?"

"I don't want to go on with medicine."

The two men looked at each other.

"I can't believe my ears," said Scott.

"I am sure you mean to be kind," said Jason, with little conviction. "But it just won't work. I can't stand it. I wish to give it up."

The doctor looked at him in a friendly way, a question in his eyes. Then he examined Jason and prescribed a tonic.

"At least it's a choice," he said.

"Now, *really!*" said the solicitor.

"Yes," said Jason. "It's true. I'm quite certain I don't want to go on."

"Then there's no point in our staying here," said Scott, offended.

"What do you want, then, young man?" said the doctor.

"For the moment, just to lie here. I want to be left in peace. It'd be kind if you left me in peace now."

"All right," said Dr. Falls. He got up, and Scott hastily left, but the doctor turned in the doorway.

"You're very unlike your father," he said.

Jason smiled, happily.

⚜

After that, he lived at the bottom of the pit of London for a year or two. He quickly used up all the remaining money, and his credit worthiness rapidly disappeared. Soon he was chalking his cuffs to keep up a façade for Mrs. Bucklingham. He pawned his textbooks and his remaining instruments. He had no means, nor had he given a thought to any way of earning a living that might suit him. What he saw at the bottom of London is a more or less blank page in Jason's memory. He was living in the silent calm of *afterward*. Slowly his odd state of mind retreated and he no longer had fits of rage. He first found a way of earning a living by chance, an idea someone gave him. It all happened because Munroe was on shore leave and unexpectedly appeared at Jason's rooms one winter afternoon. Jason was truly pleased to see him, for except for Mrs. Bucklingham, he had spoken to no one for a long time.

Munroe appeared to be on top of the world, strong now and calmer from being at sea. He took Jason with him out on the town, stood him dinner and many tankards of ale, and they talked about Hugo for a while, where he might be in the world (though they were never to find out what happened to him). Then Munroe told him all about life at sea. (Jason was never to see Munroe again after that evening.)

Because Munroe was off again the next day and because Jason had spent over a year with no one to talk to, something happened. Jason changed. That evening he broke his silence and talked to Munroe, talked and talked to his friend, who was to go back to sea, taking Jason's story with him. Hesitant at first, then more openly and freely, he told him about his life. He told his friend that he was a stranger to himself, that he was someone else, that all his adult life he had been someone else whom he didn't know.

Munroe listened to him, asking few questions. Jason did not know whether he understood, but that did not really matter, either.

Something seemed to come to an end that evening, merging into something else, so what happened later seemed right. They slipped out into the city, drank some more, talked together, and got soundly and properly drunk, going from pub to pub; then they went to a music-hall show and laughed at the performance.

Afterward they went to the rat fights. Jason had been unwilling, but his friend dragged him along, so before he could protest, a confused Jason found himself in evil-smelling premises, a famous pit in Fleet Street where Billy, the legendary terrier, had once fought. Now they were featuring a new terrier who, at its best, was supposed to surpass old Billy. The new dog's name was Jacob and he was depicted on the posters snarling and foaming at the mouth, his jaws full of rats.

The atmosphere around the pit was already heated; the early rounds were over and the pit cleared of mutilated rats. A lot of bickering was going on over whether the previous dog had killed twenty-eight or twenty-nine of the gray creatures in its prescribed twelve minutes. The twenty-ninth rat had revived during the cleaning-up operations, but by then bets had all been settled and those who had bet on twenty-eight and not twenty-nine were shouting with annoyance— they had been cheated, they yelled, glaring angrily at the fortunate winners counting their gains. The spectators who had laid no bets because they had no money, or because they had already lost it all, were also yelling—largely to add to the hullaballoo. Bookies were strolling calmly around in the chaos of raging drunks, taking new bets as if nothing had happened, calming tempers, saying this was nothing to squabble about; people should be spending their time betting on Jacob, whose round was just coming up. Good money to be made. Place your bets, gentlemen, quickly now, more gains to come! Men drank, laid bets, and yelled at each other, while the two men in charge of the pit calmly prepared it for the next bout, their high boots and leather gloves protection against rat bites. Otherwise they looked like two bank clerks with no jackets or ties: one small and fat, with a bald patch, smiling sweetly all the time; the other thin, with dark greased hair. Both were sweating profusely in the heat and were noticeably sober, for their rather special task required them to be both watchful and resourceful to avoid being injured. Jason was dragged over toward the pit, almost passing out from the extreme heat and the stench in the overcrowded place; the air was thick with tobacco smoke and the smell of sweaty drunken men mixed with the smell of vomit, dog excrement, and . . . another smell, penetrating and sweetish, nauseating, rising from the pit itself, from the worn, shiny boards where the fights took place. The sounds of music and dancing were coming from the pub next door, and for a brief suffocating moment Jason thought he was about to lose his self-control, but his friend's hand on his shoulder calmed him.

"Haven't you ever been here before?"

Jason mutely shook his head. He would like to have struggled out, but the crowd around the pit was getting more violent now that the men who had been quenching their thirst in the pub next door were back—the high point of the evening was clearly approaching. They were jammed up against the railing by pressure from behind and the impossibility of retreating finally made Jason stay. Something else was also clear to him—he wanted to see this spectacle, yes, study it, enjoy it thoroughly. In his present frame of mind, he thought he could see the truth about mankind in what was going on around him; hundreds of men stacked behind each other, old and young, some in rags, others in suits and boaters, none paying any attention to anyone else, just waiting for the rats to be let loose and the betting money to change hands. Even under the ceiling, in a special gallery, people were fighting like drunken lions for the best seats. He was surprised to see a few women among the crowd of men, most surprised to see a very well-dressed young lady—no more than twenty at most—accompanied by two black-clad men in top hats, perhaps servants or coachmen. The two men kept the nearest people away from the young woman, who was staring dully down into the pit with cold eyes. Jason just had time to see that she was very beautiful before a hum of expectation ran through the crowd. Then everything became deathly quiet and all eyes turned to the top end of the pit.

There Jacob made his entrance. He was a strange little dog, much smaller than Jason had imagined, black and white, with a short tail and pointed ears. He padded around the pit for a while, sniffing—apparently innocent and with no evil intent. But to Jason there was something ominous about him, and he did not wag his tail. He looked like Ernest, Jason's childhood dog. At a distance, he could have been the same dog. Yet the difference was obvious, terrible, though Jason could not pinpoint exactly what it was.

His friend nudged him to make him pay attention. Then Jason saw one of the two men in the pit had stepped over the rail and brought in a large metal cage. The other man had grabbed Jacob by the collar and was holding on firmly, and at that moment Jason realized where the screaming was coming from.

There must have been over a hundred rats in the cage, all of them screaming—not squealing, screaming. Jason shuddered with revulsion. Then, with a practiced hand, the man grabbed bundles of rats by their tails and flung them out into the ring.

The dog's behavior immediately changed. He started growling, very quietly, pulling at his collar, his ears flattened. When enough rats had been thrown into the ring, the man let Jacob go.

Jason could scarcely credit the uproar that now arose among the rats, most of them great huge sewer rats, scurrying away from the approaching dog, scrabbling at the wooden walls around the pit, climbing on top of each other to get up and out, but the horizontal boards along the pit walls prevented them. The rats were screaming all the time, the sound so loud it almost drowned the rising yells of delight from the crowd.

Jacob was no longer growling but silently racing from rat to rat, killing them with a snap of his jaws. If he refused to let go, one of the two pit masters was soon there to snatch the rat out of his mouth. Some of the rats tried to fight back, but the dog was so quick, they never managed to sink their sharp teeth into him. The dog was moving purposefully and soundlessly, except that little snap at each rat, and he cleared the arena at amazing speed. At the other end, more rats were now being released.

Jason was transfixed, staring at what was happening. He could see that this dog in no way resembled the Ernest he had had as a child. The difference was that the pit bull had something about him that was almost human. He was a cold, calculating systematician with four legs and a tail, a tail that did not wag but curled back up like a scorpion's. To Jason the dog seemed to be *thinking*—while Ernest and most other dogs just *lived*, played, fought, and ate. That was what was so horrible. The rat killings themselves were repulsive, yes, frightening—but their hideousness lay in the dogs' manner.

Half the twelve minutes had not yet passed. One man was heaving dead rats in great numbers out of the ring into a fenced-off area where a boy stood counting them, marking off each rat on a board with a piece of chalk. The little fat man kept supplying more rats for Jacob to catch, and the dog spent no more than a few seconds on each. As the fight stood then, it looked like a new record for Jacob, and the crowd was roaring with excitement—the boldest betting on a hundred and fifty or more. The pit bull, with crimson stains down his neck and on his nose, tirelessly continued the hunt.

Then events took an unexpected turn. When Jacob had just over three minutes left, he spotted an unusually large white, probably albino, sewer rat crouching quite still in front of him in the middle of the pit. The dog leaped at the rat, but the rat simply swerved and stopped a little farther away. In contrast to the other rats, it didn't seem to want to escape. Again, the same thing happened; Jacob, provoked, hurled himself at the rat and the rat leaped away like a white ball to another spot. Now Jacob forgot all the other rats and took up the chase. The crowd roared as if possessed—this was new and unexpected. For a long time it looked as if the lightning-fast white rat would be too smart for Jacob. Jason found himself staring as if bewitched. The great white rat bared its teeth at the dog for a moment and Jason found himself screaming—from then on he was yelling with all the others, forgetting himself, venting all his rage and aggression like the rest of the crowd, not knowing whether he was yelling for the rat or the dog.

For a moment it looked as if Jacob had caught his opponent, but then it turned out that the situation was the opposite—the white rat buried its teeth into the skin of the dog's neck, and Jacob was shaking and rattling it violently to get it to let go. It snarled and swirled around and around and the crowd's excitement rose to a new frenzy. Even the phlegmatic pit officials thumped their clenched fists into their palms and cheered. For a while it looked as if the rat would never let go. That would have been the sensation of the year, the champion dog defeated by a rat! But Jacob shook himself again and snapped at the dangling rat.

A calm and friendly voice in Jason's ear said, "Do you see Jacob wrestling with the angel."

For a second Jason was paralyzed. He stopped yelling and turned around to see who had spoken, but discovered no one. All he could see were bawling, cheering spectators, far too excited to be able to say any such thing. Nor was it his friend, because he was on the other side of Jason, yelling just as loudly.

As Jason turned back to the pit in confusion, he saw the dog had shaken the rat free. It floundered on its back a moment too long— then the dog pounced.

Seconds later the gong sounded; the twelve minutes were up. The crowd cheered Jacob wildly as he trotted somewhat wearily out of the ring. Rats were thrown out and counted at a furious rate, the two pit masters looked exhausted. The boy with the chalk carefully recorded every rat—no rat was to revive this time. The result was lower than expected because of the unexpected finale, but was incredibly high all the same—seventy-nine rats killed in twelve minutes. The crowd roared again, though it was hard to say whether from disappointment or delight.

"Are you feeling unwell?" Jason's friend was staring at him.

"What?" Jason looked up at him without understanding.

"Are you ill? Shall we go?"

"Yes," said Jason, nodding. "Let's go."

They struggled out toward the exit. The bookies were now settling the bets, and in passing Jason noticed one of them handing over a large bundle of notes to one of the servants he had seen with the young girl. She must have guessed right and won the jackpot.

They came out on the street.

❧

Jason found the girl in the snow that same evening.

He was walking home alone, unsteady and shivering, for a gust of cold air had come with the first snow, now dancing around him like small white moths, visible in the light of the gas lamps and windows before vanishing into the darkness again. If the cold continued all night, there would be quite a lot of snow the next morning. He was freezing and stumbled to his knees once on the slippery cobblestones, the layer of filth normally on them now a mass of ice.

Because of the snow, it was even quieter than usual for this time of night. He met a few lone night wanderers, a couple of girls, a few drunks, and a policeman with a long, curled mustache, the tips of it white with snow. As he approached his own street near Tottenham Court Road, he was filled with a vague feeling—a dread, a fear of being alone. It gathered inside him and gave him a nasty urge to cry. It was as if the snow and the cold, desolate winter street and what had happened that evening had opened a forgotten dam of childhood inside him. A childhood fear of the dark and of being alone.

There were almost no lights in the windows along the street; the panes were like drooping gray sails. He thought of the ships down on the Thames he had seen as a child in the fog and the rain. An image from the past suddenly came to him sharply—the plague ship. The ship had been quarantined; it had had cholera on board. The most terrible sufferings had been endured below those dead, drooping sails the crew had been incapable of furling—and then the sober yellow epidemic flag at the top of the main mast. The ship had been tied up for one long spring off St. Saviour's Dock, and passersby had stopped on the Whitechapel shore to gaze over at it. Spring never seemed to get that far. One of the harbormaster's boats went out at regular intervals, taking with it coffins and a gentleman who went on board the ship. That was the doctor. When the little boat returned, the coffins were again on it, but this time filled. As a boy, Jason had had nightmares about that ship long after it suddenly vanished one day.

He saw it again as he walked through the now thickening snow and as the distances between streetlights grew longer. He undeniably lived in the slums, perhaps was even one of their many faceless people, but that had never been the intention. He thought about his father and mother—they had presumably imagined something better for him.

Yes, he was one of the faceless. If he went down to Waterloo Bridge tonight and allowed himself to be carried off by the fierce currents of the Thames, what would that matter? Nothing at all, either to God, in whom he did not believe, or to people, whom in darker moments he did not believe in, either. Mrs. Bucklingham would perhaps report him as missing, and after a few weeks, perhaps no more than two, they would pack up his belongings and take them away. The couch was hers, Mrs. Bucklingham would probably say, and in a few years a yellowed photograph or two would be the only witnesses to his having a face, before they, too, were washed away in the current: fire and war would always appear.

꙳

When night falls people become as lonely as snowflakes floating down from a gray city sky. Now and again we fall past a streetlamp and are visible, a brief moment apart, *real*—we can be seen. We exist. Then we vanish into the gray darkness and the earth draws us to it.

ꙮ

If only I weren't so drunk, he thought, I wouldn't torture myself with such thoughts. Think about something else, Jason. Think about an amusing evening, a nice girl.

But that happy evening seemed to him nothing but a skin, an illusion, a thin wax film on a blackened dead face.

Think of a song. Yes, that was it. He could sing a song to keep him warm as he walked. He started on "Londonderry Air," but it was no consolation that evening. Then he tried "Greensleeves," but that was so gloomy. He stumbled on the cobblestones, fell again, and lay there for a few moments in the mud and snow, incapable of getting up. Then he was suddenly afraid of lying there forever, and he felt them coming, the tears he had no wish to let fall. He swore. If only he were not so drunk.

He got to his feet again; then a song came to him that consoled him. It came all by itself and conjured away the picture of the plague ship.

> Eternal Father, strong to save,
> Whose arm hath bound the restless wave,
> Who bidd'st the mighty ocean deep
> Its own appointed limits keep:
>   O hear us when we cry to thee
>   For those at peril on the sea.

He suddenly felt a little lighter. He remembered the hymn from the choir in Bethnal Green Road and recalled the carol services.

> O Christ, whose voice the waters heard
> And hushed their raging at thy word,

Yes, that helped, and it was good as he alternately hummed the second and third parts and imagined himself the soprano. He rounded the next corner and went on:

> And walkedst on the foaming deep,
> And calm amid its rage didst sleep.

Then he stopped. A body was lying in the snow in front of him beside some dustbins. He took two steps toward it, then stood quite still. It was a girl, one of the countless girls, the nameless creatures found all over the city. She was poorly dressed in a ragged dark skirt and a jacket, her feet bare and a pale bluish color against the snow—not even a kerchief around her head, her dark hair drawn back in a disheveled knot.

Jason pulled himself together, went all the way over to her, and was just about to bend down when it occurred to him that she might be dead. He felt a reluctance to touch a corpse—the plague ship again came sailing by—but nonetheless, he bent down and shook her.

Her face was in the snow. As he turned her over, the knot of hair loosened and he brushed it off her face, then squatted down and propped her up against his knees. She was very thin, even emaciated, and she had snow in her eyes and on her forehead. Although it was dark, Jason could see that her pallor matched that of the snow.

She's dead, he thought, turning cold at the thought. But she was not stiff; no, in fact, she was quite soft and supple as she lay against his knees, as pale as the snow. Rigor mortis usually sets in between half an hour and an hour later, he thought, and even quicker when it is cold. He fumbled for her throat—she was cold but not icy, and he could just feel her pulse, a faint but clear, regular throbbing.

Thank goodness, he thought, you're not dead. He brushed the snow out of her eyes and ears, then gave her cheek a few slaps. There was no reaction. He slapped her again and shook her. A few small signs of life appeared: her eyelids flickered, her mouth drew back, and a tiny sound came out of it, not a groan, no more than a small gasp.

Jason was pleased, though at the same moment he thought, What shall I do if someone comes past? A policeman? They'd think . . . hell.

"Up with you, girl," he said quite loudly.

But there were no more signs of life. He shook her hard.

"Wake up now: You can't lie here."

This time she made an attempt to open her eyes, even to focus them. But instead she rolled up her eyes, showing the whites. Jason began to worry that she was ill or dead drunk, in which case it was going to be difficult to get her onto her feet. Perhaps there was a slight smell of gin? Perhaps she had stumbled and fallen, then simply stayed there, just as he had been afraid to do. Or perhaps someone had hit her and tried something nasty, a common enough occurrence, but had then been disturbed. He looked up at the narrow strip of sky above the roofs. It was still snowing, the clouds a reddish gray from the lights of the city.

When he looked down again, he met a pair of large gray eyes staring vacantly and fearfully up at him.

"Ah," he exclaimed. "Are you feeling better?"

She did not reply, but just stared, snow falling and melting onto her cheek.

"Don't you know where you are?" he said matter-of-factly, wanting to be on his way.

"In heaven," she said.

"What? No, you're not in heaven. You're lying in the street, in Barnhart Alley. I found you."

"Oh," she said.

"I didn't think you were alive. Did you fall?" But she did not answer and her eyes closed again. He peered at the thin plain face, the sunken dark eyes and sharp cheekbones and nose. She might be seventeen or eighteen at the most, but she seemed very old, almost ancient. Those eyes—eyes otherwise found only in the very old, those who no longer know the world, who have forgotten what their names are and are waiting to die. He remembered his own grandmother, who had died when he was six. She had had eyes like that, glowing like pieces of coal in two deep round hollows. She could never remember who he was from one day to the next. Jason had been afraid of her.

The eyes of this thin, confused girl in the snow were like that, the eyes of an old person, her forehead and upper lip already showing faint lines of pain, her lips gray, almost purple in the dark. And something about her reminded him of . . .

Suddenly all London's street girls—whom he had otherwise seen only as wretched bundles of rags—suddenly they all seemed to meet in this frail sparrow lying across his knees and become real, visible creatures and in her acquire a face. Then he realized that not only old people had eyes like that; the same look could be seen in the eyes of small children when frightened or serious. Come on now, you must wake up, he thought. You'll die of cold if you stay here. You must not freeze to death.

She had meanwhile gone far away again, and by now it was really cold, well below freezing, the snow blowing. Jason worked hard to bring sufficient life back into her so that he could force a few drops of brandy from his hip flask between her lips. He had stopped thinking about cholera or that she was filthy. He had also given up worrying that someone might come; indeed, he had stopped thinking altogether and was no longer drunk. The less willing she was to get to her feet, the more eager he became, a feeling of joyous apprehension running through him, for he was still frightened and he was soaking wet and dirty. You've got to get up, he thought; then he said so aloud.

That was when he heard a peal of laughter from the street the alley ran into. Someone was standing out there laughing at them, but he couldn't be bothered to see who it was. The laughter was malicious, and he could not make out whether it came from a man or a woman. It came again several times, wheezing and hawking, evil and spasmodic, as if it hurt. Jason ignored it and worked feverishly to get the girl up and away—but she would not cooperate. He then resolutely lifted her up in his arms and set off at a good steady pace down Barnhart Alley without looking back. That would have been risky, anyhow, for the alley grew darker the farther down it he went. Behind him, the laughter faded into a last brief cackle, then ceased. He could hear no footsteps retreating. The snow was now like a carpet on the streets and he could scarcely hear his own footsteps, but he could hear the sound of his heart thumping with exertion and himself panting. Once, the girl's body started slipping and he had to heave her up in his arms so that her head fell onto his shoulder. He could just hear her faint breathing. She smelled of something, a harsh odor, perhaps a cheap perfume or hair lacquer.

Once at Bucklingham Palace, it was a matter of not waking Mrs. Bucklingham. May her ears be as filthy as the rest of her, he thought. May her ears be blocked up.

Not until he had got the front door open and carried the girl into the entrance hall did it occur to him he was taking her *home*. For a moment the absurdity of what he was doing dawned on him. He hadn't meant to, and worse than that, it was foolish of him. What might she get up to in his room? Or what would Mrs. Bucklingham do if she woke and found them? The girl ought to be elsewhere, someplace where she would be undressed and given a bed, food, and clothes. A pair of shoes. What if she died in the night? What if she developed pneumonia? She should have been in a home.

But he had never heard of any such home.

So he carried her up the stairs and into his own room. Finding his way easily in the dark, he put her down on the couch he usually slept on, found the matches on the table, and lit a lamp and the gas fire. He took the lamp over to the couch and looked down at her. She seemed less lifeless now, but that could have simply been the warm light from the lamp. Her eyes were still tight shut. He felt her hand —it was still very cold—and then he noticed she was soaking wet. Pneumonia, he thought again. With the same frightened resolution as before, he undressed her, carefully and matter-of-factly, as a parent might a child, then hung her clothes up to dry. She was wearing nothing but a blouse and skirt under her jacket, not even stockings.

Then he dried her with an old scarf. She was horribly thin. He could count her ribs and see bruises here and there. Naked, she seemed more like an overgrown child and there was almost nothing to indicate she was a grown woman. Her breasts scarcely showed, and her hips and thighs were as slim as a boy's. Her sex was disheveled, compressed like a tiny dead chicken . . . A word came to him— "abandoned."

He tucked a blanket around her and put a pillow under her head, then made up a kind of bed on the floor in front of the fire, locking the door before he started undressing. He blew out the lamp and crawled under the blanket. He looked up at the skylight for a moment—it was still snowing.

A desolate white light flooded the room through the skylight, a small patch of white sky just visible above a roof—the roofs also white, and the whiteness of it all floated in and made things seem transparent.

The girl on the couch was lying with one arm hanging slackly down toward the floor. In that light the pale thin arm became almost like glass or thin alabaster. Her forefinger was resting on the floor, the hand curved in a pretty line, a frozen, beckoning gesture.

Jason was asleep. Neither he nor anyone else would ever see the girl's arm in that light, how beautiful it was. Between the two of them, the room opened up and revealed all its objects: a pipe in an ashtray; an empty bottle, emerald green in this light; a pair of worn galoshes; a chipped cup; the violin case, all there, spread out, waiting to be brought back to life. Jason's coat hung above the stove alongside the girl's thin, now lifeless garments, but no one was there to see it all.

Then the girl pulled her arm back. She was cold.

The flower girl woke after a while. Her blanket had slid off and she pulled it back up to her chin. She looked around in surprise, then down at herself. The room and this shabby couch was to her a good place to wake alone. She saw a violin case.

For a moment she lay still, trying to remember what might have happened the night before and what had brought her here. A few random images went through her, but the whole picture eluded her. The last thing she could remember of the day before was that it was snowing. But here she was, warm, quiet, and peaceful, and she thought she was alone. She pulled the blanket even higher under her chin and closed her eyes as she smiled a contented little smile, her lips pressed close together. She lay dozing like that for a while, apparently finding it unnecessary to fathom how she had ended up there. She had woken in strange places before, so no doubt she would soon know.

After dozing for a while, she was woken by the fact that she had to . . . she had to pee.

The movement in the room woke Jason. For a moment he wondered why he was lying in front of the stove, but at once he remembered the events of the night before quite clearly. He got halfway up and looked over at the couch. The girl was apparently searching for something, bending over and looking along the couch. Jason cleared his throat and she jerked upright in fright.

"God, you scared me," she exclaimed. "I didn't think there was anyone here."

Jason did not know what to say. She was naked, and he looked away in embarrassment, though it didn't seem to worry her much. Seeing her now when she was herself was quite different from the night before.

"Are you looking for something?" he said. Out of the corner of his eye he could see she was peering under the couch and he suddenly caught on. "The pot's under the window," he said.

She giggled, crossed the floor, and unhesitantly plumped straight down on the chamber pot. Jason could not help seeing her. The girl was looking thoughtful, her gaze turned inward on herself.

She'll cause trouble, Jason thought. I'll have to get rid of her.

"Sorry," she said finally. "I simply had to." She laughed lightly again.

"It's all right," said Jason. "What's your name?"

"Emma," she said. She was standing up again now. "And yours?"

"Jason. Listen, Emma, do you know you were lying in the street freezing to death last night?"

"*Was* I?" She looked at him with genuine surprise.

"Yes. I thought of leaving you there, but then . . . Well, I scooped you up."

"Goodness," she said. Jason had expected all kinds of other reactions—perhaps he thought that this was a strange way of thanking him. But her voice was warm and she said nothing more for a moment as she thought about it.

Suddenly she went straight back to the couch and lay down. "Come on," she said, patting the back of the couch. "It's nice and warm here." Jason involuntarily got up and went over to the couch.

"What?" he said.

"Come up here with me." She glanced solemnly-slyly at him. "You can do it for free, you see, because you've been so nice."

She saw at once that Jason was angry and she looked down at the blanket.

"Sorry," she said. "I didn't mean to . . ."

But Jason was still angry, and she let out a small sob, then a few more, and then she was crying properly, though almost soundlessly.

Jason sat down on the edge of the bed, more friendly now. He knew she had not meant it badly.

"Shush," he said kindly. "Stop crying. It's all right." She calmed down and Jason stroked her dirty hand.

"Something to eat?" he said. She was still crying, but her eyes seemed brighter now and she smiled at him.

Jason got up, pulled on his shirt and trousers, and got out bread and marmalade. Then he made tea while the girl put on her dry clothes and fastened up her hair.

As they sat at the little table, Jason asked her about this and that as if making conversation with a guest.

"How old are you, Emma?"

"Sixteen, I think."

"Don't you know?"

"No." She shrugged. "Ain't given it much thought."

"Doesn't your mother know?"

"She's dead."

"Oh."

"But she never told me nothing when she was alive neither."

"I'm sorry . . ."

"She was nice, my mum. In her way. But she had such a lot to put up with."

"Yes?"

"She had five more. Kids, I mean. So . . ."

"That's a lot of mouths to feed."

"Yes. I was the oldest. So it was best I got out as quick as I could to earn some money."

"And your father?"

She shrugged.

"Mum said he played the fiddle on a boat. One of them big boats."

"He played on a boat?"

"Yes, one of them what goes to America. But I dunno if it's true."

"No." He poured out more tea.

"It's good to have something to eat."

"Were you hungry?"

She nodded.

"Nothing shameful about being hungry," she said. "Betty always says that. Betty's my friend," she added.

"She's probably right. Are you often hungry?"

"We-ell, sometimes. But I doesn't pick bread and cabbage up off the street. Rather go hungry."

There was a moment's silence. Jason could see she wanted to ask something but couldn't get around to it. She had become shy of him now.

"Do you want to ask me something, Emma?" he said.

"Yes. I mean, is you a musician?" She glanced at the violin case.

"No," he said. "I'm a student. That's to say, I was. Until a while ago."

"Student . . ." she said. Perhaps she had never heard the word, Jason thought. "Student . . ." she said again, distantly.

"Yes, I was going to be a doctor. But I play as well."

"Does you?" she said, rapidly returning to the present. "Does you play on that?" She pointed at his violin case. "How grand. That's the best thing I knows," she said. "Has you ever heard them playing in the pubs and the music halls?"

"Yes."

"Isn't they clever? I been to the music hall once. There were a real stylish gent in shiny black clothes there—them white tie and tails— he played the 'Londonderry Air,' all by himself. It was grand." Her face turned dreamy and acquired a kind of thin veil of light all around it. Jason went to fetch his violin and, without tuning it, played the "Londonderry Air." She sat quite still as he played, her eyes closed, and although he had not taken it all that seriously at first, he found himself gradually playing with more and more empathy. She was a good audience. He was playing more expressively now, with long, light strokes, and he saw the notes slipping right into her, glowing inside her, and he suddenly felt an astonishing lightness and happiness. He ended the ritardando with a quiet G, and put the violin down.

The silence was long, then she opened her eyes.

"I could see that stylish bloke at the music hall quite clear."

Jason was disappointed, but she smiled secretively.

"He had a great big mustache and almost no hair on top. But at the sides his hair was thick and bushy." She stopped for a moment, then went on. "Betty said afterward he had gold in his notes. Gold. You know"—she looked down—"I like to think that was my dad.

Maybe it was. That he'd come ashore. It could've been him." She looked pleadingly at Jason. "He had a rather lumpy nose, and . . ." She started crying again. "So've I," she said, the tears welling.

Jason went over to try to comfort her, patting her cautiously on her shoulder and back. She was sitting leaning forward and he could feel the knobbly spine through her blouse. The tears gradually ceased.

"Couldn't you play a bit more?" But Jason knew she would start crying again, and to his own surprise he noticed that he was not far from tears himself.

"No," he said. "No more now." He could think of nothing else to say. The girl accepted it without question.

"Couldn't you play like that on a boat?" she said after a while. "Like them my dad plays on. You're sure to be much better than him. Better than the bloke at the music hall, too." She smiled happily at him. Jason saw he had become a kind of god to her now, an Ares, a knight in shining armor.

"I'd never be scared at sea if you played for me all the time."

"Have you ever been to sea?" he said.

"No . . . but Betty went to Brighton once and she told me what it's like. Have you?"

"No," said Jason. "No, neither have I."

"It was so big, Betty said. Big and glittery on top, she said. And a bit frightening."

"What?"

"The sea, of course—the ocean." She said the last word very gravely.

"Here's something from me, Emma," said Jason, taking out his last half crown. "You must go and buy shoes and stockings with it. Promise me that? And perhaps some gloves or something for your neck. You'll get it cheap on Petticoat Lane."

He handed her the coin. She did not thank him, just stared wide-eyed at him and down at the coin in her hand. He could not truthfully say why he had acted in that way.

"Promise me?" he said again. "Do you understand what I'm saying, Emma?"

She was looking almost frightened.

"Yes," she said, nodding. "I promise."

Before she left, Jason asked what had happened to her the night before. She had just reached the door and she stopped, gazing ahead of her at an image of the day before. She did not reply.

"Don't you remember?" said Jason.

"Yes," she said gravely, looking at him, and he saw again how gray her eyes were. "But I doesn't want to tell you."

They said goodbye. When she had got down the stairs, she called back up to him so loudly Mrs. Bucklingham was *bound* to hear it.

"Don't forget you've got to play on one of them boats."

⌇

That was how it came about. That was how Jason found a way to earn a living. Something happened to him that evening when he went to a dog-and-rat fight and rescued a frozen girl in the snow. A few weeks later he started playing in the streets and various pubs, with varying success at first, because he was slightly embarrassed and also so out of practice, but then things got better and he enjoyed it. His constant aim was to become a ship's musician, to play in the ship's band.

A year later he met the drunken Russian.

⌇

That was Jason Coward's story.

⌇

"Excuse me, Mr. Jason."

. . .

"Mr. Jason . . ."

Jason turned around and met a pair of anxious eyes—David's.

"Yes?" said Jason, drawing in a deep breath of sea air. "Can I help you?"

"I . . . Alex and Jim sent me up to look for you. We're approaching Cherbourg and . . ."

Jason turned back to the sea—quite right, they could already see the coastline.

"Yes, of course," he said. "But we've plenty of time."

"Yes, but Alex . . . Petronius . . . and . . ."

"Well?"

"Petronius claims he's an ox. He keeps making terrible noises and we can't stop him, and Alex is raging and keeps scolding, and then there's something wrong with Spot—he's in his bunk and we can't wake him up. He's deathly pale and doesn't answer when we talk to him, and Jim and Georges have both tried smelling salts and Georges has poured a bowl of cold water over him to get him back on his feet."

Jason bit his lip. For a moment he stayed where he was, gazing out into the dusk. The images—his dreams and memories—seemed to dissolve into the air around him, then sink and vanish in the ship's wake.

"Sounds as if everything is much as usual," he said quietly.

David did not reply, but Jason sensed that the boy was staring at him.

"Ah well," he said, moving away from the railing. "I'll come and fix things. Don't look so horrified. Have you had anything to eat?"

"No," said David. "At first Petronius clung to me to tell me what it was like to be an ox, and about the martyrdom of oxen as hecatomb sacrifices in the age of Homer. Then Jim and Georges wanted to take me around the ship before we had a meal, but then we had to try to revive Spot, and *that* was when Alex started to . . ."

"Yes," said Jason. "I see." He sighed, put his hand on David's shoulder, and they headed for the entrance. "Listen now, David," Jason said. "You mustn't let them deprive you of your meals. We've still got a long evening ahead of us."

"All right," said David, looking down.

"Maybe you'd rather be back home in Vienna?"

"Yes. No. I mean . . ."

Jason looked at him and smiled. "Do you know what I think?" he said, suddenly teasing. "I think you'd thought of running off the moment we got to New York."

David glanced quickly at him.

"But I don't think you should," Jason went on. "I think you should think the matter over while we're on our way. Then perhaps you'll be with us on our way back."

David looked down again, and Jason thought he recognized the expression on the boy's face.

"I don't know what you've run away from," Jason said quietly. "And neither do I want to know. But if you've got a home, then I think you should go back to it."

David stopped.

"But people decide for themselves whether they've got a home or not—don't they?"

"Yes," said Jason. "Maybe so." He smiled faintly. "Come on," he said. "Let's go on down and knock some sense into the others."

They went below.

The same evening
La Grande Rade, Cherbourg, 18:30

———————◆◆◆◆◆———————

DARKNESS fell as the *Titanic* dropped anchor out in the harbor. The sun had gone down and the rows of portholes and windows in the hull and superstructure glowed warmly in the twilight. The sea was calm and a light bluish mist lay over the water inside the great mole.

A crowd of people from Cherbourg had gathered on the pier to see this gigantic new ship come in. The two tenders, the *Traffic* and the *Nomadic*, darted out from the quay and set course for the ship, which seemed to lie far too lightly on the clear surface. The reflections from the ship spread like floating lights on the water, and the steam whistle blasted a signal.

On board the *Titanic*, thirteen first-class passengers and seven second-class passengers were preparing to disembark—they were not going any farther. A little cargo was also to go ashore—two bicycles belonging to Major G. I. Noel and his son, two motorbicycles belonging to Messrs. Rogers and West, and a caged canary which had twittered in Purser McElroy's office all the way across—that was to go to a man with the pleasant-sounding name of Meanwell. He had paid five shillings for its fare across, but McElroy had liked its refreshing song so much over those few hours he would gladly have charged nothing. He was going to miss it.

Two hundred and seventy-four passengers came on board, some prominent first- and second-class passengers, and in steerage a number of Syrians and Armenians from various harbors in the Middle East via Marseilles to Paris and from there on the boat train to Cherbourg.

Mailbags were exchanged between the ship and the tenders.

A calm, relaxed atmosphere had spread on board after the first exciting hours at sea. After the ship had raised anchor at eight o'clock, passengers had started to retire to change for dinner, and not many were left on the first- and second-class promenade deck to see the low French coastline vanishing into the darkness. The third-class passengers had also gone inside, with the exception of the Armenians and Syrians. They were singing. Exotic, weary, and sorrowful, they were singing in the darkness around the ship—again, a ring of homesickness—this time for distant unknown villages and dawns.

After calming them all down in the cabin, Jason Coward was preparing his men for tonight's choice of music. That was quite easy this evening—the passengers would be tired and not concentrating.

The musicians were putting the finishing touches to their evening uniforms, Jim helping David turn up his trousers yet another inch, Georges thoroughly rubbing in a good dose of toilet water, and Petronius bustling about, but without letting out any more of those amazing ox noises since Jason had assured him he was a musician. Listen, Petronius, a musician, not an ox! Instead, he kept opening his double bass case again and again, looking at the instrument, closing the case, opening it, and radiating childish astonishment every time the instrument came into sight—it was impossible to say whether this was genuine or artificial. Spot, pale but in his right mind, was combing his hair on his bunk, peering into a pocket mirror.

Jason and Alex were discussing the evening's repertoire. Jason wanted excerpts from *Cavalleria rusticana* and *The Thieving Magpie*, but Alex protested surprisingly strongly against the latter suggestion.

When the ship had again come out into the Channel—this time on course for Queenstown, Ireland—and the passengers were assembled in the saloon after the splendid dinner Signor Gatti's waiters had served them, they were able to relax to the caressing notes of *Cavalleria rusticana* and *The Tales of Hoffmann*. As extra numbers, the band played the overture to *Wilhelm Tell*, two Waldteufel waltzes, and Mathe's *Pastorale* to conclude.

The Armenians were singing outside in the night; no one listened. Thus ended the first day on board.

And the Titans were thrown down into the
abyss, into eternal darkness, and chained
there in painful fetters, in the misty
Tatarus.

—HESIOD, Theogony

April 11, 1912
Due south of Queenstown, 11:10

———————

A DEEP resonant note penetrated the darkness like a ray of clear
light, making its way into his mercifully dreamless sleep and trying
to wake him, as if calling to him, as if asking: Who are you? But he
could find no name. He did not ascend through the darkness up toward the day and wakefulness until the sound rang out for the third
time—then he broke through the surface within himself, opened his
eyes, and knew: I am David.

The morning light was pouring in through the porthole. He looked
around and at once remembered where he was.

David Bleiernstern had heard the *Titanic*'s steam whistle.

For a moment he lay quite still, again with his eyes closed. The
cabin was empty; he was alone and that pleased him. He lay there in
the echo of sleep, the many confusing and unexpected events of the
previous day flitting before his eyes, though they seemed distant now,
calmer, causing him no panic.

He could see Spot as they had found him, unconscious and chalk-
white, curled up in his bunk, his eyes shut and lips dark. Jim had
noticed the immobile body, and letting out an oath, he had leaned
over Spot and shaken him. But Spot did not come round, though he
rolled up his eyes so that the whites showed. He seemed to be fighting to wake up, but with no success, and it looked horrible. David
watched while Jim and Georges struggled to bring him to life.

"Christ!" said Jim. "Here we go again."

"On the very first evening," said Georges. "What do you think?"

"It'll only get worse." Jim slapped Spot's face and shook him gently
but firmly.

"Is he ill?" said David cautiously, biting his lip.

"Ill?" Jim glanced at David. "Ill?" He bent over the pianist again. "Well, he's definitely not well."

"It'll kill him one of these days," said Georges grimly. "He'll die one of these days, if we don't look out."

Spot let out a rattling noise. Georges got up and fetched the smelling salts.

"Poor old Spot," said Jim; then he turned to David. "Better keep this to ourselves," he said. "We'll get him into shape again, then neither Alex nor Jason need know anything about . . ."

But suddenly the door opened and there was Alex with Petronius in tow.

"Oh, Christ Almighty!" snarled Alex, staring at Spot's lifeless figure. "Christ Almighty, now he's gone too damn far."

The steam whistle sounded again and David opened his eyes. Sleep had done him good and he was feeling much better. In the kindly light from the porthole everything looked considerably simpler. He had certainly acquired some incomprehensible, to some extent not entirely pleasant, colleagues, and his fingers kept fumbling when he was playing and couldn't understand Jason's imperceptible head and bow movements. Bliss in the cramped little cabin was also minimal. Petronius had happily snored as well as farted in loud combination just before he had gone to sleep, but mostly due to exhaustion David had dropped off immediately, away from it all. The first day was now over; he *had* survived and was on his way to New York.

The cabin door opened and Jim came in.

"Morning, David," he said cheerfully. "Lazy pig. Soon midday and still in bed. Jason wanted you to sleep in today, so if you want something to eat before we start work . . ."

"Yes," said David rather shamefacedly. "Is it really that late?"

"You must have been pretty done in. Get yourself dressed now, and I'll take you to the mess. You can get bacon and eggs any time of the day there. But you should shave first."

Flattered by Jim's last remark, David leaped out of bed and was down at the washroom in two strides.

"Then you can take a peek at Ireland," Jim said from the door while David was soaping his chin.

☙

Ireland. The *Titanic* had anchored two nautical miles offshore, near Roche's Point; the mainland was shrouded in mellow shadows. Jim and David had gone up to the first-class promenade deck to get a better view. Jim was in his essence that morning, pointing out the triangular shape of the cathedral just visible in Queenstown, one of Ireland's jewels. Jim was English by birth, he told David, but his wife was Irish and he also had Irish blood in him on both his father's and his mother's side. As a result he felt so Irish he could hardly bear it when he saw the country.

Two tenders came bustling out toward the ship, laden with emigrants, Jim said. "Ireland's bleeding," he went on. "She's losing her best youth, and that pleases them in London." He went on about the poverty and the shortage of potatoes, Charles Parnell and Captain Boycott, the Irish Home League, and Asquith's proposals for Home Rule. David listened with interest but without much understanding. Jim must have sensed that, because he deftly changed the subject and pointed at the little boats which had followed the tenders.

"Here come the traders," he said. "They've got all sorts of things with them, watches and clothes, shoes and postcards. They're allowed on board in first and second class because there's always someone who's forgotten to buy something in Europe for his niece in Chicago. And there"—he nodded toward a fishing smack—"there's tomorrow's breakfast. Little lobsters. Dublin prawns. Delicious. Especially with lots of butter. I think quite apart from all the emigrants, the owners would have their ships call in at Queenstown just for the prawns."

They took the stairs down to the well deck.

"I've never tasted lobster," said David. "Is it good?"

"They're like girls," said Jim. "Difficult to undress." David blushed.

They stopped on the well deck to watch the crates of shellfish coming on board. Someone was playing a melancholy tune on a flute out on one of the tenders.

" 'Erin's Lament,' " sighed Jim. "Another poor Patrick on his way to New York to work his arse off in the docks. Yes, you play on, my friend. In a week you'll be in the place of your dreams and you can spend the rest of your life longing to be back home."

David looked carefully at the emigrants coming on board, but he said nothing.

"Hey," said Jim, pointing. "Take a look up there, my boy, and you'll see your boss."

David turned and glanced upward. On the starboard side of the bridge was a short, massive man with a white beard and gold braid on his uniform. He was standing quite motionless, looking down onto the well deck, his face expressionless and his arms folded.

"Captain Smith," said Jim. "The Sphinx."

Down in the crew's mess, Jim kept David company while he devoured eggs and bacon and fresh white bread from the ship's bakery.

"Hm, captains," he began. "They're a pretty odd lot. In the old days, a captain could suddenly get the reputation for being in league with—the forces of darkness." This was said dramatically.

"Really?" said David, unmoved, and drank his coffee.

"There are lots of stories about how a captain with a kind of sixth sense saved his ship and crew. In calm seas and fog, for instance—that's the worst. Sounds get distorted in fog and you can't tell which direction they come from. And you can't see your hand in front of you. But it has happened that a captain has *known* with sudden certainty that the ship was on a collision course, or running aground, and has changed course at the very last moment. That has happened."

"Do you think the Devil whispered in his ear?" said David jokingly.

"No," said Jim, offended, "I don't. I think it's because captains often become *one* with their ships. They sort of become as great as it, with all their senses, as high as the main mast and as deep down as the main anchor. I suppose it's a necessary quality to be able to be a passable shipmaster. In the old days, an ocean trip—let's say across the Atlantic—was rather different from the stroll it is today. You must realize that."

"Oh yes?" said David, buttering another piece of bread.

"Yes, it was another matter altogether," said Jim fiercely. "No mother-dear and waiter, may I please have three scones with jam. Until about ten years ago, they had to reckon seriously on the possibility of never reaching their destination. And even if all went well, they could be becalmed for weeks, or blown far off course by storms, with foul water to drink and nothing but dry ship's biscuits to eat. Of course, situations like that depend on the captain—on his crew, when it comes down to it. All captains on today's big liners started on sailing ships."

"Have you been a seaman yourself?"

"I *am* a seaman," said Jim with pride. "Even if the agent has changed the contract. But I know what you mean, and I'll have you know, when I was young I was deck boy on the barque *Pythia* from Portsmouth. She had a captain of the really great kind, old Captain Kennedy. He had sailed the company's ships for over thirty years, the last ten on the *Pythia*. He loved that ship. He almost *was* the ship. He wasn't all that tall—oddly enough, not many captains are—but he *seemed* tall. When he was at the helm, he was like Moses at the parting of the waves. A patriarch. He used to say about the ship, I only have to want her to do it and she obeys. It was impossible to imagine the man anywhere else except on the bridge.

"But then—then came came the awful trip after the company told him he had reached the age limit. He was to be retired and had to go ashore for good the next time the ship called in at Portsmouth. That was when it happened."

"What?" said David, through a mouthful of fried egg.

"It was a gray misty morning when the ship slipped into harbor. Kennedy had been very silent all through the trip, and both officers and men probably realized he was feeling melancholy, for they all knew he had no family ashore. But no one realized just how profound his grief was. Not the kind of grief that breaks a man and makes him give in or weep, but grief that drove him to carry out his duties even more conscientiously, even more faithfully than usual. And it's also true that the *Pythia* shone like a star in the fog as she slipped in, she was that spotless and clean. The second officer had only once had an inkling of what was up with the captain, and that was one evening when he found old Kennedy on the bridge, standing there with the sextant. When he spotted the second officer, he excused himself with a rare crooked smile and disappeared below. He was not taking the sun's altitude but the moon's. He seemed to be preparing to navigate other seas."

Jim stopped for a moment, then went on: "The evening we were to call in at Portsmouth, Captain Kennedy went through all his charts and brought his notes up-to-date. He signed the documents and the logbook. Everything was in perfect order. He cleared out his sea chest, threw out all the rubbish, and gave his oilskins to his bo'sun. The next morning, when the ship reached Portsmouth, he didn't come up on deck. They found him in his bunk."

"Dead?"

"Yes. It was inexplicable. The man was as fit as a fiddle. The ship's doctor could do nothing but record *death from a broken heart* on the death certificate."

David had stopped eating. Jim glanced quickly at him, saw he now had his audience with him, and went on.

"Captain Wellem on one of the Norddeutsche Lloyd Line's big steamers was also told that his last trip had come. The same day the ship was to leave Hamburg, he collapsed on the bridge and was taken to the hospital, where he died a few hours later. The diagnosis was the same. In his will he had asked to have his ashes thrown to the wind from the bow of his ship, which is what happened. The will was dated only a few weeks before. After that the Norddeutsche Lloyd Line stopped telling aging captains that their last trip was coming up, and since then they have not been told until their last tour is behind them."

"How strange to die of something like that," said David.

"There is nothing so miserable as a captain without a ship. Imagine staying on shore after being in command of ship like this. Or a handsome sailing ship. She belongs to the captain as long as she's at sea. He performs the church services and hands out punishments and rewards. If it's a passenger ship, the ladies swoon over him and he has some difficulty keeping his admirers at bay. They all want to sit at the captain's table. All of them. Everyone wants to hear his stories. Preferably something adventurous, something about shipwrecks and Hottentots. Captains tell the most terrible tall stories and the passengers swallow them faster than they do whiskey-and-sodas. If there's a storm raging, everyone wants to be calmed by the captain personally—although he never has as much to do as he has at that particular time. People *trust* the captain. Old Captain Hayes of Cunard has an excellent trick for preventing worried passengers from bothering him. You see, even on big steamers, some people get anxious when it's rough. This Captain Hayes, then, he used to calm people's anxiety like this—if there were heavy seas and a strong breeze, but not strong enough to frighten passengers and, say, make very many seasick, he used to dress up in his oilskins and sou'wester, then get a seaman to pour a bucket or two of water over him. Then he would stump into the passenger lounge in heavy sea boots, with water dripping off him. Passengers playing cards or peacefully having tea and staring out at the foul weather would look up at this apparition suddenly appearing in the doorway. He would go right in, clap his hand to his head, and cry out bitterly: 'Look at all these landlubbers and good-for-nothings sitting around. How *can* they sit in peace and quiet with a storm raging outside, a storm such as I have never seen in all my forty years at sea.' At which he stumped out again, while the passengers sat back in bewilderment. Maybe they felt a trifle unwell, but their self-confidence was considerably bolstered. No problems with panic on old Hayes's ship, oh no."

David smiled.

"Yes, they can be real oddities," Jim went on brightly. "Take Dismal Pete, who sails for the same company as we do, the White Star Line. Thank God, we're not sailing with him. Dismal Pete loves funerals. Funerals at sea. He finds burying people at sea the most enjoyable thing of all. If a passenger happens to die, or a stoker gets knocked on the head, like lightning the captain orders the body into sailcloth with something heavy tied to his feet. None of that talk about 'We'll be in Southampton tomorrow, sir,' or 'Perhaps his parents wanted him buried in English soil,' oh no. 'Think of the risk of *infection*,' says Dismal Pete gloomily, and gets ready to send the dead man to the depths. What he likes is the ritual. The captain always reads the burial service. And Dismal Pete reads it with greater empathy and in a more grief-stricken voice than anyone else. Not a dry eye when he performs. He likes to add a few words of his own, too. Once he was disturbed in the middle of a lovely moment of that kind. A cook had had a stroke just east of New York, on the outward trip. The man was wrapped up with a sounding lead at his feet almost before he was cold. The captain was in full flow on the foredeck, beaming sunnily, but with his expression in appropriately gloomy folds, and he had just started the service, the crew standing to attention with their caps off, and right in the middle the foghorn sounded; that always calls the captain to the bridge immediately. So he threw off his coat, abandoned the prayerbook, and rushed up to the bridge, leaving the crew still respectfully standing around the dead man. Up on the bridge, Dismal Pete sees it's only a matter of a little patch of fog, so he hurtles back down onto the deck again, struggles into his coat, grabs the prayerbook, and, annoyed by the interruption, cries, 'Now, for God's sake. *I* am the Resurrection and the Life.' "

David laughed until he choked, and Jim had to thump him on the back.

"And Captain—was his name Smith?—*our* captain, I mean. What's he like?" said David when he had recovered.

"Don't know much about him," Jim went on. "He's quiet. Doesn't let on much. There aren't any stories about him as far as I know. But he was in big trouble yesterday."

"Trouble?"

"Difficulties. We almost collided with the *New York*. These ships have become so large. Difficult to maneuver. The *Titanic*'s sister ship, the *Olympic*, was in a collision last year. They're unpredictable in difficult situations, these huge boats. They set such enormous swells of water in motion. That business yesterday might have ended with us all having to go ashore again. Then it would have been over and out for Captain Smith."

"Over and out?"

"Yes. Finished. The end, that is. This is to be his last tour. Didn't you know? A kind of round of honor. If things had gone wrong yesterday, there would have been no laurels for him . . . No. Now, David, we've chattered long enough. We must get into those uniforms. We're to play after departure."

Jim took a fraternal gulp of David's coffee and emptied the cup.

Out on deck the souvenir vendors were getting ready to disembark; the hatches were battened down and the cranes on the foredeck secured.

⚓

At twenty past one, the *Titanic* weighed anchor. Steam filled the cylinders and the ship trembled. The *Titanic* swung around Roche's Point again, and the pilot was taken off to the lightship.

Then she turned in a wide curve to starboard.

A rocking movement ran through the great body of the ship and for a moment people on board stopped and looked at each other. There followed a new swelling lift, then another, the first slight breakers from the ocean ahead.

INTERMEZZO

The same day
10°W, 51°N

———◆→❈←◆———

ONE two three, *one* two three—this is going really well; "Roses of Picardy," pleasing waltzes that whet the appetite, *one* two three, *one* two three, oh, heavenly smells wafting from the dining rooms and blending with the music, tongue right inside the mouth now, young man, *one* two three, *one* two three, soon the lounge will have emptied of hungry passengers, soon they will all be seated and enjoying pastries and all kinds of culinary delights, only one last group left, *one* two three, the last lot still sitting there in their chairs gossiping about life. *One* two three. The old bass player, Petronius, keeps time with dancing movements and a slight bend of his back. He keeps time well. Spot's energetic hands strike loose chords, dominant, basic, subdominant. *One* two three. The fiddles ring out, this is going really well, bows swaying, here comes the refrain, don't come in too soon, *one* two three. *David*, hisses Alex savagely to the young Viennese Jew. *For Christ's sake, David, it's G major.* David flushes and moves a finger, and that makes quite a harmonic change, though the audience does not notice such things, they are in their corners gossiping about life, not tempted by the tempting smell of food, sitting in their corners, and *one* two three, *one* two three. They will soon get up and saunter indifferently across the soft carpets, in through the glass doors, or are they going to continue that conversation until Doomsday? How long do we have to sit here playing waltzes? The strings all singing, the ladies all clinging, the mel-o-d-y ringing. A question in his eyes, Jason nods bravely over his violin at the purser, who nods floridly back. Dominant, dominant, *sub*dominant, *dub*-dominant, subbedubb two three, subbedubb two three, two—three—and—stop.

"I think it's all right," said Jason.

"It went really well," Jim says, smiling at David.

"Something's wrong with it," mumbles Petronius, looking at his instrument. The lounge is quite empty now.

"You'll have to learn to follow better," snarls Alex.

"That was lovely, boys," says Spot.

"There's something wrong with it."

"Are we going to eat now?" says Georges.

"Pull yourself together, David," says Alex. "Did you *hear* how he . . ."

"I think it'll do," says Jason again.

"What's *wrong* with it?"

"Well, I'm going to get something to eat."

"Shall we leave our instruments?"

"Personally, I've no choice," says Spot.

"Four o'clock," says Jason. "Four o'clock on the dot."

"I'd like to know, gentlemen, whether you also think there's something wrong with my instrument."

"I'd rather know what's really wrong with *me*, sitting here at all," says Alex.

"Well, have a good dinner, all of you."

"Same to you, same to you."

"Perhaps it's a bad omen. Perhaps that peculiar deep jarring note comes from the fact that the guts the strings are made of have been taken from some unhappy ox? An ox that *wants* something from us. Perhaps that rumbling heavy note is a bad omen, or perhaps it's a good one? Not easy to say, gentlemen, not easy to say. He-he-he-he."

"I'll throw him overboard, Jason."

Petronius moved away, smiling, in a world of his own.

"I'll throw him overboard," Alex repeated.

"All right," said Jason. "As long as I don't have to hear anything more about it."

"I'm sorry," said David unassumingly, turning to Alex. "I'm sorry that I played badly."

Alex stared at the boy with hostility, then looked at Jason.

"How ever did this creature get hired?" he said.

"Now now," said Jason.

David flushed, but said nothing. Then he left them.

Jason thought about it. He looked at Alex, who was now staring straight ahead. The Russian had dark circles under his eyes and looked as if he had slept badly. Jason felt sorry for David, but Alex was exceptionally out of sorts.

Best to say nothing, he thought.

"Let's go and eat, shall we?" he said aloud.

Alex did not reply, but kept on staring ahead, then said in a low voice, "I think I ought to talk to you about something."

"Can't we do that over our food?" Jason suggested cautiously.

"No," said Alex.

The conversation was taking place astern on the boat deck outside the Palm Court, empty now during luncheon.

At first Alex stood by the railing for a long spell without saying anything, staring out to sea, clearly finding it difficult to begin. Then, without turning to Jason, he started talking.

Slowly, and with a great many pauses, he went on, Jason silently listening, unable to insert a single word.

When Alex stopped talking, a long time went by before Jason managed to get anything out.

"If that's the situation," he said finally, "then you'll have to go ashore, won't you?"

"Yes," said Alex. "I will. There'll be this crossing, perhaps one more. But you'll have to find someone to take my place."

Jason noticed he was no longer thinking clearly. To sail with anyone else, to find another companion, seemed impossible. He looked at Alex, standing there just as he had the day before, leaning heavily against the railing, staring out at nothing.

"That won't be all that easy," said Jason awkwardly.

"Oh, you'll probably find someone," said Alex, sudden anger in his voice.

"Yes, yes . . . I didn't mean that," said Jason. "I didn't mean that." He stopped for a few moments, then asked, "Have you saved anything?"

"Not much."

Jason was just going to say Alex ought not to worry, but that was not something to say. Fundamentally, there was nothing to say.

"How are you feeling?"

"Up and down."

"You must tell me if it gets to be too much."

"Yes," said Alex. "For the moment it's all right. I hadn't really

meant to say anything, at least not yet. But I wasn't . . . quite myself
yesterday. I'm still not, really, but that twerp . . . that German."

"He's Austrian."

"I thought I'd explain to you. And prepare you."

"We've been together too long for you to keep quiet about it. I'm
glad you told me."

"That was probably roughly also what I thought."

I don't understand, thought Jason. I can hear him saying it, but I
can't take it in. He's standing there. Does he understand it himself?
He looked at Alex and thought, He's my friend. He's the nearest I'll
get to a friend.

"I hope you won't let this affect you," said Alex.

"Affect me?" exclaimed Jason, offended.

"Don't worry about it. Don't let it affect your work."

Jason said nothing. How badly we talk to each other, he thought.
Perhaps we ought to have spoken more. When it comes down to it,
there are a few things I'd like to discuss with him. It's been good so
far. Perhaps we ought to have made more use of words.

"Is there anything you want to tell me?" he said, realizing at once
how stupid that sounded.

"No," said Alex. "Why?"

No, thought Jason. Why should there be? Perhaps it's not necessary.
Perhaps things can go on as before, without words, despite all this.
Perhaps we know each other best without words. Perhaps I'd no
longer know him if he told me who he is.

They stood there for a while, Alex leaning over the railing, Jason
with his back to it, both thus managing to avoid each other's eyes.

⚓︎

Alex went down to the cabin and found it empty.

The first thing he did was to wash his hands; then he sat down on his
bunk, his head in his hands. He sat like that for a few minutes, hunched
down, breathing heavily. Good to be alone. He had no appetite.

The water was rustling along the side of the ship, and above the
sound, inside his ears, was a high whining note.

He breathed deeply and held his side.

This can't be me, he said to himself. All this can't be me.

Everything around him, everything he sensed, contradicted him.
Coldly and soberly, it all contradicted him.

He tried to remember, tried to find his way back to someone who had once been himself. He closed his eyes.

Deep down in his body something was paining him, like a drop of molten metal.

It couldn't be he sitting there, not in this way. It couldn't be true. He had to find his way back. Or ahead. It might work out.

He dozed off for a moment.

Someone was in the cabin.

He was alone, but there was someone there all the same, in front of him. And he knew who it was.

The ship glides through calm breakers, the coast astern. Soon the ship can no longer be seen from the shore, and the sun starts on its way down to the horizon. There is fire beneath twenty-three of the *Titanic*'s twenty-nine boilers. The hull and bulkheads are trembling, the propellers driving her on at seventy-five revolutions a minute. The minutes go by. The ocean is opening up ahead of them. Everything on board changes rhythm, the hectic fever now quite gone. A trained eye would still be able to sense the land from astern. But no one is looking astern.

Astern, on E-deck, in the cabin by the potato washer, is Alex the Russian. He has dug out pen and paper and is sitting on a wooden chair at the little table. He sits there for a long time without moving the pen, either because he does not know what to write or because he is uncomfortable.

Then he begins to form words on the paper. The Cyrillic letters feel strange. He is writing a letter, a letter he ought to have written long ago. It is possibly too late now, but he is writing it.

Soon, he thinks, soon it will be too late for everything.

He can no longer eat, is practically never hungry. Nor does he sleep well. So why not write. He can write this letter. Perhaps the peace out on the ocean will help him. Perhaps the slow rhythm of the day will enter the letter. Soon it will be too late for everything. Every morning the sun rises over the Atlantic; every day the clocks are put back as the ship moves through the longitudes west of Greenwich. Imperceptibly the ship's day acquires twenty-five hours. He has an ocean of time. He is going to write.

ALEX'S LETTER

April 11, 1912
On board RMS Titanic

———————————

DEAR Gavrik, my dear brother,
I, your brother Sasha, am writing to you. Perhaps I ought to have
written before, but every time the thought of you and all I have
forsaken appeared, I pushed it aside. In the end it seemed impossible, because so many years have passed. I made the excuse
that I no longer knew where you were, that I would not be able to
get a letter to you. St. Petersburg is a large city and Russia a vast
realm.

But I meet fellow countrymen now and again, and some of them
regularly return home, so a friendly soul would certainly have taken
my letter with him and tried to track you down if I had asked. I could
have reached you if I had tried.

So the truth must be that I did not want to. I was afraid to write,
afraid of your eyes reading my words.

But every day, through all the years that have passed, I have
thought about you. You are there when I wake up and you are there
when I go to sleep.

A moment ago you were standing here in my cabin.

So much has happened over these years. I no longer know what
you look like, what you do. Every time there is news from home in
the newspapers or magazines here, I seem to listen in to the printed
messages, listening for your name and voice. I hear about judgments
and deportations, about secret actions, and my heart beats faster. I
look for your hand, your features, Gavrik.

Perhaps you are married, living in an official town, teaching or working for a mining company. Perhaps you have become a father. I don't
know.

146

But what I do remember is a pale, exhausted, dark-eyed student leaving home in the gray dawn to cross the many waterways of the city to go to the university on Vasilyevsky Island. Every morning you still cross those bridges in my mind, Gavrik, the same shabby bag dangling over your shoulder, the blue peaked cap you wear.

And you—how do you see me? I must be dead to you. To start with, you must have thought of me with bitterness. But gradually perhaps with pleasure. Pleasure at things lying further back than the bitter times, other things from when we were growing up, mother-of-pearl evenings in the summer, sparkling winter evenings together. One makes an effort to remember the good things about someone who is dead. At first the dead become slotted into our memory. They never come back and change it. That's what it feels like: to be dead. I am dead. It's best to get used to it.

In my mind, you are crossing bridges.

I escaped from St. Petersburg in January 1905, shortly after Bloody Sunday. I stowed away on board a Swedish boat. I was discovered out at sea and the captain made a long speech about the impropriety of being a stowaway. At least I presume that was what he was going on about, and—still in Swedish—he threatened to have me keelhauled and other tribulations. When that was out of the way, he started speaking in Russian. He had a Russian wife at home in Stockholm and he missed her on board. If I could cook a genuine borscht for him, he would allow mercy to precede justice. I could not cook borscht, but he let mercy precede justice anyway, so I peeled my way across the Baltic. Early in February (according to the Gregorian calender) we arrived in Stockholm, a pleasant little city. I slipped ashore and got by with day labor. Then I signed on a steamer that took me to England. In London, I went straight downhill. I drank, was homesick, regretted everything. But I had my violin and I played on the streets.

In the autumn of that year I met another violinist. We joined up, and we have been working together for a few years on the British-American liners and have not done at all badly.

That's been my life as a dead man. I have a little hovel ashore, a few acquaintances, no close friends.

Fundamentally this is what I have always dreaded. My own life was not of the kind I could show to my brother.

I once had a brother who was proud of me.

❧

It is possible to possess people, Gavrik. And it is possible for people to *let* themselves be possessed. I am now thinking primarily about the serfdom which is a tradition in our country.

I am thinking of serfdom of the will.

It is said of the Czarina Anna Ivanovna that in the winter of 1739 she had an ice palace built on the frozen Neva. She built it for her own amusement, for the previous year had been hard, the beginnings of disturbances and riots resulting in executions and the razing of whole villages.

The winter of that year was the hardest in the memory of man. The rivers of Europe were frozen for months—the Seine, the Rhine, the Danube, and the Thames. It was said to be so cold in Versailles that bottles of spirits exploded, wine froze in glasses at mealtimes, and in Ukraine birds fell dead from the sky as they tried to fly south.

Czarina Anna Ivanovna was a woman with a distinctive sense of humor. She liked to be entertained by dwarfs, cripples, and imbeciles. Four of her court jesters were members of old noble families with whom she amused herself by humiliating them. One of those jesters, Count Mikhail Golitsyn, became a convert to the Catholic Church, which disturbed the absolute ruler, and as a punishment she made him sit on a basket of eggs in front of everyone and cackle until the chickens hatched.

That iron winter, the Czarina had an ice palace erected on the frozen river—and it was an ice palace such as has never been seen before or since, constructed by the great architect Eropkin, who was condemned to death for treason in 1740. Blocks of ice were cut out of the clearest parts that could be found on the Neva and then welded together with water, which in that severe cold bound the elements together more strongly than any mortar could. The palace rose somewhere between the Admiralty and the Winter Palace. It had balustrades, statuettes, pillars, and furniture all made of ice. It was built by the best artists and craftsmen in the realm, surrounded by twenty-nine ice trees with ice birds perched in the ice trees, both trees and birds painted in natural colors. The palace itself was left transparent, apart from the pillars, doors, and window frames, which were painted green to make them look like marble. The windowpanes were made of paper-thin ice. The master craftsmen and their journeymen, the sculptors and building workers all surpassed themselves out on the frozen river, slaving away from morning to night to satisfy the whims of the Czarina.

Two fabulous beasts and two cannons made of ice flanked the entrance to this magnificent palace, and a full-size ice elephant served as a fountain—water spouting out of its trunk—and the ice cannons were frozen so iron-hard they could actually fire cannonballs.

The only construction not of frozen water was a wooden fence erected around the palace area to keep the populace at a distance.

The people were delighted with Anna Ivanovna's notion. Crowds also made their way out to the palace at night, when it was illuminated from the inside—it must have been a thrilling, unreal sight, with great octagonal paper lanterns with obscene motifs mounted on two spires at the ends of the balustrade, slowly rotating so that the crowd could enjoy all the pictures.

It was a palace after Anna Ivanovna's own heart, and to complete her notion, she had a bridal couple spend their wedding night inside it.

Who else but Count Mikhail Golitsyn (the one hatching the eggs) was made to marry? The Czarina teasingly ordered him to marry a Kalmuck woman of singular ugliness, one of her lowliest servants. She gave the bride the name of Busyenina, because the Kalmuck woman reminded her of that dish—spiced pork in onion sauce.

The nobleman and Busyenina were duly married, to the resounding hilarity of the Czarina. Then they were clad in furs, took their places in an iron cage on the back of an elephant, and set off at the head of the wedding procession, which otherwise consisted of more married couples—fetched from Anna Ivanovna's realm of subjects, Lapps, Finns, Kirghizes, Bashkirs, and so on, all of them in national costume and swaying on horseback and camels, or in sleighs drawn by reindeer or wolves and boars.

The procession arrived at the ice palace to the great jubilation of thousands of spectators.

In the bedroom was a magnificent four-poster bed—made of ice. The mattress was of ice, the bedclothes of ice, the two pillows of ice, and on each pillow was a nightcap, exquisitely carved out of ice.

On the tables were the most superb dishes, naturally painted and made of ice. Bottles, forks, plates, mirrors, powder bowls—wherever the couple turned, everything was of ice, even the stove and the firewood inside it.

The newlyweds undressed and went to bed; guards were posted to ensure that everything went as it should. The couple survived, and over the years, Busyenina bore the count two sons.

I think this story provides a beautiful picture of how far one can go if one possesses other people. The story is true, and I have never forgotten it.

But what about those who *allow* themselves to be possessed?

⁓

You know the broad outlines of the events that led me to escape from St. Petersburg. You must have heard about it from the police who came looking for me, or from other people.

Let me briefly complete your picture of those events.

It was while I was first violinist in the cabaret on S Street. The pay was meager, the work hard, the nights late. I was to keep you at the university, as I had promised Mother. I have to admit I occasionally considered my obligations a burden, despite the fact that I was really fond of you, Gavrik.

Viktor Zyornov was the contortionist in the cabaret. Every night he wriggled like a snake in and out of barrel hoops and cylinders, bending backward so far that his head touched the small of his back—he was what what was called a *klischnik*. Grotesque, unnatural positions for a body. He told me once they had started training him when he was still a small boy—bending his limbs, stretching him so that he would acquire the necessary suppleness. He told me it had been very painful. He himself had picked out three children with suitable bodies, and they took part in his act. He molded them as he himself had been molded.

I remember how he fascinated all the members of the cabaret company, not just his act, but Viktor himself, his way of being, his look, his face. There was something mocking in the way he regarded both

his audience and his colleagues. The three children he was teaching
—poor things—were under his influence, their souls and will as flex-
ible as their bodies. With a glance Viktor ordered them to slither
through pipes, under low bars, to do the impossible. He himself did
even more impossible things on the stage.

I think he hated everyone, and I think he hated himself.

But soon after he was hired, we all seemed to be at his every beck
and call at the theater. There were queues outside his dressing room.
The hearts of little dancers bled for him and members of the company
ran errands for him, doing their very best to please him.

I wish I could describe him in a way which would make you understand the way he influenced us, but all I feel whenever I think
about him now is a great emptiness.

He never showed any kind of gratitude or affection. Perhaps that
was why people submitted to him. Perhaps that was why people were
so attracted to him.

Although I cannot remember when or how—suddenly *I* was his
friend, his chosen friend, perhaps because I played a solo during one
of his numbers and always had to keep eye contact with him on the
stage. Or perhaps it was pure chance. Perhaps he just picked me the
way he would pick a lottery ticket.

I can see his face in front of me, feline and narrow. I can see his
smile, glittering and icy cold. I can hear his voice, soft and at the same
time with a snarling undertone.

He made me his friend. Quite voluntarily, I formed a relationship
with him, willingly submitting myself to him. He was the leader. If
he wanted to chat, we chatted. If he wanted to remain silent, we were
silent. If he wanted to drink vodka, I also drank vodka. If he wanted
champagne, it was champagne for both of us.

I loved submitting to him.

It was a serfdom of the emotions and the will.

He had no hold on me—no means of blackmail. Nothing forced
me. I let him make me into his possession.

Unhappily I often thought it must have been because I longed to
escape my burden of duty, because deep down I must have aspired
to adventure, to madness, to something other than the daily struggle
for you, for us, to make ends meet.

But the truth is that it was out of sheer indolence, sheer covetousness that I agreed to it. He made me into a thief, a burglar, and I allowed it to happen to me.

He always had an unusual amount of money for a cabaret artist. I found it difficult to keep up with his spending if we were out drinking. I asked him how he did it and he told me. He told me about his monthly burglaries, alone or with one of the children. As a contortionist he had special opportunities in the field of burglary, for a contortionist can get through the most difficult of openings.

He told me how his thievery was done and how he planned it. He never went into a house without knowing what he was looking for.

He needed an assistant to keep watch and to receive the loot outside. Would I consider it?

I was flattered. I was like putty in his hands. I worshipped him. I was pleased he had asked me, that he showed me such favor. That is how I became a burglar.

What makes me ashamed now is not that I stole. The rich villas out on Apothecary Island did not become any less rich because we took a little from them. What torments me is that I *allowed* myself to be steered, *allowed* myself to be manipulated, to be ordered, that I *wanted* to be Viktor Zyornov's aide and errand boy. He stole my will, and I let it happen.

I remember the question mark on your face, Gavrik, when you saw those rustling banknotes. Did you believe all my explanations? You were proud of me and had always been proud and grateful that you had a brother who helped you, who provided for you. I remember the childish, touching respect you—the scholar—showed for my lowly profession, the way you made an effort to talk to me about it, wanting me to tell you about the little world of cabaret. I know it rankled that you were able to study at my expense—while I never got into the conservatory for financial reasons.

You never questioned the banknotes I suddenly brought back home.

Dear Gavrik, this has become a long letter and I don't know if I have succeeded in explaining my conduct so that you understand it. Basically I am not asking for either forgiveness or understanding. I am just stating that I never had the will to do anything myself. I let everything happen to me. I was an errand boy for other people. I sat on a basket of eggs and cackled like a fool.

When Viktor Zyornov got stuck in a chimney on our last expedition, I ran away. The fact that later, after the police got him out, he informed on me and blamed me for everything, telling them I planned it all, that I was the receiver and the exploiter—today that seems no more than what I deserved.

I am very ill, Gavrik, and probably do not have long to live. I wanted to write this letter to you before it was too late. I wanted to write to you to say that you must protect what is yours, really yours. Your freedom. Never let anyone build an ice palace for you and enter it voluntarily. Whether you live a happy family life or whether you live for a great cause, beware of the snakemen.

Your brother Sasha

Friday, April 12, 1912
On board

———◆→❉←◆———

TIME at sea is different from time ashore; the hours slip by, fleeing with the light and wind. Everything becomes easy and simple. The passengers get up in the morning, have breakfast, drink tea. They think about everything they are going to do, about books and magazines they have brought with them to read. They read during the morning. They read the same line four times and their thoughts start wandering. The sea is so beautiful, the ship so small. There are such infinities of air and sky . . . Then they pull themselves together and read a few more lines. Soon it is time for lunch.

After lunch, they listen to music in the Palm Court, or stroll on deck, meet fellow passengers, exchanging a few trivial words on sports or politics—the one is as distant as the other out there. For a few days they are cut off from the busy worlds on both sides of the Atlantic. The distance between the Old and the New World steadily shrinks. And ships are laden with the world: books and silverware, Turkish baths and whiskey-and-sodas, winged chairs and hot-water bottles. Nevertheless, they are halfway, in the middle of nothing, no newspapers, no telephones, at most a telegram.

As the *Titanic* glided through the waves, she was permeated with this unruffled, relaxed atmosphere. First-class passengers ate their meals with sea-air appetites, played deck games, photographed each other at the railing, arranged spelling games and quizzes in the evenings, played cards, laid bets on the distance logged over the last twenty-four hours, on the speed and the arrival time in New York. They played squash on the fore G-deck, or went to the ship's gymnasium and worked off their lunch. They dined with friends and friends of friends in the magnificent dining room or in the *à la carte* restaurant. In second and third class, which did indeed lack some of the facilities at the disposal of first class, the hours still went by in the same peaceful way. The children played, the adults dreamed. Playing music and singing, a spontaneous swing around the lounge in third class—a piano was at the disposal of the passengers. Minor ship romances began to flower.

The crew liked their new ship once they had lost their feeling for land and the ocean opened up before them. Every day except Sunday, at ten o'clock precisely, the chief engineer, the purser, the assistant purser, the ship's doctor, and the chief steward appeared on the bridge to be received by Captain Smith, the latter in full parade uniform plus decorations (the Transport Medal and the Royal Navy Reserve Decoration). Standing at attention, they reported on their tours of inspection in their respective departments. At ten-thirty exactly, Captain Smith led the whole flock on his daily rounds through the ship, through corridors, lounges, and public rooms in all classes, through galleys and the bakery, through hairdresser salons and bars, pantries, sick bays, and engine rooms. The inspection and checking undertaken by his uniformed flock were conscientious with regard to order, hygiene, discipline, and most of all safety. Ventilators and winches were tested, a lifeboat davit examined, a carelessly placed shovel by one of the coal bunkers noted, a dirty dishcloth remarked on, a hatch battened down again, a cigarette butt on the floor in the laundry causing a sharp reprimand. After the daily round, the officers met again on the bridge, where changes were suggested and comments entered in the logbook. Then the captain conferred with the duty officer and the other officers on the bridge, informing them of the day's inspection, setting course, and giving the orders for the day.

At eight-thirty, one o'clock, and six o'clock, P. W. Fletcher of the *Titanic* blew his horn to announce that another meal was served.

Large trays of fresh rolls slid out of ovens, mountains of Brussels sprouts and potatoes were carried in to the pots, beer bottles put on ice, chickens slaughtered, napkins elegantly folded at tremendous speed.

Thomas Andrews of Harland & Wolff tirelessly darted around the ship making notes, conferring with the captain, talking to the shipowner, Ismay, and chatting with the galley boys and stokers. Shouldn't that hook be lower? Wasn't it difficult to get a hold on the largest pans? Wasn't there a place for the coal heavers to sit down and rest? Shouldn't the shelves in the linen cupboards be rubbed down with sandpaper? In that way he made himself known to the ship from stem to stern; nothing escaped his attention, and the crew appreciated this man who had created this great ship and who wished to make their work easier. Andrews was soon invited by the chef to taste a lobster, and one stewardess after another cheerfully flirted with him. The baker on D-deck baked a special bread for him (he had a delicate digestion), while the dry cleaners and pressing room on F-deck took a special interest in his clothes, sewing on a button, pulling out a loose thread, taking his suits and shirts up and down to his cabin at record speed. He was the father of the *Titanic* and the uncle of the crew. He also talked to the ship's band, inquiring whether there was enough room in the instrument cupboard, whether it was too warm or cold, whether the light was all right when they were playing in the evenings.

For the musicians the days at sea also fell into a calm and specific rhythm. They were free in the mornings, then they played for lunch and gave a promenade concert in the Palm Court. They were free from three until five, then played light music and held an evening concert. The days were strenuous and they were dead tired when they went to bed at around eleven. But there was nothing hectic about their working day; the stillness and peace also lent the music a slightly slower tempo.

David had a great deal to learn. He had to follow Jason's signals, but once he got the hang of the style and tone of the light music, their playing as an ensemble gradually went more smoothly.

There was also a lot for David to see during his free time. On Thursday he spent every free moment at the railing taking in the sea, standing there feeling himself quivering all over at the stillness and the infinity of it. He stared down into the rushing foam along the ship's side as if hypnotized, and he watched the seabirds around the ship apparently hanging quite still in the air. He was overcome and moved by the sea, which was setting new strains in motion inside him, making him feel dizzy and happy as well as slightly scared.

Otherwise the musicians spent their time reading, talking to members of the crew (Jim had discovered a stunningly beautiful stewardess whom he was systematically pursuing), or sitting in the mess playing cards and talking before and after meals.

At eight o'clock on Friday morning, Georges, the little Frenchman, told them a kind of story at breakfast in the mess. The musicians had commandeered the end of one of the long tables and were tucking into toast, eggs, bacon, marmalade, tea and coffee. Petronius was eating small pieces of toast he dipped into his coffee. Alex clearly had no appetite and soon left them. Jim sat yawning. Jason went on eating undisturbed and with good appetite. David then asked a question about the ship's name—the *Titanic*—what it really meant in English.

"The ship is really called the *Titan*," said Jason. "All the White Star Line's ship and boat names end in the suffix *ic*—the *Celtic*, the *Megantic*, the *Oceanic*—if they can't find a name naturally ending in *ic*, like *Cedric*, *Baltic*, or *Adriatic*. The *Titanic* is the sister ship of the *Olympic*, and the third ship of this class is to be called the *Gigantic* when it's built and launched. The Cunard Line gives all its ships names ending in *ia*, the *Caronia*, the *Ivernia*, the *Lusitania*, and the *Mauretania*."

Georges then took up the story: "That's to say," he said, clearing his throat, "the three sister ships in 'our' class, the *Olympic*, the *Titanic*, and the *Gigantic* to come, all have names from Greek mythology, from Hesiod's *Theogony* and the Orphic myth of creation."

"Uh?" said Jim in the middle of a yawn. He did not like mornings.

"Well, they have to name ships after something," said Jason.

"Please explain," Jim said to Georges, "why we're on a Greek ship."

"Not a Greek ship," said Georges in kindly tones. He was the orchestra's most unassuming member, although he was a Parisian, very vain and a trifle feminine, with a strong liking for toilet water and rather too elegant clothes. He had brought a mountain of books with him and was almost never seen without one, and he treated them carefully, almost lovingly. He opened them gingerly so as not to break their backs, having made sure his hands were clean before beginning to read, though he licked his finger each time he turned the page. On Wednesday he had lent Jim a book by Conrad and Jim had turned down the corner of a page. When Georges discovered this, he had looked most grieved, partly because of his beloved book, but also because it was Jim who had dog-eared it. Jim and Georges were otherwise the best of friends. The naturally convivial Jim and the little French bookworm complemented each other well and had a lot to talk about. Jim had asked Georges to explain the names partly as a way of asking for forgiveness.

"The Greek word *titan*," Georges began, "means . . . er . . . wait a minute. I'd better start with the Creation story."

"Yes, I think you'd better," Jason mumbled into his cup.

"To make it simple," said Georges, "I'll choose images which are immediately understandable. Greek mythology is sometimes obscure to people today."

"Choose what you like, Georges," said Jim to the cellist. "Get going."

"Right—the Creation. How shall we imagine it. The creation of the heavens, the world, all the creatures in the cosmos. It is best to think of the Creation as a kind of alarm clock.

"At the very beginning, before the alarm went off, there was nothing but Chaos. Nothing but confusion and disorder, I mean, gray and shapeless, no light or dark. Just like the feeling before you wake up, when you've slept for twelve hours after a bender. That's what it was like. All the elements, colors, forces, and images flying around, getting mixed up with each other, separating again and meeting again. Cronus, Time, was omnipresent.

"Then suddenly, just as when the clock starts to tick energetically before the alarm goes off, something happened in this eternal soup-sleep of all and nothing. How this happened or what caused it is way beyond my comprehension. But suddenly an egg, a shining silver egg leaped out of the mess of elements and danced through Chaos. This amazing egg seemed to be singing and mumbling and clucking, and accordion music could be heard coming from inside, as well as the sound of innumerable slender female legs dancing the cancan—good gracious, what can be inside this egg? Bang! That's it, there it is, the alarm goes off, shaking Time out of its sleep. Time begins; the egg hatches; the silver shell disintegrates and all at once Creation occurs. With one blow, everything is changed, and there, in the middle of Chaos, the world appears. Light and darkness are separated. Night is created; day is created, and the sun and the stars, and beneath it all lies the work of Creation, the world. In other words—and to use an adequate image—there is Paris and right in the middle the radiant focal point of the world—Montmartre."

"Good heavens," said Spot dryly.

"Exactly. The world. To the clanging of bells and the sound of a brass band, Montmartre expands—the world with all its creations, great and small, evil and beautiful."

"Just a moment," said Jim. "I thought you were going to tell us about the Titans and Olympians, not about Montmartre."

"We *know* you're a chauvinist, Georges," said Spot, laughing. "Montmartre is a nice place. I've lived there myself, and . . ."

"Wait, wait," said Georges. "You mustn't misunderstand me. This is a *mythological* Montmartre."

"Oh, I see," said Jim.

"I shall proceed. Our friend Time, Cronus, gets out of bed, throws open the windows, and looks out at the morning. It is a wonderful morning and he feels like breakfast. A long, peaceful breakfast."

"Me, too," mumbled Jason, but Georges continued.

"Cronus was a Titan."

"At last," said Jim.

"He was the son of Gaia, the Earth, and Uranus, the Heavens."

"I thought he was from Paris."

"Exactly. To make it uncomplicated, we can say that Gaia and Uranus were a married couple living in Montmartre. They ran one of the many establishments in that part of the city, but their marriage was beginning to crack. You can think of Gaia as a large, round, and pleasant mother, the mother of all things."

"Uh-huh."

"She had given birth to everything that existed. She had been giving birth ever since the universe appeared."

"Excuse me, but I thought it was the same morning?" said Jim.

"A mythological day lasts half an eternity, Jim."

"Pretty funny conditions in Montmartre," said Spot.

"Please don't interrupt. Gaia had given birth to the sea, which we can identify as the Seine. And she had given birth to all the Titans: Oceanus, Coeus, Crius, Hyperion, Iapetus, Themis, Phoebe, Mnemosyne, Thetis, Rhea, and our old friend Cronus. Her husband, Uranus, the landlord of the establishment, was father to them all."

"He must have been busy."

"Don't forget, he's the God of Heaven."

"So the Titans are the children of the God of Heaven?"

"Right. They are also gods, born of Heaven and Earth. There are stories about every single one of them—Mnemosyne is the mother of all the Muses, Iapetus became father of Prometheus, who stole fire and knowledge and gave them to humans, but that's going too fast. Let's concentrate on Cronus and his sister Rhea, to whom he was also betrothed, by the way."

"To his sister?"

"To his older sister, yes. But let me finish . . ."

"I thought you said Cronus had been there from the start, and now you're saying Earth, Gaia, gave birth to him?" said David.

"He was both, you see. But trouble was now brewing in Montmartre. Gaia was dissatisfied with her husband, Uranus. He was very distant—far too occupied ruling his establishment empire in Montmartre."

"A monopolist, eh?" said Jason.

"Exactly. He nipped in to Gaia when it suited him to make her pregnant. But the worst of it was that he ignored his children, didn't bother about them, didn't allow them to have any influence. The Titans had to manage as best they could as musicians, jugglers, and freelancers on the streets of Montmartre. Cronus and Rhea, too.

"Gaia bore Uranus other children as well, among them three Cyclops with one eye each, and three terrible creatures with fifty heads and a hundred arms. Uranus had these grotesque creations imprisoned in dungeons and catacombs underneath Montmartre, and Gaia had to listen to their lamentations and cries from below. Uranus was a tyrant, although he was father of all things.

"Then Gaia summoned her son Cronus for a conspiratorial consultation. Cronus decided to take revenge on his father, Uranus, and claim his and his siblings' rights. Gaia gave him a razor, and that evening, when Uranus came into the bedroom, tired and exhausted, to go to bed with Gaia, Cronus leaped at him and cut off . . ."

"Thanks, thanks, it's breakfast time," said Jason.

"Cut it off. Drops of blood fell from heaven to earth and new creatures appeared: wood nymphs, Erinyes, and the Giants. Uranus retreated for good up to the heavens, but he called out an omen to Cronus: 'The same thing will happen to you as has to me. Your son will topple you, just as you have toppled me.' That's how the Titans came to power, and the twelve siblings now ruled the establishment in Montmartre."

"And Gaia?" said David.

"She went into well-deserved retirement."

"And the monsters in the cellar?"

"Cronus was in many ways like his father. He didn't let them out. He was afraid of them. For a while, however, there was peace, happiness, and prosperity in the establishment after the younger generation took over. The problems started when Cronus and Rhea had children."

"Oh?"

"Rhea bore Cronus six children: Hestia, Demeter, Hera, Hades, Poseidon, and Zeus. But Cronus remembered his father's prediction, and to stop yet another generation coming to power, he ate his own children."

"Would anyone like some more tea?" said Jason politely.

"Just half a cup, please. He ate them as soon as they were born. Rhea was naturally desolated by this, and when she was to give birth to the youngest, Zeus, she did so in secret. She handed Cronus a cobblestone wrapped in napkins and Cronus, shortsighted and drunk with power, ate the stone instead. Rhea hid Zeus on the Île de la Cité—that's an island in the middle of the Seine, for any of you unfortunate enough not to know Paris. Notre Dame is there and Zeus was brought up in the monastery—but of course it was a mythological monastery."

"I see," said Jim.

"While Zeus was growing up, the domination of the Titans was becoming more and more untenable. The twelve Titans soon ruled over the entire city and everything happened according to their will. But Zeus grew up and became big and strong. One night he sneaked down into the catacombs, broke through the gates to the underworld, and freed the terrible monsters, the hundred-handed and the Cyclops. The Cyclops forged Zeus a weapon—a bolt of lightning—and armed with that, they went into battle with the Titans.

"The battle raged in the streets of Montmartre and was worse than any revolution. Houses collapsed, the ground shook, thunder roared. The war raged on for thousands of years, but in the morning Zeus and the monsters defeated the Titans; Zeus released his siblings from the belly of Cronus, and the Titans were thrown into the underworld and chained, with the hundred-armed monsters on guard. From then on, the Olympian gods, Zeus and his siblings, ruled, and humanity, justice, and light reigned in Montmartre. Music and joy, cancan and adventure. That's Greek mythology."

"Well, well," said Jim. "I now understand everything much better."

"Of course, I've left out lots of characters and masses of stories. That's just the basics. Very much simplified, of course."

"Yes, of course," said Jason; then he suddenly added angrily, "Gods and gods. Mythologies and religions. One is just as bad as another. We ought to be able to do without any gods."

The others looked at him with some astonishment.

"I wonder what made the shipping company name their ships after these characters," said Spot.

"They're names from the other family of gods who were defeated and thrown into the abyss. The *Olympic* is named after the third family, Zeus and the main gods. The *Gigantic* will be named after the warriors born of Uranus' drops of blood when he was . . ."

"Thanks, that'll do," said Jason.

"It was kind of you to explain all that to us," said Jim to Georges, who was now sitting sunnily radiant at the end of the table.

That was Georges Donner's mythology.

Morning. David and Jim were standing up on the forecastle. You could see the long slow waves particularly distinctly here. The crests foamed a bit. The weather was still fine, a few light cumulus clouds in the sky.

Not a ship was in sight, and the same joyous feeling of infinity again came over David. If he turned into the wind, the cool sea air rushed at him.

"Can you smell it?" said Jim.

Smell? David sniffed the air, at first smelling nothing, no odor, not real air, just chilly, with neither taste nor smell. He didn't understand what Jim meant.

"Can't you smell it—above everything else?" Jim laughed. And there *was*, after all, something in the air, a fragrance of that great open space—the air was carrying within it a whole sea, all the ocean and the skies. In a flash David realized what Jim had meant.

"Do you know what it smells of?" said Jim.

"No."

"It smells of freedom. Freedom smells like that."

David felt ill at ease for a moment, and Jim put a reassuring hand on his shoulder.

"Yes sir," he said. "Freedom. An amazing thing. Something to be afraid of if you're not used to it. Just like the sea."

"Did you grow up by the sea?"

"Yes," said the viola player. "In a little fishing village in the north. Our house was very close to the beach. When it was stormy, we used to get salt spray on the windows. But there aren't that many storms. The sea is marvelous mostly." Jim thought for a moment. "When the sun shines on it and the waves smile and almost want to talk to you, and you can run into it—I did that when I was a boy, in the summer." Jim looked across at the horizon. "Or when the fishing boats come in, laden with their catch, those great fisherman hands on the oars. The sails are furled when they near land, you see, and then they row, one-two, one-two, at a fast pace straight onto the shore. We kids used to run down and help. The boat had to be hauled up first, and then we ran around among the rocks helping. I once slipped on a wet rock and hit my head. I was in bed for eleven days." Jim did not take his eyes off the horizon. "And the smell of fish. There's something special about the smell of freshly caught cod—have you ever smelled it?"

"No."

"There's the cod in the bottom of the boat, huge and flopping and shiny. Putting your hand down in a tank like that and sliding it over the smooth, wiggling fish . . . the hull of a ship is shaped like a fish, streamlined . . . The fish is perfect, just perfect, part of the water, swirling through it, deep down. Sometimes if the water is clear you can see it from the boat as an eye-shaped, shiny little thing deep down below you. It swims in a shoal. Do you know what a shoal is?"

"No," said David.

"A shoal is when lots of fish swim together. When you see a shoal below you and the boat, it's almost impossible to tear yourself away. It's like a thousand pieces of silver gliding through the depths. You see them only for a moment when the sunlight falls on them. A shoal like that is like one great fish, moving as flocks of birds do in flight, but even faster, even more suddenly. But you can never really reach down to a shoal of fish. Sometimes when I've been in an open boat looking into the water, I've felt I'd like to be a fish like that. As silent and supple, sort of, with rays of sun on my back coming through the water from above. It must be fine to be a fish like that. And you can never get hold of them."

"If you're not catching them?"

"Yes, yes, but that's something else. There's something else. It's as if it's not the fish you're getting hold of. It stops being a fish once you've got it in the boat and it's lying there flopping around. Then it becomes a *thing*, it becomes yours. Then it is going to die."

David looked at Jim, who suddenly seemed quite serious, serious and dreamy.

"And the smell of them when they've just come out of the sea . . . that smell, like the seabed itself. It's a strange smell, fine, slightly metallic . . . about like . . . well . . ." Jim lowered his voice a little: "A little like the smell of girls when they're wet down there. But it's also a cold smell, you see, not really like girls, after all."

David was staring at him. Jim did not meet his eyes and was still looking over at the line where sky meets water.

David looked thoughtfully ahead, his face pale. Jim's words had reminded him of something.

Jim went on: "All the men in the village were fishermen, except the priest and the shopkeeper. Even the innkeeper took a turn in my father's boat, in a pinch. The boats were out for days on end, the men in oilskins and sou'westers and long sea boots. They looked terrible when they came back—fish blood and mire, brown faces, hair stiff with salt. But they always put on a white shirt on Sundays. Very pious. Very strict about that."

David had to smile.

"I don't think Jason would think much of their belief in God."

"You mean what he said after Georges's lecture this morning? Yes, yes. But Jason doesn't understand that for a fisherman . . . for a fisherman out at sea, maybe in a tiny open boat, God is the only thing he has, apart from his wits. You can go a long way on your wits, my father always said. But when your wits fail you, then you have to rely on God. Imagine the boat being wrecked, far out there . . . out in the freedom. The great sea. What use are your wits then? When the sails are in tatters and the waves are washing over the side faster than eight men can bail. There were plenty who never came back. No, out there, you have to have a god. But you go on bailing, of course.

"I've been a fisherman, and I've been a seaman. I left home young. I found out it's the same all over, everywhere by the sea. It's the same on merchant ships and on the great fishing banks. Out there, by the way, on those banks, when the boats are fogbound, they ring bells to warn other ships. The fog is thick and white and you can't see anything, and the clang of bells can be heard in all directions.

"I remember several people from home who hated the sea, for that matter—one man in particular—he couldn't sleep on the nights before he was to go out. Never. He had been wrecked on a little fishing smack and had lain with his brother on the upturned boat a whole night before they were found. His brother was dead by then, but they were clinging so tightly to each other, the lifeboat men could hardly free the living man from the dead. So for all those years he was afraid of going to sea again. All of them were afraid. They knew what could happen. But they went to sea, just as furiously as before. Trip after trip." Jim pulled his top lip down into a stern, thoughtful grimace. "No, Jason doesn't know what he's talking about. A storm comes and a shipwreck, and even if you hadn't had a god before, you found one *then*. Out of sheer necessity."

"But," said David after a while, "we're out there now. At sea."

"Yes," said Jim, turning around. "We are." He smiled. "And I'm not a fisherman. Nor a seaman any longer, thank goodness. I had a talent for music and played my way out of it."

David thought about what Jim had told him. The sea was all around them; everything was so different out here, different from his home in Vienna's Rosenhügelstrasse.

Jim told David a great many stories and anecdotes in the course of the journey, making David listen and laugh. Jim's stories were like that.

From Thursday to Saturday, the *Titanic* covered nine hundred nautical miles.

Be not afeard: the isle is full of noises,
Sounds and sweet airs, that give delight, and
   hurt not.
Sometimes a thousand twangling instruments
Will hum about mine ears; and sometimes
   voices,
That, if I then had wak'd after long sleep,
Will make me sleep again: and then, in
   dreaming,
The clouds methought would open and show
   riches
Ready to drop upon me; that, when I wak'd I
   cried to dream again.
                    —SHAKESPEARE, *The Tempest*

SPOT'S STORY

Saturday, April 13, 1912
30°W, 47°N, 22:30

———◆▸✕◂◆———

SPOT was sitting on his bunk, his head resting against the wall. No one else was in the cabin, at last no one else. Slowly it came to him that he was alone for the first time in several days, but he had no idea how long that would last. They had kept a beady eye on him ever since the first evening on board.

His movements were calm and decisive as he took a small tin, similar to the ones in which gentlemen keep snuff, out of his inside pocket.

"My snuffbox," he whispered confidentially to it. "My snuffbox." He opened it, and after making sure everything was in order, he drew up his legs so that his knees almost reached his chin and extracted a little mirror and a slim tube out of his right-hand pocket. Cautiously, with delicate gestures, he put a small quantity of the powder onto the mirror and formed it into a strip.

"Now," he said, hardly breathing so as not to blow any away. "Now, little powder, little snow . . ." The mirror was propped between his knees and he could see his eyes in it as he leaned over, pushed the tube into one nostril, and closed the other with the little finger of his left hand. He looked into his own eyes—guilty conscience stabbed at him, but that was as it should be. "Little dream snow," he said, looking at the eyes in the mirror behind the white powder. His chest tightened. Then, without hesitating, he drew a deep breath. It was fiery, but he knew what he was doing. Quickly he changed nostrils and breathed in again so the other half of the strip disappeared.

It was unusually fiery, as if a bubble had burst somewhere inside him.

"You're a grown man," he said half aloud to himself. "Not a child.

This is not a game. You'll manage." He took the tube out and stared into the mirror, then offered the few remaining grains to Helios by blowing them up at the ceiling light.

Now, he thought. Let's see. While he was still alert, he packed up the objects and put them safely back in his pocket.

For a moment he sat completely still, curled up in that position, something growing inside him and behind him, opening out through him like a flower, the flower hot and cold at the same time. It grew and grew inside him until it filled him completely; then it blossomed out, out into the room until that, too, was filled. Spot had now stretched out his legs and was sitting with his head comfortably back. He noticed that thoughts and images were coming to him from somewhere outside himself, and that was good. The room would soon be too cramped. But for a while he could stay there before having to go out and move around. Slowly, his limbs grew numb, his body tensed, and a feeling rose in him—a mixture of sickness and joy. He could hear sounds now, and it grew lighter all around him.

Spot was essentially a child of the sun, not the pale, silent, smiling nightbird he was taken for. His exterior was deceptive. In reality, Spot was not dark-haired. That was only one of the many delusions that had come after he had grown up. *It only looked like that.* In reality he had golden hair, fair and light, and his eyes were dark and clear. When he looked at himself in the mirror in the mornings nowadays, he knew it was a wicked deceit he was staring at, not quite true. In reality he was not staring at himself but at a kind of falsehood. A falsehood with bloodshot eyes. It was not true that he had thin dark hair that had to be brushed back and to the side and smoothed down with pomade.

The pince-nez was a lie, too. Not to mention his nose. Perhaps his nose should not be mentioned at all—a considerable nose, long and powerful, testifying to something strong and admonishing in him, a kind of force radiating from inside. His cheekbones were also strong, hewn out. But it was all a falsehood. He had known that the first time he had really understood himself, seen himself for the very first time and been perfectly aware that it was himself he was looking at—then it had been a rather different picture in the mirror. A little boy with golden curls and a snub nose. If he looked at himself nowadays, he searched in vain for that soft curve of face. Somewhere deep down lived the fair-haired boy, the one it all depended on. He had only disguised himself a little. Presumably everything else radiated out of that small boy, everything that had formed his face and turned his hair dark, his eyes narrow and cloudy.

Yes, he really belonged to the sun. There were days when Spot could not bear the sight of himself in the mirror, though most days it was all right. He could still work, still get through everyday things— still control the division in himself, the division threatening to tear him apart. If that happened, the falsehood and the truth would be parted in him, and the falsehood and the truth had to be in the same place. They created the human being.

He remained where he was, repeating this to himself. The falsehood . . . the truth . . . In this state the words seemed to reveal their true meaning, their depth . . .

He noticed that he was too tense and made himself breathe calmly, consciously lowering his pulse. Otherwise the shaking would start, and once it began, he would not be able to stop it. What was most important was to keep close to the sun. Stay with it.

That was where he belonged. He remembered playing for the sun on his violin. At the time, the piano had not been his instrument. He was practicing in the hall, with no one watching him. The door to the garden was open and the bright sunlight was pouring through the doorway, patterning the walls and ceiling. He could not have been very old, for he remembered he had to look *up* at the music stand. He even remembered the étude he had been playing. Inside the room it was blue and still, full of cool shadows. Perhaps he was seven. Immediately above him was the large mirror at which everyone hesitated a moment before going out or if they had company. But he was not paying attention to the mirror. His eyes kept straying toward the draperies hiding the sunlight and the garden outside. He could see the air was filled with it, the sun breathing deeply and quietly in the treetops. But he was obedient and he remained obedient to the études. He knew he had to practice before he was allowed out. Nevertheless, something was different today, for what came out of his violin was small and thin whenever he turned his ear toward the garden and everything out there. He noticed the very light itself was filled with a kind of note, a kind of hum. Without thinking, he went across to the open glass door, still playing, elbowing his way through the curtains so the sun would fall on his violin. The sound from out

171

there, which was no sound, was greater than everything, apparently familiar. Perhaps he was seven. He wanted to go out to it—he pushed aside the curtains.

The sun struck him like a sword.

He no longer had any memory of what had happened at that moment. He found himself out in the garden, on a path. He stood there playing, long, powerful strokes that made the little instrument resound so that it almost shattered, his face turned up all the time, up toward the treetops where the sun had settled. That was when he realized the summer wind was nothing but the sun touching the earth. The sun was everywhere, in the trees, the grass, in the very gravel of the path, and it was within him and around him, most of all in his violin. He walked happily around, playing wildly for whatever this was that was everywhere, hearing the humming all the time, played upper and lower registers, little cadences and trills. He sensed the notes from the sun all around him, almost as if they could be heard with ordinary hearing. He walked around and picked them up on his violin. Never before had it sounded like this and never would he have believed he could play so well without a printed note in sight, his hands finding the right grip of their own accord. Until the voice brought him back, perhaps the third or fourth time it had called.

"Leo!"

Slowly he lowered the bow.

"Leo! What *are* you doing?"

He had been in a state of bliss, and now it was shattered by the stern voice of his mother. Leo knew she would scold him.

"Haven't both your father and I told you you must practice before you may go out?"

He bowed his head.

"And look at you, playing out here. Out-of-doors! What if you spoiled your fine violin?" Then her voice quickly became gentler.

Leo said nothing. He was just longing to put his bow to the violin again, for the hum was still there behind his mother's voice, although he was standing still and had lowered his instrument, although everything visible to the eye was almost as usual. But the great notes were such that he could still reach them if he stretched out. So he let her scold and allowed himself to be led back into the hall, where his mother sat down on a chair to hear him finish playing.

As he lowered the violin again, he happened to look straight into the great mirror. He saw himself standing behind the music stand, in a light jacket and knee breeches. He saw his own face, round and soft, and he saw two quite large dark eyes. He saw the golden curls tumbling over his shoulders. Amazingly, he saw himself like that, with his instrument and bow. It was like a beautiful picture. He could not recall ever having seen himself in a mirror in this way before.

"Clever boy, Leo," said his mother. He looked in the mirror.

"Leo," he said.

❧

Leo. Leo Lewenhaupt. That was a name Spot barely dared say any longer, or even think about, and which he feared one day he would hear unexpectedly. Only once a day did he say that name to himself, quietly, into his pillow before he fell asleep at night. He was always afraid of it, afraid of what it contained, afraid of what it reminded him of, afraid of inadvertently saying it himself. But that one moment at night, when he said it to himself of his own free will, that moment was good; warmth ran through him as he whispered the name into his pillow, the name that was his secret and his sorrow. "Leo," he would whisper, and everything around him became warm and peaceful. "Leo Lewenhaupt."

The child prodigy and child of fortune. A great deal had been expected of him and he had not disappointed them, not to begin with. Leo, with his curls and brown eyes melting hearts and charming ladies and older women relatives. Leo playing the violin and the piano. Leo climbing trees and riding real horses, not just ponies, earlier than anyone else of his age. Leo recommended to the King of Württemberg for his musical achievements. As a twelve-year-old he gave concerts and his portrait was painted by a strange famous painter who kept wanting to touch his cheeks. But the picture turned out to be good and was hung in an exhibition. Perhaps it was still hanging in some museum somewhere.

Most of the time he had been deeply unhappy and afraid.

But at first nothing much was noticeable. At the beginning, when he composed his first small pieces and performed them at home and elsewhere, he had been happy. The old ladies who seemed to be made of lace and the men in uniforms and morning coats with long

173

tails—they clapped. He was pleased and proud when they clapped. His parents were also proud. They took him to more places, to more private concerts. He played the violin as well as the piano. Everyone clapped. Little Mozart, someone said. Afterward he had to eat cake and drink liqueur. He still could not stand the taste of liqueur. The officers' swords clinked. Those ladies kept *touching* him with their dry hands. His parents were proud. Gradually, without Leo really noticing it, he was given everything other children were not. His parents, ordinary German minor nobility, must have spent large sums on his clothes, instruments, and teachers. The teachers—they came and went, each one more peculiar than the last, and his technique steadily improved.

At some time or other, somewhere between the first liqueur and the fifth music teacher, he began to loathe it all. He loathed his parents, and he loathed the concerts, both public and private, the latter most of all, particularly if the house was inhabited by a prince. His loathing did not come from his gradual discovery that people in lace or with swords had not the slightest understanding of music, or that they indiscriminately clapped at performances—it was something else.

Perhaps that division in him, the chasm between falsehood and truth, began sometime during those years. The first little crack must have occurred early, so early that he barely noticed it. Perhaps it had been that morning in the garden when he had played with the sun, and his mother had come.

For the sun had touched Leo Lewenhaupt. His playing, but most of all the compositions he had begun to strew around him in the best child-prodigy manner, were filled with an echo of that great humming sound he had heard. It was still in him. It was impossible to explain to his parents or his teachers that the Leo who played at concerts and bowed with such childish gallantry had nothing to do with the real Leo, the Leo who sat alone writing down notes, fumbling along intervals, and finding the leaps, the echo of the inaudible. Only the actual music held the two together. He even had difficulty sometimes keeping them apart. It could be a soft spring evening and he might be sitting in his room jotting down something . . . something . . . perhaps it would be a little chorale or a sonatina. It was impossible to say—it had to go the way the music itself wanted. He had learned a new word—"immanent." The wholeness of the work had to be immanent in its individual parts. It had to flow just as it should, and the spring evening was soft, his pen scratching lightly and regularly on the paper. He was here. He was himself, happy. For several days he had not seen a single impresario or so much as smelled liqueur, and outside the evening breeze was rustling quietly through the trees.

A knock on the door. Come in. He doesn't know whether he thinks it or says it. He is in the middle of transposing from G minor to B major. It is his father who comes in, large, broad, round. Leo struggles with himself—what does he think of his father? Why does he *see* him so clearly, as he is, a paunch of a man? Couldn't he see him a little less clearly? So that he doesn't have to see his father as a self-satisfied old cavalry officer who has made peace with the world and his paunch, who suns himself in the growing praise of his son, and who first and foremost resembles a horse. Some of his father's closest friends actually are horses—Leo cannot understand it, but there must be something *between* his father and horses. At the same time, Leo wonders if he is not being unjust, whether it isn't that he is restless, *oversensitive*, as his mother says. So, is it himself or his father that there is something wrong with, because he can think like that? Is his father's resemblance to a sedate pony real or something he himself has dreamed up? Imagination? All this goes through his head as his father comes in. How old can he be? Not old. Was it before or after the Great Teacher that it happened? About the same time. So he must have been twelve or thirteen. Do twelve- and thirteen-year-olds have such ability for abstraction? He doesn't know. He had. His father opens his mouth and does not say excuse me. He is too pleased. He obviously has something to say, a surprise of some dimension. And Leo is obedient, a courteous child. With practice, it becomes a habit to be self-effacing, not least in everyday life. In addition, he has had to meet princes. So he looks politely and obediently up from G minor.

"Leo!" his father exclaims. "You have gotten a horse!"

For a moment Leo feels explosive things happening inside him and he doesn't know whether to laugh or cry. He smiles happily.

"But, Father, a horse!" His tone of voice—natural enthusiasm. His expression—smiling disbelief. That's how it should be. That's what is expected.

"But I already have one," he says.

"This is a real horse. A large thoroughbred stallion."

"But . . ."

"He's just arrived."

"Yes, but . . ."

"He's in the stable now."

"Yes, but where from? How has it got here?"

How will I have time for yet another horse? Leo thinks. Why did no one ask me first? What do I want it for? Where was I? G minor to B major? Inside, he tries to hum the scale he was in, but his father speaks.

"It's a present. And guess who from, young man?"

Leo is not in a state to guess.

"From you and Mother," he says unimaginatively.

"Nice of you, but you're wrong. It's . . . it's from . . ."

Leo can see that even if his father is keeping the military cavalryman's rigid mask drawn down like a visor over his face, he is about to lose self-control. He is *too* enthusiastic. He slaps his thigh as if slapping a horse.

"It's come from . . . *from there*," he says, pointing at the wall. Leo does not really follow; he doesn't understand how the stallion has come from the seamstress's room next door, but then he realizes his father means the picture on the wall.

"Just imagine . . . *he* . . . *he* has sent you a horse. As a present. Out of gratitude. My son!" It is all too much for his father and now he cracks. "We! You! You will go far—*far* . . . when *he* can send you a . . . a . . ."

Leo sees the battle is lost. He won't be able to sit here for the rest of the evening as he had intended. For when *he* . . . And what is worse, his quiet plans to allow horses to be horses and just go riding on weekends are now ruined. For what would people say if he let this gift stay unridden in the stables? His mother will have spread the news around their little town by midday tomorrow. He will have to ride the horse every day so that he can be seen by everyone. Child prodigy in the saddle on animal prodigy.

"Just what you wanted!" cries his father.

Leo sees with panic-stricken clarity how it has all happened. On one of their last rides together, his father had asked him whether he thought he would soon be able to ride a large horse, and politely Leo had replied yes, of course, but he was small still and could well go on riding Bella for another year. So his father had dropped a few words into the right ears and it had then gone on until it had reached *him* —that it was a horse Leo desired.

Resigned, Leo closes the lid of the inkwell and goes with his father to the stables, the battle lost. This was one of the major defeats, one which he remembered well. But there were also many small defeats, minor defeats in the fight against the superiority of the cavalry.

❧

Every morning he goes down and saddles the Creature. It already has a complicated Greek name and its pedigree is as long as the score of *Don Giovanni*, but for everyday uses, Leo calls him Fidelio, so that he will remember that the Creature is not what he appears to be.

The first time he rode Fidelio on his own he was frightened to death, the horse was so large and restless. But Leo was brave and put a good face on it. If he throws me, he thought, and I break my neck, that wouldn't matter. He calmed down at the thought and inwardly considered it odd, strange to be able to think like that, *mean* it, and at the same time be calm. So his fear vanished and he rode bravely. The animal was well trained, though somewhat reserved, like a courtier. As he gradually became acquainted with Fidelio, an uncommitted neutral relationship grew between them. The horse must have noticed Leo was riding it out of sheer politeness, but Fidelio had the good manners to ignore it. Leo had been able to whisper little secrets into Bella's ear, for he knew perfectly well she wouldn't tell but understood and kept things to herself. But with the Creature, with Fidelio, he never knew whether it wouldn't go back to his father. Or to *him*.

It must have been during this period that he seriously began to adopt a kind of cynicism, a division in his thinking and behavior. At the same time, he caught himself occasionally wondering whether he wasn't dangerously overstepping the mark. He would gallop through the forest shouting anti-royalist slogans or obscenities, loudly, insanely, only the horse hearing, and after the ride he would say to him, beseechingly, gravely, Fidelio, you won't tell on me, will you? You won't tell Father?

His father did not often wield the cane, but should such things come to his ears, it was not easy to say what he would do.

There were still concerts, hours of practicing, drills, more and more as he grew older, and all the time it was becoming increasingly clear to him that composition was his field.

He had begun early with little minuets and gavottes he had scribbled down after finding an amusing theme on the violin or the piano. Not grandiose, of course, but good enough for his teachers to enthuse and urge him to go on. Leo did as his teachers told him, and gradually the compositions became his secret world, the only place where he could be alone away from people. In Henkerdingen, the small town the estate lay outside, no one would speak to him naturally; either people would be exaggeratedly friendly and respectful or malicious expressions would come over their faces the moment they saw him. Things did not improve when almost the moment he had started school, his parents took him out again and arranged for his schooling at home with private tutors so that his music would not be affected. When he met other children in Henkerdingen, on the road or in the forest, they behaved much as their elders did. He could never reach them, each attempt becoming impossible from the start because the image of him, *their* image of him, always got in the way. Either people looked at him as if dazzled by seeing him—looking down or making an effort to look straight at him—or their eyes seemed to fill with gray ice. Nor was it much help that many tried pretending, and he spotted that at once—either the submissiveness, the timid respect for the prodigy, or that icy look.

His father ran the household with strict discipline. He was the image of a German officer and the minor nobility. He was thrifty, industrious, and disciplined. He never even tried to understand anything outside his everyday field of competence. When Leo was playing, his father clapped with polite enthusiasm. He always nodded off during slow movements, but could sleep to attention on horseback, so no one noticed. He took cold rubdowns in the mornings, as Leo also had to from very early on. The family fortune was not great, but profitably invested, and the estate produced a small income, so he was able to acquire the best instruments and the best teachers for Leo, and then there were the horses, of course, and fencing and shooting.

Leo had ridden almost since he had been able to walk, and there were three stallions in the stables, a mare and a pony. Everyday attire in the house was riding breeches, with the exception of at dinner. Leo hated them with all his heart, especially when they were of wool. The house had a smell of its own: stove fumes, oil, horse, and leather. Leather most of all. Those had been his childhood smells, there when he went to sleep at night and there again when he woke in the morning. But gradually he began to find the familiar smells oppressive and burdensome. He must have been about ten when he first noticed they nauseated him and scared him slightly, so he always left the window in his room open, summer and winter. His father took this as a sign of the makings of a man in him, and Leo realized there was something particularly manly about sleeping in a cold room. Fencing was also an important element in his childhood, that, and systematically shooting hares as soon as he was old enough to hold a gun properly. Afterward, he carried them home, where they were made into stew. When the autumn shoots were over, he could scarcely think clearly for several days, not to mention compose.

But he did have quiet evenings, hours when no one disturbed him, when the steeplechase of the day was over, when taking exercise, homework, shooting, riding, and meals lay like a bad dream somewhere far behind him. Only at that point did he enter into his own life, coming down from the dark loft of exile, and then the notes came. Always. He would sit at his desk for maybe five minutes with no idea what he was going to do or what he wanted to do, just sitting and staring into space, his pen between his teeth, the garden outside, and beyond it the grounds. Not a person in sight, just trees and animals. And—impossible to say where from—the first fragments would appear, faintly audible to him, like a shimmer of sound in his ears. Just two or three notes. Still not writing, he would wait until the tempo appeared, the rhythm, the breeze that had to go through him and carry him with it. Then it happened. Then the bubble inside him burst, and in a moment everything turned transparent and audible. The music was in the air around him and he simply put it down on paper. Of course, *he* was doing the writing. Of course, *he* was shaping it. But he was shaping what came to him, with a sure hand and sure instinct picking out the right forms among the thousands of possibilities. Then he forgot everything else.

When he came back to earth after sitting like that for a long time, his body would be hot and his head heavy. He would pour some water out of the carafe, his movements sluggish and confused, but after a drink he went on writing with quick firm movements, and again he would forget his very existence.

Gradually his nights also became places of refuge. He would sit from evening until it began to dawn outside the next morning, or he would be awakened by sitting bolt upright in bed after a few hours' sleep, then be at his desk in three strides, light the lamp, and go on. The cold rubdown at exactly seven o'clock would sometimes be hard after a night like that, and it was difficult to keep his attention on his teacher if he had sat up for several nights. But he clenched his teeth and completed the days. For he knew his nights would be taken away from him—at least the lamp—if they were found to be affecting his work. Or perhaps his parents accepted in silence that he sat up at night—his compositions were, after all, contributing to his growing reputation. But practicing was the most important of all, more important than anything else. Not until much later, after his childhood was almost over, did he realize why it had such priority. Composers earned no money. Soloists could become rich. And in the eyes of the German minor nobility there was something suspicious, something slightly doubtful about a composer, a person creating something on his own and giving something to the world, not permitting the world to be as it *is*. All right, you read your Goethe and Schiller and allowed yourself to enthuse over Beethoven, Schumann, and Mozart. Busts like figures in sugar icing were put in libraries and music rooms, and there was even a theater company in little Henkerdingen. But there were sides to the said gentlemen seldom mentioned, and those still alive were best kept at a distance. Not until someone is at a distance can you be proud of him. Poor Schiller had lived a pure and wretched life, truly wretched. It was incomprehensible that he did not return to his career as an officer when he had responsibilities and all. That he didn't fall back on it. But otherwise artists had a much better time nowadays. Family and friends were enthusiastic about young Leo. Just look, talented young individuals today found approval in the highest quarters, indeed, from . . . That was cause for enthusiasm. I'm proud of you, his father said. Your father and I, said his mother, are both proud of you. Both of us.

But his compositions, his own life, had to take place at a time when he actually required something else—at night.

As long as he could remember, the first hours of the day had been devoted to practicing. Piano and violin. Practicing took place in the hall, later to be made into a music room, one hour a day to start with, then longer, long wearying hours as morning, then afternoon went by. With or without a teacher. All the willpower Leo possessed went into perfecting his technique. He stayed at the music stand or on the piano stool, rarely ever shirking except when he was ill or on some rare occasion when his parents were not in the house. The three servants did not tell on him and allowed him to tumble about in the garden or sleep in.

Never again did he go outside with his violin and play with the sun.

His teachers were constantly changing. When he was thirteen, the Great Teacher came on a visit. He came from Paris and Leo trembled inwardly for days before his arrival. It was as if God were coming. God had decided to come and listen to Leo and arrived in a black calash with his coat of arms on the doors. He was God to such an extent that Leo's ordinary teachers would have sacrificed themselves to him if asked to. His parents, too—unasked. It was Leo who was to be sacrificed.

A short, delicately built man in a top hat and deerskin gloves stepped out of the carriage. When he took off his hat, a great mane of glossy black hair sprang out. His eyes were dark blue and sharp, his nose curved. Jew, thought Leo, who knew his father was not enthusiastic about Jews. But it was probably different when it was God. The maestro greeted Leo's parents, baring a row of white teeth, the eyeteeth unusually long and sharp. Then he greeted Leo.

"So," he said in broken German. "So this is the young Lewenhaupt I have heard so much about." He examined Leo's face closely.

Leo politely greeted him back.

A bare-headed servant carrying a violin case then got out of the carriage, his manner indicating the enormity of all that was entrusted to him. He was also dressed in black, like the maestro. Leo noticed that both of them seemed to glow and sparkle, their clothes shiny anthracite or coal. Then he remembered that the maestro always wore black silk or brocade; it was said to be the only way he could keep himself warm.

The violin case was also covered in black silk.

When lunch was over—the maestro had only picked at the food

and replied briefly with restraint to all the parents' attempts at conversation—they all went into the music room to hear Leo play. None of Leo's teachers was present—the maestro had expressly forbidden any "apologizing conceited pedagogic ass" when he promised to come. Leo had good, highly reputable teachers, and that kind of pronouncement would be permitted only to the greatest violinist in Europe.

Leo played. He played Mozart and Bach's *Chaconne*, a caprice by Paganini, three small pieces by Vieuxtemps, and études from Bériot's Violin School. When he stopped playing, the man in black sat quite still on his chair for a while. He looked as if he were thinking. Then he said, "Hm!" He was still again for a long while, not moving, just as when he had been listening, his eyes turned away from Leo. Leo's parents glanced uneasily at each other. But at last the maestro spoke again.

"Good. Good. But what I do not understand is what the boy is doing out here in the country. There's a lot to clean up in his playing. He ought to come to me. In Paris. My traveling days will soon be over, and I am shortly to take up a professorship. He could attend classes in Paris, although he is a German subject. Hm. He must come to Paris and he must stay five or six years. He must practice more. Six hours a day is not enough. He ought to practice at least ten, as things are. But he is still young. Small. Hm." He looked at Leo's father. "One day he will no longer be a child. And it is the child that arouses the audience's interest." He got up and went across to Leo, who looked at him in terror. Then he moved closer and cupped Leo's chin in his hand.

"Hm," he said. "You're brown. But pale under the brown, eh? Hm. Dark shadows across your cheekbones and at your temples. Hm." He maintained his hold on Leo's chin while running one finger of his other hand up to Leo's left eye and pulling up the eyelid to reveal the white. Leo was paralyzed. "Hm," said the man in black when he saw the red veins in the eyeball, his face closed and sharp, his eyes stern. Then he suddenly let Leo go as if dropping an object and turned to his parents. "Does he get enough fresh air?" he said.

There followed a long account of fencing, shooting, and the fantastic horse that had come from . . . But the maestro interrupted Leo's father in mid-flow. Again he was God.

"His playing is still far from good. But he *could* be good. Perhaps. There are certain possibilities."

"But he already gives concerts," said Leo's mother, rather taken aback by the maestro's lack of enthusiasm. "He's even . . ."

"Hm!" said God, and Leo's mother fell silent.

Leo's father dared to speak. "So you mean he ought to come to you straightaway?"

"I would like to speak to young Lewenhaupt alone," said the man in black imperturbably. "And hear him playing alone."

The parents rose with some hesitation.

"He also plays in Stuttgart four times a month. With His Honor the Court Maestro . . ." Leo's father began, but one look from the stranger silenced him. The parents left the room, confused at not hearing the maestro showering the praise over Leo they were used to from everyone else.

The maestro waited until the door had closed behind them, then nodded to the servant waiting in a corner with the violin case. The servant brought the case over and opened it. There was the instrument lying in its bed of blue velvet.

"Guarnerius," said the maestro calmly to Leo.

The violin seemed to glow as it lay there, the woodwork treated with a varnish that gave it an unusual golden-red tint. The violin did not look like an object in a case but like a piece of sunlight.

The maestro motioned for his servant to leave the room. Then he spoke.

"This," he said, "this is one of the last masterpieces by Giuseppe Guarneri del Gesù. One of his works. A violin of this kind is no longer simply a piece of craftsmanship. It can be compared with a whole symphony created by an artist. Poor Giuseppe! Poor unhappy creature! For months at a time he would wander in despair, raging and weeping through the streets of Cremona, from osteria to osteria, trying to forget his misery, unable to find the courage to finish an instrument, because he was seeking perfection . . . because the earthly violin never resounded as he dreamed it would. He kept working, despairing over never achieving it. He drank and was unhappy. Look! Look at it!" The maestro glanced swiftly at Leo. "Look at the color. Look at the neck. Giuseppe Guarneri always had the initials I.H.S. printed on the labels, the initials of Christ and a cross of roses—*Jesus Hominum*

Salvator—as if begging for forgiveness for his imperfect life and for salvation for his wretched soul, which sensed the perfect but never managed to re-create it on earth. So he was called *del Gesù*—of Jesus."

The maestro was still for a moment, and Leo looked at the instrument, saying nothing, still frightened.

"Giuseppe himself picked out the spruce for the top," the maestro went on. "As he did the maple for the back, and willow for linings and blocks inside. He produced the varnish after experimenting for ten years. We owe this violin to the Venetians. Yes. No, we owe it to the *sea*. For across the sea came amber from the coasts of the Baltic for varnish, and copal resin from the West Indies, East Indian shellac, North African sandalwood oil, mastic from the Sunda Islands, turpentine from Illyria. Across the sea came the most varied and costly paints, for the color of the instrument was as important as its resonance. Aloe, dragon's blood, brown catgut from Bombay, gutta-percha from Malaya, and campeachy wood from Central America. Everything, everything came across the sea, so the violin resembles a ship in form, and at the top of the neck, the scroll is twisted like a sea snail's house, like a conch.

"And on this instrument we venture to play! Well now."

The maestro swung his Guarnerius up out of the case and put it to his chin. For a moment they stood there looking at each other and Leo could feel his own sweat and a stinging in his armpits and down his back.

Then the maestro started playing. He played the Paganini caprice Leo had played, and he did so in a way that was at the same time fiery and icy cold. When he lowered the instrument, he again looked straight at Leo.

"Are you frightened?" he said, his expression now less stern.

"No," lied Leo.

"Hm. Now you can play the caprice again, and then we will have a little talk."

Leo played. It went rather better now that his parents were not present, but it was near the limit of his ability, particularly in the two-toned flageolet passages—for the maestro it had been a game, but Leo had to struggle and content himself with stressing them. When he stopped playing, he looked at the man leaning against the piano, still listening although Leo had stopped playing, his chin on his chest.

"Good," he said. "Why are you afraid? What is the matter with you? You're not so frightened now, are you? Now we are alone. Listen. I am willing to take you on as a pupil. When I go back, I can take you with me. Hm. What you need is proper teaching. You need to have the best teachers. Not the second-best. You play well, but not well enough. As I said before, ten hours a day. And intensive schooling. I don't know if you are still too small. I can see your parents are willing to extend themselves a long way so that you will reach your goal, that they would pack you off today if I asked them to. So I must think hard about that. Whether to ask them. Do you understand?"

Leo nodded.

"As I said, practice. Drilling. I have not got where I am today without practicing. Without drilling to the point of madness. Without having practiced until blood literally ran out of my nose. Do you see! A nosebleed! *It made my nose bleed!*" He pointed a trembling finger at his nose.

"But you are small," he said. "And you are pale under the brown. Perhaps now would be too soon. Perhaps I ought to wait a year before taking you on. Perhaps it is still enough that you are here. But on the other hand, perhaps it will be too late in a year. Hm. Difficult, you see? But . . ."

He stopped, for something was beginning to happen to Leo. While the maestro was talking, Leo had felt himself trembling inwardly. He always did when he was afraid, when he was to fence without a mask, to gallop when out riding. He trembled inwardly when he saw hares in the sights of his gun and when he was to play in public. But outwardly he was calm, always.

But not now. The inner trembling transmitted outward; it began in his chest and upper arms, faintly, but grew and grew until he trembled in his hands, his legs, his whole self. The trembling increased in strength until he was shaking all over.

The maestro looked on with a calm expression, watching as Leo collapsed in front of him, because his legs would no longer bear him. At first he sank to his knees, tried to get up again, but failed, then finally lay stretched out on the floor, racked with uncontrollable shudders, as if with cramp. He was no longer trembling but felt as if he had been torn apart. Inside himself he could hear a kind of rumble, the blood hissing in his ears and his heart hammering at a raging speed against his breastbone, a persistent throbbing in his body, every finger, every muscle tensed to an extreme, then relaxing, raging alternately.

A rushing current came and bore him with it, and he could not stop it. He said not a word and made not a sound except heaving gasps. He was fully conscious all the time and could feel his own thoughts floating like fragile bubbles up on the great roaring waves tearing at him. This had never happened to him before and he was frightened. He noticed the more frightened he was, the worse it became. The maestro, God, could just as well have been a hundred miles away. Leo looked at the black shoes and legs. Time slid away infinitely slowly and infinitely quickly. He could see the second pendulum on the clock on the wall and counted his heartbeats as he lay there. In ten seconds his heart beat twenty-six times, furiously quickly and hideously slowly. The pendulum ticked back and forth in its track, apparently stopping for a long time at each end. The distance from one side to the other seemed long, sluggish, as if the pendulum were gliding through oil. In half a second he thought, I am going to die now. I am dying. If only I had fallen off the horse and broken my neck. I'm not afraid of that. Not afraid. I was not afraid when I mounted Fidelio the first time, not afraid for my neck. It could only break. Why am I afraid now?

The pendulum reached one end.

Soon a great darkness will open up and swallow it all. I can feel it there, just behind everything, beneath everything. And it is hissing. The darkness is hissing. And yet it is still, pitch-dark, silent. But it is there, beneath everything. I am afraid.

The pendulum reached the other end.

But I am afraid they will find me like this, that Mother and Father will find me like this. He will run out and fetch them and say your son has had a fit, an epileptic fit, he is dying, you must come . . . and they will come and find me like this, *no no no*! Not that, not that . . . ! I can feel them. I am floating away. I can see them sitting waiting in the living room, waiting for the decision, sitting there, thinking about their prodigy son, are there . . .

Everything was turning black.

The maestro stood still, watching what was happening for a few seconds, his expression troubled. But he had seen a great deal in his time and he thought he understood something, slowly, without really being able to put it into words. So he calmly knelt down beside Leo, stayed there for a few seconds, then took hold of one trembling arm, which was shaking so violently he could hardly get a grasp on it. But once he did, he did not let go. He forced the hand into his and pressed it to Leo's chest, patting him cautiously with the other hand, then began to stroke Leo slowly across the shoulders and chest. That helped. When the trembling eased a little, Leo looked up in anguish.

"Don't go," he whispered. Then he began to shake again.

"No," said the maestro. "I won't go. Do you want me to call your mother and father?"

Leo desperately shook his head.

"No? All right, I won't."

The maestro went on calming Leo.

"Hm," he said after a while. Leo was still lying on the floor, but was almost still now, only a shudder occasionally running through him.

"Hm. No cramps. So not epilepsy. I've seen that before and it's not that."

"It's never happened to me before," whispered Leo. He could feel the tears coming into his eyes.

"You mustn't be afraid of me."

"No," whispered Leo.

"You are afraid of a great many things." He smiled for the first time, showing those sharp teeth. "You don't want to be sent to Paris. Is that right?"

"Yes," whispered Leo. "But it's not just that."

"So. Then there's something else, eh?"

"Paris would . . . ten hours a day . . . I really want . . ." But he had no words for what he wanted to say.

He had never said it to anyone before.

"Hm."

"I want . . . I sit up at night and compose. It has to be at night. I already practice so much, there's no other time but at night."

The maestro smiled, and there was now almost warmth in his smile. His eyes suddenly seemed friendly and wise.

"So that's what the matter is," he said. Leo swallowed, then nodded, and went on to tell him of the concerts, his parents, and how his secret nights turned out.

"If that's how things are," said the maestro, when Leo had finished, "there's little I can do for you." He smiled again.

"I'd like to develop my technique . . ."

"But that's not the main thing?"

"No."

"Hm. Now hear what I have to say. Listen. As you know, there are composers who are musicians and musicians who are composers. But there are also more one-sided people, composers who are competent musicians but have never played in public. And there are soloists with no imagination whatsoever, virtuosi, who can scarcely compose a ditty. Unfortunately, I am one of the latter. The little I have composed is not good. Even if I *dreamed* it well. Now you must listen very carefully. The composer is in this case the one who is blessed. *Never* let anyone tell you anything different. It is the composer who creates music."

Leo said nothing.

"But that is not my field. You may possibly become a very good soloist, *perhaps* one of the greatest. The fact that you have given concerts here in Württemberg means little. Child prodigies enchant people—that's all. You cannot play properly yet. But you could learn. If you want to."

"Don't . . ."

"Yes?"

"Please don't say *that* . . ."

"Ah. I understand. Well, young man. For the time being, you must obey your father."

"Yes," said Leo quietly.

"As you are used to doing."

Slowly, Leo started crying, quite soundlessly, the tears welling out.

"Give me your hand."

Leo held out his hand and the maestro took it in his, examined it, measuring the length of the fingers in relation to each other. Leo had long, slim hands, the muscles and sinews arched. The maestro turned the hand palm upward and gazed at it for a long time. Then he let it go.

"Good," he said. "Listen. Dry your eyes now."

Leo at once stopped crying and wiped his face. The maestro went on.

"I'll fetch your parents now. But remember, to be gifted is double-edged. It is a gift—that lies in the very word—and it is a great burden. I can predict many lonely and difficult nights for you. I can tell you that you will weep a great deal and you will have a great many miseries. For you have to pay for the greatest bliss. In music you commune with God. This is what people don't understand. Hardly anyone. But the man who carries on a conversation with God, devoting himself to its language, its music, whether he writes it or practices it —he is condemned. He must pay, for he experiences something others do not.

"I can tell you nothing about your compositions. I have not heard them. But I am still willing to take you on as my pupil. But not yet. It can wait. You must be able to decide for yourself first and not let others decide for you."

He got up and went over to the door. "And now I'll find something to say to your parents."

"May I say something?"

"Please do."

Leo was silent for a moment; then he said, "Thank you."

"That's all right, little brother."

❧

It is early morning and he is out riding. He has been riding at a slow pace along the river and through the village, the prescribed routine, but now he has come out on the other side and the red-tiled roofs are behind him and open ground ahead of him. It is spring and the fields have been plowed; the smell of earth is everywhere. The grass is not yet green and lies like withered hair along the edges of the ditches.

No one can see him now, and he sets off at a gallop. He leans forward over the horse's neck, afraid of being thrown, afraid the horse will trip on a molehill and fall. But he rides on even faster, faster and faster, the wind blowing in his face and the horse's hooves drumming. He starts shouting aloud as he rides, words pouring out of his mouth, words he finds it hard to believe he has in him. Some of what he shouts is quite impossible to understand.

Half an hour later, when both he and the horse are at last exhausted, he slows down and rides through the forest, following a path for a while, inwardly empty. He is just like last year's colorless dry grass;

the horse snorts and gasps with exhaustion. Leo cautiously pats his neck.

"Fidelio," he mumbles tonelessly. "My gift." Then the last abuse of the morning comes, softly, wearily. "Devil take you."

He comes to a small clearing on a slope and slips off the horse into the gray grass, sitting by the horse's forelegs for a moment, looking up at him. From down there the horse seems enormous, his eyes two huge red marbles, the sun shining into them. He can see they are covered with a thin, moist membrane. The horse shifts his head, snorting down Leo's neck. Leo shudders and draws away. He looks up into the horse's face and gets to his knees. Fidelio has an S-shaped flash on his forehead. Leo bangs his own forehead against the horse's with small determined movements.

Kick, he thinks. Kick.

But Fidelio just stands there expectantly. Leo can see his eyes just above his own. Then he gets up, moves away a few steps, and sits down in the grass at the foot of a small ash tree, leaning back against the trunk and stretching his legs out. The ground is still chilly; above him are the bare treetops, not yet sprouting out. Spring is late, and the absence of life in the forest suddenly puts him in an even gloomier mood. It is as if this amazing state of *pause* in nature, this feeling of no-man's-land, will last forever and ever. He knows it is now that things are happening. But this growth is not visible, and worse, he cannot feel it. He can never remember such a bloodless spring before.

In the dry grass, right next to the trunk, is a small flower. He had almost sat on it, but then he spotted it and moved away a little. The flower is white, but he doesn't know its name; it is the only one in sight. In the summer when he is alone in the woods and no stranger can see him, he often lies among the meadow flowers—flat out and resting. He can't do that now. Instead, he lies on his stomach and studies the little white star-shaped flower. He can see it is not quite white and that the petals have splashes of purple in them. What is it called? He thinks hard, hyacinth, iris . . . he knows nothing about flowers. But it is white and purple and is by a tree, alone. He closes his eyes.

Everything has quickly become as it was. God, the great God and maestro from the numerous concert halls and salons of Europe, the virtuoso with fire and brimstone in his playing, had gone the same day he had come. But Leo remembers the little smile at the end, in the music room, as well as the snake-like smile as he said goodbye to Leo's parents. In the music room the smile had had something human about it. Leo did not have to go to Paris. His parents were disappointed—or pleased? It was not easy to say. We ought to wait another year, the maestro had said, and at that moment their disappointment showed on their faces, particularly his father's—wasn't *his* son good enough? But they quickly consoled themselves with the fact that he did not have to go just yet, his mother in particular. As long as he was at home, a more immediate glory was reflected on the family. His music lessons went on as before, but with an extra hour's practice after the evening meal.

He was soon going on his first real tour.

"He is both small and large for his age," the maestro had said, whatever he had meant by that. Leo never really understood the great man who had come to see him. When he saw him in his mind, he seemed frightening. Perhaps that was why Leo had begun to tremble. It could be. But in the middle of all that cold, everything that was superhuman about the man—in the middle of all that, there was something else. He *had* consoled him. So Leo often thinks that the man in black is the only person he could talk to about real things. Could he talk to his parents about them? Or the court maestro, Gösch? Gösch was a gnome with warts on his head. He played technically very well and taught excellently—but it was dead, all of it was dead. The great stranger who had played like brimstone—what had he said? He had said he had practiced until the blood had run out of his nose. Had Gösch ever done that? Gösch had no blood in his veins. Formaldahyde ran through them instead.

To practice like that, Leo thinks, you have to have some idea of perfection. You have to have had a glimpse of the impossible, and that glimpse must be such that it never gives a poor devil any peace or rest once he has seen it.

It was almost as if Leo were grieving over not going to Paris, but nausea rose in him every time he thought about the dark stranger and what life would be like with such a teacher, alone, in a large strange city with no time to write music. He was relieved he had not had to go.

The violent inexplicable attack Leo had had in the music room that afternoon had never been repeated. His parents would never know about it.

What had it been? Leo did not know. Only, now and again at night, if particularly tired and overworked, he would notice a faint trembling in his chest and upper arms, just as it had started that day, but never anything more. He slept on it and in that way forestalled it. But the feeling of something deep down inside him not being what it appeared to be, that there was nothing but a veil over an evil darkness —that feeling stayed with him. After the scene in the music room, days had gone by before he felt more or less well again. His composing was still going sluggishly, but the little he had done was good.

Leo turns over on the grass, the sky above the treetops high, light, and blue, the clouds white. He can stay a few more minutes before going home.

But there is something. Someone is looking at him. Without knowing how, he suddenly knows that someone's eyes are on him. Where? Someone among the trees? Guardedly, he gets up, brushes himself off carefully, and looks innocently around. He can see no one, yet cannot free himself of the feeling.

Someone is looking at him.

He takes a few steps over toward the horse. Everything is quite still—a faint rustling from the forest, nothing more. He must have imagined it. Don't forget you've got to buy ink in Henkerdingen. Again he looks around and suddenly hears a faint growl.

He stiffens. The sound is coming from the woods behind him. He leaves the horse and walks in that direction, and the sound increases in strength, then becomes barking. A dog emerges from a bush, two steps, large and black, a kind of German shepherd. It stands barking at him. Cautiously, Leo moves closer. The dog does not wag its tail and its ears are back. It is black all over, its coat shaggy, not a pedigree dog, a mongrel, dirty, its front paw injured. It must have been in a fight.

"It's all right," says Leo coaxingly. The dog growls, looking furtively at him. Leo can hear the horse is uneasy. The dog has no collar, not even a rope around its neck. A feral dog. Its coat bristles even more, and the growl turns into a kind of deep, ill-omened howl as Leo takes another step nearer. The dog looks as if it is going to leap at him, and Leo is sure it can bite if it wants to.

He stands still, the dog two strides away. Why does it pause? Why doesn't it take a leap? Then Leo realizes it must be protecting some-one, somewhere behind it.

Someone is crouched down in the bush, scarcely discernible in the thick undergrowth.

"Come on out," he says calmly.

A small figure rises, hesitantly, a little girl, younger than he, perhaps eight years old, in a ragged green skirt and brown jacket. Her face is scratched and her tangled hair hangs down, knotted and dirty. Leo can't remember having ever seen her in Henkerdingen. She is looking at him and she is frightened. He doesn't know why. She bites her lower lip and looks wide-eyed at him. She has a kind of scar on her face, a gash running up from one corner of her mouth, the skin puck-ered all around it. Harelip. Then Leo sees she has two rabbits in one hand.

Poaching, he thinks. The land around here is private. "Is the dog yours?" he says. The child's eyes grow larger, but she says nothing.

"Have you been there long?"

She remains mute, but shakes her head. She is incredibly dirty and scared to death.

"I won't do you any harm," says Leo, but he can see she doesn't understand what he is saying. She looks worriedly around; then she opens her scarred mouth and a stream of words in a language Leo has never heard before pours out. He can't understand a word. Then she suddenly stops.

He has to smile, and he shakes his head as a sign that he doesn't understand. But something happens to him, as if he had nevertheless understood something in those strange sounds. Her face gives him something to think about.

Then she starts talking again. She is calmer now, and this time a German word appears.

"My brother. Brother," she keeps repeating, and at last Leo understands.

"You're out looking for your brother?" he says.

She nods eagerly. The dog has also calmed down now, but is still watchful, looking askance at Leo. Leo smiles again and points at the rabbits she is carrying in her hand. There is blood on her bare arm.

Snares, he thinks, and shudders, reminded of the autumn shoots. He points at the rabbits, rubs his stomach, and says, "Eat?"

She nods eagerly but says no more, just stares at him, the scar on her mouth revealing a tooth.

Leo realizes he is late.

"Goodbye," he says, waving cautiously. Then he goes over to Fidelio and mounts him.

She is still standing there as he rides away.

⚘

He met the girl twice more in the forest. She always came upon him without warning and he never found out what her name was or who she was. The dog was always with her. As they could not talk to each other, it was a matter of her simply looking at him while he was resting after his ride. The nearest she ever got to a conversation was sitting down beside her dog and looking across at him. And Leo, who otherwise avoided people's eyes, noticed he did not mind. She didn't know who he was, didn't know about the child prodigy, young Lewenhaupt, so his image did not get in the way. Instead, she saw *him*. The first time, she had two more rabbits with her; the second, she was empty-handed. Something else happened on the second day— the big black dog came over to Leo and licked his arm.

"Have you found your brother yet?" Leo asked her. She did not reply. Her gaze turned inward and she again repeated the word: "Brother."

Leo thought about the Great Teacher from Paris.

That same day, at their evening meal, his father said, "Some Gypsies have come into the forest. Vagrants."

"How awful," said his mother.

"I've spoken to Schmidt and Stub about them. They think they're probably poaching. Stub has found a few snares."

"But something will have to be done, won't it?"

Leo pricked up his ears.

"Stub and Schmidt are taking the other men with them this evening."

The next day Leo saw no sign of the Gypsy girl. He rode around a little as if searching, almost missing her, but he did not find her. So she had been chased off the night before, together with her people.

It didn't really matter. They would have moved on a few days later anyhow. But he was sad, and also worried in case she had told anyone she had met a German in the woods, a big boy on horseback, in which case they would think he had reported them. Would she be made to pay for that? He thought about that scar, the harelip, and wondered whether she had had it since birth. It had looked bad. Were people born like that?

Leo heard the horse snorting uneasily. He looked up.

The black dog came out of the undergrowth. Alone. It padded straight up to him and sniffed at him. He patted it and it licked his hand. Its coat was good to feel.

"Poor old thing," said Leo. "All alone, then?" He took a good hold on its coat.

For a moment he looked into space, then got up and smacked his lips at the dog.

"Come on," he said.

It followed him all the way home.

It now follows him everywhere, is his dog. His parents' protests are to no avail. The first day he brought it back was the most difficult. But he managed it.

"What's *that?*" said his mother, pointing at the dog stretched out on the floor in front of the music stand. "What's *that?*"

"It's a dog. My dog."

"I can see . . . *your* dog?"

"Yes." He answered from far away. He was practicing, the dog lying sleepily on the floor, listening. It is not particularly musical, but all the same, it was listening. Leo went on playing all the time his mother was talking. It was more difficult for her to get through to him that way. He was deep in arpeggios, but quite firm when he replied.

"Who in heaven's name gave you permission to . . . Where did you get it from . . . ?"

"It was given to me. I'm its owner now." He played on.

She looked at him, doubtfully, close to tears. Could this be her Leo, usually so amenable. She looked at the big black dog with distaste.

"It's filthy."

"I'll give it a bath."

"And it's bleeding."

"Only a scratch."

She didn't know what to say, but then it came—half suppressed: ". . . rabies!"

She looked horrified. He stopped playing and looked straight at her.

"The dog is to stay with me." Quietly, clearly, and at that moment the dog thought fit to let out a growl.

Leo turned back to the score again and went on playing. His mother was still hestitating, wanting to say something more, breathing heavily as if about to have one of her asthma attacks. Then she went away.

Leo played on, the dog lying on the floor. It gave him a rather nasty feeling of malicious pleasure to know he had just horrified his mother. She was usually quite kind and never hit him, much kinder than his hot-tempered father, whom she could calm. But this feeling was not directed at her. It intoxicated him and he smiled to himself as he played. The arpeggios became perfect.

The dog stays. Even his father's attempts to persuade him, coupled with concealed threats, have no effect. The dog is allowed to stay. Leo is astonished that he has really found the courage for this defiance, he, Leo, usually so compliant to all commands, advice, and admonitions, doing everything he is told even when he knows he won't be able to. He is as suddenly inflexible as steel. The dog is his. It is a gift. It is to stay with him.

Apart from this, he says nothing about it. His parents are confused and find him unrecognizable. The dog stays.

For a while he and the dog search the woods together again to see if the girl with the harelip or any of her people have come back for it. In that case he would give the dog back. But he never sees her again. Is she sad because she has lost her dog? Does she ever think about it, or the German boy on horseback?

Every morning when he goes riding on Fidelio, the dog follows just behind, never letting him out of sight, even when he gallops. At first the horse was nervous at having this shaggy creature at his heels, but gradually he got used to it being there, reluctantly, just as Leo's parents had. The dog and Leo have become friends and it growls at everyone else. Only Leo can feed it, only he can pat it. His parents, teachers, and the village people are frightened of it.

Of course, gradually his father began to appreciate having a life-threatening dog in the house. He went so far as to talk about having the old rottweiler put down and replacing it with the big German shepherd, adding it to the kennels by the stables.

When Leo heard of this suggestion, he reacted. He growled at his father, noticing the way his hackles rose. He snarled. Got up and left the dinner table.

His parents sat back, resigned. Leo is changing. Though perhaps it is just that the changes are only now becoming visible.

He gives concerts throughout that autumn. The dog goes with him on all his trips, lying in the dressing room waiting for him, weighty, black, silent. When Leo comes in after the applause, it gets up and pads over to him. Then the whole concert vanishes from his mind. He never tires of squatting down in front of the dog, looking at it and shaking its coat. He never finds out whether that glass-clear gaze is stupidity or wisdom. The dog is utterly unmusical, ignorant of who Leo is. It is a stranger.

But *before* the concerts . . . Leo himself realizes he has changed. Before concerts he is overcome with a nervousness bordering on anguish, like the state he was in when the maestro came to hear him. Hours before the concerts, it can take hold of him and hurl him into pitch-black fear. The same happens again in his dressing room before concerts. He keeps thinking about all the people out there in the concert hall. They have come to listen to him. He can sense with a kind of clairvoyance that they *are* there, coughing, glancing through programs. Every time his thoughts wander in that direction, he starts trembling. He is to play for them. They will listen. Every mistake he makes, the slightest tremor, they will hear. These are proper concerts, and he is no longer a child prodigy. The audience is critical. He himself must answer for what he is going to play. In his mind, he goes through the program, the pieces becoming insidious traps, and it all becomes a leaping from one ice floe to another in a deep cold sea. *There*, in the scherzo, he is uncertain, and *there*, in the trio, and *there* . . . What he had done a year ago without fear, indeed with loathing sometimes, but without anxiety, without giving it a thought now has become a nightmare he cannot wake from. He has to go out on the stage and do what is expected of him, also what he does not know if he is capable of.

Sometimes he used to vomit up everything inside him before he went out to play, taking the taste of gall with him onto the stage. As he leaned over the basin in his dressing room, feeling as if all his entrails were trying to get out, he was beyond all help. He chased everyone out of the dressing room, his mother, father, teachers, the concert society's representative, not wanting them to see him in that state. It was humiliating enough already. Soon he had to go on and feel the thousand eyes of the audience on him.

Nor could the dog help him then.

Not until afterward. Then he always took the dog for a walk to thank it for waiting.

One evening he is walking the dog as usual through the evening-quiet streets of a small provincial town. Where can it have been? Perhaps Giessen—it is humid, oppressive weather, the smell of marsh . . . He is walking through the streets with his black dog, calm, relieved the concert had gone well. He had gotten through all the dangerous places, managing to leap perfectly from ice floe to ice floe . . . Sometimes fear could overcome him so fiercely that parts where he thought he was quite safe suddenly became dangerous, almost insuperable, the relatively safe floes beginning to sway ominously so that he could barely save himself. But that night it had gone well. He is relieved, but not happy. Is he ever happy? The tension in his stomach has abated and all he feels is a slight tenderness in his midriff from the vomiting before the concert.

The streets are dark, the shutters all closed. If he meets anyone, he flattens himself against the wall in the darkest shadows. The town lies in flat country, so it is difficult to orient yourself and he has no idea where he is. But he is not afraid of getting lost, and he also has the dog. He lets the dog choose the way.

He turns a corner and stops. In front of him is a lighted doorway, a gentleman's house, a landau outside it. Five people are getting out, two women and three men. They are dressed up as if they had been to the theater or a concert. Of course. Them. He had seen them in the third row. Two married couples and a young man. They stop outside the front door, one couple clearly about to walk home, and they are saying goodbye. Leo wants to slip past, but stops and listens. They are talking about him.

". . . superb, the Mozart."

"Oh yes. And Paganini. Wonderful music."

"A virtuoso."

That kind. Leo decides to go on. He has heard all that before. But one of them, the young man, says something that makes him stay.

"But he was nervous."

"Nervous?"

"He was white as a sheet. Never seen anything like it. And his upper lip was gleaming with perspiration."

"Now you mention it, Jean, I—"

"It's true!" said the young man. "And his whole being, so tense, so dispirited. I can't say I enjoyed it. There was something unnatural about it all, something—"

"But the music was beautiful."

"Yes, but don't you see, it was all good, yes, excellent, as long as you closed your eyes. But when I saw that young boy . . . I don't know . . . Didn't you also get the impression that it was a kind of exhibition, a kind of circus . . ."

"That's the art, Jean. Think of Mozart. He was also exhibited like that. It's the talent that has to come out."

". . . like a trained horse."

Leo walks on, straight ahead, looking neither right nor left. Their voices recede behind him. The tears run down his cheeks and he lets them run.

⚜

He walks for a long time, finally coming to an open square in the middle of the town in front of the palace. He sits down on a bench.

A horse. A circus horse.

He is suddenly aware he has become a circus act, just one in his father's stable, and he has been so for a long time. He sits there, his mind empty, the dog lying at his feet, one thought in his head, and it grows in him, filling him more and more. It is no longer music. It is no longer art. It is dressage. And where is a dressage horse to find meaning in what he does? Where is *he* to find meaning in music when the actual performance of it has become an acrobatic number? Dressage. He laughs as he weeps.

—✳—

That was one night. He sat on that bench, chilly, unwilling to return to the boardinghouse, wanting to disappear in the dark. The clock tower struck one, then half-past. The palace archways and windows were dark, as if they were giving off the darkness, which ran and trickled through them out into the world. He felt like this palace. He *was* like this palace.

Then it happened. In the stillness he heard notes. Trumpets. Horns. Bassoons. Music calling to him, triumphantly, violins lamenting, and all the time, drums, thundering like horses' hooves.

He sat bolt upright. Now! Now it was there. He had not been able to compose for a long time—he had come to a full stop and all attempts had run out in the sand, the most painful state for anyone trying to create. Not being able to. All artists come across this lethargic meaningless horror sooner or later. For Leo this meeting with nothing had come early, perhaps too early. But now, this evening, the music had him again, the real music. He fumbled in his pocket, in his jacket and waistcoat. Not a single piece of paper. Not a stub of a pencil. The notes became steadily clearer and stronger. He got up. Where was he? He had a room at the boardinghouse where he had paper and ink. He could sit there.

He ran through the streets, the dog ahead of him. Something was calling in him. He himself was calling. Home! Home! The dog pulled him along and he found the right house and managed to collect his wits, pulled the bell and was let in by the housekeeper in her nightgown. Your mother has been beside herself. Walking up and down wringing her hands, Oh yes, she has, has she? Well, where's my room? Ah yes, thank you. Good night. No, don't wake her. I'll speak to her in the morning. He made his way in, closed the door, and lit the lamp.

—✳—

This is his dream. Once, when Leo was small, his father took him to a riding exhibition in Stuttgart. His father was leaning back in his seat and gazing with pleasure at the ring, where six faultless white horses were going through their paces in formation and performing their feats, red plumes on their heads swaying in time with their movements.

This is the dream. A horse rears up on its hind legs and totters clumsily forward—"almost like a human," a voice whispers, perhaps his father's. But now it has become the voice of the dream. *Almost like a human.* It is rearing. The trainer is in front of it in a top hat, his whip raised. The horse looks uncomprehendingly at the dark figure, its eyes panic-stricken with the effort of standing on two legs. It whinnies and shows its teeth. Its body is tense and unnatural. It takes three steps, three four five six, slowly and uncertainly. It is a torment for it to rear and it looks as if it is crying.

This is the horse's dream. They are racing through a white morning—the town with its red roofs is there, and a boy is sitting behind a window, writing. The dream is abruptly interrupted by the crack of a whip, and then it is up on two legs again, showing its teeth, and a violin laments, pianissimo at first, then louder and more discordantly against the underlying drumming theme.

This is the music. As red as the dancing plumes, a streak of blood trickles from the horse's eye.

Leo draws bar line after bar line down the paper. As usual when he sits like this, not thinking about it, they become slightly crooked, gradually inclining to the left. He fills the space in between with inky blue notes, draws another bar line, then another.

It is still within him.

He stays there a few more minutes listening to the sequences that had been interrupted—what does this mean, how did that happen? He straightens up and smiles wearily at himself. He looks out the window and sees it is late and early at the same time. It must be six o'clock already. Then he looks swiftly through the sketch—it is for full orchestra, something he has scarcely dared to do before. He looks at it and reads through it. He does not understand it. He does not understand what it *is*, does not recognize himself in it. He has never composed like this before. It's not bad, he thinks, almost with surprise. It is the beginning of a symphony.

❧

After that, the rest of the tour is simpler for Leo. A peace descends on him, a kind of distance from everything around him which makes it easier to endure the concerts, the long days of traveling, and the company of his mother. It is simpler to comply, because he has other things to think about.

His mother has always had asthma, with a few mild attacks off and on. But in the end, particularly after the dog joined the household, it seemed she was using her asthma against him, as a weapon. The attacks became more frequent and more severe. Leo could not believe she produced them deliberately. Nevertheless, that is what it seemed like.

In a way he can see why the attacks keep coming. He knows it is his mother who has to suffer when his father is angry with him. She always goes between them. Her asthma serves to protect both Leo and herself. That is almost the worst part of it. Once or twice on the tour he has had to heat a kettle of water, put some ether oil from his mother's flask into the water, and help her to inhale it under a towel. He feels no sympathy for her at these moments, no compassion. Her long, shrieking breaths are repulsive to him, as is the sweat glistening on her forehead and the impotence in her eyes. He almost hates her. He can read the reproach in her eyes. Her asthma attacks seem to come from *him*, as if *he* were the illness.

The morning after he had been out all night, she had an attack of that kind. But that morning it was different. It did not worry him and he was too tired to hate her. He was empty and laid bare, incapable of feeling anything special about it. He simply helped her out of sheer habit. Quietly he accepted her reproaches, first the looks she gave him and then the scolding about his disappearance the previous evening.

Then something seemed to dissolve between them, as if they no longer regarded each other in the same way. He saw it quite clearly and he also saw that she sensed it. Something had happened. He ordered a cup of bouillon and helped her drink it.

Quiet descended between them.

Then they went on. The attacks ceased.

In the evenings, alone in one of his many rooms on the tour, he takes out the draft he had written that night, polishes it a little, and rearranges a few minor items here and there. He still doesn't understand that it is he who has composed it. It is completely different from anything he has done before. It has another voice. He cannot comprehend what it contains. He takes walks to think about it. He sits down and tries to find a continuation for it, but the silence continues within him, though a few small ideas are communicated from his usual source of melodies, themes, and sounds, but nothing resembling what he wrote that night, nothing that can be used.

He goes on speculating even when he has returned home, the quiet autumn all around him. The joy of creating ordinary small pieces has gone. They all seem pointless, banal, and traditional, with no distinctive features in comparison with the ominous sketch lying on his desk.

Besides, all things are distant—his parents, the house, practicing. He is free and imprisoned at the same time.

Instinctively he starts to study everything he can find on harmony and composition. He reads back numbers of *Neue Zeitschrift für Musik* and studies different scores. But that is no longer sufficient and does not help him. With that little sketch he seems to have taken a stride into a world of new sounds and new themes—a whole new way of composing. A world in which he has to fumble and feel his way ahead. But he is no longer able to; his palette is not large enough to enable him to go on, and the knowledge he lacks cannot be found from reading.

In that way something dies.

⚜

In that way something happens. It is time for the fall hunt. Distant shots rend the cold, clear air. The ground is frosty every morning and the shooting stars rain down at night.

One early morning, Leo and his father are walking through the forest, as usual carrying their guns barrels upward; in line with his father's strict shooting principles, they have only two cartridges each. Then no shots are wasted.

They spot a hare in a clearing. His father is quickest, much quicker than Leo, and in one movement he is ready and has the gun at his cheek. Then there is a shot and the hare is dead.

They go over to it.

"Excellent," says his father, picking it up. "Fine little specimen."

"A good shot," says Leo.

"Well," growls his father, "I don't know. We were quite close. Very close, actually."

"But all the same."

"I've done better. That kite, if you remember, was much farther away."

"Yes, it was."

"And it was in flight."

"All the same," says Leo, "that was also a good shot."

"Yes, maybe so."

"You were quick."

"Very quick. Yes, I was very quick."

"You'd have got it even if it had started running."

"Yes, that's true. I would have got it."

"Father, I'd very much like to study composition."

His father says nothing.

Then he guts the hare right in front of Leo's eyes.

Leo, Leo. This is the moment. This is the moment when you make the wrong choice. At this moment you can be free if only you have the courage. You can defy him, tell him you're going to study composition anyway, whether he likes it or not. You know you'll manage to get through it on your own if necessary. But you don't say so. You don't defy him. You don't want to be free. You have been plucking up your courage for days and now you betray yourself by not using it. Your courage ebbs away. You acquiesce. You say, "Yes, Father," and bow your head, while at the same moment you know the consequences will be difficult years and that every year will be a battle with yourself until the next time you have gathered up enough courage and such a moment comes again.

"Aren't you going to Paris? To that, that . . . You are going."

"Yes, Father. But composing—"

"You can do what you like . . . on the side. Your career comes first."

"Yes, Father. But—"

"I'll pay. I've paid large sums already. There's no question of studying composition. What use would that be? What will you *live* off? There's nothing more to say. You will go to Paris. One day you'll thank me."

Later he is sitting in the stables, just back from the hunt, but he can't bring himself to go indoors. He wants to stay there for a while.

Fidelio snorts and lowers his head toward him as he sits leaning against the horsebox wall. The black dog is dozing at his feet.

One day you'll thank me.

In the warm darkness of the stables Leo puts a curse on himself. Now he is going to Paris. One day he will thank his father. He looks down at his hands and grasps his gun.

Then he shoots Fidelio and the black dog.

He had only two cartridges.

That same night Leo dreamed he was out alone on the autumn fields and it was growing dark. In the dusk he saw a figure, a huge man towering over the treetops in a red coat, his face like copper and feathers. Leo was both frightened and calm at the sight of him. The stranger then pointed at the hills and the horizon, where two stars had just risen.

Do you see those two stars?

The stars were golden and clear, clearer than any real star in the sky. One was directly above the other.

Yes, yes. I can see them. That's where I want to go. If only I can get to them.

Everything in Leo was being pulled toward the stars out there in the heavens.

Then the upper star faded and disappeared.

When you reach the star that is left, you will die.

Then the dream ended. He slept calmly for the rest of the night and dreamed other dreams. But Leo remembered that short dream for a long time afterward; long after he had arrived in Paris, he often thought about that dream.

Spot sat up in his bunk with a jerk. The air all around him was heavy with time. He must have been there for a long time.

He looked around. The cabin walls seemed to have come closer, as if they had grown in toward him. The monotonous sounds from the ship, the rustling, creaking, and tinkling pressed on his eardrums. Something was hurting.

The ship was gliding through the night; the porthole was black. He was sitting there, a passenger, a traveler, a temporary minor musician without so much as a name to cling to.

He was a traveler, a constant traveler.

This journey had really started in the landau bearing him away from his childhood home, when he was seated inside, trembling a little, trembling because he was afraid and alone—and at the same time happy to have got away. That was the day he had started this great journey which had brought him here, away from his own name and his own face.

In Paris he always had the feeling of being on his way; his pleasant student room in Montmartre was like a carriage or a ship. When he closed the door behind him and was alone inside it, he could feel it moving. In the daytime, as he walked the streets, he seemed to be sailing along rivers and streams, strange wild waterways—the Orinoco, the Mississippi—the avenues—and poling his way through unchartered deltas, tributaries, and marshes—the side streets and alleys.

He also went on journeys and expeditions into music. He went to concerts and listened to music he never knew existed, music he had never heard anyone mention in Henkerdingen or Stuttgart. He visited countries no German geographer had yet discovered, met the Eskimos and Mongols of music—the impressionists, moderns, people who wrote music unlike anything he had ever heard before. He felt as if he had come tumbling down from the eighteenth century; even aspects of his clothing indicated previous centuries—only the wig missing—and he rolled down like a stone through a hundred years of time, arriving at the party in the wrong attire, his baggage full of insane clatter, then searching like a madman among his many effects for something he could use, searching and searching, throwing out wigs and hose, rapiers and walking sticks, pink beribboned minuets, plaster busts, knickknacks and medallions, and *Grosse und Kleine Stücke für Violine*, the whole great mess, hurrah! On this journey he tasted costly dishes, fairy-tale drinks, and scents from the *Arabian Nights*—everything, everything was like champagne.

He was taken on in the maestro's class, and the teaching was one long avalanche of practicing, new and yet more new pieces, indefatigable working on details and appoggiaturas, a musical Witches' Sabbath. The maestro stood listening like a magician among his pupils. Listening to them. There were twelve in the class, nine boys and three girls from eleven to nineteen, all tremendously different, twelve novices in witchcraft, twelve fellow passengers. With new friends, Leo went to concerts and exhibitions; he wept and laughed, learned that there were other drinks besides liqueur and port wine, clattering off with them along quiet Sunday-morning streets and going on outings and trips into the country. He discussed literature and art with them, but most of all music, music, music. He fell in love in turn with the three girls in the class, and they in turn fell in love with him. That was also a journey.

But he set off on another kind of journey as well, a journey through fevers and mists, making his way into illness. Not long after he arrived in Paris, he caught measles, then chicken pox and mumps. He fell ill with those three childhood diseases one after another and took a long time to recover. In the middle of chicken pox, he was taken to the hospital. His fellow students were not allowed to visit him, but the maestro came regularly and examined him as well as all the remarkable colors and shapes he gradually took on. His protected and overworked childhood now seemed to be losing its grasp on him, and he had to experience everything that all children have time for all at once. He had not had *time* to be ill.

Because he was fifteen, his illness was protracted. He was in the hospital for two whole months with rashes and blisters and swellings, and at times his temperature was high enough for serious concern, but he was fiercely opposed to informing his parents. The maestro agreed on that point, on the whole, apparently taking Leo's illness with great calm despite the fact that it came in the middle of the term.

The hospital was run by Catholic nuns, all of them friendly and slightly distant. They hummed at night as they went from bed to bed, watching over the ward. To Leo, in a mist of fever, the humming turned into the sound of the sea, of glittering waves carrying him through the darkness. He had never seen the sea in reality, but he dreamed he was Odysseus lying chained to a vast bed, floating on a mythical sea, listening to the Sirens singing. When he had recovered, he wrote a little scherzo on the bedridden Odysseus.

But something else happened before that. As soon as he was well enough to be up and about, the maestro brought his violin to the hospital and Leo played for the sick and the nuns. The violin sounded different, a different instrument to hold after being in bed for so long.

He had not been able to bring himself to look in the mirror while he was ill. Once had been enough, when he had chicken pox; he looked so terrible, the sight made him worse. But when he was about to be discharged and found himself standing in front of a mirror, putting on his own clothes, he saw a stranger. He screamed in horror at the stranger in front of him, a thin, pale young man, with high cheekbones and a sharp nose. His lips were gray. He stared at the stranger without really believing what he saw. He raised a hand, and the stranger in the mirror also lifted his hand.

His hair was almost black.

For a long time he found himself shrinking back whenever he saw himself reflected in a shop window or a barber's mirror. Only his hands remained the same. He recognized those.

Then he grew, so that his whole wardrobe had to be replaced. He was sixteen, then seventeen, and he rapidly became one of the best pupils in the maestro's class.

The maestro was apparently always the same, unchangeable, imperturbable. What he had prepared Leo for about the teaching turned out to be true: ten hours a day. The maestro had stopped giving concerts and was now devoting himself entirely to teaching. He drove his students hard. He was always just as stony, just as mercilessly critical, just as precise and unsmiling, no sign ever appearing of the intimacy that had arisen between them when he had visited Leo.

The students knew of the maestro's achievements, his brilliant career and reputation. They trembled before him. They practiced hard. They knew him, but no one knew anything *about* him.

Then one evening Leo was walking home together with two of his fellow students, Jean-Cyr, a boy slightly older than Leo, and Danielle, whom they called Danielle in the Lions' Den because of the mop of wild red hair into which her face had a tendency to disappear. It was Saturday night and they had been to an evening concert, then gone dancing. They were in high spirits, a bright cloud of laughter all around them.

Leo and Jean-Cyr failed to notice the figure in black they had passed, the boys being absorbed in foolish chatter ("Listening to Mozart is like drinking champagne with your ears"); Danielle listened entranced. But she must have had her eyes about her, because she stopped her two cavaliers by tugging at their elbows.

"It's the maestro," she said breathlessly. It took Leo and Jean-Cyr a few moments to realize to whom she was referring. They stopped and stared at the half-lurching, half-creeping figure who had emerged from a side street just as they had come by. He was filthy dirty and did not appear to have seen them.

"Shall we . . . ?" Leo began uncertainly, but the others knew what he meant. The maestro would not necessarily want them to see him in this state.

"Perhaps he would prefer . . . to manage on his own," said Jean-Cyr quietly.

They could hear the maestro mumbling to himself, but not what he was saying. They were at a loss and Jean-Cyr had turned pale. The whole situation was inconceivable, even against nature. It *couldn't* be the meticulous, rigid man they knew from their lessons—it just *couldn't* be the great, world-famous artist falling into the gutter over there. What they were looking at was a wreck, a sick dog, growling noises coming from him. His face was quite different, the features blurred, the eyes almost unseeing.

Then Danielle took charge.

"Come on," she said. "We must help him. A policeman might come along. Or he might injure his hands."

They went over to him.

"Can we help you, sir?"

"Ah . . . no, but isn't it . . . ?" He was looking at them from far, far away, as if not really recognizing them. The look in his eyes showed he was trying to pull himself together.

One doesn't ask one's professor if he is drunk on such occasions, but . . .

"Are you feeling ill, sir? Has something happened to you?"

The answer was some time in coming; the maestro's voice was hoarse and slow.

"Ah," he began. "Nothing whatsover has happened. What-so-ever.

No, oh no. On the whole, generally speaking. But it's gone now. Ah yes. All of it. Yes, it has . . ."

"Gone?" said Danielle as they slowly piloted the maestro unsteadily down the street. "Gone? What's gone?"

"All of it. All my money."

"What are you saying, sir? Has someone stolen your money?" Danielle was still doing the talking; she seemed more practical than the two boys.

"The money? The money? Yes, I told you. It's the money that's gone. Ha. Damn the money, for that matter. Damn the money."

The three young people looked at each other. Leo could feel a faint nausea rising in him at the sight of the maestro. It reminded him of something, something disquieting.

"Have you lost it, then?" he interjected.

The maestro suddenly looked sharply at him.

"What a lot of questions! Well—young Lewenhaupt? Yes, it is young Lewenhaupt, isn't it? The brat from Schwabenland? Hm? The spoiled piano-playing brat with the curls? Don't you deny it. I recognize you. I've seen you as you were, I have, I know all right. I know your innermost secrets, don't forget that. What are you doing out on the streets at this time of night, young man? Hm. Shouldn't you be doing your homework? You have to practice *more*, young man. Practice more. And ask fewer questions."

Shocked, the other two gazed at their teacher.

Then he took a turn for the worse and a constable came over to them to ask whether everything was all right. Danielle, pale around the gills, told him it was all right, the gentleman was only slightly indisposed. The constable shrugged his shoulders indifferently and disappeared, muttering, "Indisposed."

Leo absently helped the others to steer the maestro along, aware now of what had happened to his teacher. It was painful to think about. He hoped the maestro would say nothing that would help Danielle and Jean-Cyr to understand what he had been talking about. Then a little farther down the street, out it all came.

"It was turning into a nice game of baccarat. I had already won a tidy sum at *à cheval*—one two three four—was it four? Five? I think I won five times running. Now I'm ruined. So this is what it feels like to be ruined."

Leo nodded faintly at the other two.

"There's a gambling den down that street," Leo said in a low voice.

"For that matter," the maestro added, almost lecturing, "for that matter, I've managed to gamble away everything I had, everything I've earned in twenty years. It's incredible how quickly fortunes come and go nowadays. Though they go faster than they come. As I said, I spent twenty years making mine. I have—let me see—pawned everything I possess, to be precise. You have to be careful when it comes to money. But tonight I got into debt after the last round. Then my violin went, too, and that was tiresome. I had to . . . hm . . . had to put it in writing that the violin was theirs, their very own, before they let me go. It was very unpleasant. Ah well."

Leo let go of the maestro.

"Not the Guarnerius!" he cried. "Not that?"

The other two also stopped and stared at the maestro as if he were a stranger.

"Yes," the maestro sighed, looking down, for moment apparently sober; then he went on jerkily: "Giu-seppe Ghu-huarneri's little riddle-fiddle."

"It can't be true," whispered Leo. *"It's not true."*

The maestro looked up, and if the three of them had not known before what was meant by a person being crushed, they now saw it in his face. But then the face darkened and he frowned, glowering at them.

"What's the matter with you all?" he snarled. "Don't you know who I *am*? If you dare so much as insinuate that . . . and what do you know about anything, anyway! Brats. What do you know about anything!"

They looked down.

"Anyway, anyway . . . it was really a bad instrument, a wretched violin," the maestro went on nonchalantly. "Not worth keeping. I'll win it back. Sure to. Nothing to worry about. Tomorrow or another evening. Sure to."

"Christ!" said Leo.

"Leo!" exclaimed Danielle, looking at him. Leo said nothing more. Then they went on helping the maestro along.

But however it happened—there he was at eight o'clock on Monday morning as usual, correctly dressed, his face blank. Danielle,

Jean-Cyr, and Leo had spent Saturday night and most of Sunday deliberating on what they should do. The only conclusion they came to was that they should keep their mouths shut. They now met the maestro's gaze with some nervous confusion as he surveyed his class, but there was nothing unusual to be seen and his eyes dwelt no longer on them than on the others. Not a muscle in his face moved. He said the usual polite good morning and opened his violin case.

A glint of gold, and the Guarnerius lay in the maestro's hand.

He began to teach.

The three of them never mentioned the matter again, nor did the maestro ever make any reference to what had happened. It really did seem as if it had not happened, as if it had all been a dream.

They never found out whether the maestro had managed to win back his instrument, or whether one of his many benefactors had helped him redeem it, or had guaranteed a loan. In the end, they almost forgot all about it. It was best to forget. In some ways, they were thankful not to look any further into the maestro's double life, because then they didn't have to know anything *about* him.

But the incident left something behind in Leo. That glimpse of understanding, of *recognition*, which had come over him when he found the maestro in the street.

That was one of the many stages in his journey.

His studies went on for six years, during which the students were not allowed to give concerts on the express orders of the maestro. Nothing incomplete was to be brought out into the light and no student concerts were held until the last two terms, when they had to prepare themselves mentally for their final diploma concert.

It was worth thinking back on those six years—a great deal of work and more practicing than before, with very little time left over for composition. But all the same, Leo was satisfied. It was a help not having to perform. In that way, drills and the exhausting work of perfecting became a task in itself, free of the thought of audiences, performing, and circuses. It was a help not living with or having to see his parents. Those first six years in Paris became something other than what he had feared. He learned a great deal.

Sometimes he almost made himself ill with longing to be able to work properly on writing music. But the stimulus from his theory teachers and from everything he heard at concerts and everything he discussed with his friends to some extent made up for the loss. He also felt profoundly uncertain about the many new trends in the music world, the many new languages. His own knowledge and means of expression were insufficient, stemming as they did from another period, another atmosphere. Everything new inspired and confused him. Apart from a few minor pieces, he wrote very little. He pushed composition aside and stuck to the violin. The symphony he had started lay untouched.

At regular intervals the thought of his cowardice, his lack of willpower, rose in him, and he thought about the curse he had put upon himself. But everything else that had happened to him, all the work he had done, took the edge off such painful thoughts. If nothing else, he met students of composition he could talk to, and his theory teachers were quietly patient when his attempts at writing music occasionally affected his real work. They were usually satisfied with him, and it was probably not only the maestro who had some inkling of what he really craved.

But that, too, the decision about it all, he pushed aside, postponing it indefinitely.

Over those years, young Leo Lewenhaupt also learned how to get along better with people. Many of his fellow students were just as rare birds as he was and had been through some of the same things. He could talk to them. He could discuss serious matters if necessary. But first and foremost, he could talk about all kinds of other things as well, silly and serious, and think up things with them—jokes and outings—because so much was tacit between them. Leo had never had any friends before as a result of his strange isolated life as a child, but also, he *was* special, different. Friendship has to be something given, something natural.

Of course, he made a great many mistakes at first in his relations to friends and teachers. He was clumsy, not used to mixing with people. To begin with, he had been rather impatient, superior, spoiled, self-absorbed—*standoffish*, quite simply. Fortunately, he had not really noticed it himself, and by the time his stay in hospital was over, the sharpest edges had been rubbed off. He not only grew out of his clothes and was able to exchange them for more normal attire for a young man—but he also seemed to grow out of himself, as if he himself had molted.

All his early life, his childhood, was cast off him, disappearing just as his old face had disappeared.

It all went inside him and there became a chrysalis.

￼-ᵥ-

Leo wrote home punctually once a month, like a clerk, dispassionately varying the form of the letters with no regard to what had really happened to him. He told them what he presumed they wanted to know. He scribbled the letters on the last Sunday of each month, and on Monday morning copied them in his best and most meticulous handwriting—the impersonal handwriting he knew his mother appreciated.

The replies came back just as punctually, mostly containing the same old admonitions and the latest exciting news from Schwaben. His father was noticeably uncommunicative when it came to horses and shooting, presumably incapable of mentioning them after what Leo had done. So his father's letters were mostly blusterings of various kinds. His mother had again become absorbed in her old interest in the royal family. She always had major or minor sensations to relate. She never mentioned her asthma—that appeared to have left with Leo.

So the falsehoods and pretense continued between them, once a month.

Otherwise he avoided as much as possible thinking about his parents as well as what he had left behind. He never went back to Henkerdingen in the holidays. It was conspicuously easy to persuade his parents that work kept him away, and the holidays *were* short. He spent the first summer alone in Paris in the suffocating, unbearable heat of the city, enjoying every moment of it. He was free, he was alone, and he did every mad thing he could think to do. At first his imagination stretched only as far as simply roaming around the darker underworld of Paris, in daylight, then at night. He was content simply to walk around *seeing* everything that had previously been forbidden him. After a while, he began to participate; then one evening he went back to his room and found to his astonishment that he was so drunk he could not stand up. The next morning he swore a solemn oath that he would never again try to see what it was like to be drunk, then got drunk every night for a week.

That was the first summer. But he spent the following summers with one or more of his friends, either going out to the country with them or going home with one of them. Jean-Cyr came from a town near Marseilles.

So for the first time in his life, Leo saw the sea. He realized what a mistake it was to have been born in Schwaben, damn it all, so far inland, with forests and horses and guns and hares. A mistake must have been made somewhere, a cosmic exchange. Waves were what he should ride, and his tools were fishing rods and nets. He was of the sea. The sun was reflected in the sea. He belonged to the sea.

Spot sat up in his bunk again, peered around, then smiled.

"Leo Lewenhaupt," he said to himself. "They were good years. Good years. Golden years."

He dug out his snuffbox and pocket mirror again, then started preparing another strip of cocaine.

Golden days. Glittering light from those days flickered around him as he sat there.

Why, he thought, why had he never asked himself at the time about where he was going? About why his face had changed? Would everything have been different if he had stopped and asked? Did he have any idea at the time what was going to happen? Had he known it deep down inside? Perhaps. Perhaps.

He thought about the sea as he had seen it that first time. He considered the sea a great friendly creature on which he had sailed away in Jean-Cyr's dinghy. It had been like being carried on the back of an older brother.

He saw the sea in front of him, one misty September day, as it lay there, quite calm and still, as if waiting.

He also thought about Danielle, Danielle in the Lions' Den, that fifth and next to last year after he had been to the sea, when he had made love to her.

Spot sniffed cocaine off the pocket mirror and again blew the last grains up at the ceiling light.

He was no longer smiling.

Intoxication took over immediately; he trembled faintly and closed his eyes. He thought about Danielle. He thought about that spring. From then on, his memories were only evil.

♈

April rain in Paris. That light, swirling moisture makes everything shiny and clean, filling the air with the smell of street dust and stars.

It is Saturday morning and Danielle comes panting in from the rain, breathless after having run up the stairs, her red hair like fire around her head, spattered with raindrops, her arms full of paper bags and an enormous bunch of flowers.

"Look, Leo!" she cries. "I've been to the market. Look! New carrots and lettuce. And *asparagus*! And fresh green peas." She crosses the room to the tiny kitchenette and starts unpacking the vegetables, first the lettuce. She has found fresh spring lettuce, emerald green and tiny.

"And the zucchini is in," she says, waving two green objects. "And look at this." She goes over to him as he sits there on the bed and thrusts the big bunch of flowers into his face.

"I've ruined myself on the flowers. Look. Anemones. Aren't they lovely?"

It is a sea of blue, red, and violet.

"And daffodils," she says. "And tulips."

The flowers are wet from the rain and smell stronger than usual. He is filled with their scent.

"Spring's come!" cries Danielle.

He smiles bleakly up at her. She ruffles his hair.

"I've bought bread and wine and cheese, and two lamb chops. You can have the biggest if you're really good. Perhaps."

He is still holding the flowers, and she has rushed back to the sink again. Then she starts to prepare the food. She has more or less moved in with him, but she has kept her own address largely for the sake of appearances and because she has to have somewhere to practice.

"Now let's make some lunch, Leo. That'll be terribly good for us."

He should have got up off the bed long ago. He should have put the flowers in water, helped her with the meal. But he stays where he is.

"A real spring feast, in other words," he says, making his voice as enthusiastic as he can, but she can hear something is wrong. She knows him very well. She drops the asparagus and looks at him, properly this time.

Then she sits down beside him. "Leo, Leo, you mustn't cry."

"No," he says. "I won't cry."

He is trembling as he lies in her arms, and far away he can hear her whispering quiet, careful words.

"What's the matter? Leo, what's the matter?"

"I'm sorry," he says. "But the mail came while you were out."

"Well?"

"There was a letter from home."

"Has something happened?"

"No. No. I suppose you'll think it's silly, but . . . but they want me to go back home for the summer."

"Well?"

"I haven't been home for four years. I think I simply *must* go this time, but . . ."

"Leo . . ." She holds him tight.

"Mother writes . . . she writes to say they would like to give a concert or two, now that I'm at home so seldom. A private concert. Just like in the old days. And . . ."

"Is that so bad?"

"Danielle, you don't understand. You don't know what they're *like*. I can't say no. I know perfectly well what it'll be like. They've planned it all already, and I bet you anything the invitations have been sent out. And there's sure to be an impresario hanging around in the wings. It'll be just the same as before. Just the same. And I . . . When I read the letter just now, it was as if everything went black. I thought—"

"Leo," she says. "It's only a concert."

He stiffens and jerks away from her.

"That's easy for *you* to say," he says in a stifled voice. "You're always so clever. You can just get up there on the stage and do what you're going to do, just like that, before curtsying and leaving. You don't have any nerves."

That is not true. She looks down, trying to hide that he has hurt her.

"You have no idea what they're like. Do you remember I once told you I shot my horse and my dog, just before leaving home? Can you believe that they were more bothered about the horse, the poor horse, than about their *son*, who had actually shot it, who had for some reason or other shot it. They were touching in their concern for the deceased. But it was my horse. And it was a good shot. Bang in the middle of its forehead. You should have seen Father fussing over the body. *I* was sent to bed after he had beaten me. I wasn't even allowed to wash the blood and muck off me. Do you think they've ever even *thought* about what made me do it?"

"Yes, Leo. I think they actually did. They're fairly sure to have."

"What do you know about it? What do you know about it?"

She holds him again.

"I haven't given a concert for four years," he says after a while. Then out it comes. "And I hope . . . I hope I never have to again."

The next moment he starts trembling, trembling as if he were being torn apart, exactly like that time in the music room, a cold darkness growing all around him. He had almost forgotten what it was like, had persuaded himself everything was different now. But in reality everything was just as before, and oh, he had imagined, imagined— there was such a lot he had imagined. He had imagined he was free.

He could hear her voice as if it were coming through soft material. "Leo. Dear Leo."

⚜

A long time afterward, the world is more at peace and he is lying in her arms. He opens his eyes and looks at her. She is troubled. She's a fine girl, honest and brave, from a good home, and she has read everything. There is a strange person living in that lions' den. She is sitting looking at him and she is troubled.

He smiles cautiously up at her. He has almost calmed down now.

"I would really like to be with you this summer," he whispers.

"But surely you're not going to be there all summer?"

"Probably. If I know them."

She strokes his forehead and looks searchingly at him.

"I wish you could come with me," he says after a while.

"You know that wouldn't be decent," she says, smiling.

"Yes, it would," he says. "As long as you *would* . . ."

"*Would . . . ?*"

He interrupts her—"The flowers!" he cries, holding up a daffodil he has been lying on; they are nearly all crushed.

"Never mind the flowers," she says. "What was it I perhaps *would* . . . ?

"To be honest, Danielle, I don't know how one . . ."

She smiles.

"It's usually done like this," she says. "You kneel before the desired one, hand her a flower, and then you ask."

He holds out the daffodil and looks at her, a question in his eyes. That is as far as he can go.

"This is probably terribly foolish," she says. "I think you're fairly mad."

He shakes his head.

"I think it's just because you don't want to be alone."

"No," he says. "Danielle."

She grows serious.

"Yes," she says. "Yes. Yes."

He pulls her down to him and they cling to each other.

Then, when it is afternoon, she says, "Did you mean what you said?"

"Yes." He is still quite giddy. "Of course, I meant to ask you whether you would . . ."

"Not that, Leo. I mean the other thing. Did you really mean you never want to give concerts?"

She is looking penetratingly at him. He does not know what to say and thrusts his face into her shoulder.

"All right, all right," she says. "So be it."

They ate the lamb chops for dinner instead. Danielle had the biggest one.

⚜

So they went to Henkerdingen together, and it was dreadful, just as bad as he had feared. His mother was beside herself with pride, nervousness, and curiosity. They hardly recognized Leo. His mother clapped her hands and cried out in dismay, and his father was embarrassed to find that Leo was now taller than he. They looked searchingly at Danielle. She was soon to be displayed to everyone. It did not improve matters that Danielle knew little German and his father

had an ingrained distrust of all frog-eating Gauls. He entertained his
guest with grim stories about the 1871 war. The whole summer became a play, a performance. Leo bravely acted his part and he *did*
give the concert, and two more. He could see Danielle struggling to
keep a straight face, striving to converse with his parents, to be
friendly. He knew she was doing it for his sake, but it pained him to
see her walking arm in arm with his mother, like sisters. His father
gave him a long lecture on the duties and joys of matrimony and Leo
had to go out and run it off afterward, otherwise he would have been
ill. Everything was stuffy, stuffy and oppressive. The concert was
dreadful. He thought he had changed, that all that evil lay behind
him. Now his old self came back, and he trembled and was afraid and
vomited. Things were happening inside him, upheavals, incomprehensible processes. Danielle had to bear the brunt.

She always had to bear the brunt.

When they were alone, he took it all out on her. He realized it, but
could not restrain himself. It simply poured out of him. Even then he
did not understand what an egoist he was, the way he was behaving.
It was to take many years before he understood what he had done.
Had she loved him a little less and answered back . . . But Danielle
was one of those rare people who *bear*, and she bore with him, and
she listened to him and held him and put up with most things. His
whole childhood rose in him again. She bore the brunt. Oh yes, the
old Leo was still living within him, changed, masked, and far more
sophisticated in his self-absorption. Him, him. All that summer was
about him. Danielle said nothing. But she cried on the train on their
way back, and she had dark circles under her eyes.

They married at the end of September, a simple civil wedding in
Paris, for neither of them was a believer. Leo's parents had started
making plans for the wedding, and his mother had insane expectations
of an outstanding white event, but somehow or other Leo had managed to stop them when he saw the panic in Danielle's eyes. That
cost his mother an asthma attack and four days of icy shoulders whenever they brushed past each other in the house, but he had his own
way.

They married, moved into a tiny apartment, and both continued
their studies.

All that autumn violent upheavals kept happening inside Leo, conscious and unconscious feelings rising and falling, although outwardly

he was calm. At the New Year, Danielle had to hold him and watch over him for several nights when he had an acute anxiety attack. It became more serious when the student concerts started, for Danielle also had her own struggles with them, but he hardly noticed. He neither helped her draw up her program nor even replied when she suggested they play duets. They had often done that before with great success and both had enjoyed it. But now Leo did not answer, as if he had not even heard.

In between he drank a little.

One evening in March he threatened to ruin his hands by holding them over the gas flame and keeping them there until they were so badly burned he could never play again. She had to pull them away by force. He was miserable, almost angry with her because she had seen him so degraded, this time, and many times before.

"I don't want to anymore," he said. "I don't want to be a soloist. I want to compose. That's all I want to do."

This time she gave the same answer, though not until after a long pause. So be it, she said quietly and resignedly.

"In God's name," she said.

That was how it came about that Leo never received his diploma, much to the exasperation of his teachers and fellow students.

Danielle passed with flying colors, and by the winter they had a daughter.

Ten years of your life, Leo Lewenhaupt. His life as a composer had lasted ten years. And that was a lie. All a lie.

Ten years of new studies. Of insane projects never finding fruition. Bills kept coming. Leo's parents no longer contributed anything after the final break, and Danielle was too proud to accept anything from hers. Leo's habits were expensive—more expensive than he himself realized, and they also had little Josephine. If things had been right between them and in Leo's work, they would have survived those years, but Leo took little part in his own life. Even his daughter often left him unmoved. Occasionally he was frightened of himself.

Danielle steals across the floor, three-year-old Josephine in her arms. He can hear them as he sits there writing, but he knows he must

grant his daughter the delight of frightening him. They stop just behind him. Then Danielle leans over his shoulder, Josephine thrusts
her little head into the hollow of his neck while both of them cry
"Boo!"

Josephine chuckles at the terrified face he makes.

"Again!" she cries. "Again!" Danielle lifts her up and they do it
all over again. Josephine's hair is golden and curly and tickles his face.
He sniffs. Her very body seems to be fragrant, sweet, like cinnamon.

"Again, again!"

"No," says Leo. "I think I've been frightened enough for today.
I'm working."

"Papa workin'."

"Yes, Josephine." He looks down at the little face turned pleadingly up at him, wanting something of him. She is his child, *his* child.
What does she want of him?

"Danielle," he says abruptly, "can you take a look at this. What do
you think of it?" He hands her a sheet of music. She stands looking
at it, frowning. Leo does not look at the child, but he can sense her
expression, disappointment, her mouth turned down.

Danielle fetches the violin and plays through the bars.

"It's good, Leo," she says. "It's good."

"Yes, do you think so, too? Don't you think so?"

"If I'm to say anything," Danielle begins carefully, "it's only a
thought—it's a bit stiff at the end here . . ."

"Stiff?"

"Nothing much *happens*. G, C, E—maybe it isn't so unexpected?"

He bangs his hand on the desk in annoyance.

"Stiff!" he cries.

"Papa *workin'*," says Josephine thoughtfully.

"Yes, but you asked me what I thought, Leo. Don't you want me
to be honest? I said I thought it was good."

"Yes," he says meekly. "You did."

He knows she is right. He knows the sketch he has done is ordinary
and like everything else—but not himself. That's the way it goes
most of the time. He has an idea, two to three bars, a promising start,
but then it dries up, becomes dust in his fingers, trickling out into
insignificant generalities.

Is he too proud to admit it? Or too cowardly?

"Would you keep an eye on Josephine?" says Danielle. "I must go out for a while."

He sighs heavily.

"Will you be long?"

"No," she says quietly. "I won't be long."

Josephine crouches down and looks up at him. What shall he do with her? After a while, he also crouches down. They say nothing. A moment or two passes before they find something to do.

They draw.

"Look now, Josephine, I'm drawing a boat. Sailing on the sea."

"Not draw boat," she says cautiously.

"Don't you want to draw a boat? Look at the boat," says Leo in a strained voice. "It's sailing beautifully. And a boy's fishing in it."

"Not draw boy."

"Oh well, we'll draw a little girl. A little girl in the boat."

"Not boat."

"As you like," says Leo resignedly, dropping the red crayon. "What do you want to draw, then?" He is clearly not much good at either composing or drawing.

Josephine looks long and searchingly at him, and that look to him seems terrible.

"Papa *nice*," she says. *"Nice."* Then she puts her arms around his neck. He holds her, not knowing what to do, clumsily running his hand over her head. He is made to think about a little boy playing with the sun, but who couldn't play. It's a thousand years ago, a thousand sun-years. And he is made to think about another little girl who sat in the grass looking solemnly at him. They did not speak the same language. They were far away from each other. A thousand years ago, that, too. He thinks about it all as he strokes and strokes this little stranger's hair.

These were great times in the world of music, just as they were in the worlds of art and literature. Things were being composed in new ways; there was a whole new mode of expression. Discussions raged between classicists and the new Germans. Programs changed, premieres were howled down or greeted with frenzied applause. New truths were being sought, new languages, one revision following another, with absolute music and the myth of genius. Then new myths came, and new concepts.

In all this, Leo Lewenhaupt fell short. But he composed, major and minor pieces, with major or minor success, barely sufficient for a living. He was considered promising by a great many people, but they felt that his great breakthrough was yet to come.

The fact that he was able to compose as he had always wanted to did not bring him peace, did not free him as he had hoped. Leo sensed the truth and that was what destroyed it all, namely, that it was a lie. It was all a lie. He had no mode of expression of his own; he was incapable of breaking through his own limitations and finding a language which was genuine. What was his, what arose immediately, was of a past age. So he developed inhibitions, scruples, and periods of total block, of powerlessness.

He realized quite soon that he had probably drawn his bow too hard, that he was meant for something he was not able to do, but he could find no way back. His own pride and cowardice stopped him. He could have turned, but he had an inkling of what was perfect and he was more than sufficiently gifted to know the difference between what was great and genuine and what was false. And that—knowing, but not being able—that made him ill.

Then there was his self-love—if only he had managed to *see*, if only he had managed to take part in his own life. But more and more the dream he lived for receded, the dream of being able to hunt with the great hunters on the wide-open spaces, the rich hunting grounds. The dream of the sun.

Oh, how he could dream! He dreamed of everything he was to write, great beautiful dreams, but on paper they all turned to ashes. So he wrote less and less, in the end writing practically nothing.

If only he could have seen. Instead, he destroyed Danielle, the finest person he had ever met, and he destroyed her without wanting to see, almost deliberately. He could have understood, but he made himself blind, just as he had when he entered into this marriage. Out of anxiety of being alone? Wasn't that why? Wasn't it?

This responsibility and guilt were to burden him for the remainder of his life. After six years, Danielle managed to pluck up the courage to start giving concerts again, but something in her had been broken.

Nothing was as before, and her playing lacked concentration and balance. So she started to teach, something for which Leo inevitably showed his contempt and which she herself truly disliked. In this way, Leo's self-contempt and self-absorption infected everything around him—and her. She was still courageous, braver than she had the strength for. She must have promised herself something when he had proposed. He was a child who did not know it. He never even considered helping her to keep that promise. For had *he* really promised anything? Did he try to keep anything?

He was a man with no means of keeping promises. His whole life consisted of promises he did not keep, so he lied. Both his work and his life with her died because the essential ability was lacking, the talent it depended on.

And so, without love, he slowly destroyed his own life.

After nine years Danielle left him and took their daughter with her, their actual departure quiet and undramatic, in keeping with Danielle. She had paid all the bills, cleared everything up, and put all the papers in place, indeed, written little lists for him. Then she calmly and matter-of-factly told him she was still fond of him, more fond of him than she cared to think about, but that she did not think he understood what it meant to be fond of someone.

Leo probably knew what she meant, but there was a scene and he was contemptible enough to beg her, implore her, accuse her, attack her, and heap reproaches on her. So she just left, right in the middle of it all.

For a few months he felt better than he had for a long time, enjoying his freedom. Then winter came and he found himself doing nothing but yearning for her, for her hands, her embraces, her words. He tried to get her back, but she did not answer his letters. He longed for his daughter, whom he had never really been able to care about —he used the gas-bill money to buy a china doll for Josephine and lied in the accompanying letter to Danielle, saying it was money he had earned from compositions. So he had to manage without gas for a while.

But it was his own loss occupying him, not his wife and daughter. He cultivated that loss.

He was twenty-nine and had gray streaks in his hair.

He buried himself in his work, a last terrible journey through de-

spair. Every stroke of the pen had now become as loathsome as concerts and appearances had once been.

❧

He tried to write a symphony, as a starting point using the old sketch,
a theme from long ago, from a cold and amazing night in Giessen.

He put all he had into his work, clinging to it as if to a life buoy.
It was to save him, take him to a place where everything was right
again, where there was no longer a dividing line between falsehood
and truth.

❧

"Well well? Isn't it young Lewenhaupt?"

"Who? Me? . . . Maestro!"

Leo leaped up from his chair, almost tipping over his glass of absinthe, and pressed the maestro's hand.

"May I sit down?" The voice was as before, carrying through the
noise of talk and clinking glasses. It was dark in the cramped premises,
but Leo could see the maestro had also aged, though the eyes were
the same, and the sharp little smile.

"Well," said the maestro. "It's been a long time."

"Yes. How many years?"

"The years . . . let's not think about them. When you get to my
age, you don't like thinking about them. It's as if they have become
a forest. And one day a wind will come through that forest and the
trees will fall."

"Five years, at least."

"Sure to be. How are things going?"

"Very well, thank you."

"Really? I'm glad to hear it. I must say, Lewenhaupt— Well, shall
we have something to drink? What are you drinking?"

Leo nodded at his glass.

"Precisely," said the maestro. "Waiter, let's have two more of these.
Well, where were we? Danielle."

"Precisely . . ."

"I must say, Lewenhaupt, I expected something of you two. Of
both of you. Really expected something."

"So did we, actually, I'm afraid."

"And now you're here." The glasses of absinthe came. "Do you often come here?"

"Every evening."

"Ah well. And your composing?"

Leo was still for a long time; then he said, "Maestro, last night I went and heard Debussy. *Après-midi d'un faune.*"

"Oh yes. I was there, too. I didn't see you."

"I was standing. At the back."

"Well?"

"I listened. I wept. With joy and anger. His music is like a parasol. He walks with it under his arm, and once down by the sea, he opens it up, orange and big and beautiful."

"Yes . . ."

"I wept. Can you remember . . . Do you remember you once predicted many tears and many difficult nights for me?"

"Yes, Leo. I remember."

"I have been composing for several years now, Maestro. You've heard some it, I know that. Tell me honestly. What do you think?"

The maestro was silent for a while.

"To be honest," he said, "your pieces all show good musical talent and good craftsmanship."

"Yes?"

"But no more."

Leo was still for a long time. Then he said, "I once had a language. It was *our* language. The musical language of Europe. The mother tongue of Beethoven, Mozart, and Haydn. It was suited to elevated, intricate artistic expression and could at the same time be simple, universally understandable. I grew up with that language. I lived in the sound of it from when I was small. Then I grew up and found that language had been taken over, exploited, made banal. By the petty bourgeoisie. By Herr and Frau Biedermeier. By my parents. It was used for pretty little pieces—for sale for pianos in thousands of homes. The *universal,* what is that now? *Waltzes.* The waltz kings borrow phrases from our musical heritage—for mass production. The waltz kings get rich."

"Very rich," said the maestro.

"And the content . . . gives itself away in the banalities of Offenbach. The language which was ours, in which I could express myself, has been destroyed. The Biedermeiers have plumped their fat back-sides on it. The way to a true, artistic mode of expression goes else-where today, into something else, something new."

The maestro looked at him with interest.

"And," Leo went on, "it has been like that for a long time."

"Yes," said the maestro. "It was like that before you were born."

"Yes! Yes! I discovered that when I came here to Paris. I discovered I had been a knickknack, an ornament, nothing else. Of Meissen porcelain. And I was put on display. Anywhere they thought they could line me up."

"Yes," said the maestro, nodding. "You looked terrible."

"And I thought I could wipe out the lie. I thought it was enough to sweep everything aside, smash that porcelain figure. I thought it was all right to clear the air, begin again, in the truth. Create a new language. I wanted to be rid of the lie. But I myself was part of it. It didn't work."

"I'm not sure I quite follow you."

"Maestro, I heard Debussy's new piece last night."

"Yes?"

"I can't create. I haven't got what it takes. Not what is for *now*. My abilities seem to slip through my fingers."

The maestro stared at him. "I presume you mean this, Leo?"

"Yes. I *hear* no music any longer. It has gone. And I myself have done away with it."

Again the maestro was still.

"And that time," Leo said. "In our music room, when you . . . you didn't tell me that—"

"Well now," said the maestro. "Don't say I didn't warn you."

"No," said Leo. "I didn't mean that, either."

The maestro emptied his glass. "That," he said with a grimace, "tastes awful. It's for infants. Not for grown men."

Leo wasn't listening. "But I can't stop dreaming about it!" he exclaimed. "That's all I *want* to do. It's the only thing I've ever desired, to write music. To compose something great, something true!"

The maestro looked at him, a momentary glint of malice in his dark eyes.

"Many are called," he said gently, "but few are chosen." He smiled briefly.

"And you . . . are you one of the chosen?"

"Leo. Little brother. You could have been an excellent violinist."

"But not one of the chosen, not there either?"

"No, perhaps not."

"But I knew . . ."

"Yes, Leo. You *knew* everything. You were very good. Had the techniques at your fingertips. Literally speaking. Just as you almost certainly master the techniques and theory of composition."

"But what is it it depends *on?*"

The maestro looked at him in surprise. Then he laughed. He laughed long and loud. Leo was annoyed at first, then wondered. He had never heard the maestro laugh before.

"Leo, Leo," the old man said, "I apologize for my untimely laughter at such a serious and self-searching moment. But I am over sixty and I have never found out what it depends *on*. What it is that separates the genuine from the false, the genuine from the superficial, and what it is that makes one person an artist and another a craftsman. To tell you the truth, I don't even know on which side of the border I myself am."

"I want to die, Maestro."

"Nonsense! Do you have creditors?"

"There's another outside the door every time I go home."

"Then you won't die. There's still someone who needs you."

"For Christ's—"

"Now, now. Don't fly off the handle. You have a wife. You have a . . . isn't it a little daughter?"

"Yes. Josephine. She'll soon be ten."

"They're waiting for you."

"I can't go there. I don't even think she would have me. And even if she would . . . I wouldn't manage it. I haven't got what Danielle and Josephine need."

"Leo, my prediction still holds good. You have many tearful nights before you. The journey has only just begun. The journey lasts longer than you think. It's always like that. *But you will carry it through!*" He almost shouted the latter. "You *must* carry it through, at all costs, regardless. Regardless of where it takes you."

"Even if I can't create?"

"Of course you can create, Leo. You're richly equipped. The question is just *what.*"

Leo shook his head.

"Well, you'll see. Wait and see. Anyway, I have to tell you that I've given up teaching."

Leo looked up, startled.

"Look," said the maestro. He laboriously removed his gloves and held out his hands. They were curled up like claws. "Arthritis," he said.

"Does it . . . hurt badly?"

"Not really. Only when I play." He smiled again, and again that glint of malice played in his eyes.

"My God," said Leo.

"So nowadays I just go around thinking. I am waiting. I can still handle the chips. And I have enough money. One has one's sources. It was because of my hands that I gave up giving concerts, by the way, and started teaching. I noticed quite early on that it was coming. That's why I always wore black silk. For warmth. And now I'm here."

"My God," mumbled Leo again.

"I still have my Guarnerius. I had really thought of giving it away. Deep down, I had thought of giving it to you. Just imagine, I think I decided the very first time we met that you should have it, when the time came."

"No," said Leo. "Anything else!"

"Don't worry, you won't get it."

"Thank goodness."

"It's worth . . . more than money. But . . . but can you think of anyone who might have better use for it? . . . I mean, it just lies there in its case."

"No," said Leo. "Who could that be?"

"Leo. You're a fool. Can you remember when you were still in my class and how I had to think for you all at regular intervals? Yes, for you, too. I thought through the piece, thought aloud for you so that you would learn to see intentions and lines as clearly as mathematical reasoning. Don't you remember?"

"Yes, I do."

"Now I will do your thinking for you again. As you can't do it yourself. I was thinking, Leo, of leaving my Guarnerius to your wife. Can you give me her address?"

"To Dan—"

". . . to Danielle, yes. Danielle in the Lions' Den. Serious little

Danielle. Who once picked me up off the street. And who . . . as far as I can make out . . . has picked you up several times over the years. She is to have it."

"But she . . . she doesn't give concerts any longer."

"No, Leo," said the maestro acidly. "She doesn't. I can't think why. I don't even want to think why. But . . . and here again I have to do your thinking for you . . . perhaps she could start again."

Leo gaped.

"The most important thinking," said the maestro, pointing to his head, "is not in here between the ears. Primary thinking is here," he went on, clutching his chest with his deformed hands.

Leo said nothing.

"And now," said the maestro, "I must go. I've sat here swallowing this slop long enough. Ugh!"

"Wait," said Leo. "Wait."

"Are you afraid of being alone?"

"Yes," said Leo, looking down. "Where are you going?"

"I don't think you'd like to know. A place where I go when my hands ache."

"Where?"

The maestro looked piercingly at Leo. "I don't know whether it would be right," he said. "In the state you're in."

"Take me with you."

"Listen, Leo. It's at your own risk."

"Yes," said Leo.

"You'll have to be responsible for every step you take from now on. No one will come along and pick you up."

"At my own risk," said Leo.

They left together.

❧

That was how Leo came to visit the Association des Assassins for the first time. The place was well concealed in a shabby courtyard in the twelfth arrondissement, two floors up, quiet and dim, with a row of separate cabinettes along a long, dark, winding corridor. A hunchback in a turban took their coats and hats, then showed them into a salon lit by red lamps, with soft carpets and Oriental ottomans; a few people were already seated in a semicircle around a low table. Leo recognized some of them, a painter, a writer—then he realized where he was.

The hookah was on the low table in the center of the circle.

"Stranger, are you seeking pleasure or relief?"

"He's with me," the maestro said sourly. "He's to have nothing. He's just looking around."

"Sir, if you'll excuse me—you know that guests are not allowed here."

"Nonsense," said the maestro. "Do you know who I am, little gnome. Get back to your cloakroom. And get a doctor to change that bandage on your head. It's too tight."

"Relief! Relief!" exclaimed Leo. Someone from the semicircle around the hookah hushed him. Leo had been watching them and seen their faces softening and changing as the effects took hold. "Relief," he said again, almost pleading. "Relief."

The hunchback threw out his hands and smiled acidly at the maestro.

The maestro sighed; then they took their places.

Unaccustomed and uncertain, Leo inhaled the smoke for the first time. The maestro leaned over toward him.

"At your own risk, Leo," he said.

"Yes," said Leo, nodding and smiling. He had to smile because his mouth had turned unspeakably dry and his lips stuck to his teeth when he tried to speak.

"You're a child, Leo."

"Yes," said Leo. "Yes, I know. I want this."

"I thought as much," said the maestro, taking a pull on the hookah himself.

Leo watched the air melting away and become flickering colors. Far away somewhere he could hear music, an echo of the great hum, the hum of the sun filled with solemnity that had been all around him, raising him to great dreams and then letting him fall, fall down into the dark. Again he was approaching the sun. Again he was a child, and there was no line between falsehood and truth, no line between what he wanted and what he was.

That was Leo's first visit to the Association des Assassins, and it amused him slightly that it was the maestro who had taken him. Leo often went back. He found a kind of peace there.

⚜

Leo. Leo Lewenhaupt. That was your life. And when a few months later you fled from your creditors and the failure of your symphony, you shed your name. No one was ever to hear it again.

A great many other names followed.

You are resigned now, Leo, totally resigned. There is silence inside you and all around you. There is no music. Once you were a little boy in the sunlight, and that little boy was sliced in two, between what was *him* and what was his language. He became a liar without wanting to, and thus no longer a whole human being.

You are a dead earth sailing through empty space. You listen but do not hear. There is no heaven.

But you can still go on living. You can try to live with no resistance, with no dreams—until life fetches you, or death. You can try to go *through* nothingness. You speak foreign languages. You can live everywhere. You can play the piano in cafés and for the waltz kings. You can hide in the palm courts of hotels and in the second violin of seductive melodies of human dreams. One day something will happen and then you will no longer exist. But you, Leo Lewenhaupt, child prodigy and knickknack, liar and seeker of the truth—you will live on. You will live on in every banal tune the light orchestra plays. You will live on in the beautiful dreams of cultivated audiences. You will live in the truth and in the falsehood. You are there in the battle songs of the workers and the sophisticated soloist's dream of the greatness of the human spirit. You will live on in everything that creates. One day perhaps someone—or something—will heal your wounds, and you, Leo, the human being, will be whole again. One day you will be yourself again, whole, and you will speak the truth, will be able to love, and you will sing.

❧

Spot got up off the bunk, went over to the cabin door, and put on his hat and coat. He wanted to go out, needed to go out and walk.

He laughed lightly to himself. As he stood there, thinking back, everything seemed almost simple, so simple it all almost dissolved into nothing. But he knew—deep down he knew that what *now* seemed simple was evil and insuperable when he was sober.

Ah well, he thought, shrugging it off. All defeat, all of it. It just *seems* great because it is about myself. Everything about myself is supposed to be so very great and important. In reality you have man-

aged to save the world from yet another arrogant semi-talented artist.
And Danielle and Josephine? You should never have married. What
had you to offer another person? It was good that she left. Best like
that. She should have gone before. I wonder if he gave her the violin.
Perhaps she is playing again.

He tied his scarf.

All defeat, he thought. That's the story of your life.

He hurried out the door.

❧

That was Spot's story.

❧

He almost collided with a small figure in the corridor.

"Spot," said the voice, strange and distant, through walls of time.
"Spot."

The air seemed to be full of shapes bulging and rippling all around
them.

Spot laughed loudly. He was feeling good now, the air full of time
and sounds playing for him, playing all the things he otherwise no
longer heard. And he had remembered, and thought, and he knew he
himself did not matter, that he did not *exist*. When it came down to
it, he did not exist.

Spot realized he had to get up on deck to the stars and the sea. He
laughed again. Then he recognized David.

"Come with me," he said warmly and gently. David hesitated for
a moment, looking intently at the pianist.

"I'm asleep, you see," said Spot in German, with a natural intimacy.
"I've committed the little sleep." He laughed again, this time at the
expression. David looked at him anxiously and said something. Spot
could make out the name Jason, but at that moment the name said
little to him. Jason. Jason was something far away and had nothing to
do with him. But this David, on the other hand, this sympathetic
young man—they had tuned the piano together. That was true. Spot
laughed again. He had to explain a thing or two to this young man.
David, David. What was it the others had said about David? Something. Something mean. It would be good if I could give him a helping
hand on his way, Spot thought. He took David's arm and pulled him
along.

David had no idea what was up with Spot and responded to the warmth and friendship suddenly coming from him.

"I'm going up on deck to look at the night," said Spot. "And you're to come with me." Spot really could *see* David now, see him properly. He could see him with all his senses—not dully and apathetically as usual. David was a young boy, almost a child, and Spot had a great deal of childhood in him that evening. So David had to come, too, for Spot wanted his company in all this. So with no more fuss, he took David by the arm and pulled him along.

David went willingly, though wondering. As they moved along corridors and up stairs, Spot was chatting and laughing, and it did David good to hear him, although there was little coherence in what he was saying. But David enjoyed the warm friendship, even if he could not understand it.

They came up onto the promenade deck. That late, there were only a few night strollers out, so they almost had the whole deck and all the stars to themselves. Spot let go of David once they were out in the fresh air, then flung his arms out. He crossed over to the railing and stared out across the sea, now dark and calm, the sky a little cloudy on the horizon. It was impossible to see where the sea ended and the sky began. But above them, in the zenith, it was cloudless and all the stars were out.

"Look!" said Spot. "Listen!" Then he was quite still.

David looked. And David listened.

This is what he saw. Among a thousand others, the ship is also a star sailing through the night. White foam gushes from the bows. The hull trembles. Lanterns send spears of light out into the darkness. On board—people behind portholes and lounge windows. Millionaires and galley boys. The nightshift of stokers going to work in the bowels of the ship, the weary evening shift tumbling into the washroom and washing off the coal dust and grease, calling to each other in hoarse voices. Then they fall asleep almost before they have stretched out in their bunks. The ship is a star. Waiters and deck boys are playing cards in the mess. Three members of the ship's band are drinking tea and rum. In the first-class smoking room, William Stead and Major Archibald Butt, President Taft's advisor, are peacefully discussing prospects for peace. Otherwise the smoking room is empty and the ship is about to settle down for the night. But out on the third-class promenade deck a young couple are walking back and forth, arms tightly around each other, back and forth without speaking. They have no desire to go inside. A star of dreams.

David and Spot stand there sensing all this. Listen. Listen. A faint singing is coming from the ship. It is humming. Just as it hums in telegraph antennae. Morse signals are going out through the ether, out into the great night. The wireless never sleeps. John Phillips, the wireless operator, is on duty, sending words out into the night. Words and dreams. Wireless telegraphy is incomprehensible, even Phillips thinks that, although, as opposed to the general public, he has some idea of what is happening when the signals go out. He has chosen his profession because it has something of a dream in it. It is a sober, quiet profession, in which you have to listen.

Totally different is the enthusiasm of the passengers, particularly in first class, for the entertainment offered by the wireless. In the purser's office, they can fill out telegraph forms—just as they can ashore—which are then sent up to the Marconi room through a tube. There the wireless operator, for twelve shillings and tuppence for the first ten words, and ninepence for every additional word, sends the telegram on. The passengers send greetings and messages, many of them saying nothing and a few important, until far into the night. To and from all the other steamers crisscrossing the ocean that night. A worried American woman has sent a message to her nephew on board the eastbound *Caronia*. DON'T FORGET YOUR SCARF WHEN YOU GO ON DECK IT IS COLD AUNT GEORGIA. A gambler, one of the many impossible to get rid of professional poker players on the Atlantic run, telegraphs a colleague on board the *Olympic*, sailing east: BUSINESS IS GOOD ALL WELL HAL. The poker player has had luck on his side on the trip (they *always* do, however they manage that)—so he can afford to send a longer message to a girl in New York—God help us, a whole Shakespearean sonnet. No doubt he has something to make up for. It does not come cheap. Phillips dutifully thumps out the poem, word by word, to the shore station at Cape Race, where other wireless operators are sending the messages on via the American telegraph network. The signals tick constantly on into the small hours. Phillips has dark rings under his eyes, for a coil had gone the night before and the station was silent while he and Bride, his colleague, repaired it. The telegraph forms have piled up and he hasn't slept for eighteen hours. His back is bowed as he taps out the words, sending the passengers' worries, playful jokes, witticisms, and information, small and great. The antennae hum, and through the night come messages from other ships, either direct or from Cape Race. Some of the messages are to the captain. The *Livia* and the *Puck* report fog near the American coast. The *Borderer* reports ice. So does the *Hellig Olav*. The *Mesaba* reports ICE BETWEEN 41° AND 50° NORTH AND BETWEEN 49° AND 50° WEST STOP LARGE ICEBERGS ALSO FIELD ICE DRIFTING STOP PLEASE INFORM CAPTAIN. Papers with incoming and outgoing messages pile up. The North Atlantic night is full of sounds, full of the humming song of the telegraph, from the coast of Ireland to Newfoundland, signals running through the night, fragments of words, about the weather, about ice, and bits of pure dreams.

That is the ship. If you listen really hard, you seem to capture all the other bits and pieces rising from the ship, all the dreams of the night, torn from their waking connections. Breathing in dark cabins. A child sleeps safely beside its mother in third class, dreaming about a dog, a nice retriever. A stoker dreams about his wife and son back in Southampton. A girl lies half asleep, thinking about some green woods in Ireland. There's something fine about those woods where she once had an adventure. The captain is asleep, too. Heavy and white-bearded, his expression stern, he is lying stretched out on his couch, a figure on a medieval tomb, a king or a knight in stone above his remains. Captain Smith sleeps lightly, as captains have to. He sleeps and his dream is awake. His dream is the ship.

The ship glides on through space, its course staked out. It is holding course well. Now and again a wandering star glides by somewhere out in the darkness; a lantern appears just above the horizon, glints, and disappears again.

High up in the crow's nest the lookout is peering ahead: a calm, wide-awake eye in the darkness between the sea and the stars. He is a seaman and is not cold. Beside him he has a telephone with a line to the bridge. The helmsman is standing like a cross at the wheel, immobile in the faint light from the instrument panels, looking out, out into nothing.

A ship of dreams. Spot and David at the railing. David's face changes as they stand there—a long time. He is dreaming himself.

+

"Well," said Spot. He is more himself now. "Well, David. Where do you actually come from?"

"I'm Viennese," said David after a slight pause.

"Oh yes, that was it. And what are you doing here on board?"

David did not reply.

"Jason," said Spot. "Our good friend and leader, Jason, says you've run away from home. The others think so, too."

David remained silent.

"Listen," said Spot kindly, "I don't want to pester you."

"Thank you," said David in a small voice.

"You don't pester me, and you came up here with me. I have my secrets, too."

David did not look at him.

"But there was something about you just now, when we were looking out. Is it a girl?"

David was quite still.

"So it does have something to do with a girl," said Spot cautiously. "Am I right?"

"Yes," said David. "You're right."

Spot hesitated, then said, "Should you take it so badly?"

David turned to face him, his eyes glittering, but he said nothing.

"So it's a love story of *that* kind," said Spot. "A real love story."

"Yes," said David. "A real love story."

Oh, du lieber Augustin,
Alles ist hin!

—OLD VIENNESE SONG

DAVID'S STORY

———◆●◆●◆———

IT was one of the last days at the summer camp; a kind of farewell atmosphere already permeated the large yellow main building. Not one of the hundred and twenty boys wanted to do what he was told any longer, as if they had to make use of their last moments of freedom, a final reason to get up to some devilry before the city and their parents again placed everyday limitations on them.

The camp leader, Captain Rindebraden, was in despair, to put it mildly—particularly after what had happened that day.

The captain was a powerful ex-cavalryman in his mid-sixties with a curly red mustache. He wore wool even at the end of July, had a modest state pension, having retired after a bullet wound, and was now employed as the leader at a summer camp. He tried his best to put into practice the ideas of Baden-Powell for the training of youth, combining them with his own ideas of what he called "wholesome living." This wholesome living was a kind of ideal state of existence best achieved by following a regimen the captain referred to as his Health System. The System consisted of gymnastics, and hot-and-cold baths, combined with foot care, eight hours' sleep, and lamb's-wool socks with fingers for each toe like gloves. Rindebraden himself wore, or so he said, only linen underwear beneath the wool, and he impressed on the boys that every mouthful of food—oatmeal, too—was to be chewed thirty-two times.

Understandably enough, Captain Rindebraden had some difficulty carrying out parts of his System with the boys at this summer camp, but things ran smoothly for the most part. The boys from the capital were often close to total exhaustion for the first three weeks of their month's stay, owing to all that fresh air, running around in forest and field, and not least because of the captain's exercises, which consisted to a large extent of twisting. After such a day's routine and a final cold shower at night, some boys found to their astonishment that they were asleep before they had even reached their bunks. So there was not much time for mischief. But the same thing always happened during the last week of their stay, however hard he had driven them. The boys, all between ten and fourteen, were now fit enough for the program and as a result had a deplorable excess of vitality. So they invested it in illicit expeditions after bedtime, in orgiastic visits to the dining room, in playing hooky and lounging about, and not least in visits to the other side of the water.

The last was a particularly severe offense.

The handsome camp building was near Ischl, in gentle wooded countryside by a lake. The girls' camp was on the other side of this lake.

The girls' camp was run by the same foundation and roughly along the same lines. Agreement between the two camps was perfectly clear—the two sexes were to be kept totally apart. Nevertheless, it was impossible to prevent some of the older boys from sneaking out to take part in clandestine meetings on the other side, or—which was most typical—simply to *look*. Rindebraden understood what was going on inside them. As an officer, he also had a good idea of the strategic enterprise and planning which went into these expeditions, and this boded well for the male youth of the Double Monarchy. The boys came from good solid bourgeois homes in Vienna, sons of doctors, master craftsmen, engineers, and lawyers. Nevertheless, this excess, this . . . *need* had to be tamed. Tamed and reformed. Into chivalry and moderation. On the whole, no harm ever came of these outings, and the captain was fair when he meted out punishment . . . not *too* strict.

But today . . . today things had gone beyond all reason.

⚜

This is how it had all begun: Just before dinner, Hannes Schachl had gone over to David and whispered, "Coming with me during the afternoon rest period?" David hesitated. Hannes was his age but bigger and more mature.

"Where to?" he said, to gain time.

"You know where." Hannes and David were in the same class at school and knew each other from before, but Hannes occasionally had ideas which . . .

"*There?*"

Hannes nodded. "*There.*"

"God, Hänschen, we'll get caught."

"All right, I'll go alone." But he kept on looking at David.

"I've no desire to spend tomorrow weeding."

"Neither have I," said Hannes. He smiled broadly, his lips clamped together and his arms folded across his chest. He had shot up this last year and was now pleased to be able to look down on his friends. His eyes were always filled with a dangerous desire for adventure, and it was an honor and privilege to be asked to go on expeditions with him.

"If it's just the two of us," said Hannes, "no one'll notice. We won't do what Dieter, Rüdiger, and Schnellkopf did yesterday. Obviously you get caught then."

"How are we going to do it?" said David, glancing up at his friend. David had just turned fourteen and thought his childhood had gone far too quickly. His bar mitzvah was coming up in the fall, so this was probably his last summer camp.

"We'll leave the blankets so it looks as if we're still there. Then we'll meet behind the shed, in the bushes. If there are two of us, one can keep a lookout."

"Right!" said David, briefly shaking Hannes's hand.

⚜

All went as planned, and after crawling laboriously and for ages through the undergrowth along the sports field up to the edge of the forest, they ran through the woods until they came to the water.

"This is it," said Hannes. "We have to take a wide swing around the paths so we come down through the woods on the other side." He was now the leader of the expedition, and David obeyed. As they made their way through the undergrowth, orders kept coming at regular intervals from Hannes: "Down!" "Duck!" "Still!" and after they had thrown themselves down for the third time in the best Cherokee fashion, David couldn't contain himself any longer.

"Yes, Captain!" It came with a grin, for his friend really did remind him of Rindebraden, with that assumed solemnity and all.

"Idiot," said Hannes.

"Captain in training!"

"What?"

"All right, Captain in training . . ."

Hannes won the fight and was just about to force a sign of defeat out of David when they heard voices.

"Down!" David whispered it this time and Hannes obediently threw himself into the pine needles. The voices were quite close, a number of voices, and the worst of it was that they were girls' voices. Though to be truthful, these two Indians did not really know whether that was the worst or the best. That depended. As they both went to a boys' school, they hardly ever saw any girls except their sisters, or else at a distance on the street and at the Burg Theater. Neither of the boys knew anything much about girls. These persistent raids on the girls' camp were made mostly out of curiosity, almost an urge rather than deliberate attempts to achieve human contact. Of course, some boys at school were always saying they had kissed girls, and a few free-spirited ones even claimed to have done *it*, but the only concrete evidence they had was an eyewitness account of Rüdiger, who had once been seen actually *talking* to a girl in the street.

Only the most forward boys ever got any further than looking from a distance at the girls in the other camp. One or two lucky forward ones had recently gone further. They had both talked and shared three pieces of forbidden princess cake with some of the girls at a secret meeting after sunset. The others, ordinary mortals, contented themselves with looking, perhaps able to see a leg when a stocking was rolled down or a shoulder when a girl scratched a mosquito bite.

So it was not all that strange that both Hannes and David almost choked when they saw through the grass a whole *flock* of girls on their way through the forest, all of them in bathing suits. They were making the slightly frightening noise of a lot of girls' voices, laughter, and exclamations. The flock passed only a stone's throw away, and David and Hannes had to fight for self-control.

Once they were out of sight, Hannes looked at David, who had turned quite pale.

"Let's follow them," said Hannes, his expression indicating that they were making a great sacrifice.

"Yes," said David, nodding. He had a feeling this might be a turning point in his life and his friendship with Hannes.

They crawled after the girls without so much as snapping a twig.

"Where are they going?" whispered David fiercely. He couldn't understand why the girls were heading into the forest away from the lake.

"No idea," whispered Hannes back, his mouth full of pine needles. They crawled on. It was a lovely summer day; a warm and lazy wind blew through the trees. As they crawled on, the scent of the forest floor, of grass and moss rose in their faces. The treetops waved above them, glossy green and summery. Just the right kind of day to play hooky and be in the forest. If it hadn't been for those girls . . .

"Yes," Hannes said suddenly.

"Ssh."

"I know. They're heading for the tarn."

"What tarn?"

"The little tarn the stream comes from. We went there last year."

David nodded. He remembered the place.

Now that they knew where the girls were going, they could keep at a greater distance. Ten minutes later they came to the little tarn.

They found a bush on the ridge above, wriggled into position, and, hidden by the foliage, began their observations.

The girls had all started bathing—swimming, spluttering, and splashing in the cold water. David was surprised that he could see no counselor with them. But Hannes nudged him and pointed.

"Look . . . there she is. The Wolf Mother." The Wolf Mother was an older girl, eighteen or nineteen. No one really knew why she was still at the girls' camp, only that she had a kind of unofficial position as counselor there. It was said she was the niece or sister of one of the adult leaders, so was allowed to come each year. So *she* was there to supervise . . . Everyone knew she was a terror. She was brusque and hostile, and had caught some illicit visitors several times. And she was merciless. In addition to that, she wore *pants*. The girls were also afraid of her—or so it seemed.

She was standing there keeping an authoritative eye on her subjects in the water and on the banks. David cleared his throat; he could see that Hannes, too, was not entirely at ease.

But they soon had other things to think about. The girls were coming up out of the water. Then there were some deliberations, the Wolf Mother barked out a few orders, and most of them started taking off their bathing suits.

Two hearts stopped beating up on the ridge.

Bathing costumes were hung up to dry; some of the girls jumped in again, others dried themselves and lay down on towels or straw mats. David and Hannes stared and stared. David watched one of them in the water, a girl his own age with soft round breasts. On the ground lay one of the largest of them, almost a grown woman, between her legs a thick blond mat of hair. Hannes simply couldn't keep still. Some of the girls started getting dressed as their suits dried, obviously bashful, although they thought they were alone. But there were still many—marvelously, frighteningly many—naked bodies in and around the pond. The Wolf Mother was standing on a rock, watching them all with a satisfied expression. Every time the girls approached her, there was a loud tittering.

"I don't believe it," whispered Hannes, their eyes at that moment on the pointed breasts of a less developed, younger girl bouncing as she jumped about in the water.

"Wouldn't you like to be down there with them?" whispered Hannes. For a moment David was uneasy.

"What? No. Well, yes." Hannes grinned and glanced over at his friend. When David turned his eyes back to the bathers, Hannes crawled back a little, then rose to his feet, and before David could blink, Hannes had grabbed his legs and pushed him down the slope. David was so surprised, no sound came out of him, and even before he had rolled right to the water's edge, Hannes had disappeared. A wail went up from the girls and an order rang out at once: *"A boy! Grab him!"*

He presumed it was the Wolf Mother and knew he was lost. Two of the older dressed girls were over him at once, holding him down. The naked ones grabbed their clothes and covered themselves, some slipping on bathing wraps. David lay there, resigned, cursing Hannes with all his heart.

"Well now . . ."

He looked up. It was the Wolf Mother. "What have we here, then? A nice little suckling pig?"

Then the giggling started—oh God, not that . . . Still rather uncertain after the shock, David looked up into a hard, bony face above broad brown shoulders, the face and cold eyes of the Wolf Mother.

"A dark-haired little demon, eh? A Ruprecht the Scamp?" The

giggling increased at this comparison with St. Nicolas's masked companion. David swallowed. "Sit up!" He sat up. "Anna! Resi! Go on
up there and see if he was alone."

"Yes, Fräulein Schlinger." They almost seemed to curtsy with their
voices. David was petrified.

"A nasty little boy brat." The Wolf Mother smiled mockingly as
she stood in front of him with her feet apart and her hands on her
hips. The giggling and tittering had become laughter. They had him
now—he was at their mercy. Worst of all, David was sure Hannes
was now lying somewhere on the other side of the tarn watching this
degrading spectacle with amusement.

"I think he was alone, Fräulein Schlinger." Again that curtsy in the
voice.

"So we have a solo visitor from the boys' camp. How amazing."
Another wave of laughter. "And what is this little man's name?"

David did not reply.

"You must know it is customary to leave your visiting card or in-
troduce yourself properly—in the company of *ladies?*" The Wolf
Mother's voice sharpened and her eyes narrowed even further.

"Right! The name we can find out later. No problem. And how
long, sir, have you been up there in the bushes?"

No reply from David. He was thinking about the comments that
would appear on his report when the time came.

"So—a long time, then," said the Wolf Mother. "And why, dare
we ask?" Giggles all around. David did not reply. The Wolf Mother
hauled him roughly to his feet.

"Lost your voice, too, have you—as well as your mind?" She was
holding him hard by his collar, and David saw her rage was genuine
and deeply felt, particularly the hatred in her eyes. She flung out a
hand and pointed at the circle of girls.

"I suppose you were here to *look*. To satisfy"—she cuffed him—
"to satisfy your dirty little mind." A mumble came from the girls, as
if they all now realized the grim truth when the Wolf Mother used
such fearful words. David stared up at her in terror. He could see her
teeth. They seemed to be quite blue.

"Or," she went on acidly, "perhaps you were here to take a look
at your beloved, eh? Your little girlfriend? Hm?" More laughter, this
time uncontrolled. "Wanting to see her with no skirt on?"

David desperately shook his head. Indeed, he had no girlfriend. But the Wolf Mother interpreted this as a yes.

"Aha, exactly. That's it. Well. So would you be so kind as to point out which of them is your chosen one? We are not going to have any more of this." David looked at her in despair. She had clenched her teeth and was pointing at the girls, all of whom were now quite still. "Now show me which one it is," she said, threateningly friendly. "If not, you understand, then . . ." David did not doubt for a moment that she would beat him until he could no longer stand. But he just shook his head slightly, his eyes sliding from one face to another: the tall blonde who had been lying in the sun, a small dark girl with a snub nose, another with kind eyes and round breasts . . . perhaps he could say it was her . . . but something told him he could not. His eyes flickered on from hostile to laughing eyes until a dark gaze met his—a tallish, slim girl with dark hair and a white forehead. As his eyes met hers, she moved her lips. She was looking straight at him, quite openly.

David shook his head and the Wolf Mother was at once on him.

"So," she hissed. "The time's come for your thrashing. Resi, bring a suitable sapling. And quick!" David's heart sank.

Then the Wolf Mother was standing there with a sapling in her hand.

"Well now," she said. "Will you unbutton voluntarily or do I have to do it for you?" David was near tears and quite incapable of moving.

"So there's only one thing to do," said the Wolf Mother.

"*No*," said a voice. The Wolf Mother stopped and turned around. David saw it was the girl with the dark eyes. She took a step forward. "He's my sweetheart," she said firmly. "No one may touch him."

It was quite still; even the Wolf Mother was irresolute.

The dark-eyed girl went over to David. She was the tallest of them, and all the time she was looking terribly serious, her forehead even whiter than before. She looked straight at him. Someone giggled.

"Right, Sofia," said the Wolf Mother harshly. "As this little creature is your . . . beloved, then you may administer his punishment. Is that understood?"

"Only on the hand," said Sofia without taking her eyes off David.

"Right," said the Wolf Mother. "Get going."

Sofia nodded.

She did it. It hurt, and David saw from the way she turned her eyes away that she also found it painful. Neither of them made a sound, though David heard her give a little gasp when it was over. Then her eyes met his again, and without a word she went back to the others.

David had to give his name in order to be allowed to return to his camp. It would all come out, anyway. So he walked back alone through the forest, tears in his eyes all the way, partly because of Hannes's betrayal and partly because of the shock of what he had seen and what had happened. The blows on his hand had also hurt, but the tears were mostly because of the dark look and that little gasp from a girl called Sofia.

❧

Captain Rindebraden was striding up and down the floor like a walking thunderstorm, getting more and more agitated. David stood paralyzed in front of him, listening to the claps of thunder, until finally he was beaten and sent to bed with no dinner.

He found Hannes sitting on his bed in the dormitory, clearly waiting for him.

"Was he very angry?" he said. David did not even condescend to glance at him, but calmly started undressing. He was pleased the beating had not made him cry, though he couldn't have looked unmoved, because Hannes said, "I didn't know they'd be so crazy."

David started putting on his pajamas.

"I just couldn't stop myself," said Hannes quietly. "I won't say anything about what I saw—afterward."

David still said nothing, but just looked at Hannes.

"And you *said* you wanted to be down there with them," said Hannes, attempting a smile. David got into bed.

"Was she horrible, the Wolf Mother?"

"Good night," said David.

"And who was the girl with the stick?"

David hoisted himself up onto his elbows.

"Listen. I have been told not to speak to anyone. I'm to go straight to bed." He sounded sullen.

"Oh," said Hannes looking at him. "It's just that I'm awfully sorry. That's all I wanted to say."

"Yes," said David; then after a moment's thought: "I'm not really angry."

"Did he ask if there were several of us?"

"I haven't told on you," said David.

Hannes sat quite still for a moment.

"Right," he said. "I'll go now. Good night."

David lay awake for a while. It was unusually peaceful in the dormitory, and he could still see the clear blue evening light through the window. He had not gone to bed this early since he was quite small. Something about the light out there, the stillness of the big room, and the sounds of activity coming from outside made him remember what it had been like when he was really small. Or when he had been ill. But at the same time he felt he had grown, was almost an adult, anyhow more mature than this morning. When he closed his eyes he could feel his body extended under the blanket. His hand still hurt, but there was also something else. He could feel himself filling all his limbs—right out to his fingertips, like when a hand is thrust into a glove. He was filling his body completely—it was he, it was his, while at the same time what he was filling was nothing but an object.

He opened his eyes. Nor was he really angry with Hannes any longer. Maybe not with the Wolf Mother, either. Maybe. In any case, he wasn't angry with Hannes. He could feel a triumphant joy that he wasn't angry. How amazing! And his joy increased in spite of the Wolf Mother and the captain, as well as his teachers and all those in authority back in the city. David would have liked to laugh if he had had anyone to laugh with. He smiled as he lay there and again closed his eyes— Then he thought about the girls.

He would sink through the floor with shame if he ever met any of them again, but as he lay there alone, he thought about them. He extracted the scattered, chaotic pictures from the afternoon, seeing those naked bodies quite clearly before him, and that excited him, but he controlled himself and lay there for a while, dreaming, dozing . . .

Then he saw her, those large dark eyes, that dark hair. He sat up abruptly and shook his head, turning hot and cold with shame, a fearful gnawing shame. His defiant joy seem to leave him, and again filled with the humiliation of the afternoon, he buried his head in the pillow and swore silently and desperately. He was glad this was his last camp, truly pleased he would not have to come back again next year.

As he was thinking that, he fell asleep.

When his bar mitzvah came, back home in Vienna that fall, it was essentially a somewhat superfluous ceremony. That afternoon when he had sneaked after girls with Hannes, David had already discharged himself from childhood without really knowing it.

He saw the dark-haired girl, Sofia, once more before camp came to an end, on the last evening. David had finished the interminable weeding—part of Captain Rindebraden's system of punishment—and had gone down to the lake with Hannes to skim flat stones. It was light enough for them to be able to see the circles in the bright water, and then they sat talking for a while. The friendship between them had in some way been consolidated these last three days. By the time they had to get back to the house, the two of them were in a good mood.

The gravel crunched as they walked up the path, and there she was, in front of them. They stopped abruptly, David at once recognizing her, her eyes as large and serious as before, her forehead just as white—no, whiter now in the darkness. Hannes looked inquiringly at her. David's first impulse was to run away, but Hannes nodded knowingly, said a grown-up and brief "Good evening" to her, then walked on alone, the gravel crunching as his footsteps receded.

She took a step toward David, then another. At each step, David could feel a kind of paralysis creeping over him. Then she was standing quite close to him.

"Do you come from Vienna, too?" she said.

"Mm." He could not find his voice.

"I had to get away this evening. It's the campfire and singing and all that." She smiled cautiously, her eyes still on him. David had never heard of *girls* also going on forbidden expeditions. He wanted to run away.

She took hold of his hands, just like that, and examined them closely. They couldn't have looked all that good, because she frowned. He also had dirt in the sores after all that weeding.

"Does it hurt?" A smile again slid across her face. How can anyone be serious even when they're smiling, thought David. He looked down.

"No, no." He shook his head. "It doesn't hurt." She didn't let go, not then, but stood like that for another moment, his hands in hers. Run, David, run! David could feel waves of humiliating shame rising and falling inside him. He didn't know girls could be like this—so serious, so challenging.

"I go to Schönbrunn on Sunday mornings," she said. "Quite early. Early enough to see the Emperor if he's leaving for Ischl."

"Yes," said David. She let go of his hands, put hers on his shoulders, and leaned against him.

For a moment or two, all reality merged into two hands on his shoulders, a warm face, a mouth. Then he tore himself free and rushed up the slope.

"David!" she called after him.

⌖

The next day David was back in Vienna, taking with him what he was sure was the worst report ever.

He handed the envelope to his father in the office of the music shop. His father looked him sternly up and down as he opened the letter. Then he read it, rubbing his graying beard.

David stood waiting. If he had managed the captain's thunderstorm, he could probably manage this, but he wasn't quite so sure now.

"David," said his father, after he had read the letter, "come here." David obeyed. His father looked him up and down again, then looked straight at him, this time his expression no longer stern but almost tender, sorrowful. Carriages and trams were rattling past outside.

Then his father cuffed him over the ear.

"You'll soon be going through your bar mitzvah," he said. "Our home has always been modern—if I may say so—not Orthodox, and I'm afraid these things mean much less today than when I was a boy. Things were different then. I would have liked you to go through some of what I did, some of the *solemnity*. But . . . well, you see, it was not common then for young Jews to mix with other young people. And as far as I can see from this letter . . ." He frowned. "Perhaps morals were better then, customs stricter." He stopped, his expression rather strained. David's father almost never talked so openly to him, particularly about morals and faith. He ran a music shop, selling instruments and sheet music and talking seriously and at length about music, taking his children to the Burg Theater and bringing colleagues and musicians back for evenings at home. But on his faith, Judaism and morality, he largely limited himself to simple maxims. David couldn't remember ever seeing his father like this. He seemed almost moved. Otherwise, he was stern and dismayed if he ever had to punish his children.

"I think we'll leave it at that," said his father. "What remains, really, is your acceptance by the congregation as an adult man. I don't know what that means to you young people today. But from now on I have no desire to punish you. This is the last time. That is a promise."

David looked wide-eyed at him.

"I hope you will eventually realize what that means," his father said. "From now on, any punishment you receive will be self-inflicted."

David nodded without understanding. What his father had said did not come back to him until much later, and by then they were no longer his father's words but a voice inside him saying them.

"But don't do anything like that again," said his father. "It is unmanly, and a gentleman should not behave like that."

"No," said David.

"Welcome back home," said his father. "Did you have a good time at camp?"

"Yes," said David. "But this year was the last time."

"The last time," said his father, nodding.

"But it was good. And I made a new friend."

"Really?"

"Hannes—Johannes Schachl. The lawyer's son."

"Excellent."

"The camp was good," said David.

David's home was a large old-fashioned apartment in the thirteenth Bezirk, on the second floor in a courtyard in Rosenhügelstrasse, one of those quiet, calm streets where the bourgeoisie of Vienna grew roses, tulips, and ornamental flowers in their front gardens. Because the street ran up a little hill and also in an east-west direction, it received a great deal of sun, so rosebushes grew unusually large, the roses of all shades from red to the pinkest of pinks to almost purple. They were the pride of the street, and the front gardens literally overflowed with them.

David's father ran the music business, as his father had done before him, and in time it would be passed on to David. This was as certain and obvious as the fact that the Emperor would be buried in the Imperial Tomb, as were his predecessors. Like his neighbors, Herr Bleiernstern was one of the sacred, ordinary bourgeoisie, and his home was, accordingly, solid, good, and well cared for. David and his sister, Mira, had grown up in a household in which everything ticked and worked, was as stable and as satisfactory as a well-kept clock. On Sunday evening their mother and father went through the household accounts and the business accounts for the past and coming weeks, and the surplus money was placed in a secure account and good investments. Their father added up the dividends once a year, and there were always so and so many kronen and heller more than the year before.

David's early world was one of absolute peace, of kindness, security, justice, and industry; of good glass, heavy plush furniture, and handsome cupboards with lion's feet. He learned to play the violin and the piano—the instruments his father played best—while his sister learned to play the cello and the flute, their mother's instruments. In the evenings, the family made music together, or alternately, the parents read great novels to the children, always good literature of an educational nature, from Goethe to Kipling, and the whole family enjoyed the readings. Only on festive days did their father read out of the Torah, and they dutifully paid a visit to the synagogue, though as in all Viennese bourgeois homes, faith was a matter for the private sphere, not worn outside for public display, like the Eastern Jews in the second Bezirk. Faith was fundamental and a matter of course— invisible, like blood itself, not something they talked about.

Only very rarely, as when he had handed over the letter from the captain, was David able to understand from his father that this had not always been so. In fact, his father was a believer, if not in form, at least in his attitudes. If he was no longer able to vouch with his clear good sense for Jehovah's personal involvement to the advantage of the Jewish people, nevertheless that faith was still somewhere inside him, now largely expressed in observations of the most important aspects of tradition. Nor had he had the children baptized in church, as many other Jewish families had begun to do. Neither David nor Mira ever learned Yiddish. Their father had abandoned the language for good when he married, for their mother was German-speaking only. It came back to him only when his brother came on a visit from Prague, or if a piece of music particularly moved him—never more than a few sentences or phrases, but said with great warmth and in a melancholy tone of voice unfamiliar to the children. That voice came from another era and other latitudes, speaking through their father, an echo of flight from Russia two generations earlier, the sound of long afternoons reading the Torah in the congregation's shul. Both David and Mira liked that lamenting tone, especially as their father otherwise spoke the most correct and down-to-earth business Viennese. At regular intervals, when his father took David aside to instruct him in the ways of the world, he would speak in the same dialect and use the same petit bourgeois tone of voice thousands of other fathers used all over the imperial city.

"Whether Jew or Christian, the best way to serve God is to carry out your work or profession well, build your home and your trade. Those who are industrious and careful are the ones who build, who build the world."

Like thousands of other sons in the same city, David nodded thoughtfully at the words of his elders.

"My generation," his father would say, "went through the after-effects of the wars. We learned that rebellion and great gestures do not change the world—thrift, work, and friendly rivalry do. Careful accounts, hardworking efforts. My father's generation saw the empire in chaos, and that necessitated composure. Europe has seen no war for a long time. Now that we shall soon be handing the reins over to you who are young, you should know that your home is in order. Perhaps you find us old-fashioned at the moment, but you will soon see why everything is as it is. Our home is richer, you should know, than when *we* took it over, well cared for and well run. You will run it more efficiently so that you in turn can hand it over in even better shape to your children."

Everything in moderation, that was the elders' fundamental axiom. The unchangeableness of security and solidity seemed as eternal as the Danube itself—the river would always go on flowing. The sons, however, had begun to be different, and David in his turn was to do things which shook and hurt his father. In some ways those things were connected with David's stay at the summer camp at Ischl, his friendship with Hannes, and even more with his meeting with a girl he knew little more about than her name. All that was to come later. Later, David was to realize that security and solidity, as far as his father was concerned, were connected with a fairly conscious desire for assimilation. Tens of thousands of Jewish citizens like his father lived all over Austria, and they were more or less indistinguishable from the tens of thousands of average Christians in the same middle-class belt.

David himself scarcely ever gave such things a thought, indeed was hardly aware there was any difference. "Citizen first, Jew second," his father used to say. Only the strange melancholy mixed with tenderness his father had shown in his office that day told David his father knew something that David was not to know about. His father remembered something his whole family had borne, and he wanted it to be forgotten with him. The time seemed to be ripe. David and Mira became ordinary German-speaking Viennese children.

So David went through that somewhat superfluous ceremony, his bar mitzvah, read in the synagogue, was dignified, and said a prayer at the family dinner. Uncles, aunts, second cousins, and cousins of sisters-in-law all came from far and near—the most distant uncle had long earlocks, which made David feel rather alien in his own home. He received his presents in the afternoon, a flashlight, a selection of Dickens, a tie, some scores, a tie pin, a blue suit he could grow into, and a shaving kit, which was to remain unused for a few years (so it seemed, sadly). He had been given the new suit before the great day so that it could be shortened in time. All of it, everything—the world, the suit, the shaving kit, and the city around him, the streets and grounds, life, books, and music—all of it was there to grow into. And his father would never punish him again.

Johannes Schachl was confirmed that same autumn.

A quiet winter followed, with a great deal of snow, particularly after the New Year. The snow lay in drifts in the streets, changing the appearance of buildings and trees. It lay like gray cataracts on classroom windows in early-morning classes, turning the room blind. Herr Schulze spoke English in a refined manner, his well-trimmed goatee rhythmically wagging up and down with methodical philological precision. On this particular bleak January morning, he seemed to have already droned on for a long time in that blind room. The tiled stove had been stoked up well before school started, and as a result the heavy dry air made it a struggle for the twenty-two boys to keep awake, as if the heat were filling their ears, closing them up.

Hannes Schachl's back at the desk in front of David slowly started sagging, only to straighten with a jerk now and again, then start sagging again. The movement was as monotonous and boring as Herr Schulze's grammatical goatee, now analyzing a sentence from *The Tempest* for the tenth time.

David tried hard to concentrate, fixing his eyes on something away from Hannes's back. But his thoughts were digging secret little tunnels in the thick layer of warmth and weariness, and they soon started wandering.

This winter had been different from any other for David. He had moved up into the second senior class, and things were more adult, more serious; the classroom showed signs of this. His previous classroom had had a sweetish smell of chestnuts or candy. It had been for children, and now, in his new classroom, the smell was different, sharper and more acrid. His teachers were strict and impersonal, somehow simply part of the smell of the whole school. David did not like it. Nor did he like gym, where the smell was of pungent discipline, the penetrating smell of sweat.

All of them were weighed down by the burden of homework.

But this winter had also confirmed and expanded his friendship with Hannes Schachl, whom David had really known only superficially before camp. It was a good friendship. They were very different, both outwardly and in temperament. David was calm and quiet, considered to be something of a sissy. He was slender. Hannes was tall, strong, and impetuous. Hannes boasted of more or less invented deeds, while David stuck sternly to the truth. So even if they could not really believe it, they had stepped into the ranks of adults, though they still had mock fights when no one was looking. In discussions that could seem to be parodies of adult hair-splitting (neither David nor Hannes could say whether they meant them seriously or not), they always took opposite sides. David preferred Brahms; Hannes, Wagner. They argued benevolently and lengthily on such matters. They pushed each other into heaps of leaves or the many snowdrifts on their way home from school. They spent time in each other's room and had dinner in each other's home. David was always received with great friendliness by Hannes's parents, despite the fact that Herr Schachl openly supported the anti-Semite Karl Lueger. But nothing was ever said or implied about David's origins—not between the two friends either.

Books were what first and foremost strengthened and expanded their friendship. That winter they both discovered poetry, which alongside their fights constituted an important part of their time together. This was an amazing discovery, that they could read poetry and actually benefit from it—poetry that made the room lose ceiling and walls; poetry that made simple volumes, their pages carefully cut, become picture galleries filled with watercolors and stained glass. Poetry, written by poets, *young* poets still walking around the world alive, some of them even in their very own city. Not only David and Hannes made the acquaintance of literature at the time—the same thing happened to several of their friends, in the middle of the boring everyday gray of school. It became their first literature. It belonged to them, the young, and was closed to adults.

Typically enough, David preferred Rilke's tender beseeching, while Hannes set more store by Hoffmannsthal. In the other arts—music, drama, and painting—new things were appearing, things which broke with all the old, conventional, and academic. The boys sensed something was *happening*, and that was good.

These were their first fumbling steps on a road which in time was to take some of them far away, estranging them from their fathers and causing them sorrow. But as yet it was enough that there were writers who were not neatly lined up in the bookcases of good citizens, and whose lines were not analyzed in the classrooms of Royal Imperial Vienna. As yet it was sufficient that a concept such as imperial was given another color through poetry, new depth and new meaning—omens in the world of the imagination. As yet they had not got as far as reading other things—fearful things that were almost impossible to understand, the literature of bombs and revolution, unmentionable Strindberg, and dubious Wedekind. As yet no one in their circle of friends had begun to write their own poems and articles, then to sneak into cafés where writers sat and hand over their neatly written manuscripts, hoping for an opinion. The great political discussions had not yet come, except as shadowboxing à la David and Hannes's rounds on Wagner versus Brahms.

Nor was God really on the agenda yet; He was still in the wings waiting for His cue.

During his bar mitzvah, David had not really thought about God, except in conventional symbolic terms, almost as an extension of the aesthetics of the ceremony, the synagogue, the scents and light inside it. The conscious question about God did not yet exist for him, as little as any kind of experience of the actual enigma. The nearest he had come to that was probably on the evening in camp when he had been sent to bed, an experience with no concepts and closely connected with the experience of time and body, the experience of love. So those fields came to be linked in David's mind without his having a name for them or indeed any understanding of them. Basically he thought most about love—without really noticing he was thinking about love nearly all the time.

One thing now was the continual dirty postcards, the smutty talk that could overwhelm them in their free moments, almost like the smell of school, stern and rather unpleasant. It was shameful, an awkward desire and more or less dreamed-up experiences—or implied experiences with cousins and neighboring boys, a girl in the entranceway, or hurried hands and rustling taffeta at a young people's dance. Little of that matched what the poems had to say. And what the poems had to say little matched the love life they sensed in the streets and alleys, on public sale. Nothing matched.

But it was something else—and these were David's moments—to hear the sound of rustling leaves on still nights when the clock tower struck cautiously on David's window, waking him. Awake but full of dreams. He had never dared go to Schönbrunn early on Sunday morning; in fact, on the whole, he had no desire to show himself anywhere near Schönbrunn. He was afraid of a dark clear gaze, a pair of large eyes that saw through him and found no resistance in him. He feared the conscious certainty living in those eyes, so different from what he saw in other girls, who mostly giggled shyly like children.

Those eyes. Never go to Schönbrunn. David protected himself, unconsciously and with all his strength, against what was to come. But on such nights, with the striking of the clock his companion, he yearned for her and would then whisper at the window, whisper nonexistent words, wishing that everything would begin. Take me with you, he would whisper to Time as it went by. Take me where I have to go.

Sometimes sleep is clairvoyant. Sometimes a definite sound wakes you, a definite word or sentence. And in your sleep, in your dreams just before you wake, you already know what is going to wake you. Long before a mother or father or sister has opened the door and said, It is morning, the sun is shining, it is pouring—long before that, you have *known* just those words would be said, that you would be woken by just that. On those occasions, time becomes something outside yourself. That was what David's sleep was like that fall and winter. He had a presentiment of everything that was to happen, and he protected himself, while longing for it. It was fall and winter. He was with Hannes. He had left childhood and stepped into his own time. He progressed in his knowledge and education, played in a string quartet, went to the theater, and read poetry. He slept soundly at night and was woken out of his deepest sleep, or slept in the middle of his clearest wakefulness. So he was not entirely surprised when Herr Schulze's pointer crashed down on the desk in front of him with a deafening bang—unconsciously he had heard the crash long before it woke him.

He looked up guiltily.

"For the third and last time, Herr Bleiernstern. For the third and last time," the teacher said angrily, and David pulled himself together, ready to answer the question. "You are asleep, Herr Bleiernstern," said the teacher. "And you must not sleep. You must analyze." The class buzzed. "Analyze *A brave vessel, who had, no doubt, some noble creature in her, dash'd all to pieces*. A demerit for you, Bleiernstern, a demerit."

"I'm sorry I fell asleep, sir. I didn't mean to."

"It'll be a demerit. Well? *A brave vessel . . .*"

Miranda to Prospero—one of those terribly boring things with no context, nothing to do with the world, especially if looked at from a grammatical point of view. But as David sits there, he is without knowing it a kind of Prospero—a sleeping, unconscious Prospero who knows everything and sees everything. He is in the dim warm classroom, and outside, it is snowing even more heavily—what *is* there about this day? No answer to that, of course, but as he walked home from school, David's annoyance over the demerit was completely external and seemed to have nothing to do with him.

Hannes was walking beside him, the snow under the soles of their boots hard-packed and glistening. Teams of handsome brown horses trotted past with vapor coming from their nostrils and streaks of sweat down their legs and flanks. It was a little milder and the snow had stopped for a while, but was soon to start again. The sky was heavy and reddish-gray above the Vienna afternoon.

"Want to come home with me to do homework?" asked Hannes, as they came to the corner where they had to decide. David had not thought of doing anything else except spend the afternoon with Hannes on homework and then literature, but on an impulse, vague and dreamy, and slightly surprised, he heard himself saying: "No thanks, Hannes, not today. I'm supposed to meet Father at the shop."

Hannes nodded, also slightly surprised, then smiled in farewell and disappeared up his own street, an avenue of linden trees. As he vanished quickly and cheerfully into the dusk, David watched him, feeling rather lost but not knowing why.

He started walking the long way to the center of the city. He never usually went to see his father without notice, and as he trudged on, he wondered why he had said that to Hannes, to whom he always told the truth. He could have taken a trolley, but decided there was no hurry and he had plenty of time. He walked on along the streets, his schoolbag under his arm, and it began to snow again, the snow affecting him strangely, so that the thickening traffic seemed to be seen through a scrim in the theater: a cavalry regiment, a brewer's dray, ladies in fur hats and muffs, dark façades, messenger boys running in the vanishing light. Through the driving snow, they all became mellow shapes apparently flatter than usual.

Once at Graben, he set off toward his father's shop, which was situated on one of the side streets, small but with a very good reputation. He looked up at the cathedral—the zigzag pattern on its roof had disappeared in the swirling snow.

What was he really doing here? He suddenly realized that he shouldn't go to his father's shop, that he should change course. But he went on dutifully, rounded the corner, and came up the right *Gasse*.

A few meters from the shop, he stopped as if bewitched. There, in the street, in the snow, was his father, bare-headed and coatless, his back to him. He was gesticulating and talking to someone beside him, a policeman in a helmet, writing in a notebook. Some passersby had stopped to watch. Behind the two men, the plate-glass window had been smashed; splinters of glass protruded darkly out of the great hole. Inside, in the window, was a smashed violin, and snow was swirling in through the hole and settling on instruments, scores, and piano.

David stared at the broken window. Neither his father nor the policeman noticed him. He kept staring at the splinters of glass and the snow driving into the darkness of the shop. His father's voice came floating through the air: ". . . don't know what it means," he was saying, and the policeman said something about a meeting that had been held. David saw his father standing there, bare-headed, waving his arms about, and suddenly he felt he was watching a stranger. I should go over to him, he thought, let him know I'm here, ask if I can help. But the instrument dealer over there was a stranger; the shop, too. David was nothing but a passerby, stopping for a moment to see what was happening—only a broken shop window and not part of his heritage, nothing to do with him. He pulled his cap down hard over his forehead and walked past the gaping wound in the plate-glass window, half shocked, half ashamed of himself. He hurried up the street and vanished around a corner and into the evening. It was already almost dark and the darkness was good and soft and saved him.

He did not look back.

※

She notices him as he comes down the alley, and despite his thick winter clothes and cap, she sees at once it is he. He is walking as if coming from his own funeral.

She thinks about his name, then says it aloud, but he doesn't hear. She half runs through the snow to catch up with him, then stands in front of him to bar his way.

A moment goes by before he looks up. He draws a deep breath; then he presents his face to her.

"It's you," she says quietly.

"Yes." He looks at her, not particularly surprised.

"So it's you." She is just as serious. She is just as serious, even when smiling, as now. She quickly takes his arm. No one can see them here. They walk on together.

"I've waited for you at Schönbrunn every Sunday morning. But you knew that."

"I knew. I couldn't come."

"Never mind. It was all right, anyway. Just waiting."

"Yes, it was all right."

"It was necessary. But it was beginning to be enough."

They walk through the alleys. She puts her hand carefully on his; then she stops him and again stands in front of him.

"Your hands are cold. Here." She pulls his hands into her muff and holds them there. They stand like that for a while. They stand like that for a snowy century. He drops his schoolbag without noticing, the flap opening and some books falling out.

"I've been to buy a paintbrush. I thought I'd paint a picture. Of you. As I remembered you. I'm going to be a painter."

He nods. "I don't know what I'm going to be."

"No."

"But I'm not going to stand in a shop and sell instruments."

"No. Shall we go and have hot chocolate first?"

"Yes. Chocolate."

"But we won't go to Novak's. I usually go there to have chocolate with some cousins. We won't go there."

"I also have a lot of cousins."

"We'll just walk the streets until we find the right place."

They walk, she with her arm under his again, and she disappears with him, takes him with her. Some schoolbooks are left behind in the snow, the flakes melting on the covers. White, white. The evening is dark as they go on.

⚜

"Say what you like about children never obeying their parents, but this young lady here, she just wants to paint and paint. Just like her mother. I wish she'd find something else. Be a bit more disobedient."

"Mama!"

"You see . . . ?" Frau Melchior sighed cheerfully and knowingly at David. "She keeps trying to bring up her mother, that's what she does."

David looked down in embarrassment, but Sofia intervened. "Mama, you're frightening David."

"Do you see what I mean? Well, not that a little upbringing might

not be needed on my part. Ever since my blessed husband—er—
died, I've been, how can I put it, extremely distrait. Yes, I think you
could say that. Distracted. Sofia has never had a proper upbringing.
Just so that you know, Herr Bleiernstern. Oh, is it all right if I say
David? You've got such a long surname. I mean, this house, just so
you know, is frequented by nothing but painters and sculptors and
actors and those, those—well, people who write. Poor Sofia has never
had a proper upbringing. Please excuse me for being so free. But
you're probably wondering why she is as she is. She's certainly been
neglected. As her mother, it's best I say so outright before you find
out for yourself, David. Otherwise you seem to be a courageous young
man. Now *she's* bringing me up."

Sofia sighed and looked in despair at her mother, who really did
seem to be enjoying life, sipping her tea at various points in her long
monologue. David sat there with his cup, answering in words of one
syllable, his face flushed.

"And now," said Frau Melchior, "now she's come here claiming
space in my studio. Sofia, I must tell you straight, this can't go on.
Can't you do something . . . something sensible? Learn French or
collect stamps or go to dancing classes like proper girls do."

"Mama, you know I hate dancing. And I don't want to be like
proper girls."

"Just imagine, David—yes, I'll say David now—every morning she
gets up and starts *painting*, now, in this fine weather."

"It's raining, Mama. It's been raining for days."

"Nonsense."

David ventured to say something. "It's true, Frau Melchior. It actually is raining."

"Eh?" said Frau Melchior. "Really? You see, David. That's what
I'm like now. Distrait. Yes, well. I hope you don't take after me too
much, Sofia, and more after your father. Otherwise perhaps *you* may
well have to suffer," she said, turning abruptly to David. David
flushed again. "Now, where were we, where were we . . ."

"We were talking about *painting*, Mama. The studio. I brought David along to look at some paintings, didn't I, David?"

"Exactly, precisely," said Frau Melchior. "Exactly. And then I go
and I lay claim to you. Sofia dear, I thought there must be something.
I've hardly seen you in the evenings for the last three months. You,

who's otherwise always at home on your own. So when you at last appear dragging your find with you, I think the least you could do is to bring him in here so that he can have tea with *me*, your mother and next of kin. She is talented, by the way," Frau Melchior went on, turning to David. "God knows where she got it from. I myself paint extremely mediocrely. Perhaps from her father? My blessed husband, Adalbert, was a mine owner, just imagine, a *mine owner*! It sounds awful, doesn't it? But he was basically a lyrical soul, Adalbert, he really was. That's more than can be said of those brothers of his who come here every year or so. You see, when my late husband, the mine owner, *became* that—deceased, I mean—and left us this, the house and everything else, well, good heavens, the mine, too! I almost forgot, the whole works, with gold and diamonds and . . ."

"*Iron ore*, Mama."

". . . and all that, then his brothers naturally took over the actual running of it, yes, they took over. Two really unpleasant men, that's what they are. Men of the world. Never show their faces here, except when they rush in to arrange for those penances, or whatever it is we pay for the forgiveness of our sins . . ."

"*Taxes*, they're called, *Mama*! Capital levies."

"I call them penances. That's the sum we pay the state if we are to be forgiven for all the mad things we do."

"Oh, what nonsense, Mama. Taxes are what we pay the state so that the state can administer for the benefit of all. You know that perfectly well."

"All right, all right," said Sofia's mother. "But come now, Sofia, I've seen what kind of books you read at night."

"At night, Mama?"

"Kropotkin, eh? And Marx. And this . . . that Baldian . . ."

"Bakunin, Mama."

"So don't you go talking about the state and the benefit of all, Sofia, my little bomb-thrower."

David had the impression he was drinking tea with his whole face, an enormous teapot, apparently bottomless. They were in Frau Melchior's living room, a lofty, rather bare room, the furniture, pictures, and objects expensive, yes, some priceless, but the room had a feeling of having been scraped together. Two paintings had been taken down and turned to face one wall, leaving white squares on the wallpaper.

A Roman bust was serving as a paperweight on the escritoire. An enormous cage containing a neurotically fierce canary hung over by the window. When they had arrived, it had pecked David's finger, shrieking in triumph—its name was Franz Josef. The room was confusing and charming, reflecting its occupant, Frau Melchior, now enthroned in an armchair opposite David, dressed all in white with a red silk shawl around her shoulders. She was tall and had the same long, slim neck as Sofia. But Frau Melchior's expression was mildly distant, as opposed to Sofia's serious, determined features. The two of them both resembled and were very unlike each other. David had heard about Frau Melchior before. She was fairly well known for her painting, but perhaps particularly for her salons, which attracted leading names. David was feeling slightly faint.

Light from the rain and melting snow was trickling in and settling on stacks of books, pictures, and furniture. In that light, Sofia was at home. David could hardly take it all in. She was wearing slippers, and a stab of delight went through him every time he saw her feet, which she had drawn up under her in her chair as a child does.

"Wouldn't you like a little more tea, David?"

"Thank you, but I think . . ."

"Mama. We've sat here over an hour drinking gallons of tea with you. May I now take David up to the studio?"

"All right, my dear," said Frau Melchior, looking at Sofia with undisguised pride. "David?"

"A thousand thanks for tea, Frau Melchior," said David, getting up. "I hope you will excuse us."

"Of course, David."

Sofia was already heading for the door. Frau Melchior took David's hand and pressed it in farewell. For a moment she was quite calm, her face collected. She nodded at him, serious and appealing. Then she smiled.

"*Auf wiedersehn*, Frau Melchior."

"*Auf wiedersehn*, David . . . and thank you."

⁂

After long dark stairs and corridors, they were in the great attic room under the roof which served as a studio, the light from the skylights soft and white. Sofia closed the door behind her, then flung her arms around his neck with sudden tenderness.

"Were you terribly frightened by her?" she said, speaking into his shoulder.

"Frightened?" He had never seen Sofia like this before.

"So many of them are frightened," she whispered. "She's . . . different. I was so afraid she would frighten you."

"No, Sofia."

"I thought, as you come from a home where everything, where things are ordinary—and here everything is quite unordinary."

Shyly he ran his hand over her head.

"Of course it's difficult anywhere else but at home."

"But she's all I have," Sofia went on. "All I've ever had. It's true only actors and painters and so on come in and out of here. Always have, all through the years. When I was small I thought things should be like that, but then I realized why those uncles of mine never came here with their families. Not that I like them particularly, either . . ."

"Sofia, Sofia . . ."

"Last year she forgot Christmas," said Sofia. "She's been like that since Father died."

"I did wonder how much was acting and how much . . ."

"Genuine? Of course it's acting, all of it. It's a manner she's adopted. She knows that, and so do I. But it's genuine all the same. Because she can no longer take off the mask. It's been like that ever since."

"When did your father die?"

"Oh, when I was small. He . . ."

"Yes?"

"He died down in a mine shaft. That's what they say."

David asked no more, but went on stroking her hair.

"There was some kind of scandal, I think, but it was hushed up. Since then Mother's been . . . a little odd. But she lives and breathes for art." Sofia stopped for a moment. "Do you remember that first evening when I told you I used to go and have hot chocolate with my cousins at Novak's? Well, it's a kind of obligation in the cause of my upbringing. My uncles don't think this house is good for me, and they've told my cousins to be good company for me, although they like me as little as I like them—and the funny thing is, Mama fully agrees with my uncles on that point. Oh, David, do you think all this is . . ."

"No, Sofia." David smiled into her hair. "Not at all."

"It was an uncle's idea to send me to camp last summer. He's very progressive and goes in for Healthy Living, so . . . Anyhow, David . . ."

"What?"

"She liked you, especially that 'It actually is raining, Frau Melchior'! If she hadn't liked you *then*, she would probably have thrown you out. That has happened occasionally."

"I liked her, too, Sofia."

"Yes, but because of that you can come here now. She doesn't mind. You can come here. So we don't have to walk the streets all the time."

Oh, how they walked the streets. They have sat in cafés a little, too, but they have mostly walked and walked around streets and parks, white and still, afternoons and Sundays. Stolen, precious hours between school and homework. They have walked and walked, all through that late winter, close together, talking, silent, smiling. They have stopped quietly in entranceways and behind trees. They dare not walk in Prater, for fear of being *seen* by someone, but they have been to Wienerwald, got soaking wet and caught cold. The evenings have been late for David, and he then has had to catch up as best he can with his homework—his parents think he did it at Hannes's. But every morning he is wide-awake, hurries to school; the schoolday goes like a breeze. Then she meets him on the corner of the linden avenue, where he says goodbye to Hannes. Hannes nods wisely at them. He probably feels responsible for them, for it was he who quite literally pushed David into it. He tells no one.

They talk to each other. They talk about books they have read and read poetry to each other. They talk about the trees, and invent stories about people they see. She is so different. Girls just aren't like this. Gratitude rises through David and out into the world, for being allowed to experience all this, in secret, true, but free, years before morality permits it. David buys a thin silver ring for her, the vendor smiling at him as he disappears with the little parcel, his face scarlet. She gives him a medallion. That was the day they went to the museum and were almost evicted because they couldn't stop touching each other. A very young public nuisance. She is like that. It is like that. Different.

※

"Show me your pictures, Sofia."

They go through the studio, past Frau Melchior's many colorful still lifes. David sniffs the air a little and realizes where the sweetish smell on Sofia's hands comes from, the reassuring smell of oil paint and turpentine.

Sofia has her things in one corner, a picture in cool colors on the easel. She quickly covers it, then takes out a folio.

"I'll show you the drawings first," she says, her face lighting up as she smiles. She quickly presses his hand.

They spend a long time looking at Sofia's pictures.

※

A quiet, dark, gable-windowed room, almost like a monastery cell. It takes a few seconds before he sees the pretty light coming from the stained glass in the window, a semicircular shape, a blue cross with roses around it. Seven roses.

You live here? Up here?

Yes.

It is so . . . so lovely here. The chair and the table. And the bed.

I had another room before. I lived somewhere else when I was smaller. This was some kind of chapel, I think. My grandfather was an alchemist, three hundred years after his time. This was his room. I wanted to live here.

And you sleep here.

I sleep here.

Sofia, Sofia. Tell me. The shapes of light running and running. Tell me.

What shall I tell you?

Tell me about the stillness. Tell me whether it was as still around you as it always was around me.

Yes. It was always still around me. Always still through all the years. Even if I walked through the noise and laughter down there.

Down there.

Everyone came down there. All the famous people. Actors and

painters. All those people you've seen on the stage at the Burg The-
ater I've seen here. They talked to me.
What did they talk about?
So much. Nothing at all.
Did you ever show them your pictures?
Never. Never my pictures.
Did they ever come up here?
Never. My beloved. Hold me.
Sofia. What's the matter?
Once one of them—one of them. I was only twelve.
Sofia.
He touched me. He broke the stillness. So deeply, I was afraid. I
don't want to talk about it. An actor. So much was happening in the
house at that time. He touched me so deeply. I was changed after
that. Hold on to me. I don't want to talk about it. David, everything
became different. I was afraid. Promise me one thing.
What shall I promise you?
Promise me you'll never leave me.
I promise.
Never leave me. Never let me go.
I promise.
Never lose me.
I promise.

⚜

Walk into the years, Sofia Melchior and David Bleiernstern, walk on.
That's how you grow together. You will exist through sunlight and
wind. You long for each other when you are separated by family,
holidays, and exams, not frightened longing, not unendurable or sick
longing, but still and humble. Letters written on calm summer evenings by a lake, a hand taking the letter out of the *poste restante* box
to be read on the tram home. Still, growing. For you, David, she
becomes what draws you to her. It is her. The way she looks when
she is standing outside in the street waiting for you. Her words are
your prayers. Her hands are bells ringing for you.

There are days when the sky touches the earth; out in the Wienerwald the sky often touches the earth without anyone seeing it,
apart from you two. In the end it becomes almost ordinary. Do you
know you two are holding up the world? Saving it from going under

any moment? Do you know, as you sit in Sofia's quiet room looking through art books, that you are bearing everything? That when you let your eyes rest on van Eyck's great altar painting in that book, it is so that it will never be destroyed by fire, never be crushed to dust.

Long live the revolution! For these are the days of revolution and upheaval in all fields. The old are to go, fixed opinions and views of the decaying empire creaking at the joints. They will soon be gone. Soon a new sunny world will dawn. The Emperor, the power of the Church, dogma in art—they must go, all of them. Long live the oppressed! Long live freedom! Long live free love! All that is written. Sofia has unlimited access to freethinking literature and has read it all, and David keeps up with her as they grow older, become sixteen and seventeen and are still growing up, and in toward each other.

❧

Quiet city streets in the sun. The city wakes after a long winter, people stroll in the streets, couples arm in arm, children laughing.

The city streets of childhood and youth. Living in a large and beautiful city is all that is worthy of a young person, cornices and rosettes, carved entrance doors, curved streetlights—oh, how beautiful, how beautiful when it rains, when the sun shines. The quiet buzz of voices in cafés, gray streaks in the marble tables, the waiter nodding kindly, bringing the newspaper and café-au-lait, the schoolbag left on stone steps, lilacs in the park smelling of lilac.

What is most beautiful is when you are two—two people walking down the street, arm in arm. He is young, his face pale and immature, his hair thick, dark, and curly. Of course, he is wearing that ridiculous blue suit, and for some reason he has a hat on—he should never wear a hat—it looks as if it had landed on his head by accident. And she? She is wearing a red-and-black costume, low shoes, and is carrying a muff. Of course, she sees his hat and the suit he is lost in. Why can't men dress naturally? Either their coats are too big or their ties look like suicide attempts—long ago things were different, she thinks. He would be wearing a toga. Or a huntsman's suit and cape. But she does not say what she sees. She smiles.

"So *elegant* you are," she says, straightening his tie. He looks uncertainly at her, smiling in embarrassment. He has never ceased to be shy of her.

There are other couples like them walking the streets.

God, how good it is to be seventeen. The city is never so beautiful as then. Everything; all the buildings have a powdery shimmer of emotion about them, are in love with each other, the lines and curves of the façades playing with each other, so that it might cause moral indignation, but it doesn't, because it is blameless in all its sensuality, young and pure. The architecture of the city reflects whether people of the time are able to love or not, clearly visible in the surrounding forms. Now they walk down Graben toward St. Stephen's Cathedral, a monument to love, fearful, eternal, unwavering. *It* stands. It is a mountain, it is a thicket of thorns in stone, black and stern.

It is so beautiful the two of them stop for a moment, just looking at the soaring towers, the stone arches running from midships to starboard. Birds flying.

"Just think of the blood spilled to build it," one of them says.

"Yes, inhuman suffering."

"The power of the Church—fearful."

"In the new state, churches will be turned into museums. Into meeting places and assembly halls."

"Yes. Just think that people agreed to it all. Didn't grumble, although they had to hew stone for years and pay taxes for the priests to put up their building."

"In the new state, churches like this will come into real use."

"So they haven't been built in vain."

They stand looking at St. Stephen's Cathedral, what they have read and thought pouring out of their mouths. The power of the Church and those priests *are* terrible, they know that perfectly well. But she smiles and says, "Let's go and look at the stained glass."

The colors in there are intoxicating, the building losing its weight and severity below the vaulting and becoming light and open, like crystal spheres, like outer space, the stained glass hovering around them.

Silently they walk from window to window. He has taken off his hat and holds it in his hand like a piece of lost property.

She grasps his arm. "Look."

It is the window with the roses; they stay there a long time, entranced, gazing.

Afterward they cannot bring themselves to say anything more about the people's sufferings, even if they know what they know. The cathedral is too beautiful, after all. They go out into the daylight.

Before the two of us could talk to each other
everything was like the shapes of light as it runs through
colored glass.

Talk? Converse? Of course. Gradually a small circle of young people of their own age has formed. Some want to be artists, others enthuse about politics; some want to be this or that. They have found a small café where they meet at regular intervals, after rounds of galleries, theater performances, and evenings of music. Sofia and David have slipped in with them. They sit at round tables, slightly less embarrassed, a little more certain, a little more open. The axle of the universe runs straight through them as they sit talking themselves hoarse, on every subject between heaven and earth. Newspapers and magazines circulate. Hannes is also with them now. He has had his first poems published under a pseudonym in a very small magazine, but everyone knows it is he, the seventeen-year-old, who has written them, and as good friends they praise him to the skies. You would think he had written the *Marienbad Elegy*, and in reality he almost feels he has, although the edition of the magazine runs into only three figures. Slowly, all things fall into shape. Everything is talked about here, important things. From all the discussions and spiritual conversations at home, Sofia is used to asserting herself, and she manages quite well. David is more silent. She secretly squeezes his hand under the table while the conversations go on—a little current of stillness from her to him. The conversations—when David tries to recall them—seem to go something like this:

"Kierkegaard," says someone. *"Joy and Rapture."*

"Schelling," says another. "Good God!"

"Kritik der reinen Vernunft," says a third, secretively striking the table.

"Liberation of the masses," slips in from another conversation running parallel across the table. "Marx and Engels."

"I think that Wedekind . . ." a fat youth inserts loudly and cheerfully, drowning the politicians. Words and names.

"Anyhow, when Herzl says . . ."

"While J. P. Jacobsen, describing . . ."

A thin, sickly youth at a corner table cries: "Nietzsche!"

The gathering shudders and everyone nods devoutly. They had forgotten Nietzsche. He can't be passed over. For a while they talk about him, then conversations dissolve into a series of dialogues, and a number of elders of the Church swirl through the air. Ibsen Ibsen, Hauptmann Hauptmann, mumble, mumble. "Wagner!" someone suggests, but is soon hushed.

It is possible to sit and listen with quivering ears and, as David does, then run to the library and feverishly hunt out the names which—more or less to impress—have been self-confidently flung out that afternoon. That is what their circle is like, brave young men and a few brave young ladies. Here they have a place in which all theories, connections, and mixtures can be tried out. Slowly they crystallize, who tends toward art, who wants to write, who is to devote himself to thinking. And who does not want to be anything, ever.

David did not know which direction this was taking him, and that worried him a little, but it was so much better to be with his friends and Sofia than at home. He was profoundly impressed by her, everything she knew and was involved in. If she made a decision, she did so calmly and seriously, with no fuss—from deep conviction. She began working for various idealistic purposes, taking responsibility, working at her painting, reading—always herself and sure of herself.

Best of all was walking together in the Wienerwald, where they never talked about art or politics but largely about flowers and plants. She knew about plant life, the difference between valerians and marsh marigolds, pine and spruce. As they walked she kept saying the strange names of flowers. "Pussyfoot," she would say. "Columbine." David had never been particularly attentive in botany class and had never been able to connect dusty herbariums with living flora. When he was in the countryside and saw a blue flower, he just called it a blue flower. He knew there was a Latin name for it, but he did not know what it was. But Sofia had drawn all the flowers and named them.

They often walked in silence in a kind of dream, strolling through inner landscapes. Once when Sofia had shown him the metamorphosis of rose leaves from those innermost to those on the extreme edge, he had gone straight to the piano at home and without a second's thought written a brief tune, a melody of roses. Sofia had picked a flower and placed the leaves in a row on a smooth stone so that he could see the way the outer, sharp, heart-shaped leaves grew smaller and rounder, more delicate, becoming in the end a tiny little monocotyledenous shape. Then, with no transition, came the actual stamens, the lovely inner form of the rose. He had seen the way the rose was a variation on one single theme, the heart shape of the rose leaf. All this had gone into his little tune.

Later, when he played through it in a more sober mood, he did not really know what he thought of it. Was it idyllic? He did not play it to anyone, even to her—just as he had not dared show her or anyone else the poems he had written. To take them to a magazine, to an *editorial* office, as Hannes had done with his . . .

He buried them in a drawer like a secret, afraid to look at them and perhaps find out what was wrong with them. The same applied to the tune.

Many things happened that spring. At the beginning of April, Sofia moved away from home, or at least halfway. No special event caused it, no dramatic departure, just a calm decision that the time had come to begin to tear herself free. She had long been taking painting lessons and was going to try to take the art school entrance exam in the fall. At home with her mother, she said, there was seldom any peace and quiet to work in. Nor any space. Frau Melchior protested approvingly. Sofia found an attic room in Laimgrubengasse which served as a combined studio and apartment.

Changes also came about in their relationship. The quietly growing friendship between them changed color and temperature. An incomprehensible vehemence would overcome them quite suddenly, and they could go on kissing until they could scarcely stand, almost until they were bleeding, while at the same time they had to push each other away, slightly scared. They had indeed *talked* about love. They had *read* about and discussed love. But to find powerful adult desire in themselves—that was strange, and frightening. For they have grown and grown toward this point, the tenderness slow and cautious between them. They have embraced each other, held each other's hands, touched each other, kissed each other formally and solemnly. Now all this seems to have blossomed, inexplicably and wildly. They are nervous, rather sensitive to each other, occasionally irritable. Now and again she will ask him to let her go, leave her alone, or . . . Or something might happen. Or they don't know what. At the end of April a day comes when she throws him out of the studio.

He has come as usual after school one afternoon to watch her work and to do his homework in a corner somewhere. Then perhaps they will go down to a café or just for a walk. He runs whistling into the entrance of Laimgrubengasse, goes up the stairs, and bangs on her door. She opens up, a paintbrush still in her hand and her hair tousled. Her eyes are large and bright, larger than usual. He goes in, puts his schoolbag down, and is just about to sit, but something is different. He goes over to her as she stands by the easel, and she is waiting for him. He puts his arms around her. Then they are lying on the paint-spotted floor, pulling at each other, their hands running everywhere, until she suddenly cries out, loudly, pushes him away, and tells him to go.

"David! No! You must go. Go now."

He gets up, ashamed, confused, strokes her shoulder carefully, and asks for forgiveness.

"Go now."

"I didn't mean it."

"Don't talk nonsense," she says soberly, her face twitching. "Don't say anything, David." She is not looking at him. "Go now. Don't come back until I tell you to."

Since then he has had a terrible week, a leaden week. To add to everything else, his mother and father are now aware of what they have suspected since Christmas, namely that he is not with Hannes Schachl every day. They find new and unimagined, almost conspiratorial features in their son and heir. They had not expected this of him, certainly not *and where have you been, young man?* Neither does Herr Schachl or his wife know where *their* offspring is at any time. Both Hannes's and David's reports cards are appalling, and *as long as you live under this roof, you must* . . . Mira, his younger sister, has of course spied on him and tells her parents what she knows—she is at that age. She can tell them about the circle of friends in the café and that David is mixing with dubious . . . but she knows nothing about Sofia. What does that matter? David has waking nightmares about never seeing her again; his life is wasted and all is over. His father makes a long speech but does not punish him, just stands there talking, gently, decently, and helplessly. A faint contempt for his father rises in David—long live the revolution! But somehow or other he manages to soothe his parents, to persuade them he will better his ways. He goes out, makes his way through the city, and can't be bothered to see either Hannes or any of his other friends. Can't be bothered with anything. The days, fine spring days, are as gray as lead. He thinks about her, thinks about her body melting against his own down there on the floor, and he flushes, then pales from shame, delight, and grief.

April comes to an end. Then it is the first of May and the heat of summer arrives, lying like a cloak over Vienna from early morning, the days sultry and school miserable. According to instructions, curtains have been put up over all the classroom windows, so that—in case it should undermine society—pupils will not be tempted to look out at the fine weather—thus celebrating the arrival of summer.

David suffers all day. Then, as he drags himself off after the last lesson behind the crowd, not answering anyone except a dejected "Maybe" to Hannes's suggestion to go home with him—there she is at the entrance, waiting for him for the very first time at the gate, quite openly and unembarrassed. He stops in front of her without a word. Some boys spot them and laugh insolently, but Hannes manages to distract them and get them to go with him. David and Sofia remain standing there. She is looking down, not at him. He dares not touch her.

"Are you coming to the May Day celebrations?" It's true, they had talked about it and had a vague agreement. He goes with her, still without saying anything.

It is hot, the atmosphere in the parks and streets slightly strained, people's faces shiny in the sudden sultry heat, irritable, not relaxed. Instead, life acquires a new feverish haste. Spring—life returns.

They walk along the Danube Canal on their way to the park, not daring to hold hands; rather, *he* dare not, using the old no longer valid excuse that someone might see them—Just who? she asks—but she realizes he does not want to, so pretends she doesn't want to, either.

Every time they brush against each other it is like a thunderstorm inside them. Their faces flush from the heat, but it is not just that. Once they stop, she wants to kiss him, but they have to tear themselves free from each other the moment their lips meet. Her face is trembling. She looks down, down all the time.

They get to the May Day celebrations, brass bands and speeches in the park, beer being drunk from outdoor tables. There is also a feverishness about the celebrations. In the oppressive atmosphere, the speakers seem to feel the revolution is about to happen. So do the crowds, caps soaring into the air, people cheering and shouting. Then they start singing.

He dares to hold her hand in the crowd. They have exchanged not a word since they arrived, during neither the speeches nor the music, scarcely daring to glance at each other. But now she puts her hand into his—or does he put his into hers? Their hands are warm and moist, and he can feel the small patches of hardened skin on her palm. She has a good hand, a hand that works and is shaped by that. A hand in which there is meaning. He suddenly sees the way that hand holds everything, paintbrushes, a pencil, a book, an iron. This is the hand that holds the hairbrush when she does her hair. Now she is holding him.

A woman gets up onto the rostrum in the twilight. They recognize her from previous meetings—one of the really famous, lonely ones, up there on her own, a frail, middle-aged lady speaking on the women's movement. The amazing thing is that she manages to speak so that the beer-swilling, hot and weary workingmen quiet down and look slightly ashamed. She talks about the heroines in the struggle, famous names, Louise Michel, Emma Goldmann, Rosa Luxemburg —she herself is alone and has no mission—she speaks equally of anarchists and socialists. A certain amount of coughing from the bearded members of the organizing committee shows that this is not entirely approved of, but she ignores them. She is a very good speaker.

"Rosa Luxemburg," she says, "goes in and out of prison for the cause of the revolution. And we? What do we do?" The atmosphere has become slightly recharged, no longer tipsy shouting but changed into an enthusiastic seriousness in the audience. New listeners keep appearing, attracted by the sudden quietness of the crowd, and they hush the brass band.

She goes on about Rosa Luxemburg, describing her so that they can almost see her, her glasses, her limp, always with newspapers and pamphlets in her bag.

"A weak woman, yes indeed, *only* a woman, perhaps you would say, gentlemen." Muffled laughter. "But the exterior deceives you as always."

David glances at Sofia. Her eyes are shining and she is listening entranced, as he is. But they are holding hands hard, not for a moment forgetting they are holding on to each other. Suddenly, in the middle of Rosa Luxemburg and the movement in Germany, Sofia turns and fixes her eyes on him, squeezing his hand. He starts when he sees her eyes, the way they have changed, now unnaturally large and dark, almost as if the pupils are wide-open and not contracting. His own eyes . . . he realizes they are the same, for her eyes become even more amazing as they look at each other. They leave. In the middle of the applause and cheering, they have to go. They hurry past the brass band, past the yellow lanterns of the café, through the dark park under trees heavy with foliage. They half run through streets full of elated laughing red faces, holding hands all the way, knowing they cannot let go, knowing they cannot take a tram—the light inside the tram would destroy everything.

They run all the way to Laimgrubengasse.

They are up in her attic room; the door slams behind them. She takes off her cloak and flings it over the chest of drawers, then opens the window. It is hot up there from the sun on the roof. He goes over to her as she stands below the window and he fumbles for her.

As they kiss she notices everything growing, as if her body is growing, as if objects, the air, and the darkness are all growing. Most of all, he is growing in her arms. His neck seems to give way when she blows into his ear. And she realizes . . .

They are standing in the dark, a step from each other, looking. Then they undress.

"You're warm," he whispers as they get into bed.

The softness of her skin is almost more than he can bear. At first they just lie holding each other, looking at each other. She is afraid now, because she *wants* to, because she wants to almost too much. It is like slight nausea. He kisses her carefully all over her face. He, too, must be anxious.

She pushes him away cautiously. He gets up on his knees in the bed in front of her.

Rosa Luxemburg goes in and out of prison for the sake of the revolution, she thinks bravely.

"Come," she whispers.

He swallows, the blood draining from his cheeks, and she is also pale.

"Come now," she breathes.

He goes into her. She lets out a sound and he can see her squeezing her eyes tight shut. Then he buries his face against her throat.

The rest is like a wave rising and hovering, a long time. At first they fumble a little, not really daring to test out whether they can go further. Then their movements become surer, the one able to feel what is happening to the other. She throws her arms around him, breathing in time with his breath.

Her will and desire lie in that breathing; he can hear it, feeling it in the whole of her, even stronger than his own. Now he goes even deeper inside her: her face—he catches a glimpse of her face, dissolved as if she is weeping. She clings to him, letting out a series of small, lamenting cries. He has never seen how beautiful she is before. They have to guess their way ahead, for no experience exists, which means the discovery bears them with it and makes it simple. It is very simple—he is surprised how simple it is. She clings even harder to him and looks like a goddess. He whimpers.

Afterward they lie still together, and she sees his face. Narrow, as if he had acquired new features, and she holds hard to his curls.

⚘

It happened twice that night. Twice they were the sea striking against the shore, the wave rising, then still in the sunlight, and in the rapids of the wave they glimpsed a little child with its arms raised, in the middle of the wave between shore and sea.

Two more times. Then morning came, and with it the rain. They could hear it gurgling and running down the roof, faint rumbles of thunder far away. Gray morning light slid into the room. They slept at intervals, dreaming and waking, mixing with the sounds of the rain and the warm skin-close memories from the night still on them. Somewhere between waking and sleeping, he suddenly whispered, Can you smell earth?

Earth, she mumbled. Earth? But it really was earth, a fresh scent of humus.

Yes, she whispered, you're right.

But earth, he mumbled, in the middle of the city, how can that be?

Not all that odd, she said sleepily. All this—she thumped the roof beam above them with one hand—is fairly raw and moldy. That's earth, too.

She stroked his stomach and he lay listening to the gurgling rain, breathing in its scents and that of mold. Of them.

There are potted plants outside the window, too, she said.

But—he said.

Don't say anything more, she said. Sleep now.

Her body was filled with a warm, sated darkness. She wanted to be still, not talk, never talk again. Obediently he turned and lay with his face against her throat.

Another gust of rain came from out in the countryside and swept over the city in light, fine waves, the drumming on the roof increasing, a soft sound which he listened to, listened and floated into. He was breathing.

And with the rain came sleep.

Always, always still around us; nothing and no one gets by. No voices, no words. I scoop into the dark well of my childhood and let you drink from it. You are the answer to a question I never even knew existed.

That was how their relationship changed that spring: secret meetings, the inexplicable connection that started in Ischl, almost three years earlier, between two children on the edge of a pond—this *between them*, not knowing what it was, what caused it. They found a language, a form. It changed them. They both became very different in a short time. It is perhaps hardly necessary to say that after this revelation they were seldom seen in the café circle. They withdrew from almost everything, all their activities, the string quartet, organization work, painting lessons, theater visits, gallery rounds, and—on David's part —any deeper involvement in school and homework. They drank from each other. They loved each other to exhaustion, to anemia and malnutrition, and were very very happy. David was so happy at this time that when—kindly and fraternally—Hannes one day tried to urge moderation (David was doing really badly in some subjects now, and Hannes, who had an inkling of what was going on, was worried on his friend's behalf)—David burst into tears of happiness. Happiness over all that had happened; tears because these were emotions with-

out logic. He tried to explain as he dried his tears. He tried to explain
to Hannes that he worshipped her. He tried to explain everything
that cannot be explained, that he had found poetry in life, and that
he—a chosen one—had found what the Poet in *Wiederfinden* called
"meiner Freuden süsser, lieber Widerpart." (David and Hannes had been
taken aback by the concept of *counterpart* a few years earlier, considering it exaggerated.) But Hannes the poet pretended not to understand what David meant. Hannes had known a girl or two himself.

"But, David, it's only a girl," he said.

"Only a girl?"

"Yes. The world's full of them. With all due respect to Sofia, but
. . . you can't get *married.*"

"Who's talking about getting married? We *are* already . . ." David's
voice failed him, which was just as well, for otherwise he would have
said something pathetically poetic. Instead, he said, "Hannes, I don't
think you understand."

"What I mean, David, is, be careful not to let your emotions run
away with you to that extent, both of you. You're still young . . . yes,
yes, *we* are young. I don't mean to sound superior—but you're mad
if you . . ."

"That's the worst bit of bourgeois smugness I've heard since the
days of Captain Rindebraden."

"The world also has its practical side, David. Listen to me. I don't
mean to spoil things. But you should realize this—*you both* should
realize this, you who are to be radical social beings. I think you've
gone mad."

"In that case it's the most enjoyable state I've ever been in."

"The world is *not* as poetry may here and there mislead you into
thinking it is. A static state of happiness of that kind simply doesn't
exist, can't exist. Believe me. I try to *write* poetry."

"Yes, but you don't know anything about this. Couldn't it be,
couldn't it *possibly* be that for *once*, one time among millions, the universe has pulled itself together and poetry is right? And so this is *the*
only . . ."

"You're a romantic. You have no idea what you're talking about.
You'll be terribly disappointed, or you'll get hurt. Sooner or later
something will penetrate your blind happiness. Something or other
will reach those lofty clouds of happiness and *crash.* Your fall will be

great. Listen—you—the two of you—are hardly ever seen at the café nowadays. Right. It is none of my business, and you're welcome back, together or apart. But it is worse that you'll flunk your exams. It's only a matter of time before your parents find out about Sofia. The Melchior family is well known, and maybe there's already talk about it. It'll come out, you can be quite sure. I've heard your father talking to *my* father. Yes, I have. Herr Bleiernstern had a confidential man-to-man chat with Herr Schachl. An unusual alliance. You should have heard them. It's true Papa is worried about these poems of mine and is wondering what will come of me—but that's a trivial family affair in comparison with your father's worries over you after your last report card. Your father's worries are monumental. You should have heard him asking Papa, asking and asking, cautiously and courteously, whether he *knew* anything. Papa knows nothing, but it *will* come out, David, sooner or later. This is none of my business, either, as your friend. A friend does not interfere. I'm just pointing out some consequences. What really worries me is that you are flying so high, binding yourself so closely . . . What is going to *nourish* it, this love? What is its substance? David, I'm afraid you'll make yourself unhappy, or her."

"You don't understand, Hannes. I should never have tried to explain. I *have* to bind myself. *Have* to fly high. *Am* already bound. I have no choice."

"Oh, you ass. You mooch around, young and stupid, with dirty collars and as white as a sheet, talking about poetry and nonsense. I wish I had never pushed you down that slope."

"But you did. You did it."

"Yes," said Hannes, after a while. "And the worst thing about it, the worst thing, is that I wish it were you who shoved *me* down. The worst thing is, you scoundrel, I envy you. I envy you like hell."

David grinned.

"It's no laughing matter," said Hannes. "Things will go badly for you. To the dogs. I'll have you know, David, I actually . . . This is a secret no one knows, but I still say my prayers. I have never been able to break the habit."

"What are you saying . . . ?" David began in disbelief

"Shut up. I have to tell you I include all the good people I know, as well as you, you two before anyone else. Don't think it's anything special. It's more like mental hygiene. But I include you two because you understand it least of all. Because you're caught up in some kind of idiotic dream. I pray that you won't be unhappy."

David looked down. It had all become very painful. Hannes looked embarrassed and they parted without much warmth.

Hannes did not seem to understand, and David soon forgot their conversation, just as he had forgotten that gray week before May Day. He and Sofia went on as before. The fact that David did not actually fail his exams might possibly be put down to Hannes's "mental hygiene" prayers, and the whole affair continued to be kept from David's parents.

Sofia was quieter than before, tender and gentle with him, though sometimes rather distant, almost anxious. But if he asked her about it, she did not reply. The new situation seemed both to unite and to separate them. Making love enabled him to see other sides of her, other faces he did not know. At those moments she was a stranger, a stranger he loved.

Then the summer holidays and separation came. Sofia was to go to the country with her mother, where she was to catch up on some of her neglected painting. David was mostly to stay at home.

David was not afraid of separation. He was in a perfectly calm mood on their last day, when Sofia asked him to tea with her mother. So what happened was strange. He talked brightly, used to the situation now and no longer shy with Sofia's mother. They talked about the weather, politics, summer activities, and an exhibition or two, all in Frau Melchior's fluttery absentminded way. David was in the middle of a sentence, his gaze straying from Frau Melchior to Sofia on the sofa, when suddenly he felt tears in his eyes, and then they incomprehensibly overflowed. Frau Melchior gave him a quick, observant glance, then turned to her daughter.

David got up, excused himself, and in some confusion wished them a pleasant summer before heading for the door.

Sofia followed him out, and they stopped in the corridor.

"Sorry about that."

"That's all right." She took his hand, smiling gravely. "It's all right, David."

"It'll be miserable without you."

She shushed him, finger to mouth. She stood looking at him, erect and clear-eyed, as if at a distance, in the way she looked at a painting. Again, she seemed a stranger.

He was about to say something, but she saw the tears returning. "Go now," she said. "Don't make it difficult. Goodbye, David."

He stayed for a moment, seeing how changed she had become recently, and somehow it was this that had overcome him in the living room—the contrast between then and now. She had become so amazingly beautiful, so adult, holding herself differently, features of her whole self different. *He could see it on her from far away.* Perhaps everyone could see it and would understand if they thought about what they saw. Perhaps even Frau Melchior understood. This Sofia was a new Sofia, and he had a part in that new person. He clenched his teeth and controlled himself.

They said goodbye.

That summer—that summer David lost all his shyness and reserve with her. Letters, letters, pages and pages of loneliness and longing. Her letters came back, calm and collected, almost reproachful in their undemonstrativeness. He paid no attention and wrote so that the ink flew, wrote poems, abandoning all inhibitions and mailing them off to her. He missed her; a loss which on previous partings had been calm and almost beneficial now became an emotion overwhelming him completely, physically hurting him, an obsession, a fever. He beseeched her to come home as soon as possible. He went on long, melancholy walks alone, talking to himself, talking to *her* as if she were there. Passersby turned around and stealthily stared at him.

She came back in September. It turned out she had been home for several days when David heard at the café she was back. He bought flowers and a much too expensive art book and rushed up to her room in Laimgrubengasse.

He poured out all his longing and loss and joy, kissing her, embracing her, talking and talking, telling her how terrible it had been without her, smilingly but clearly reproaching her for not letting him know as soon as she was back. Didn't she know he was dying of longing? Dear, darling, beloved Sofia, *dying*, pain, misery, suffocation. But it was good to see her, wonderful, marvelous, now they could be together all fall. He would drown her in love, in gratitude, in flowers; look at these flowers, they're for you, and this book, too, of course, *I can't live without you.*

She smiled at him, kissed him in thanks for his gifts, but it was as if something had been withdrawn or had come between them. David was confused.

Then they went to bed, hastily and carelessly. At the most important moment, he sensed that this was going all wrong, but he exclaimed yet again that he couldn't live without her.

She gently but firmly pushed him away from her, turned on her side, and hid her face in the pillow, either miserable or angry.

"Sofia, I'm sorry. What did I do wrong? You mustn't be miserable. You must always be happy. I want to see you always happy. It's just that I want to have you with me, always."

She refused to be consoled or pacified. Not like that. It took a while before they got back to the same sense of peace—after he had stopped talking and trying to console her, but was lying on his back looking miserably up at the ceiling, she suddenly turned to him, put her head on his shoulder, and fell asleep.

The following weeks were almost as before, though they were both more outward-looking. They started going back to the café, to galleries, theaters, and concerts, and they attended meetings and lectures. Sofia had passed her entrance exam, and art school now occupied most of her time. She buried herself in work and also started mixing with her new friends from the school. David adjusted his whole way of life to the pain he had felt when she was away. He stuck to her, his whole life merging into a thin, invisible thread tying him to Sofia. He did not stop writing poems to her. He could not be with her enough. He did not stop telling her how fond he was of her and that he would never be able to live without her.

In November, the Burg Theater put on Part One of *Faust*. The production was greeted with enthusiasm by the regular audience, particularly the part of Faust. But the evening Sofia and David went there was a surprise.

The auditorium had started humming quietly as the audience waited for the curtain to go up. The performance was already a few minutes late.

A man in a dark suit came onstage.

"Your Highnesses, ladies and gentlemen. The Royal Imperial Theater wishes to inform you that due to illness, Herr Maier is unable to perform the part of Mephisto tonight." A disappointed hum of surprise ran through the auditorium. "However, at very short notice, Max Jänner, the court actor, who has recently been living in Berlin, is now back in Vienna on a private visit and attended yesterday's performance—at very short notice, Herr Max Jänner has agreed to take the part of Mephisto, which—as Your Highnesses and honored audience will well remember—he has also previously performed on this stage."

The atmosphere in the auditorium was at once transformed, the audience now seething with enthusiasm and expectation, one or two even calling out Bravo. A few years before, Max Jänner had had all Vienna at his feet; he was the darling of the theater, and he had broadened interpretations of the great classic roles. Everyone agreed he was a brilliant actor, but he had unfortunately recently transferred his activities to Berlin, incomprehensibly. Many considered it a sign of arrogance. *Berlin*, of all trivial little places! However, Jänner's exile was for the moment forgiven, and the audience applauded, happily surprised, drowning the theater representative's apologies on Jänner's behalf should an occasional slip occur because of Jänner's lack of knowledge of the staging of this particular production.

"He is supposed to be good," David whispered to Sofia. They were in cheap seats way up under the ceiling. "Have you ever seen him before?" Jänner's days of glory in Vienna had been just before David had started enjoying theater.

"No," said Sofia. "I've never seen him before."

She gripped David's hand.

The curtain went up. They had scrapped the Dedication and the Prelude in the Theater and gone straight into the Prologue in Heaven.

The Seventh Heaven. Clouds and veils. Clusters of angels and stars swaying hither and thither in graciously choreographed movements. Tonight the audience did not seem entirely taken by this charm, nor did the three archangels particularly move them, although their recitation was excellent. The audience was expecting someone. The Lord God was already waiting, unapproachable and silent, on his throne.

The angels' part was coming to an end.

A dark shapeless figure sidled onto the stage, gliding, insect-like, then suddenly straightened up a little, face still hidden by the cloak, and flung out one arm, a bat wing unfolding in one swift movement.

A white face came into view, cold and expressionless—but it seemed larger, *clearer* than the masks of the other actors. Then, as if from elsewhere, the figure's voice sliced into the audience, filling the whole auditorium, although it was not much more than a whisper:

> *Since you, O Lord, are with us here once more,*
> *To ask how we are going on at large,*
> *And since you viewed me kindly heretofore,*
> *I thought I'd make one, too, in the ménage.*

A chilling breeze ran through the auditorium. Sofia squeezed David's hand. She was cold, too.

> *Your pardon, if my idiom is lowly,*
> *My eloquence up here would meet with scorn,*
> *Pathos from me would cause your laughter solely,*
> *If laughter weren't a thing you have forsworn.*

The figure had until now stood still, but then he grimaced scornfully and—in an almost invisible leap—was beside the Lord's throne, ingratiating himself. The first laughter rose from the auditorium, the kind of laughter that sticks in the throat. The scene went on. Mephisto made his wager with God for Faust's soul. David was riveted, amazed at the diction and technique of the actor. Jänner made every word of Mephisto's ring icy clear, and his movements were grotesquely drawn. But at the same time he seemed relaxed and natural.

Sofia did not let go of David's hand. When Mephisto growled that he had no desire to associate with the dead, but loved fresh, living young bodies, Sofia started so violently, David turned to her. Her eyes were bright. Her nostrils trembled, and she seemed not to notice she was gripping his hand so hard, or that he was looking so closely at her.

When the first scene was over and Mephisto had left the stage, Sofia relaxed and once again seemed to be aware of where she was. She let go of David's hand.

The tragedy went on, and to a great extent it was Max Jänner's evening. He overshadowed them all, Faust and Gretchen, *playing* with them, apparently pulling invisible strings, humming inaudible, tempting, seductive melodies. Now and again Jänner had trouble with his cues and finding his right place in the bigger scenes of the Witches' Kitchen and Walpurgis Night. But he commanded both stage and audience so superbly that those failings seemed almost to be elements of Mephisto's demonic temperament. He *did* the unexpected, not saying exactly what was expected of him, literally refusing to behave. It was difficult to know where he stood. This created a special tension on the stage between the actors, but the acting did not become stiff or nervous. It acquired an immense concentration and at the same time amazing lightness, all stemming from the character of Mephisto. He commanded them all.

David was overwhelmed, amazed, shuddering with delight. Sofia was pulled along, too—almost more fiercely. Every time Mephisto was onstage, she squeezed David's hand even harder and turned rigid, just as she had during the Prologue. She did not want to go out during the intermission but sat on the stairs with her head in her hands, miles away, answering him as if in a daze when he asked her if she was all right. She stayed there while David went out for a glass of water and some air—this was almost *too* good.

After the performance and the thunderous applause were over, Sofia was still pale, just as distant. She did not clap or smile; the rigid expression on her face was unchanged. Max Jänner had to come back onstage time after time for bows. He had taken off his devil's hat to reveal an unexpected corn-colored mane of hair; smiling broadly, pleasantly, and wearily, he seemed almost unnatural, waving to the audience and picking up all the flowers hurriedly purchased during the intermission.

Sofia was quiet when David accompanied her home. They had been walking for almost half an hour before she returned to normal and he dared speak to her, and even then she replied only in monosyllables.

Once back in Laimgrubengasse, she threw her arms around his neck and drew him hard against her, whispering something into his ear; then she thrust him away and disappeared inside and up the stairs.

He walked home, wondering.

He saw nothing of Sofia for the next two days. He was in a strange mood, having slept badly. He knocked on her door, but she was not at home. He thought of going to see whether she was with her mother, but it would have been awkward to barge in without an invitation, so he comforted himself with the thought that she had a great deal to do.

On the third day, he went to the café to see Hannes, and there she was, quite unexpectedly, at the same table as Hannes, who was listening to Sofia talking to a third person, an adult David did not know.

David went across to them and slapped Hannes on the shoulder. Hannes looked up. What did his expression mean? He was smiling in confusion, his face changing color as he greeted David but couldn't get the words out. David slipped over to Sofia, who had not noticed him and was still talking to the stranger. David put his hand cautiously on the nape of her neck. She started and looked up.

"David," she said, smiling. "How nice to see you."

It was David's turn to be startled. This was not the way she usually spoke to him. The stranger had also spotted David and rose, holding out his hand. He was a tall, well-built man in his forties, well dressed, with pomaded fair hair and glasses. His features were regular and broad and his eyes bright blue—a sympathetic face, almost glowing with equanimity and goodwill. David shook his hand, a large, warm, safe handshake.

"David," said Sofia, "this is Max Jänner. Max, this is David Bleiernstern."

"Glad to meet you, Herr Bleiernstern," the tall man said. "Sofia has told me about you."

David's thoughts came to a full stop for a moment; then he realized what he had heard.

"Delighted—Herr Jänner," he mumbled, flopping down into a chair. Was it possible? Was this pleasant, almost delightful person the same man who had had the whole Burg Theater shuddering the other evening? Word had spread about the performance and Vienna was quivering with the sensation. They had urged Jänner to repeat the performance, but the real Mephisto had recovered and Jänner had collegially refused all requests. Now he was here. David could not make the connection. At the other tables people were staring with greedy curiosity at the actor and the three young people.

"I hear you and Sofia were at the theater together on Wednesday," said Jänner, seeing David's astonishment and wanting to help out.

"That's . . . that's right," said David. "We enjoyed it immensely."
He flushed with embarrassment.

The actor nodded.

"Nice to be back in Vienna," he said. "For once. Yes, for once."
He kept his eyes on David all the time and David smiled shyly
back. "Nice to meet young people. Things happen among the young.
Your friend young Schachl writes poetry. It's encouraging to see
such currents among the young. I've actually read some of Herr
Schachl's poems in the *Ahorn*—I try to keep up, even from where I
live now—we were just discussing the poems when you arrived,
David."

"Oh yes," said David, unable to find anything else to say, his head
quite empty. The actor sensed his embarrassment and calmly went
on.

"I was just saying to Schachl I found his poetry very musical,
though I have to say it doesn't yet have the necessary transition of
thought. But it's immensely musical."

"Thank you once again, Herr Jänner," said Hannes proudly. Then
he launched into a lengthy account of the difference between poems
read aloud and poems recited, which turned into something David
could not really follow.

When Jänner replied, it was with reserve and natural confidence,
and at regular intervals he glanced over at Sofia and David as if to
bring them into the discussion, smiling at David several times, clearly
trying to get him to overcome his bashfulness. He succeeded eventually, though not until later on in the evening. David was trying to
fathom his own confusion, to find a logical explanation for it all.

Sofia must have seen this, for while the other two were talking, she
said quietly, "Max is a friend of Mama's. He used to come to our
place a lot."

"Oh, I see," said David, but his confusion remained. He looked at
her, but she avoided his eyes. "I thought you said . . ."

"What?"

"No . . ." said David. "Nothing. Where did you meet him this
time? At your mother's?"

"Yes," said Sofia. "He wanted to see me again. I was just a child
then. He went to see Mama—he wanted to meet her again, too—
and she sent me a message. The evening before last."

"Oh," said David. "How nice." He smiled at her despite the corrosive unease, almost anxiety, rising in him.

"Max very much wanted to meet you," Sofia went on. "That's why we came here. I thought you might be here. But Hannes was. He'll probably monopolize Max for the rest of the evening."

An image flashed through David's mind, an image of a smashed window and a gaping hole. Something was bothering him, something he could not remember, something he had to recall. Sofia was still not meeting his eyes but gazing at Jänner as he spoke, her dark eyes wide.

"What about a little something to drink?" said Jänner cheerfully.

A bottle arrived on the table.

The rest of the evening was horribly painful, in that David's embarrassment did indeed vanish and he thawed out. Not used to alcohol—two glasses were enough to make him tipsy—he wanted to show them he was not embarrassed, not afraid, did not feel the anguish piercing him like splinters of glass. So he talked to the actor, loudly and incoherently, smiling and laughing. He wanted to know how you could play the part of the Devil without being the Devil yourself when onstage? Didn't you have to have a bit of the Devil *in* you offstage? Know him? Know him personally? He asked the question very provocatively and Sofia looked annoyed, but Jänner replied good-temperedly.

"My dear young friend, that's a very difficult question. More difficult than you imagine. If the Devil exists—which I personally very much doubt—then he's a creature of such hideous evil and such loathsomeness, I don't think anyone would manage a personal meeting with him. He would be like all the world's fears and all the world's evil laughter concentrated into one figure. No one could portray a creature of that kind on the stage. It's not the Devil I portray."

"No?" said David. "Who is it, then?"

"I try to portray an actor being the Devil. I think that's the only way to do it. Think about it—it's not as simple as it sounds."

"But this actor, this buffoon, he must also have some evil in him at that moment, be inspired by some kind of cruelty to be effective."

"Yes," said Jänner gravely. "I think that's true."

"Exactly," said David angrily. Sofia grasped his arm to stop him from talking, but Jänner put his large hand over hers to calm her and went on.

"The amazing thing," he said to David, "is that the evil the actor has to incorporate within himself—and it is true he has to find it in himself—the amazing thing is that it will never be effective on the stage until he *controls* it, until he sees through it and *overcomes* it. He can't perform an active, *personal* evil. That wouldn't look particularly evil. He has to transform it. And the funny thing is that when it gets to that stage, that stylization, then—for him, the actor—it's no longer a matter of evil or dark forces within him—it becomes a new force, a force of light. The audience sees it as a current of darkness from the blackest of hells, while he experiences it as light, as goodness, as something helping him. That's important. You have to differentiate between the substance and the person, between illusion and reality. The point is that it has to *look* evil. In reality, the representatives of evil, those who commit evil, frequently look innocent and harmless. But a harmless Mephisto would be nothing but a joke on the stage."

Sofia and Hannes nodded solemnly at the actor's words. They had clearly learned something—but David thought it all sounded like a play on words, a game which removed from the concepts their irrevocable meaning. Had he been sober, perhaps he would have regarded it differently, but David was now feeling a horribly active evil beginning to glow inside him, burning all through him, directed at this friendly and attractive actor sitting opposite him. He noticed Jänner did not remove his hand from Sofia's until she herself withdrew it—and that was several minutes later. David could feel tears choking him, and he felt like tipping the table over and flying at Max Jänner's throat. Sofia—sitting there watching that clown, that fool, that . . . that brilliant, superb artist. She kept staring at Jänner, wide-eyed and open, and he touched her hand again, that slim white hand that was David's heaven. David was grief-stricken at the sight, and he became very drunk. Later he remembered he had talked and talked, babbling on and on, but without being able to rock Jänner's confidence or make any impression on Sofia. He remembered saying something terrible very loudly, and that Jänner, considerately and carefully, to avoid a scandal, had helped him out onto the street, where he had been very sick. Jänner had cleaned the worst up with his own handkerchief. It had all been very humiliating. Then Sofia had come out, looking miserable, and she had neither touched him nor said good night but just disappeared arm in arm with Jänner.

Hannes helped David home, walking around with him until he was presentable enough to face the displeasure of his parents.

"Don't pay any attention," he said as he calmed David down and they were walking around the block for the fourth time. "Ignore them. He's going back to Berlin soon. Are you listening, David? He's going back to Berlin."

"Hannes, I feel terrible."

"You're just drunk," said Hannes.

"No, it's something else. What *is* the matter with me? I'd like to . . ."

"You're jealous," Hannes told him. "But don't be. He's not worth being jealous of. Just a stupid actor with a fancy name."

"She *went off with him.*"

"Yes, she did. *You* couldn't take her home, could you?"

"No . . . But couldn't you . . ."

"Me? I had to take *you* home. Was I supposed to leave you in the lurch? Or perhaps *Jänner* was supposed to take you home and go up to meet your parents? Pull yourself together now, David. Anyway, his name isn't Jänner."

"What do you mean?"

"That's his stage name. His real name is Errschling. Herrgott Errschling, if that's any consolation."

David had to laugh despite his misery.

"Don't let your emotions run away with you like this," said Hannes. "You're like a feather in the wind."

"Yes, but didn't you see how they . . ."

"Yes," said Hannes. "There were one or two things . . . but that doesn't necessarily mean anything, David. Take no notice."

"Why did she bring him to meet me? That's the cruelest insult I've . . ."

"Now now," said Hannes. "Don't you think it might be because she wanted to give you the pleasure of meeting a famous actor? *You're* the one who has behaved stupidly and insultingly tonight, David, and I'm sorry I had to see it."

"I know," said David quietly. "It's just that I was terribly—frightened. You see, Hannes, I've promised her to . . ."

"No," said Hannes firmly. "I don't want to know anything about what you've promised her. She brought him along because she wanted you to meet him. She didn't bring him along for his own sake! She must have thought you admired him, and to tell the truth, so did I. You've talked about practically nothing else but that performance of *Faust* for the last two days."

"Yes, Hannes, I see all that, but there was something *more* than that, something *else*. Something . . . something *between* them."

"Don't pay any attention," Hannes repeated gently. "Just pretend nothing has happened. Jänner said he was going back to Berlin in a few days. He's performing there all this season, and the next. When you see Sofia again, tell her you're sorry you behaved so stupidly, and then I think you should try to forget the whole thing. Forget Herrgott Errschling. Otherwise it'll only be disastrous."

"Yes," said David gratefully.

"Are you feeling up to facing your parents now?"

The next time he met Sofia—a whole week later—he did as Hannes had advised and apologized for his behavior. Sofia seemed to be herself again, and her rather dismissive aloofness had disappeared. Instead, she was more loving to him than she had been for a long time, almost overwhelmingly, as if she was also asking forgiveness for something.

It confused him, but made him happy. Jänner was not mentioned between them for a long time.

Nevertheless, all that fall and winter there was an unease, a kind of undertone of uncertainty, of danger. Something *had* happened, something *had* changed; something unsaid was gnawing between them. First and foremost, it was clear from the fact that Sofia's moods kept changing. Sometimes she was just as usual toward him, just as close and tender as before, but then suddenly, for no apparent reason, she closed up, looks and words becoming distant. For days she would avoid him, blaming her work, and she *was* really busy. But that had never stopped them from being together before. All this worried David profoundly, and he again started showering her with poems and written endearments, attentions large and small, presents, books.

She seemed to have bouts of grief and David lacked the courage to ask her why. Deep down, he sensed it had something to do with the actor, but he did not dare talk to her about it, clinging to the hope that if he pretended it was nothing, all would be as before. It never occurred to him to console her, to understand what *Sofia's* grief was in all this. Instead, he made it quite clear that he was unhappy, reproaching her with a thousand remarks for being so fickle toward him. One day in the New Year, he happened to see an envelope in her studio, face down on the chest of drawers, with the sender's address visible—*Berlin 3, Max Jänner* . . .

"So you correspond with that Jänner, I see," he said, icy with jealousy.

"What?" said Sofia from the easel, rather surprised. "Max? Yes, we write to each other now and again."

David would have given a great deal not to have seen that envelope. They had had a good afternoon together, he and Sofia, almost as in the past. They had run through snowdrifts and played tag; then they had sung together. Now all that had been spoiled. The envelope had spoiled it.

"So you have time for *him*," he exclaimed. "And last week you were so busy you didn't even so much as want to see me."

She put down her brush, came over to him, and looked closely at him.

"David," she pleaded. "Don't be unreasonable. Please."

"Unreasonable," he said, hurt. "I think it's you who are being unreasonable. What are you up to with that man?"

"Up to?" said Sofia, turning her eyes away. "We correspond. He's an old friend of the family—Mama's, mostly. I told you."

"When we were at the theater, you told me you hadn't seen him before."

"Did I? I don't remember."

"You're lying," said David dismally.

"David, I really can't remember ever saying any such thing. Perhaps I thought you were asking me whether I had seen him on the stage before . . . which I hadn't. David, it's true."

David looked at her. Her eyes—there was dark despair in them and they flickered. Was she lying? Did she have to lie?

"And what," he said between clenched teeth, "do you and Jänner find to correspond about?"

"About . . . lots of things. Art. About what is going on today. What we're doing. David, what does one write letters about? Anyway, that's none of your business."

David said nothing for a moment.

"Have you also noticed," he then said quietly, "have you noticed we don't talk about everything the way we used to? Not always. Something has changed."

"Yes, David."

"Do you exchange thoughts with *him* now?"

"What if I do? David, you don't even want to understand. You're always talking about yourself. Everything is about your loss, your love, about you and me . . . all the time. Tell me what you think it will come to, between us? Will it just go on and on like this until it ends in a proper marriage contract and so on and so forth forever and ever? You can't mean that. I'm not like that, David. We must move *on*." She fixed her eyes on him, without mercy. "You must understand that *I* want to move on. I want to be older, and I want to learn. I can't get everything from you. I have to be free."

"Is that what you have to be?"

"You can't grow under a lid."

"I'm not a lid."

"Yes, David, sometimes you are a lid." She smiled at him, a bit uneasily.

"What do you want me to do?" David cried.

"You must be free, too. Free and courageous. Just as you were when you rolled down to us out at Ischl. Just as when you refused to say I was your beloved, although you saw I wanted you to say it. As free as when you ran away from me that last day at camp. Like that whole fall when you didn't go to Schönbrunn on Sunday mornings. You must be like that for me to love you."

"Don't you love me, then?"

"No," said Sofia. "Not here and now."

"But I love *you*!"

She did not reply.

"Did you hear what I said, Sofia?"

"No, you don't," she said. "At this moment you just want to own me."

"Nonsense," said David. "There's no sense in what you're saying. What do think Jänner wants of you, then? Do you know what kind of reputation he has, by the way?"

She did not reply, and again that desperate look came into her eyes.

"Is it *him* you love?"

No reply. Her eyes were quite blank.

"Once," David began, his voice beginning to fail him, "once you told me about—an actor. About something that had happened when you were younger, very young. Was that . . ."

"Yes," said Sofia, nodding quickly. "It was he." She was breathing quickly, frightened.

"Do you want to tell me about it?"

"No," said Sofia. "No. It's too late. I could have told you before if you'd asked. I don't want to talk about it. I can't any longer. You've written too many poems to me in between."

It was as if something inside him had simply been mercilessly crushed. He noticed with astonishment that he felt like hitting her.

"That time," he said, "you asked me to . . ."

"Be quiet, David. Can't you be quiet. Yes, yes. I know what I said. But you didn't understand then, and you don't understand now."

There were tears in David's eyes. All he wanted to do was to get out, to get away from it all. He was cold and numb all over and felt he would be sick if he stayed another minute.

He went across to the door; then suddenly she was in front of him, grasping his hair and raising his face. She looked at him for a few strange, shining seconds. A glimmer of bright inexplicable joy ran through him. Then he rushed out into his dark misery.

❧

Go into the night, David Bleiernstern and Sofia Melchior. Go into the night separating you. Tonight the roads are leaden gray and without light and you are traveling through a country with no milestones. There you are to go, into the kingdom of parting, and you will go tonight, each of you, on your own.

No limit to the night. If only one could remember dreams, if only one could know what one does not know. In the depths of sleep someone walks past and summons you, summons you away. The way goes forward, into the darkness.

Tonight you will dream about her, David. Will she dream about you?

You are both alone. You are no longer *you two*. You are You and

You. You two have been created in light. Now you and you will be created in darkness.

☙

"David? Is it you? How nice. So . . . er . . . very unexpected, I must say. It must be at least two months since we . . ."

"Good evening, Frau Melchior. I hope I'm not disturbing you."

"No, not at all, but . . ."

"Are you well?"

"Yes, thank you. Life has its bad and good moments; only the other day I broke a vase, an expensive one, too—but on the other hand I had a nice letter later that day, from my old friend . . ."

"Could I come in, Frau Melchior?"

"Yes, yes, of course, David. By all means. What am I thinking about. Don't stand out there in the wet and cold. I have one of my little gatherings tonight—you know, the usual bunch, but if you don't mind, at last you may . . ."

"A thousand thanks, Frau Melchior. The maid didn't want to let me in, so I asked her to fetch you."

"But, my dear David, you're soaking wet. Is something wrong? You look wretched."

"Is Sofia here this evening?"

"No, David, not yet. But I'm expecting them in the course of the evening."

"Them?"

"Yes," said Frau Melchior, suddenly quiet. "But you knew, didn't you? Max Jänner's in town. He's been here a week or two now. Largely for her sake, I think. He's out with her now."

"Yes, Frau Melchior, I know."

☙

Rainwater and melting snow splashing along the gutters, David shivering in his thin coat as he stands on the street corner, opposite Laimgrubengasse, an empty, desolate street. They had not seen him in the murky twilight. They had not seen his face, or his eyes. How long has it been now? They had come smiling past him down in Graben, she close to him in the rain, and they had not seen him. He had followed them from café to café and stood outside. How long had it been now? Is he still up there with her? They had slipped smiling in through the entrance. How long? The light is on in her window. Or is it the neighbor's? He leaves. He walks away, away, walking for hours and years. No one on the streets that night, the kind of night people stay indoors. Everyone he meets is no one—they have no faces. He goes away. But he must not leave! He must stay. He must stay and care for her, watch over her. He has promised to, promised her, forever. He rushes back through the rain and again stands on the corner. He has to. Are they still up there? Is the light on? How long has it been? The actor has been in town quite a while now. David knows they have been seen together. Tonight it had been too much to think about and he had gone to find them and had found them. They had not seen him. How long now? Time becomes a thick mass he has to struggle through as it clutches at him with every step he takes. The light is not on. The light up there is not on. For a moment his despair is too great and he wants to scream. Then he remembers Frau Melchior is having one of her evenings.

"Just say so, Frau Melchior, and I'll leave."

She looked at him with a harassed expression.

"Nonsense," she said firmly. "I can't have you going around like a wet dog because of Sofia."

"I've been standing outside for a long time."

"My dear departed Adalbert went around like a wet dog just before he died. It was not funny. It's best if a person comes into the warmth then. Let me take your coat."

"Thank you so much."

"We'll be quite a number tonight, David. I don't know if you want to meet my guests."

"I really came to talk to Sofia, I haven't spoken to her for three months. She doesn't want to see me any longer and she doesn't answer when I write. And now I've heard she wants to . . ."

"That's right, she's trying to get into the Academy in Berlin. Says she's too tied down here. Ah yes, a mother's burden is a heavy one. Before they're old enough to walk, they're off to Berlin. Anyway, David, Sofia has always made up her own mind. She's always been like that."

"I've always liked coming here, Frau Melchior. I don't know whether I've ever properly said so . . ."

"Yes, David. I know."

"Then you must have realized that Sofia and I . . . that Sofia and I . . ."

"Sofia has never been very communicative, David. While I chatter away, she is silent. But I was able to see that you made her very very happy."

"But now . . ."

"David, can't that be enough? Do you really think the happiness you gave her just disappears? Do you think she's forgotten it?"

"But this Jänner . . . Frau Melchior, I don't want to make things difficult for you, but he's taking her away from me."

"Max Jänner is unusually talented and a rich man. He is helping her. There's always been a—special relationship between them, ever since the first time he came here. Now she's grown up. She wants to go to Berlin. He is helping her."

"He has everything and I have nothing."

"Sofia is happy when she grows, when she changes. Do you begrudge her her happiness?"

⚜

Soaked, he slips up the stairs, lets himself into the apartment in Rosenhügelstrasse as quietly as he can. His parents are in the living room with Mira, his father reading aloud. David steals along the corridor and into his father's study. It is dark in there. He stands still for a moment so that his eyes can get used to the dark. His father's voice from the next room is level and deep. Only a year ago and he would have been able to sit there in the gentle lamplight, with Mira and his mother, listening to *The Jungle Book* for the third time. Now it is like a country he can never visit again. He himself has become an Akela, the lone wolf, or a Mowgli, the human being among the wolves, a wolf among people, as it seems to him. He roughly shakes his head, no longer able to think sensibly. Now. He sees the bureau, above it the portrait of his father as a lieutenant in the infantry. He slips through the darkness, over to the desk.

In the passage, just as he is about to slip out again, he bumps into Mira. She looks at him in horror. He signs to her to keep quiet. She goes over to him and strokes his arm, childishly affectionate. Stay, her hand says. Stay with us. I don't know what's happening to you, big brother. Stay.

His father's voice from in there: "Are you coming, Mira?"

David knows his sister. He knows she will not keep it to herself. "David's here, Father."

His father is at once at the door.

"Well . . . I must say. I must say. Now I'd like an explanation of what's going on, David. You haven't been to school for . . . is it four days? Five. And where have you been since this morning?"

"I must go now, Father. I have an appointment."

"You're to stay, David. I'm not sure what's afflicting you . . . whether it's a . . . er . . . a young lady or a gambling debt. But you can rest assured I'll help you find an amicable solution, inasfar as that is within my powers. Your mother and I are worried."

"I understand, Father. Don't worry. I must go now."

"No, David, I think that's enough. We have a right to know where and what . . ."

"Goodbye, Father. Look after yourself, Mira."

"David. *David!*"

". . . this young man is David Bleiernstern, a friend of Sofia's—of our little family—he happened to come along . . ." Indifferent, dutiful, courteous glances from artists who had no eyes for anyone but other artists. The conversations went on and David sank down into a chair. Frau Melchior gave him an apologetic, resigned smile; then her presence was required elsewhere.

How long had he sat there? Had he dozed off for a moment? When he opened his eyes again, he saw Sofia and Max Jänner coming into the room, arm in arm. Jänner greeted people right and left, and everyone flocked around them. Sofia's eyes were shining. David saw Frau Melchior's anxious face as she tried to forestall the couple, to tell them he was there, but David was already on his feet and pushing his way through the crowd.

"Sofia!" he cried. "*Sofia!*" He stood in front of Jänner, in the light of Jänner's face looking kindly and understandingly at him.

"David," said the face. "Are you here?"

Sofia's voice, from far away, as if warning him: "Max . . ."

"Let go of her, Jänner. Would you kindly let go of her arm." He heard his own voice rising to a falsetto, not giving his words the right dramatic content—on the contrary. Someone laughed. David refused to allow himself to be affected. Nervous quiet, the whiff of an amusing scandal. Frau Melchior, loud, confused: "Isn't it time for another pot of coffee?"

"Are you threatening me, David?" said Jänner, smiling in disbelief.

"I know who you are all right," said David quietly. "Herr Herrgott Errschling!"

"That's no secret," said the actor. Then he laughed in a superior way. "Come now, David, let's sit down and talk about life. Herrgott and David, in peace and quiet."

"You bastard," said David. Absolute silence. Sofia's voice penetrating.

"You don't understand, David. Why do you have to hurt me like this?"

"I'll kill you," David said to Jänner. "I'll kill you if you don't let her go. She's mine. I'm hers. We belong to each other. You have no right to steal her."

"So say the Ten Commandments," said Jänner, laughing quietly, then turning serious. "Sofia has come to me of her own free will," he said. "That's life, David."

"Are you saying . . ." David looked at Sofia, who was crying now, without a sound. She had let go of Jänner's arm. A voice came from far away. "Shall we throw him out, Frau Melchior?"

"I'll kill you," David said again. The actor smiled benignly at him. "You're making a fool of yourself," he said.

"Yes," said David. "I am perfectly aware of that. I look both innocent and ridiculous. Think about that, Errschling."

Jänner frowned.

"Be careful," he said. "Why don't you go home? Why do you torment Sofia? You're compromising yourself and her. You're not doing anything to *me* by coming here and causing a scandal, but what do you think Sofia says about a little Jew boy, a little smart-aleck coming and . . ."

Calmly and collectedly, David unbuttoned his jacket and put his hand in the inside pocket.

"Sofia is a fine girl," Jänner went on, "and if you really want to know, if you really want to rub salt into your own wounds, we are . . . Sofia and I are . . ."

David was standing with his father's revolver in his hand, the safety catch off, aiming at Jänner.

"Put that down," said Jänner calmly.

"Just go on where you left off," said David. "Just tell me, Jänner."

Silence, an occasional sob from Sofia. Then Frau Melchior at last.

"There's to be no shooting in this house. This is a house of artists and peace."

Jänner smiled crookedly.

"Give me the gun," he said, but he did not move. "Sofia *is* fond of you. I also set store by you, although you're an idiot, but I was as friendly as I could be to you because *she* . . ."

The sound that followed was more like a shriek than a shot, slicing into everyone's ears and shrinking the room. David had fired into the ceiling, raising the revolver and firing up into the air.

"Get him," said a voice close by. "Get him before he reloads." But David had already dropped the gun. Someone fumbled for his arm, another firmly grasped his shoulder, then a clear strong voice cried, "Let him go! Let him go! Don't you dare touch him!"

They let him go. He left. He left with Sofia's blessing.

"You're stark staring mad. Young Werther and his great passion with inclination to metastasis. A *revolver*, for God's sake. *The whole city is talking about it.*"

"Yes, Hannes."

"Your father has been to see us today. He's a broken man. You've broken him, David."

"Yes," said David, remarkably easily and quietly.

"The police have been here, too."

"The police?"

"Jänner has reported you. The police will probably want to investigate, regardless. This kind of thing can't be hushed up. But he has reported you. He had some kind of attack after you made your exit. The police are looking for you, your father's looking for you—I must be insane."

"Thanks, Hannes."

"You can't *live* in this garden shed. Spring will come to you as well."

"What do you think I should do, Hannes?"

"Do? Don't you think you've done enough? There's one thing you simply must understand—you can't compete with a man like Max Jänner. You can't win over him. That's not the way to win love. He *is* someone. You are no one. Sofia will not be attracted to you as long as you don't have anything of your *own*, a tension in you, a stretch of road you've walked alone. Something *you* have devoted yourself to, something *you* burn for, something *you* have seen and transformed."

"I know," said David. "Perhaps that's what I realized as I stood there pointing a gun at him. You know, everything turned out so different from what I had imagined. I had taken the gun and money plus my passport from Father's desk. I was determined to kill him, make myself into a murderer, and then try to get away after I'd done it. Rather guilt and flight, I thought, than him having Sofia. Then I was standing there, aiming at him—that friendly generous goodness of his just churning around inside me, his words sort of glancing off me. Then an amazing thing happened—I realized I actually *could* do it. That it would be quite simple. At the same time I realized that he probably didn't like me particularly, either. So I thought I might as well *not* do it, if I didn't *want* to. It was so easy—just choosing not to do it."

Hannes looked thoughtfully at his friend. "It was a wise choice," he said.

"I thought, So he's like that. There he is, and here am I. Everything was so fragile—sort of thin—and I thought, Why on earth shouldn't he win over me? What's wrong with him having the last word? So I chose not to."

"But you fired?"

"Hm. Only because I have no idea how to put the safety catch on a revolver. I was afraid it might go off by accident."

"Hah."

"The funny thing was, I wasn't thinking about Sofia being fond of him. I wasn't really thinking about her at all, or about myself, basically, or about Jänner. I just *saw* him, if you understand."

"No, I don't."

"Neither do I, really."

They were quiet for a while. David was sitting with his legs drawn up beneath him on the big table in the toolshed in the Schachl garden, where he had spent the night. He breathed up at the cracked window, his breath turning to a cloud of vapor in the raw, cold air—he watched it for a while.

"You know," said Hannes, "don't think Sofia isn't fond of you. She is. I know that."

"Have you . . ."

"Of course I've talked to her. She's been here twice. She's very hurt and furious with you. As furious as you can be only with someone you prize very highly. She's completely beside herself."

"And Jänner?"

"I don't know what there is between them, as I told you. Perhaps it's a lot. But she mentions him only in passing, so to speak, and is angry with him for reporting it to the police."

David sighed, sending up another cloud of vapor toward the window.

"I'm going away now, Hannes," he said. "I'm going this evening, as soon as it gets dark."

"Going where?"

"Out into the world. Fleeing. Just as I planned to do. I've got my passport. I'm terrified, but I'm going, pleased and satisfied. It's the only thing I really *want* to do, after yesterday. In a way I'm doing what Augustin the musician did."

"What?"

"Don't you know the story of Augustin?"

"No."

"I thought everyone knew it. Augustin was a musician in Vienna over two hundred years ago. He played the bagpipes and was a cheerful, happy musician, but far too fond of his drink. One evening in 1679, during the plague, he got drunk in a tavern—times were gloomy in Vienna for a musician and the smell of corpses hung over the city. On his way home, Augustin had to cross a churchyard. The plague was raging at its worst at the time and the mass graves were open. Augustin didn't look where he was going in the dark and fell down into one of them, down among all the corpses. He lay there, in a fog, until the next morning, then was woken by the carters flinging down new corpses. He realized where he was, in a mass grave. So without thinking he broke out into song and sang a little ditty:

> *Oh, du lieber Augustin,*
> *Alles ist hin!*

"When the gravediggers heard someone singing down in the grave, they were terribly frightened and thought perhaps it was a ghost. But the tune was so cheerful. When they looked over the edge, they saw Augustin sitting astride one of the corpses as he sang:

> Oh, beloved Augustin,
> Everything is gone!

"They hauled him out of the grave and he lived for many years, grew old and full of days, and his song was never forgotten. That's the story of Augustin."

"I've never heard it before."

"I'm leaving, Hannes. I'd better do so while I still have the courage. I'm feeling cheerful, easy—like Augustin in the grave, breaking into a cheerful song whenever things were damned awful."

"Mad," said Hannes. "All you can do is give yourself up to the police."

"No," said David. "I could have shot Herrgott Errschling. I didn't. And he knows that. So I don't think he should have reported me."

"What are you going to do?"

"Now *you're* asking me what *I'm* going to do, Hannes. To tell the truth, I don't know. But I'm going to ask you to pack a small bag with the barest necessities for me. And I think you should go and have a talk with Father . . . explain to him that I'm leaving. Ask him if he will give you my violin and one or two other odds and ends."

"He'll only insist on knowing where you're hiding."

"No," said David. "Not if you tell him I want my punishment to be self-inflicted."

❧

It was quite dark when David slipped out of the Schachls' garden shed with his suitcase and violin. He knew the railway station might be watched, but he was not afraid as he walked along, feeling calm and clear-headed, almost confident. If they caught him, then they caught him. The assassin! The dangerous criminal! He smiled to himself and started off down Hannes's avenue of lindens.

"There you are at last," she said beside him in the dark.

"Yes," he said. "I'm going away, Sofia."

She nodded. Said nothing. Stood still. He dropped his violin and suitcase and put his arms around her.

Now he was consoling her.

After a while she said, "It was unusually foolish of you, what you did last night."

"Yes," he whispered.

"Cowardly, too." She abruptly stamped her foot. "And you never gave a single thought to me, or to Mother."

"No," he whispered heavily. "No, Sofia. I'd better go now."

"Yes," she said. "That's best." She put out a hand and ran it over his head. "I'll be going to Berlin regardless, David."

"I know," he said.

"And I'm still fond of Max."

"Yes," he said. "I don't expect . . ."

"You're so beautiful, David." She kissed him, then put her hand on his forehead. "You're hot."

"Travel fever, perhaps."

He looked at her. He saw her again, sitting on a tree stump in the Wienerwald with her sketchbook over her arm, her face tense, clear, hands moving swiftly. He saw her asleep. He saw her standing there in the dark. Nothing that exists is ever lost.

"I must go now," he said.

"Everything's a journey sometimes," she whispered. "Where are you thinking of going, by the way?"

"I don't really know."

"Then it's sure to be all right."

"Maybe. I must go now. There's a train to Munich at eleven. I'll go on from there—to England, I think."

He was still standing there, and she put her arms around him and pressed hard against him, pressing him hard to her. Then she let go and peered out into the dark.

"It is beautiful in April."

"Yes."

"Something happens to the air in April. Here in Vienna everything becomes so transparent."

"Yes, it's beautiful. It'll probably be transparent in other places, too."

"I'll miss you, David."

🌱

That was David Bleiernstern's story.

Così tra questa
Immensità s'annega il pensier mio:
E il naufragar m'è dolce in questo mare.
— LEOPARDI, *L'infinito*

Thus, in this immensity my thoughts do
    drown:
And it is good to suffer shipwreck in this sea.

April 14, 1912
14°N, 42°W, 10:30

———◆✦◆———

T HE ship was sailing into an unusually clear and still Sunday. The sea was shining as far as the eye could see, the air cool and the sky light.

This calm out in the middle of the ocean was special, so even less experienced passengers who had at first ensconced themselves in their cabins now wrapped up well and came up on deck to stand along the railing, respectfully admiring the North Atlantic. The ship forged ahead, breaking up the sea into foam for a few moments before the calm settled back again.

Captain Smith's service in the first-class dining room had a large congregation that morning. As standing orders prescribed, the service was for everyone, so steerage passengers were allowed up into the magnificent dining room. So many people were present, the room seemed quite cramped. Some of the first-class passengers looked disapprovingly at the crush, but most were well-mannered enough to ignore their less-well-off fellow passengers, though one or two mothers and nursemaids clutched a little anxiously at their small children.

A great many children were on board, so there was much gurgling laughter and exclamations in Welsh and Irish, and some of the youngest were crying. Children, hushed by their mothers, stared wide-eyed at chandeliers and pointed at all the amazing things to see.

At exactly half past ten, in full uniform, Captain Smith appeared before the congregation, dignified and formal, the company's prayerbook in his hand. He calmly surveyed the congregation and once or twice stroked his white beard; then he opened the book and began the service for the first Sunday after Easter.

The ship's band was playing for the hymns. The evening before, Jason had straightened his tie, brushed his hair, and gone to see Cap-

313

tain Smith to discuss the order of the service. They always adhered to a selection of well-known hymns because of the mixed nature of the congregation, everything from Anglicans, Roman Catholics, Presbyterians, and Methodists to some more obscure religious denominations—there were also a great many Armenians on this trip. Jason could not really remember which god was worshipped in Armenia, but if the Armenians appeared at the service they would at least be able to hum along with the rest and not feel excluded. One Sunday on the *Mauretania* a few years earlier, a group of Muslims had strayed into the service and been so taken by the music that they had begun to sing in upper registers to "Praise the Lord the King of Heaven," an occasion Jason thought back on with delight. Although he had no faith himself, he felt the services were important regardless of what the captains of the various ships made of them. This was the only time during the trip the ship's band played for the other classes. Jason had come to enjoy Sunday mornings very much, and he took particular responsibility for them. Conscientiously he went to Captain Smith to see how he liked to conduct the service. The captain turned out to be a phlegmatic, almost sleepy man who patiently listened to Jason's questions and answered them with a "Yes" or "No" or "Do as you think best."

Jason did as he thought best. His ensemble stood lined up by the piano and played "O Christ, Our Joy, Gone Up on High." They had to pay special attention during hymn singing, particularly in the morning. Congregations always sang unevenly in various keys, and half of them did not get around to starting the verse until the accompaniment was five bars ahead—so the beat had to be firmly marked. To a large extent this fell to Petronius and his double bass, but unfortunately he was once again being utterly impossible. He had been scatterbrained and vague ever since early morning, mumbling incomprehensibly to himself and laughing without reason, although he had behaved fairly well these last few days at sea. Now he was staring vacantly, with a strange smile on his face, playing more or less at random, now and again stopping completely and letting his eyes roam around the room as if he could see everything and nothing, smiling rapturously, clearly totally unaware of where he was. Annoyed, Jason signaled to Spot at the piano. Spot understood and hammered away at the bass like a madman and saved the situation for Petronius.

Jason sighed to himself during the captain's sermon, a traditionally maritime address and like every other captain's sermon he had ever heard. This could not go on any longer. However much it hurt, Jason would have to tell the agent in London when he got back. Old Petronius would have to stay ashore for good now.

Otherwise everything had gone well so far. Spot had kept his head, as far as Jason could see, and David had managed his part well. He hoped he would not run away in New York. But Alex was as white as a sheet, his forehead glistening with strain. Jason sighed gloomily again.

Captain Smith's sermon came to an end; then he read the blessing. Jason Coward put his bow to his violin and launched into "O God, Our Help in Ages Past."

⚜

The rest of the day went by calmly. The staff was beginning to know the ship now: where the cups were, where the stairs led to, where the keys to the linen cupboards were, and which way the doors swung. Everything was running more smoothly. The sounds were more familiar, as was the ship's special way of behaving at sea. After running around from morning to night during his first few days on board, smoothing out difficulties, Mr. Andrews could now take things more easily. He was enjoying a pot of tea on his own in the Palm Court, tired and satisfied. She was a good ship, stable at sea, little vibration, kindly disposed toward the passengers, and beautiful to look at. She had not been tried in heavy seas yet, or at top speed, but that was to happen the next day, Monday. Andrews was satisfied. He drank his tea. There was no music in the Palm Court on Sundays, so it was quiet and peaceful up there, a comforting April light coming through the window.

The hours merged into a long, clear series, as they do at sea. On the stroke of midday, the *Titanic* sounded all her steam whistles and the engine-room telegraph was tested in all positions, according to company instructions. The duty officers were gathered on the wing of the bridge in the fresh air, sextants out. The height of the sun was measured and their position noted, then passed on to the purser to be pinned up on the notice board in the smoking room and the largest corridors. *Since Saturday midday: 546 miles*—that was twenty-seven miles more than the ship had logged the day before. The passengers began to discuss whether a new speed record across the Atlantic was being attempted, but the more nautical among them had already calculated that the *Titanic* had not exceeded twenty-two and a half knots underway. The record holder, the *Mauretania*, could do twenty-six. But the next day they were to decide the new ship's maximum efficiency, fire under all boilers, and wagers laid.

Sunday morning passed. The passengers strolled around, took Turkish baths, dipped in the saltwater pool, played squash, and rode on the electric camel. Card games were prohibited on Sunday.

Lunch was over, then tea. In the Marconi room, the wireless operators were writing out Saturday quotations from the stock exchange in New York which had been transmitted from Cape Race overnight and had to be distributed before two o'clock—millions never rest. It was hard work, and some important as well as less important messages were pouring in at the same time.

"13:42 from the *Baltic*, eastbound from New York to Liverpool via Queenstown: GREEK STEAMER ATHENAI REPORTS ICEBERGS AND LARGE ICE FIELD TODAY 41°51'N, 49°52'W STOP BEST WISHES TO YOU AND TITANIC ON MAIDEN VOYAGE STOP CAPTAIN STOP." The message was immediately handed to Captain Smith on the bridge, where he was talking to the shipowner, J. Bruce Ismay. Ismay liked to play captain and stuffed the copy into his pocket. Later, with a self-important look, he showed it to several passengers.

"13:45: Message from the German ship *Amerika* to the United States Hydrographic Office, Washington, D.C., picked up on the *Titanic*'s receiver: AMERIKA PASSED TWO LARGE ICEBERGS AT 41°27'N, 50°8'W ON THE FOURTEENTH APRIL." But at that moment the wireless operator was so busy with share quotations the message was ignored and never reached the bridge.

At about half past five that evening, the air temperature dropped rapidly and it turned bitingly cold outside in the course of a few minutes, falling 10 degrees to 33°F, just above freezing. The passengers retreated into the warmth. With regard to the ice warnings on the ship's course, Captain Smith gave orders to set course slightly farther southwest than would otherwise have been the case.

It grew dark. By half past six the temperature had reached the freezing point. The stars came out and it was very clear.

The ship's band had had a quiet day, as they did not have to play in the Palm Court or at lunch. The members spent the time in various ways. David had listened to even more of Jim's reminiscences and tall stories. Spot had slept. Georges had read, and Alex and Jason had sat talking in the mess over tea and a smoke.

No one knew where Petronius had been all day.

At seven, they were to play at dinner; Petronius did not appear. His double bass was also missing. The huge instrument was no longer in its case by the piano.

This made things difficult for Jason. He could lead an orchestra with a confused bass player, even with a drunk, mad, or sleepy bass player, but it was fairly impossible with no bass player at all. The members of the band shrugged their shoulders and looked at each other. Purser McElroy stared at the place where Petronius should have been. They did the best they could, a waltz from *Der Rosenkavalier*, "Life on the Ocean Wave," a selection of ragtime, the popular "Oh! Oh! Delphine," and "Girls on the Film." The passengers assembled for dinner.

During a break, Jason sent out a search party. Spot, Georges, David, and Jim trawled the ship from stem to stern, but although they met some pleasant girls on the way, Petronius appeared to have sunk into the ocean.

After dinner, the band went on playing light music on request, but it soon became more noticeable that Petronius was missing. A young couple inquired kindly whether the nice little bass player they had seen at the service had been taken ill. Yes, yes, said Jason with some embarrassment. Yes, unfortunately he's been taken ill. The couple gave him a tip to take to the sick man, and in some confusion Jason put it in his pocket.

Purser McElroy came over to them. "Where is your bass player?" he said in an ominous voice.

"No one's seen him since—just after the service," said Jason.

"Have you looked for him?"

"Everywhere."

"Hm," said the purser. "There's always something with you musicians."

"Yes," said Jason. "There certainly is."

"He can't have jumped overboard," said McElroy sourly. "He *must* be somewhere."

"Yes, indeed," Jason said. "We'll go and have another look. He has taken his double bass with him."

"Taken it with him . . . ?"

Jason nodded, blushing.

"Do you mean to tell me he's dragging that huge thing around the ship?"

Jason nodded once again.

The purser rolled his eyes, said nothing more, and left them.

"I wonder," said Alex, "whether there might not be something in what the purser is saying."

"What do you mean?" said Jason.

"That he might have jumped overboard."

"Nonsense."

Spot interrupted them.

"He's not *that* mad, Alex. I don't believe it."

"Well, he's gone too far this time." Jason sighed. "I thought so at the service this morning."

"You should have thought that many trips ago," said Alex.

"Now listen," said Jim, "you all know Petronius. He's odd and—well, not quite right in the head, but he's quite harmless, both to himself and others."

"After the service," said David quietly, "he was going around as if he was looking for something. That was the last time I saw him, before Jim and I went to get something to eat."

"Good, David," said Jason. "Have any of you seen him since?"

The others all shook their heads.

"Peculiar," said Jason. "Peculiar. Right. Right, now. Our audience is waiting for a gripping rendering of Lincke's 'Verschmähte Liebe,' with or without the double bass."

They tuned up.

"The only thing I don't understand," said Spot at the piano, "is why in heaven's name he has taken his bass with him."

⚜

In the merciful darkness, deep down in the bowels of the ship, the wailing sounds of a double bass were wildly ringing out.

There was a ghost living inside Petronius's double bass.

The same evening
On board, à la carte *restaurant*, 21:05

———◆◆◆———

WAITERS glided from table to table with discreet, world-weary movements. Cutlery rattled against porcelain; cut glass sang. Signor Gatti, the headwaiter, stood at his desk supervising everything with a gaze Jehovah would have envied on the Seventh Day.

Everything had to run smoothly. Dinner was an artistic production. An act of creation. Everything had to be perfect. No waiter was allowed to serve a plate with the slightest spot of sauce on the edge, rough seas or no. If a guest showed any sign of rising, at least two waiters were to be there to assist.

Signor Gatti and his senior waiter were responsible for serving the most difficult guests, such as those who must never be kept waiting for their coffee. Never. Never should they have to signal to the waiter. That was imperative. Gatti believed a *look* in the direction of the waiter would be too much of a strain for some guests. So the aristocrats, the millionaires, and perhaps a few multimillionaires were surrounded by serving *spirits* in jackets and bow ties, genies Gatti himself had trained to fathom the desires of guests and preferably carry them out before they were expressed. Signor Gatti thought a waiter—the perfect waiter—should be a mind reader and seer. Gatti himself was a theosophist, so he had personally undertaken to serve the famous editor and spiritualist W. T. Stead on this trip and was trying in every way to make contact with the newspaperman. But Stead appeared unaffected and was looking phlegmatically down at his truffles with his ordinary bulldog expression. Gatti did think once he had caught a spiritual message for champagne—but when he brought a magnum to the editor's table, he was met with a look of bewilderment and the bottle had to be removed.

After that, Gatti reverted to ordinary means of receiving orders. But as he stood by his desk, he was still dreaming of a restaurant where waiters were mind readers and mediums, and where negotiations over the wine list occurred via astral bodies.

What a tremendous idea! What a restaurant it would be. They would all come there after their meetings, the great spiritualists and theosophists, Sir Arthur Conan Doyle, Madame Besant, Dr. Steiner. And—oh joy—Krishnamurti. It was indeed a stupendous idea, almost an inspiration. If an opportunity arose during the course of the journey, he would certainly drop a word or two in the ear of Mr. Stead, who was now being served his brandy. Or perhaps he should write directly to the Theosophist Society in London. Waiters would have to have the Gift. Perhaps there were a great many unemployed young men with the Gift. Men who could be trained in the professional skills of an *à la carte* waiter. Oh, what prospects! The supernatural was the future. Almost everyone who was anyone in this technical era was thinking in that direction. Had not Gatti himself overheard Mr. Stead talking to Benjamin Guggenheim about some damned Egyptian mummy the other evening? Ah, now the Astors were leaving. The headwaiter rushed across the floor, the air flattening his shirtfront. "Good night, Mrs. Astor, Mr. Astor. I hope you have a pleasant evening."

Ah yes, the multimillionaire was newly married. He smiled at his young wife and she cooed back, and they left a handsome tip behind them.

Gatti floated back to his desk, silently humming one of his native country's many songs on *cuore, amore,* and *dolore.* How amusing that *coeur* rhymed with *doleur* and *herz* with *schmerz.* But not in English. It was probably too cold in England. But the English, they could think and make money, not like at home, where they just shouted hurrah. Ah, Italia! But in English . . . just pain and brain. Where was he? He was in the Spiritualist Restaurant.

Luigi Gatti's dreams came to an abrupt halt as strange noises started coming from the entrance of the restaurant.

A small gray-haired man with a goatee, carrying a massive object and waving something long about in his other hand, was pushing his way in past two waiters trying to stop him. His appearance was alarming and he was shouting loudly and incoherently. People looked up, forks halfway to their mouths; waiters stopped in their tracks, dishes poised, and stared. The little man forged his way with astonishing speed across to the headwaiter's desk, stopped in front of the perplexed Gatti, and bowed.

"At your service," he said. "At your service. You are Italian? *Siete italiano, Voi?*"

"Excuse me," said the headwaiter in his irreproachable English. "But who are you and what are you doing here—with a double bass?"

"I am a musician," cried Petronius. Then Gatti recognized him as a member of the ship's band. "Do you understand? *Mu-si-can-te,*" Petronius went on. "But in reality—in reality I am probably something else. So much else. And soon I will be immortal. I have had my eye on you, Mr. Headwaiter, and have been able to sense that you are a man with spiritual interests. And now the moment has come."

"The moment?"

"Now you will see. Please may I have your permission to tell the company what I have heard in my double bass?"

"Heard in your . . . *ma che diavolo sta facendo?*"

Petronius had put his instrument down, and with no further request for permission, he started playing madly and unmusically, with wild, thrashing movements.

Deep screeching sounds came from the double bass.

"Listen," shrieked Petronius. "Listen to what it *says*. Ladies and gentlemen, *signore e signori*. Bam-bararam. Baba. Listen. Tara. Ha-ha."

Guests hurriedly started to leave. Gatti was standing with his arms out in a rigidly abandoned gesture. He was extremely upset, and to crown it all, the man was Italian. This was all extremely distasteful.

"The moment has come," cried Petronius as he scraped away on the strings. "Now it is here. At last. *Sentite,*" he cried, glancing happily at the headwaiter. "*Che dice la musica! 'E venuto il termine. Finalmente. Viene stanotte.*"

Gatti wiped the sweat off his forehead. Scandal. Scandal. Oh, now the Strauses were leaving, that sweet little American couple—the two old people had ventured into the *à la carte* restaurant for the first time that evening, sober and modest as they were. Now they were hurrying out.

The headwaiter came to his senses and remembered his dignity. He counted to three, then called out to his serving spirits.

"What are you hanging about there for? Make him stop."

⌖

In the cabin, however much Jason tried to talk to Petronius and calm him down, he simply could not bring him back to reality. Summoned by the purser, Alex, Jason, and Jim had had to guide and half-carry their crazed colleague down all the stairs, drag him along the corridors, and put him to bed, shaking, shivering, and babbling.

"It's true," yelled Petronius. "It's quite true. I swear by the memory of my great-grandfather. I heard it in my double bass. At last, at last I shall no longer have to endure it."

Alex glanced at Jason, but said nothing. The purser had already given Jason a dressing-down and Jason was clearly unhappy about the whole incident. "I'll inform the agent, Coward," the purser had said. "I will tell him. This is scandalous, and I hold you responsible."

Jason sighed and looked indifferently at Petronius's shivering figure on the bunk.

"I can't make out what he's babbling about," he said. "Pour some whiskey into him, Jim. Then perhaps we'll get some peace."

Jim produced a hip flask. Petronius drank greedily, cleared his throat, and swallowed.

"Good God," said Jim. "He's emptied it."

"I'll get you some more," Jason assured him.

Slowly calm descended on the cabin, the patient occasionally crying out some incomprehensible word, until he at last fell silent.

"Delirium tremens?" said Alex.

"He doesn't drink much," said Jim. "And it's not like that."

"General insanity," suggested Jason. "I'm fed up with it. He's fired. That is, if we haven't all been fired."

"Don't worry too much," said Alex. "I'll talk to the purser tomorrow morning. It'll work out all right."

"Do you think so?" said Jason. "Where are the others?"

"Up in the second-class dining room," said Jim. "They're accompanying a service. A priest among the passengers didn't think the captain's service was sufficiently godly this morning, and he's invited anyone who would like to come and sing hymns for an hour or two. The others were asked to play for them."

"Good," said Jason wearily. "You'd better go up and help them. I'll stay and keep an eye on him."

The other two left and Jason sat down on his bunk and started reading a bird book he had found in London. Petronius was snoring, loudly and peculiarly, as if his madness had settled in his lungs.

The double bass, large and dark, stood in the corner.

PETRONIUS'S STORY

THE road. It was the beginning and the end, birth and death. Everything ran along it, day and night, forests and towns.

In his mind he always saw the road stretching ahead of him, yellow, scorching hot in the sun, winding for miles through the countryside, crickets chirping in the undergrowth and grass along the roadsides. Otherwise everything was dead in the middle of the day. Perhaps a snake lay sunning itself in the dust, perhaps a lizard. No birdsong at midday, and even the wayfarer is resting. There is always a small grove or a shady tree where he can go and take a breather, perhaps a spring, too.

He had walked miles like this, exhausted, sweaty, dusty, thirsty, and wretched. But the road had always been the only happiness he knew and he would not have exchanged his pilgrim's staff and sore feet for anything.

The road was eternal. It was thirst, and it was also calm waters.

Out in the countryside, too, right from the start up in the mountains of Umbria, he had thought about the road every day, looking at it as it wound its way like a ribbon of artificial gold in the midday sun, carts and wagons trundling along it laden with wine and barrels of oil, vegetables, and meat. All year round, the carts creaked along, through the villages and onward on the long way to Rome.

In the opposite direction, from the big city, came merchants, peddlers, and wayfarers from other landscapes, traveling players, musicians, all of them stopping in the little village, some for a day or two, then going on. The road was like a river carrying all things with it, a

324

river of images: a silent old friar with a staff and brown habit, a bird vendor with cages full of small twittering blue-and-yellow birds, but also hawks and falcons. All travelers had tired, distant eyes when they stopped at the village, the miles they had traveled and the thought of the miles to come apparent on their faces. The road was a river, carrying them all with it, and the villages were the backwaters, of course.

Even when he was a small boy he had thought about that word, "backwater," and as long as he could remember, the road always seemed to want to take him quietly with it. The other village boys also found everything coming and going on the road exciting, but it had exercised a special attraction for the young Giovanni Petronio Vitellotesta.

❧

One day when he was twelve, a marionette theater came to the village.

Just outside the lower gateway, in the shadow of an old wheelless wagon, Petronio had his permanent lookout spot. He could sit there all day just watching what the road was bringing with it. When he thought no one could see him, he got into the old wagon and whipped up the horses with a long stick. He could see himself quite clearly thundering away on the wagon down the valley, a cloud of yellow dust behind him.

They laughed at him in the village and called him the Demon Driver. But Petronio paid no attention and just smacked his lips at his horses. He often slipped away on longer rambles up and down the road and into the valley away from the village. His father, who was the village butcher, had forbidden him to do this in case he met robbers or other rabble. Petronio had had many a slap for defying his father and going on his own. But he simply *had* to go alone. That was best, and as long as he was careful, no one saw him.

But on ordinary days he sat on the wagon outside the south gateway, and that was how he had first seen the marionette theater rattling up the hills, the little wagon drawn by two tired brown horses, three people alternately driving the horses or running behind pushing.

"C'mon, there! Giddyap!"

A stab of joy ran through Petronio, and he leaped down from his place on the wagon. He recognized the approaching wagon although it was many years since it had last been there, so long ago he could remember very little about it. This was great news, so he ran back to the village shouting out what was on its way, something he had never done before.

Long before the wagon reached the gateway, it had acquired a crowd of children behind it.

✢

At that time his name was Giovanni Petronio Vitellotesta. His family's unusual surname—calf head—stemmed from the days of his great-grandfather, the memory of him preserved in it forever.

This first Vitellotesta was a headstrong, singular man with book learning. He had been to both Rome and Venice but, for some unknown reason, returned to the village of his birth to become a butcher. He was immensely strong, big-boned, and of a violent temperament —the reason why, together with his occupation, he acquired the name.

Great-grandfather was also called Petronio (his great-grandson had been named after him at an unfortunate moment). After having worked for several years in his native village, the great-grandfather had taken a wife. She was young and haughty and also headstrong, and she had perhaps taken a lover—who knows?—but for whatever reason, for a long period only six months after her marriage she had denied her husband his most elementary rights. She had "shut the bedroom door," as it was referred to in a slightly revised way in the family legend. This embarrassed the butcher, and after some weeks of the door remaining closed, his rage increased. The whole village was talking about it, for keeping anything a secret was quite impossible, and the butcher was not only suffering physically but also humiliated. Anger and unreleased energy were bottled up inside him, and he dreamed of revenge, a pithy revenge, a way of regaining respect from his wife and neighbors.

One evening, after he had thumped in vain on the door of the little bedroom, the fatal idea came to him, a revelation of what he must do in order to regain his honor.

He went down to the slaughterhouse. A calf's head, fresh that day, was hanging on a hook, large, heavy, and bloody. He took it off the hook and, after working on it for an hour, made himself a mask out of the great head, with small holes in the neck for eyes. He put it over his own head like processional headgear. It was very heavy and tight, and he found it difficult to breathe inside, but when he looked in the mirror on his way up to his wife's bedroom, all his hopes were confirmed. Indeed, even more so. He had had to take his clothes off so as not to soil them, though perhaps with other intentions in view, and the calf's head looked as if it had grown out of his naked body.

Standing outside the door, he started making the most horrible noises, roaring and bellowing, stamping on the floor with his bare feet, and thumping his chest. Perhaps his voice was distorted by the mask, or perhaps his rage was so great his voice became inhuman. Anyhow, he achieved his objective. His wife opened the door and the effect was formidable.

When she saw the naked figure in the moonlight streaming in through the window, the horns and distorted eyes, blood and fat glistening down his torso, and she heard the insane noises the creature was making, she screamed, a scream from her very depths that could be heard all over the village. She fled back into the room in order to throw herself out the window. The butcher realized he had succeeded beyond all his wildest expectations. He raced in after her to stop her, for he had not meant her to do herself any harm. But to his wife, this monster had simply come in after her, seized hold of her, and was refusing to let go. She screamed even louder, waking the neighbors, who then poured into the street with lamps and candles, most of them in their shifts and nightshirts.

What they saw was indeed strange. The butcher's wife had managed to tear herself free from the monster's embrace, and she came rushing out of the house, still wailing with terror, the monster behind her. The sight of a stark naked man with the head of a calf naturally also had its effect on the new arrivals. They hesitated for a few paralyzed seconds as woman and monster rushed by, but then, as one man, they all set off after them, the men grabbing hoes and rakes in passing. Clearly this was an evil spirit, a demon, one of the demons of hell from the depths of the black night, which had come to haunt the village.

"Maybe it comes from the moon," cried a young man with an ax.

He had heard of such things. Perhaps the monster had already eaten the butcher, suggested another. It must have been attracted by the smell of blood, said a third. General opinion was that it had to be killed.

So a grotesque procession rushed down the little main street in the direction of the piazza; first the wailing wife, crazed and half fainting with terror; then the naked, minotaur-like master butcher glistening with blood; and finally a mob of nightshirt-clad men shouting and brandishing axes and crowbars. More and more followed. Women crossed themselves and hid their children, so as to protect them from this bloodstained brute. One woman fainted, and the priest stood in his doorway looking as if the Day of Judgment had come.

Had it not been for the noise and fuss they were making themselves, the pursuers might have heard the ogre calling out quite human words, if somewhat indistinctly: "Wait! It's me. It's Petronio." But neither his wife nor his pursuers heard him. It was also difficult to run with the heavy calf's head on, and to his horror he now noticed that he couldn't get it off, as it seemed to have clamped itself onto him.

His pursuers came closer, their weapons raised. Just as he was catching up with his wife, he slipped on some garbage and fell to the ground with a crash. The men were instantly on top of him, four holding him down. He would undoubtedly have been killed if one of them had not suddenly called out: "Wait! It's the butcher."

The men stood up uncertainly, their lances still raised. They looked in confusion at the hideous creature squirming on the ground. The butcher?

"Yes, look at this," someone cried. "Here's his moon mark." He pointed at the large birthmark on the butcher's right arm, which did slightly resemble a half-moon. "I'm sure it's the butcher. I've seen that mark ever since we used to go swimming in the river as boys. *Veramente.*" Then several more recognized the birthmark.

They could now hear the butcher's voice coming from inside the calf's head. He himself knew little of what was going on outside, and as something had got into his eyes, neither could he see anything, but he realized his life was in danger and begged to be helped out.

Amid total silence, the calf's head came off and the butcher's ordinary head was revealed, bloody and terrified. An impressed mumble rose from the stricken crowd around him. This was impossible, surpassing the most fearful fantasies. And the butcher was naked.

The butcher pulled himself together and looked around. Then he got up and walked calmly over to the fountain, where he rinsed the worst of the blood off him. He then went resolutely over to his wife, now sobbing on the shoulder of another woman in the crowd and unaware of what was going on.

"Come now," said the butcher. "We're going home."

He took her by the arm and pulled her along behind him, looking neither right nor left.

As he did this, the mumbling sank to a low whisper, then faded away. Deathly silence settled on the piazza.

The butcher took his wife home with him. No one knows what he did with her there. Everyone else went quietly back to bed. That was the end of the Night of the Calfhead, as it was called from then on.

The butcher's wife never again denied her husband what the law and the marriage contract demanded, and they had a great many children. Superfluous as it is to say, the wife was never herself again. Something in her was crushed, and after the Night of the Calfhead she almost never spoke again, her eyes becoming transparent and vacant. She was said to have gone mad, and little shudders went through people when the butcher was mentioned. A man who could behave like that had to be watched out for. People turned away from him in the street, and his wife was glanced at with compassion and some uncertainty. And, of course, the whole story also gave rise to hilarious laughter.

If he had not known it before, the butcher now was also a marked man. People came from far and wide out of sheer curiosity and his business boomed, becoming large and reputable, with many assistants. But over the years he grew moody and irritable, and in his old age he more or less ceased speaking. He grieved when his wife died, and it is very possible that he regretted his brilliant idea. But if that was so, he did not show it. He was a man who stood by his actions, and he lived his life with the dumb dignity of an ox.

That was how the family got its name, Vitellotesta.

Such was the family legend. Petronio had heard it a hundred times, in both censored and uncensored forms. Other villagers with no family pride to preserve told him that his great-grandfather had been stark naked. Some also maintained that his great-grandfather's manly state had been of a kind that offended public modesty, but most people doubted the butcher could have kept it up after coming out onto the street.

Petronio's mother and father had never made any mention of such matters, but they used to show him the two stumps of horns left from the calf's head in question. Some wise soul had preserved them, and later on they had been returned to the family. The two stumps were household relics, set in the wood of the very door the wife had refused to open. The parents always showed the horns to the children with a degree of formality, only on holy days, and when a serious and sacred oath was to be taken, they made their way to the little bedroom, which was otherwise kept locked. Members of the family looked with respect on the gray pieces of horn, shiny with wear, a memento of the great-grandfather from whom the family name had come. They always spoke of him with a mixture of gratitude and relief, gratitude because the butcher's business gave him his reputation and wealth, relief because they were, thankfully, not inclined to such insane actions. They were healthy and normal, and periodic insanity of that kind had not otherwise occurred in the family. They were good people and God did not allow retribution to fall on descendants.

There was one exception. Young Petronio was the next youngest in a family of eight children, and he was named after his momentous great-grandfather when it turned out he had come into the world with a half-moon birthmark on his right arm, exactly like the one that had saved his minotaur great-grandfather. The discovery caused a great stir at the childbed, and the two women helping crossed themselves and shook their heads. Still exhausted from the pains, the mother cried out that this child would bring misfortune on himself and others, and God help the little innocent who already at birth showed any resemblance to such a man.

The child was promptly given the name Giovanni Petronio so that there should be no doubt about whom he resembled or according to circumstances ought to resemble.

As Petronio grew older, it was clear he was different from the others—although he did not resemble his great-grandfather. As the youngest son, he should really have gone to school and become learned, but he showed little or no interest in that direction—the opposite of his great-grandfather. Very early, Petronio began his escapades along the road or in the wooded mountain country around the village. He sat on the wagon outside the gateway, keeping a lookout. He neglected school, and neither cuffing, admonitions, nor beatings helped. Every time he was brought back after disappearing from his school desk in the middle of a lesson, or having wandered along the road without permission, Petronio met the flood of abuse with a surprised and hurt look, as if they were scolding him for something he had not done, or had done with good intentions. He never seemed to remember the last time. Eventually, after some consultation with the priest, who also functioned as the teacher, his parents took him out of the village school, tired of wasting money on keeping him there when he always ran away. The priest was also tired of fetching him back.

A family council was held by the horns in the bedroom door and it was decided that Petronio should now assist his father, brothers, and the others in the slaughterhouse. But the same thing happened there. If they sat him down to rinse intestines in the yard, they could be certain if they left him alone for five minutes he would be gone and the intestines left lying as fly bait in the heat of the sun. Nor was it any good leaving one of the assistants to keep an eye on him, for they all complained, just as his brothers did. Petronio's career as a butcher thus came to an end after a few months. So his name did not reflect his choice of profession.

His parents kept on scolding him, though largely out of habit. Petronio often had the impression that they really wished for things to go all wrong for him in life, and once or twice he had felt quite ashamed because in the course of a day he had not given his mother any real reason to complain. But he was not very good at thinking up mischief.

On the other hand, what he did without thinking, without meaning any harm, caused his parents great worry and grief, and the cuffs became more frequent. What he really wanted to do, what he liked best, was to roam around or sit in the wagon outside the village.

"It's the first Petronio in him, poor boy," his mother said to the other village women, shaking her head. This meant the villagers were extra kind to Petronio, but it was not a kindness he particularly enjoyed, for it was the same kind shown to the sheep that was to be slaughtered the next morning. One of the women would come and thrust a fig into his hand, or a piece of sugar, saying, "In God's name, child, here you are, for having such a name." Then she would perhaps shake her head while Petronio thanked her as best he could. "Don't thank me, thank the Mother of God."

Otherwise his life was good. He was by no means disliked in the village, and he was fond of his brothers and sisters and parents and they of him. Nevertheless, to him they seemed somewhat uneasy, especially when they brought up his name and heritage. Then Petronio would feel there was some kind of shadow, an invisible difference between him and the rest of the little world he knew. He had often run away from home and stayed away a night or two at a time, sleeping in haystacks or under a tree, though he always returned. But the desire to go farther and see another valley or perhaps a big town—that desire sometimes grew unbearably strong.

When the theater troupe came to the village, Petronio was twelve, thin and small for his age, with quick movements and clear green eyes under his brown fringe of hair. There was something squirrel-like about him, something light and fleeting and dreamy. In this he was also different from the other village boys, who were slower in most other ways. Petronio was very musical, sang well, and could play both the fiddle and the guitar.

He also had a talent no one knew about, and which was to a great extent to set the course of his life.

He could *see*.

As he sat on that wagon outside the village, or roamed along the roads and paths, he saw things no one else could. Rocks and trees could be buildings and palaces, and suddenly a bleak, deserted landscape was populated with figures, amazingly beautiful and noble figures which both existed and did not exist. When he was alone, he could *see* these figures as clearly as he could his own brothers and sisters. Just north of the village on a mountain slope was a little clearing where there was a spring among the boulders, always gurgling faintly, so faintly he had to stop and listen with his whole self to hear it. It was a special place, and he was perfectly aware that someone was living there—a beautiful girl in bright clothes. He had often seen her. She was the same age as he, but her clothes were made of the finest gossamer fabric he had ever seen, and her eyes were thoughtfully melancholy. So Petronio realized the girl in the spring was not only twelve like himself but also ageless and timeless, as if she had always sat there guarding the water.

He saw many such figures, but he never spoke to them; nor did he ever tell anyone about them. In one way these strangers were more like brothers and sisters to him than his real siblings—he felt he was like them, and never doubted he had really seen them. Elves, fairies, dark *condottieri*, lovely maidens. Who were they? He called them the Beautiful Ones. One early Sunday morning, before anyone was up, Petronio saw a whole procession of them going through the village, the only sound a faint silvery tinkling, like the little bells of a jester.

Another time he saw his great-grandfather with the calf's head under his arm, walking deep in thought in the forest below the village. Petronio the younger did not make himself known, nor did his great-grandfather appear to notice Petronio as he sat in a tree watching the old man going past on the path.

Petronio gazed at the sturdy old man. He looked sad, walking along there. Were they alike? He thought about his own reflection and could see nothing of it in the old man's face. No, they were very unalike, and yet there was something familiar, something that bound them together. The calf's head the old man was carrying as if it were a great burden seemed to have something to do with it.

That was Petronio's childhood, and perhaps it is not all that surprising that he ran away with the marionette theater the morning after its performance in the village. The theater had invited the whole village to a feast that evening. The colorful wagon could be made into a stage, and young and old flocked to the piazza. When darkness fell, lamps were lit in front of the theater's blue curtains and the performance began. Petronio had helped put up the stage and had managed to push his way through to a place right at the front. Enthusiastic cries from the villagers came from behind him as the plays went on, robber stories for the young and love stories for the older people, all great fun and pleasing, the audience laughing and clapping as wine bottles were passed around. But Petronio sat riveted throughout the whole performance without really following it. The marionettes bewitched him. They were alive; there was a golden shimmer in the air around their gracious figures. In reality they did not need strings. He had never before experienced what this meant: to have *life*. They were like his secret siblings—the Beautiful Ones, and they were talking to him. While the puppetmaster roared out the words of the villain and the hero from above, the real voices of the marionettes rang out softly and clearly through the night air.

You must come with us, the voices whispered. *We know you. We are your companions. You belong with the few.*

After a great many encores, the performance was over and Petronio—half dreaming—went that night to say goodbye to the objects and the houses in the village. He would never come back. He crept home and packed a little bag, and early the next morning, an hour after the theater company had departed, he slipped away and followed the road, followed the marionettes.

⚘

You belong with the few. Perhaps it was true. For Giacomo, the puppetmaster, a large, friendly-looking southerner, made no objections to Petronio joining his little company, which consisted of two assistants in addition to the master. The puppetmaster looked at the boy with satisfaction and asked whether he was the boy who had helped put up the stage the evening before. Yes, Master, replied Petronio, that was me. Did you enjoy the show? the master asked. Petronio had no idea what to say and looked pleadingly at Giacomo in his confusion. Good, said the master. You can look after the horses.

For several months Petronio was horsekeeper and errand boy for Giacomo's troupe. That was how his traveling life began, and he got along well with the road, which always took him farther, providing him with more and more new things to see. That was how he saw the towns of Campagna and Tuscany, the sea and ships, and how he saw Garibaldi's triumphant entry into Rome.

Gradually he started handling the marionettes. They were delicate, rare beings. At first he learned how to look after them, retouching them with paint when necessary, hanging them up properly so their strings did not tangle, and mending their costumes.

Then Giacomo bought a violin for Petronio so he could play during a dance number for two marionettes they had made especially for it. They were slim, light figures, with extra-thin strings. It was a very successful number, not least thanks to the young Petronio's sympathetic and amusing playing.

Finally he learned to work the marionettes, which was the most difficult of all, demanding alertness, discipline, and strength in arms and legs. Getting a marionette to walk naturally across the stage requires months of practice. Petronio grew up, came out of his dream world, and stopped seeing things that were not there; indeed, almost forgot about them, just as he had put his memories of home behind him. But the marionettes continued to be his best friends, if in a far more tangible way. He became a very skillful puppeteer. In his own mind, Giacomo had decided that Petronio would be his successor. The young man was gifted. Giacomo also had a child of his own—an only daughter, Giulia. She was Petronio's age, and Petronio and Giulia got to know each other in the cold months when Giacomo gave his players time off and went to winter quarters in Rome with his wife and daughter. Young Petronio went with him to Rome and helped him put the wagon and marionettes in storage for the winter. Giacomo took the boy home with him, let him sleep in the kitchen, and found winter work for him in an inn. Pretty little Giulia was very fond of Petronio, that was obvious, and as Petronio and Giulia grew older, the matter seemed quite clear to Giacomo: He could look forward to a happy old age with a clever and gifted marionettist as husband to his only daughter.

But something in Petronio resisted the idea of marriage when Giacomo first brought the matter up—although Petronio was also very fond of Giulia. Perhaps his great-grandfather was haunting him, or perhaps it was his wanderlust and need for freedom. He put the matter off, postponing the betrothal. But by the time he was twenty-one, he was head over heels in love with Giulia. She hurried things along by meeting him at the end of his working day at the inn, and they went on long walks together along via del Corso.

Nevertheless, Petronio begged to be allowed to remain a free man for one more year. The master agreed, and Giulia concurred with some reluctance, but Giulia's mother, a determined woman, masterful and stern after having borne the responsibility alone for so long, preached a sermon to Petronio. He must not let young marriageable girls wait longer than absolutely necessary. He could wait for one more year, at the most, but after that he must bear his share of the responsibility as part of the troupe and for his last years as part of the family. He had to seal the pact, so to speak. However much he was in love with Giulia, this made Petronio uneasy, for it all reminded him suddenly of the slaughterhouse back home.

Then spring came and the road was waiting for them. It took them far away that year, as far as green Tuscany, and on their way they saw rain and sun, prosperity and need.

They saw the pellagra districts in the north, poverty-stricken, thin, sick farm laborers, so poor they quite literally had no salt for their food. The shortage of salt brought on pellagra, an illness that ended in madness, often suicide. Salt was expensive and in the hands of a monopoly. Added to the salt shortage, famine was widespread, and for the first time Petronio did not enjoy playing for the children in the countryside—children with hollow, sunken eyes and skin stretched tight over their skulls, their smiles angular and shriveled. The laughter of the adults was hoarse. The troupe had a play in their repertoire about a rich man who ate himself to death—a burlesque— a brief sketch in which the marionettes grew fatter and fatter each time they came onstage. The play was amazingly successful with the farm laborers, but that same night soldiers came and chased the theater company out of the village—for there had been trouble after the performance.

In the tiny village of Pazienza, they gave their first performance in the piazza as usual. The village was poor and gray, marked by its warring past, with towers, walls, and bulwarks everywhere.

The ruling family's palace was on a hill outside the village, a handsome yellow stone building erected over a hundred years earlier. It was surrounded by a park containing cypress and deciduous trees, rose gardens and fountains. Despite the palace's apparently inviting beauty, from a distance there was something unapproachable, rather dead about it, as if eyes were peering from high windows. The del Vetros lived there. Contessa Francesca del Vetro ruled over Pazienza and the land around it; she was the seventh generation to do so.

She was hard on the villagers, but the rulers of the house of Vetro had always been harsh and the Contessa Francesca was neither better nor worse than any of her predecessors. The palace was said to be haunted by an unusually obstinate ghost, which refused to leave the contessa, her children, staff, and servants in peace. It had resisted the most persistent attempts to exorcise it. The ghost made life for the inhabitants of the palace a misery, wiping out all joy in the del

Vetros' souls, consuming them, sucking the life force out of the contessa's two children—pale, delicate twins of nine, a boy and a girl. It was obvious that they had grown up without joy, for they were both as white and transparent as alabaster. The ghost must surely have robbed them of joy and light—just as it had all previous members of the family, even when the counts had lived in the old palace in Pazienza itself.

Who was the ghost? That was not easy to say. They had tried to find out, searching in records and annals; in earlier times they had gone as far as to ask the ghost personally. But he was a silent man, in a simple gray cloak. Very pale. Very quiet. Never a word from him, never a rough action. No windows broken, no clocks stopping, no wailing at night. Just quiet, patient waiting. The ghost *was* there. It was always there, putting its curse on the life and doings of the del Vetros. He could have been anyone, an old unhappy *condottiere*, a priest, an earlier count who had put a curse on his successors. But the family had got used to the ghost's presence and endured its joyless existence. The people had to suffer instead. Only the other day the wages of the laborers in the fields had been reduced yet again—that was the ghost's fault. The del Vetros' life was joyless, without grace or music. There were never parties at the palace, never any dancing or singing. That was not like the family and it was all the fault of the ghost.

But other people laughed and told the marionettists they should take no notice of such talk. No one had ever seen a ghost—at least not in the last two generations—it was just an old wives' tale. The contessa herself was responsible for reducing their wages and for the consequences—she and the administration. As the players were to go out to the palace, it was necessary to scare them a little. But they shouldn't be frightened. It was all nonsense, and good luck to you out there—though it is true it's a joyless place.

It so happened that Contessa Francesca had heard that the puppet theater was in Pazienza, and as it was said trouble had arisen in a village farther south after a marionette theater had visited the place, her first thought had been to chase the company away, but then she changed her mind. The contessa had been a widow for seven years, and she filled her days with hard work, making herself as strong as a rock. But when she heard the words "marionette theater," a kind of crack appeared in her and something trickled out—a tinkling sound like a jester's bells. She looked back into her own memories as she sat at her desk. Then she remembered seeing a puppet theater when she was small. Her father had taken her to the market in another village and a troupe of players there had had a marionette theater.

It was the most amusing and beautiful thing little Francesca had ever seen, and she had begged her father to let her go again.

Now she was thinking about her own children, Cristiano and Maria.

As she sat at her desk, she took out a piece of crested notepaper and quickly wrote a few lines, sealed the letter, and addressed it: *To the visiting marionette theater in Pazienza.*

She summoned her secretary.

"Deliver this at once," she said.

The faint, clear echoes from deep down in Francesca del Vetro transformed the day for her. Her children were having a French lesson with their governess, and she went and told the governess she was free to go, then took the children out into the park to tell them about the marionette theater coming that same evening. Then she told them about when she was small and had been taken to a puppet theater and how lovely it had been, with those little dancing figures so like humans—only much more gracious and lighter than humans ever are. She was really talking to herself more than to the children—the twins sensed this—and as she went on, they exchanged looks of amazement. The contessa thought the memories were opening up like a gateway into the light, and she described details from the performance she had seen, much more than she could truly remember. But the bright spring day, the jester's bells, and the dancing marionettes had suddenly come alive in her. She noticed to her own surprise that she was looking forward to the evening. And it would amuse the children. "You'll find it all great fun," she assured them. "You'll laugh and laugh, just as I did that time."

"Did you do nothing but laugh, Mother?" said Maria in amazement.

"Yes, my child," said the contessa. "It was very amusing. I remember a puppet dressed as Arlecchino—like in the carnival. And another that danced. They were marvelous, I promise you. This evening we'll be able to see it all again."

"Yes, Mother," said Cristiano. "How lovely for us."

⚓

At six o'clock the Giacomo Marionette Theater rolled in through the gateway and started creaking up the long avenue leading up to the palace.

The windows stared at them in the twilight.

The head manservant showed them to a place in the most private part of the park behind the palace, where the contessa and her children were to sit on the terrace and enjoy the performance.

Petronio was uneasy. They rigged up the stage, made all their preparations, and lit the lamps. The park behind them was large and deserted, the mansion windows mostly in darkness.

"Well now," said Giacomo. "Nervous?"

"I don't know," said Petronio. "They've put out only six chairs. The audience will be small."

"Small but profitable," said Roberto, the third player.

"We must do our best," said Giacomo. "They're sure to be wealthy. If this succeeds we can go back to Rome earlier than usual this autumn. That'll please Giulia, Petronio."

Petronio did not reply, but started getting the marionettes ready. He missed the inquisitive glances from children looking on as the theater gradually emerged, the laughter, and the expectant questions.

At eight o'clock, the contessa and the twins appeared together with their governess and two supercilious-looking young men, clearly the contessa's assistants.

Francesca del Vetro greeted the three players and bade them welcome. She turned out to be a tall dark-blond woman with a rather sharp face, a slightly bowed neck, and small hands.

"The children are delighted," she said to the bowing Giacomo. "Very good of you to come."

"Thank you kindly, Your Highness," said Giacomo, bowing even lower.

The children, two small figures in pretty clothes, the boy in a sailor suit and the girl in a white dress, greeted the players politely. Then they all sat down and the players vanished behind the stage.

The performance could begin.

❧

It is one thing to play in a piazza full of smiling, cheerful people who have already had a little wine and have been laughing even before the performance. In those cramped and pleasing circumstances, the audience seem to become one and laugh as much at other people's laughter as they do at what is actually happening onstage. A piazza is a good place, a warm place. Voices carry well, held in by the house walls. The audience join in. The children shout at the marionettes, and the adults explain things to them.

But it is quite another matter to play with a large dark park behind you and a dimly lit palace in front, with an audience of six marble statues sitting stiffly on rococo chairs on a deserted terrace.

Halfway through the first sketch, Petronio could see it was not working. So could the other two. Nothing was happening out there. As the witch was creeping up on the princess, the children were supposed to cry out—they had to cry out, be terrified. It was that kind of play, and there was room for all kinds of variations according to the atmosphere outside. Now they were playing out into *nothing*—and it was terrible. Petronio peered through his secret spyhole to see whether his audience *was* still there, and there they were, all sitting bolt upright on their chairs without moving. He could not see their faces, only the outlines. Perhaps they were asleep. He made the witch let out an evil, cackling laugh, but nothing happened. The play became forced, bad, peculiar—they could feel it themselves as they struggled to keep it going. Although it was a warm evening, they felt cold all around them.

The contessa was also disappointed. She remembered she had been carried away on a cloud of bright laughter, and now this was nothing but a dark and extremely ordinary evening on her own terrace. The theater seemed small and rather shabby, the voices weak, although they were speaking as loudly as they could behind the scenes. She recognized the puppetmaster's voice and she could also see the marionette strings quite clearly. The illusion was not working, and there was once even a real muddle on stage—the leg of a marionette got caught and simply would not free itself, although someone above was frantically tugging at the string—in the end, a hand came down and put an end to the misery, while a voice desperately tried to make a joke about God's hand intervening in the most surprising places. But it was not the least bit amusing, and the joke was in bad taste.

She looked at the children. Perhaps *they* . . . ? No. The girl was yawning and the boy was looking down at his knees, occasionally glancing dutifully up at what was going on onstage. The governess and the two secretaries kept glancing knowingly at each other.

Francesca del Vetro suddenly felt great rage rising in her—to think that she had even thought of bringing the puppet theater here at all! All that bright joy which had made this day different from others seemed to have been wiped away, and now she was sitting there with a hurt feeling of emptiness.

The play came to an end and the children clapped politely.

Behind the curtain Petronius was thinking, They have learned that, they have learned to clap, perhaps they have been taken to the theater and been bored, so they have learned to clap in the right place.

"What shall we do?" he whispered to the master.

Giacomo shrugged. "Don't ask me," he said. "It's like playing to a wall." He looked as if he would rather put an end to the evening altogether, but then Petronius had an idea.

"Comedy doesn't work," he said. "I don't think plays will work at all. Not dialogue and action. What about the dancing number?"

"We haven't used it this year," objected Giacomo.

"We'll improvise," said Petronius resolutely. "I'll go out and play in front of the stage. You do the best you can. Otherwise I think we can forget our fee."

The master nodded gloomily. Roberto ducked into the wagon to get the two special dancing marionettes, and Petronio fetched his violin and went out front. He was not thinking primarily about their fee but about how they could blow a little life into tonight's audience—as a matter of honor.

"Ladies and gentlemen," he said. "Not to mention all the highnesses great and small . . ." God alone knew how this would go. "As you see, I have a violin with me." He moved closer to his audience. The two superior gentlemen were deep in conversation and not listening, but Petronio turned first to the thin, white-faced children, who looked as if they longed to go indoors. "This is a magic violin," said Petronio, wondering how to go on. "I bought it from an Eastern wise man I once met in Civitavecchia—that is, he can't have been all that terribly wise, because I got it for next to nothing—it looks like a fairly ordinary violin, doesn't it, but what is special about it is that a *spirit* lives inside it. And when I play on the strings, the spirit wakes up. The sound of the violin brings dead things alive. Marionettes, for instance. Just watch now . . ."

Petronio was hoping they were ready behind the scenes and that they had heard what he said—voices carried very badly on the terrace. Cautiously, he put his bow to the violin.

The curtain went up. Two collapsed heaps lay on the stage. That was all right, they had everything in place, even the dark backdrop with the half-moon and glittering stars.

Petronio moved close to the children. I hope the others will let me go on for a while and won't start the marionettes dancing too soon.

He let a note slide off the violin, then another, and another, carefully, quietly, praying. He leaned over the children. The marionettes remained there, lifeless heaps.

"It's not working," he said to the children. "It won't work unless you help me. I forgot to tell you—the spirit's magic works only if you want it to. Only if you really and truly *want* it to."

"There's no such thing as magic," said the boy, looking up and fixing his cold blue eyes on Petronio. "Nor spirits."

"No magic?" said Petronio, making the violin play a falling bewildered note. "Of course there's magic. Spirits, too. Are there not, Your Highness?" He turned to the mother, who was also looking on his attempts somewhat coolly. But she nodded courteously and said, "Yes, of course. Don't contradict our guest, Cristiano."

"You must want it, too, Your Highness," said Petronio. "You must make an effort. So. Shall we try again?" He looked at the children. The boy sat as before, but something was happening to the girl, something about her eyes, two tiny stars just visible in them. Petronio thought angrily to himself, There *is* magic. Spirits, too. I've seen them myself.

Then he began to play, and the marionettes came to life.

Something did happen, but when he thought about it later, it seemed impossible and unbelievable. With his violin Petronio invited the marionettes to dance—a melancholy, beautiful little dance under the moon. He carefully followed the marionettes' movements and played up to them. Everything worked as it was supposed to, the strings invisible against the dark backdrop and the light just right.

Suddenly the dance came alive and there were no longer puppets dancing but living creatures, apparently growing larger in the dark, apparently lamenting, apparently singing in time with the violin. Infinitely carefully, the marionettes touched each other, started dancing together, found each other like two lost children in the forest.

Petronio was still uncertain of the outcome and hardly dared look at his audience, but when he heard the boy hush the two conversing gentlemen, he knew things were going all right. He played on. He was surprised at himself; strange tunes suddenly poured out of his instrument, tunes he did not know, wonderful old-fashioned tunes, beautiful and seductive. Giacomo and Roberto backstage must also have been affected—never had the marionettes danced so well before, as if the two separate little dancers had first come into their own right in this place, as if *they* didn't quite fit in on a piazza among hundreds of noisy people. Here they felt at home.

A spirit really did seem to have taken up residence in Petronio's violin and seized him, seized them, steering them all.

Petronio grew warm, and it was warm all around them.

Then the melody changed character and the marionettes danced an amusing rhythmical number with funny great leaps, the comical aspect of the marionettes coming out without disturbing their sorrow. They floated through the air.

The children laughed quietly, then shifted to the edge of their chairs as if to get closer to what was happening onstage, to be close to those white figures in the darkness.

Petronio looked at the contessa.

Francesca del Vetro was weeping, and he realized it was life that had come at that moment.

When the children started clapping in time to the music, he knew he had to stop. He played the dance tune one last swirling time, then stopped. The figures onstage bowed, at once solemn and melancholy again.

After that, he took the risk of fetching one of the comical characters from the wagon, a jester. He took it with him onto the terrace, its strings and wooden holder quite visible, and got up on one of those handsome chairs to be high enough, then made the marionette walk on the terrace and frolic and do somersaults. He made it talk—the children could perfectly well see he was doing the talking, but that did not matter, just as it did not matter that they could see him working the strings. There was life in the marionette whatever he did now. Giacomo and Roberto came out with a marionette each, a Pierrot and a Columbine, and together they improvised a sketch on the terrace, each of them standing on a chair—the governess and the two gentlemen had to stand.

The children were laughing easily now, the boy even clutching at his stomach. They begged for more, so the troupe did a quick extra number from the stage, the one about the rich man eating too much. Afterward, the children were allowed to look at the marionettes and touch them in farewell. Then the governess took the two of them off to bed.

Contessa del Vetro went over to the three players. She had pulled herself together and her expression was now collected, but her eyes were clear, as if light and dancing.

"Thank you so much," she said. "That was very pleasant."

"It is we who should thank you, Your Highness," said Giacomo proudly, and he bowed.

She looked at them, somewhat uneasily, then turned to Petronio.

"You played very well," she said. "Very well. The melodies were . . . They seemed to be saying something."

Petronio bowed his head, but he did not reply.

The contessa bade them good night, glancing at them one last time, then hurrying into the house.

The head manservant showed them to their rooms. On the way through the corridors they walked in silence, neither talking nor laughing as they usually did after a successful performance.

At Petronio's door, Giacomo said, "You played very well, Petronio. Our fingers seemed to move by themselves as we worked the marionettes. It was very . . ."

"Good night, Master," said Petronio.

"Good night," said Giacomo.

Roberto and he were taken farther down the corridor, and Petronio opened the door and went into the little room allotted to him for the night. It was many years since he had slept alone in a room, and he was looking forward to going to bed.

He lit the lamp and started undressing.

"Not bad," said a voice.

Petronio started and turned around. A man was standing with his back to the closed door, a servant presumably.

"Oh," said Petronio. "I didn't hear you come in. I'm sorry, sir— am I perhaps in the wrong room?"

"Not at all," said the man by the door, stepping into the room and sitting down on the bed. "Not at all."

He said nothing more. Petronio looked at him in some confusion as he sat there in the faint light of the lamp. A large, broad-shouldered man, he had an air of of great calm. It was hard to see his features, the light from the lamp making them blurred and indistinct.

"Why . . . er . . ." Petronio began. "What can I do for you?"

"That was excellent, what you did with the violin," said the man in a strange foreign voice. "First class, if I may say so."

"Thank you . . ."

"I'm a musician myself. Violinist. That is, I was, once upon a time." He smiled.

"Well, I wouldn't really call myself a musician," said Petronio. "I just play a little, when the time seems right."

"Yes," said the man. "You are a musician. You're one of the musicians who will be remembered."

"Nice of you to say so," said Petronio politely. "But do you really think the children and the contessa . . . that they will remember those few notes?"

"I'm not talking about them," said the man, turning to Petronio, his features still unclear. "I don't know whether they will remember or forget this evening, although I think it was memorable. But I'm talking about something else. Petronio Vitellotesta—you will be remembered long after you are dead and gone."

Petronio had to laugh.

"Now you're exaggerating," he said.

"No," said the man. "I know what I'm talking about. There are plans for you."

Petronio could find nothing to say, and the stranger was also silent for a moment.

"I was a musician with Conte Lorenzo del Vetro," he said then, rather gloomily. "Court musician."

"Were you?" said Petronio. "How interesting."

"But Conte Lorenzo smashed my violin in a rage. I had played for his wife—a serenade with lovely melodies for dancing and love. Quite innocent, by the way, nothing that could cause offense. But his wife was young—a child, really, much younger than Conte Lorenzo himself. So he must have thought—well. I thought it extremely unreasonable of him to smash my violin. Truthfully, I did think the Contessa Laura was very . . . very beautiful. Melancholy. I wanted to cheer her up. And perhaps I wanted to . . . But I don't think he should have smashed my violin."

"It's a wonder you wanted to stay at all," said Petronio with feeling. "I really think you would have had good cause to leave the moment he smashed your instrument."

"That was exactly why I stayed," said the man.

"Oh . . ." said Petronio.

"I was silenced, you see. Interrupted in the middle of that cheerful serenade. In the middle of . . . Something was about to happen to the contessa at the very moment I was interrupted. I couldn't leave before I had completed it."

Petronio could not really see the connection.

"Did this happen a long time ago?" he asked.

"It has been a few years."

"Well, well. Am I supposed to be sharing this room with you tonight?"

"If you like."

"What?"

"If you wish me to stay, Petronio. I owe you a great deal."

"Excuse me . . . I don't really understand. Did you attend the show?"

"I was the spirit in your violin," said the man. "I thought it was such a good idea for you to say that."

Petronio opened his mouth to say something, but then closed it abruptly. The man went on.

"So I thought, All right, he shall have a spirit in his violin," he said, laughing.

Petronio stared at him, looking into his face.

346

"This count . . . Lorenzo del Vetro . . ." he began uncertainly.

"A brutal man. If only he had contented himself with just slitting my throat. But he had to go and smash my violin as well. Smashed it in front of me and the young contessa, against one of the pillars in the hall—yes, it was down in the old palace, of course. They lived there at that time. You know, he smashed it while it was still resounding."

"I see," said Petronio.

"Very unchivalrous of him. I have been walking around here ever since. Following the family, following the blood, so to speak."

"They say you're the cause of the hardness and lack of joy in the del Vetros," said Petronio rather daringly.

"It's not true," said the apparition. "I am a quiet and gentle man. I haven't even shown myself in recent decades. On the contrary, it is the del Vetros' obstinate, cold harshness that has kept me from freedom. It *is* a house without joy. The musicians I could use to finish playing my serenade never come here. Not musicians like you. This evening is the first time I've succeeded."

"I feel very honored, Signor . . ."

"You can call me Michele," said the apparition. "That was my name."

"A great honor, Maestro Michele."

Petronio was not entirely sure how to converse with an apparition. He looked at the figure, the gray cloak, the worn boots. The face was clearer now, finely drawn in harmonious lines. He seemed to be a very sympathetic ghost.

"Right," said the ghost. "It may be that when Conte Lorenzo killed me in front of his wife after having smashed . . . that may be the main cause of the del Vetros' coldness, and lack of musical ability. I'm sure my constant presence has also had an effect. But . . . from my present position, I often think it could be the other way around, this matter of cause and effect."

"I'm sorry," said Petronio. "But I know little about the sciences."

"It's very simple," said the ghost. "Let us say the cause of something that happens on a Saturday is to be found on Sunday?"

"I don't really understand—what happens today can be blamed on something that will happen tomorrow?"

"That's right. Just as a puppeteer knows what will happen to the

347

marionette in the next scene, and so is prepared for it. If the good fairy is to come in from the right, he will put the princess on the left, so that the fairy comes unexpectedly upon her. The puppeteer knows that—the one who pulls the strings knows what will happen. But not the marionette. That's what it's about."

"Oh," said Petronio.

"The reason why the princess goes to the left is apparently because she wants to stand in front of the mirror to comb her hair. But in reality it is because the good fairy is to come."

"Ah . . ."

"But she doesn't know it. That is, not usually. This has been a very fine evening, Petronio, in every way. I myself am very happy now that I can rest in peace. You are a special young man, Petronio, who has inspiration and sees things other people don't see."

"That's true . . ."

"Perhaps this fine evening was the reason why Conte Lorenzo smashed my violin. So that this evening would happen. So that you would come here and I would be able to tell you what I have to tell you, before I go."

"Go where?"

"An interesting question."

"Yes."

"I have a message for you, Petronio. I shall disclose to you what the puppeteer wants of you."

"I don't understand . . ."

"You'll understand. I can tell you what will happen to you, and there is a definite reason why I must tell you. I began by saying that you will be remembered . . ."

Petronio stared at the ghost, and for the first time in their conversation he was frightened by him.

"Do I frighten you?" said the ghost. "Personally I would have preferred not to do this, but just to thank you for giving me a reason, then going away and letting you find out about it for yourself, as it happens."

"I don't really know," said Petronio. "Is it dangerous to know such things?"

"You will resist, I promise you, unfortunately. You will try to persuade yourself that all of this evening and our conversation never happened. You will do everything you can to forget what I am now going to say, even if it is very beautiful and very honorable."

"Beautiful and honorable . . ."

"Almost like when you played for those two children this evening. Only much greater."

"Now wait a minute," said Petronio. "You say this is *necessary* . . ."

"Yes," said the ghost. "It has to happen, as far as I understand it, even if it is horribly difficult for you from now on. One might even think it was a punishment. But in reality . . . in reality it is a reward."

"I think it's rather unpleasant to think . . ." said Petronio after a while, "to think that one is hanging from strings like a marionette and can do nothing about it either way. The marionette doesn't have to know it is going to be eaten by the dragon, for example. And who decides, anyway. Who is it holding the strings?"

The ghost smiled kindly.

"I thought you would ask that," he said. "The answer won't tell you much. You could call it the heavens, or the stars in the sky. But deep down, it is you yourself."

"Me?"

The ghost rose to his feet.

"I prefer to whisper," he said, "when I tell you your destiny—if you don't mind." He leaned over and cupped his hand around Petronio's ear.

It grew warm.

Then he whispered it.

The words had hardly entered Petronio's ear before he burst out laughing, wild skeptical laughter. The ghost vanished and Petronio was like a swaying twig a bird has just left. He went on laughing in the darkness, laughing like a maniac, shaking his head, desperately, agitatedly, happily, unhappily.

⚓

Petronio never married Giacomo's daughter, Giulia, although he tried his very best. In the meantime she had fallen for someone else and was unyielding despite her parents ordering her to marry Petronio, and despite the fact that Petronio beseeched her with his very life.

Nor did he take over Giacomo's marionette theater. It burned to the ground one night in the south, and Giacomo died in the flames together with his marionettes as he lay asleep in the wagon. It was actually Petronio's fault, for he had forgotten to put the lamp out in the wagon when he left.

Petronio's life was the road and its thousand trades and activities. It was many countries, more troupes of players, and a circus. It was happiness and unhappiness, success and failure. He became bass player for a circus because one evening he lost his jacket with all his savings in it, and if he was to survive he had to take whatever work was offered—the only work he found was as bass player in a circus, although he could not play the double bass and told the circus director so. He was hired anyway.

He became a musician and traveled far and wide, a colorful series of events, images, and people making up the road, and through it all murmured the knowledge the ghost had given him. For years he had managed to forget it, and then it sprang up again, and kept on reappearing. It was the cause of the breakup of his only marriage, in Marseilles. It gave his life an unattached, impetuous character. As the years went by and Petronio grew older and finally became a ship's musician, this knowledge of his became unbearable. He had to find a place to hide from it, and he hid in madness, detaching his head from his body, taking his thoughts away from each other and putting air and laughter and light between them as best he could, to forget and not be tormented.

Now and again his knowledge burst through, and then he defended himself with whirlpools of foolishness, talking as much nonsense as he could find.

On April 10, 1912, he boarded the *Titanic* of Liverpool by pure chance, because a musician had fallen ill a few days earlier and because he himself had happened to stop by the agent's office. He went on board, and the following Sunday he heard a voice in his double bass—as if an apparition had hidden itself inside the instrument.

That was Giovanni Petronio Vitellotesta's story.

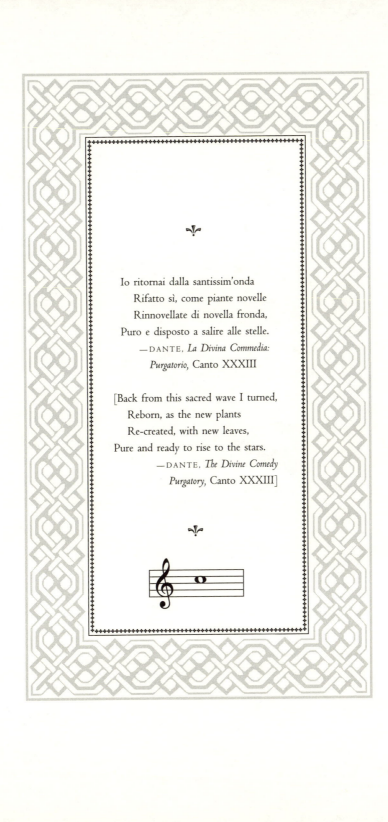

Io ritornai dalla santissim'onda
Rifatto sì, come piante novelle
Rinnovellate di novella fronda,
Puro e disposto a salire alle stelle.
—DANTE, *La Divina Commedia:*
Purgatorio, Canto XXXIII

[Back from this sacred wave I turned,
Reborn, as the new plants
Re-created, with new leaves,
Pure and ready to rise to the stars.
—DANTE, *The Divine Comedy*
Purgatory, Canto XXXIII]

April 14, 1912
41°46'N, 50°14'W, 23:32

———— ◆•✕•◆ ————

IT is cold and clear. The ship is doing twenty and a half knots through the night; the stars are dazzlingly bright. It is so clear, celestial bodies can be seen the moment they come up over the horizon, the stars just on the horizon sharply divided by the line of the earth as if by a scalpel.

The sea is dead calm.

In the crow's nest fifty feet above the foredeck, between sky and sea, lookouts Frederick Fleet and Reginald Lee are staring out into the night. They have been there since ten o'clock and there is half an hour left of their watch. They have had orders to keep a special lookout for icebergs because of all the incoming warnings and the exceptionally calm weather.

They are not talking to each other. They have divided up the world between them into two fields of vision.

The stillness in the air and the sea is not pleasant, lack of movement making it difficult to see, and there are no reflections of lights, no outlines or contours. The sea looks like black ink.

All at once one of them says, "Fog."

A smoke-like fog is suddenly ahead of them, just beginning to slide over the foredeck, and a swift, icy cold current runs through the air. The two lookouts stare ahead.

It is 23:40. Without hesitation Fleet suddenly bangs the crow's-nest bell three times, the signal for danger ahead. Then he lifts the phone and rings the bridge.

"Hello. Hello! Is anyone there?"

A metallic voice answers.

"Yes . . . what did you see?"

353

"Iceberg dead ahead."

"Thank you."

The officer on the bridge rings off. Paralyzed, the two lookouts watch the great mass of ice looming up out of the darkness ahead of them. It is a huge iceberg, almost as high as the crow's nest, frosty mists drifting away from it like veils. The iceberg was only about a hundred yards away when Fleet spotted it, and now it is right in front of them.

"We're heading straight into it," says Fleet, and they brace themselves for the crash. They have done their duty and all they can do now is watch. They know that down on the bridge, somewhere below and behind them, orders are being given. The helmsman is swinging the wheel and the officers peer out into the darkness.

An eternity seems to go by before the ship swings to port. From the vibrations they realize the engines have been put into reverse. The seconds pass and slowly the bow swings away from the iceberg. The ship glides on. They've cleared it. A whispering sound rises as the iceberg glides along the starboard side, splinters of ice loosening and falling onto the deck.

A slight shudder goes through the ship all the way to the crow's nest.

Then all is still, the great black mass disappearing into the darkness astern. The engines stop.

"That was close," says Reginald Lee.

Less than a minute has passed since they spotted the iceberg.

※

The captain is a light sleeper. The moment the vibrations from the engines change, his eyelids flicker, and through his sleep he can feel a slight unnatural sideways movement in the body of the ship.

He is awake. He starts dressing, puts on his jacket and uniform cap, and goes onto the bridge.

"What was that?" he says.

※

In the depths of the ship the warning bells are ringing. The water-tight emergency doors have been closed and red lights are flashing.

Firemen and engineers climb the emergency ladders and disappear through the manholes.

In contrast to the officers on the bridge, they know what has happened. The gash is over three hundred feet long and water is cascading in on the starboard side, into the forepeak, into aft holds 1, 2, and 3, and boiler rooms 5 and 6.

☙

Thomas Andrews is working in his cabin, number A36. A vast heap of blueprints, plans, charts, specifications, lists, and technical shipping compendiums lies in front of him; he puffs on his stubby pipe as he makes notes. He is about to go to bed and is so absorbed in completing his report he notices nothing. A few minutes earlier he had heard a deep singing sound, like air in a waterpipe. He registered it, uneasy for a moment that something might be wrong with the plumbing, but the sound disappeared. He is writing.

Someone knocks on his cabin door. This late? Andrews puts down the papers he has in his hand and laboriously gets to his feet.

The knocking is repeated, more urgently this time.

"Yes, yes, I'm coming."

Purser McElroy is outside.

"Good evening, Purser. What can I do for you?"

"Captain Smith requests your presence on the bridge immediately, please, sir."

Andrews looks at his watch. "Now?"

"Yes, please, sir. At once. We seem to have run into something in the dark."

☙

Midnight. Phillips, the first wireless operator, has just handed over the headphones to his assistant, Bride, who has been kind enough to relieve him two hours earlier than the watch requires. It has been a hard day and Phillips is ready to turn in. He is taking down his suspenders by his bunk in the wireless operators' quarters just off the Marconi room when someone bursts in. He turns around, yawning.

"Yes . . . ? Captain, sir!"

"Sparks, we hit an iceberg a few minutes ago. I'm expecting a

complete report on the damage within minutes. Will you please be
ready to send out a request for assistance."

In a flash, Phillips remembers the many reports of ice during the
course of the day, including one or two that never reached the bridge.
He hauls up his suspenders again.

"Yes, sir . . ."

⚜

". . . and the situation is horribly simple. The ship can stay afloat
with two watertight compartments full of water—never mind which
two." Andrews nervously patted his pipe. "She can float with the
three bow compartments full, and in calm weather she can keep afloat
with the four bow compartments full. But she can't float with the five
full."

Silence fell on the bridge.

"For architectonic and practical reasons," said Andrews, "the watertight compartments don't go all the way up through the ship, as
we know. They go up only to E-deck. The five first compartments
are filling up now, relatively quickly, but it's difficult to know how
much water she's taking on per minute. We don't know the size of
the hole. When the first five compartments are full enough and the
ship lists, the water along the corridors of E-deck will inevitably begin
to fill the sixth and seventh compartments."

"How long have we got?" said the captain gravely.

Andrews calculated rapidly on a piece of paper.

"An hour to an hour and a half," he said. He was pale. "A little
longer if we're lucky."

The captain looked at him. My last trip, he was thinking. He
cleared his throat, looked at his officers, and raised his voice.

"Gentlemen. Orders. All hands on deck. All lifeboats made ready.
Passengers roused and ordered to the lifeboats. Yes, that's true." He
paused. "I've just thought of something."

They all knew what had occurred to him. The captain had suddenly
closed his eyes and grimaced painfully.

"First Officer," he said quietly, "what's the lifeboat capacity?"

"Eleven hundred and seventy-eight places, sir, with full boats."

"And the passenger list?"

"One thousand three hundred and twenty souls, sir."

"And a crew of over seven hundred . . ." the captain began.

"That's what the regulations prescribe, sir. In relation to tonnage."

"Orders," said the captain. "Women and children first. This must be carried out in complete calm. No panic. Officers arm themselves, to be sure. I repeat: *No panic*. Take any action to stop outbreaks of hysteria."

"Excuse me, Captain," said Andrews, "but do you really think it wise to suppress all sense of danger—I don't think many people have noticed the collision, at least not on the upper decks . . ."

"There must be no panic," said the captain firmly. "It must be carried out in an orderly manner. I'll give Sparks his orders, together with our position. Then we must pray to God and hope we stay afloat until help comes."

"There's a ship to the northwest," said Second Officer Lightoller. "I saw its lights when I was out on the wing of the bridge."

"Send rockets and signal with the Morse lamps. Are my orders understood?"

The officers answered as one.

"Right," said the captain. My last trip, he thought. My last trip.

Come Quick Danger. From *Titanic*, 1:12:
CQD . . . CQD . . . CQD . . . CQD 41°46'N, 50°14'W REQUEST ASSISTANCE HAVE STRUCK ICEBERG TITANIC CQD.

From the *Parisian*, eastbound:
HULLO OLD MAN I HAVE A HEAP OF MESSAGES FROM CAPE COD STATION TO SEND ON STOP DO YOU WANT THEM TRANSMITTED?

From the *Titanic*:
CQD THIS IS CQD 41°46'N, 50°14'W.

From the *Parisian*:
SHALL I INFORM THE CAPTAIN? ARE YOU REQUESTING HELP?

From the *Titanic*:

YES PLEASE COME IMMEDIATELY STOP.

From the *Prinz Friedrich Wilhelm*, westbound:

WHAT IS GOING ON OLD MAN?

From the *Titanic*:

HAVE STRUCK ICEBERG STOP WE ARE SINKING STOP.

Sunday, April 14, 1912
Musicians' cabin, midnight

———◆◆◆◆◆———

DAVID had woken without knowing why. It could not be long since they had gone to bed. Something had woken him, a sound, a movement, as if someone had shaken him gently.

He had been dreaming one of those light dreams that come just after sleep sets in. Something about Sofia and her room in Frau Melchior's house in Vienna, Sofia in front of that window with the seven roses. It had been a clear, quiet dream, nothing but that one image.

He lay in the dark for a while, trying to go back to sleep. He could hear the others breathing and Petronius snoring.

What had woken him? Something was different.

Then he noticed that everything was quite still. No creaking, no vibrations, no sound of water rushing along the side of the ship.

For a moment he thought they were in the harbor. He fumbled for his watch hanging on a peg on the wall. He peered at it for a long time, unable to make out in the dark whether the hands were on one or twelve.

Someone coughed in the bunk below him and sheets rustled.

"Spot," whispered David. "Are you awake?"

"Yes."

"Are we still?"

"Seems like it."

"Why?"

"Don't ask me, David. I've been awake since Jason put the light out. I sleep badly and lie here thinking. A quarter of an hour ago there was a kind of shudder, as if we were going over ground . . . then the engines reversed and stopped. Then they ran at half speed for a few minutes. Then they stopped again. They've been stopped ever since."

"Is something wrong, do you think?"

"We may have met a ship needing assistance. Medical help, for instance. Things like that happen occasionally."

Suddenly they heard a roaring, wailing sound from outside.

"What's that?"

"Huh. It sounds—it sounds as if they're letting steam out of the boilers. Strange."

Jason's voice, wide-awake in the dark: "Can't you two give us a bit of peace."

"Sorry, Mr. Jason," said David. "But we're still. And Spot says . . ."

"What's going on?" said Alex angrily.

"No idea," said Jason. "They're letting off steam. Someone better go and take a . . ."

There was a knock on the door. Jason was quickly out of his bunk, across the floor, and opening it.

"Good evening, sir, I'm sorry but . . ."

"Purser? Mr. McElroy, sir?"

"You're to take your musicians up onto A-deck at once."

"What? Excuse me, Purser, but it's . . ."

"Captain's orders."

"What's going on?"

"The passengers are being woken and the atmosphere is somewhat confused. A little music would perhaps have a calming effect."

"Waking the passengers?"

"Yes, so you must come at once. We've struck something. An iceberg, it seems. There's no danger, but for safety's sake the passengers are to go into the lifeboats. If you would play, it would all seem more . . . more like a drill, almost."

Jason looked at the purser in astonishment. The man was quite serious.

"Oh well," said Jason, yawning. "Yes, of course, of course. We'll come."

"Many thanks," said the purser, and was gone.

Jason switched on the light.

"Up!" he said. "I can't imagine what all this means, but we've got to get up and play."

"Uh?" came a sleepy voice from Jim's bunk. "Play? Now?"

"Get up and into your clothes!" said Jason. "Perhaps we can save the last shreds of our reputation if we hurry a little."

"This is the stupidest . . ." mumbled Georges.

"They'll surely understand the absence of the pianist," said Spot. "I have my private little nocturne to play here in my bunk."

"No," said Jason. "We are all supposed to get up."

"Petronius, too?" said Alex peevishly.

"Him especially—Petronius, Petronius! Wake up now."

"It's the whiskey."

"He has to come, too, even if he just stands there as decoration. Hey! Wake up." Jason shook Petronius roughly.

"Iceberg?" said Jim in a low voice. "Did he say an iceberg?" He sounded slightly worried.

"Yes, that's what he said," sighed Spot, pulling on his uniform.

"Ah!" came expectantly from Petronius as he opened his eyes.

The corridors were crowded. Stewards and stewardesses were knocking on doors and waking passengers. People were pouring reluctantly toward stairs and exits, confused, talking, some with life belts under their arms. Some had noticed the jolt and realized something was wrong. Some had seen the clerks from the mailroom retrieving soaking wet mailbags. But most were wondering what the point of all this was.

The musicians at once noticed something wrong on the stairs— their feet seemed to hit the steps in an unfamiliar way.

"The stairs are crooked. The ship's listing," said Jim. "She's listing to the fore, I think."

They came up into the first-class lounge and were received with applause. A large proportion of the first-class passengers had assembled there, some of them still in their evening clothes, others clearly annoyed at being woken, and the arrival of the ship's band created some relief. Jason Coward and his six musicians made their way to their corner by the piano. Spot had carried Petronius's double bass up, and he now handed it to him, thrusting the bow into his hand. Petronius clutched the instrument.

They started with a selection of ragtime, and that was clearly popular. The passengers had decided to take all this inconvenience cheerfully, like good sports. When the band played Irving Berlin's latest hit, "Alexander's Ragtime Band," some of the younger couples started dancing and others clapped in time with the music. Waiters who had just gone off duty had been hauled out of their bunks and were now running around sleepily serving refreshments.

The boat deck could be seen through the windows. Some white lumps were lying on the deck along the railing on the starboard side. Ice. Two men in dinner jackets, who had still not gone to bed when the alarm went off, were out there with their highballs, breaking lumps of ice against a deck chair to put in their drinks, laughing and smiling.

Then the band played waltzes.

Out on deck, dark-clad seamen hurried back and forth, frantically busy with the lifeboat davits.

A ship is lying on the horizon to the northwest, and on the starboard wing of the bridge, Quartermaster Rowe is sending up rockets at minute intervals, on the orders of the captain. Attempts have already been made with the Morse lamp, to no avail. It is a quarter past one in the morning. Rockets race away and explode in the distance high up above the *Titanic*.

She is now lying noticeably deeper in the water.

The other ship does not react, the only ship not to wake up tonight. Like a blind eye, it stays on the horizon for hours to come.

"But you *must* get into the lifeboat, madam." To put it mildly, the officer is desperate.

"Nonsense. I'm not getting into any lifeboat. At least not without Herbert, my husband."

"I'm sorry, madam, but those are my orders. Women and children first. Your husband is sure to come in a later boat."

"I can't think what use all this is. I'll complain to the company. The sea is perfectly calm, the electricity working, and the music playing. It's very cold outside. I prefer to stay indoors. The doctor says my bronchitis . . ."

"The *Titanic* is sinking, madam."

"*Surely, you must be exaggerating.*"

362

❧

The first lifeboat, starboard number 7, had been lowered at a quarter past midnight. It had room for sixty-five people, but owing to lack of enthusiasm among the women in first class, there were only twenty-eight on board when the officer gave orders to lower the boat. It was lowered largely as an example, to show that things were serious.

Similarly, at ten past one, the starboard lifeboat number 1 was lowered with only twelve passengers on board, including Sir Cosmo and Lady Duff Gordon, who found it safest to be in the forefront. Port boat number 8 was lowered with thirty-nine on board.

Port lifeboat number 6 also had twenty-eight on board, while starboard number 5 still had room for twenty-four people when it was ordered to be lowered.

Later the demand for places grew.

❧

Walls were collapsing in the depths of the ship, corridors started filling up with water, and luggage began to float around.

The third-class passengers in steerage, mothers with large families, sturdy men with large hands, poor Jews and confused Armenians—they are all trying to get up and away. *They* had felt the collision. What had seemed like a faint jar on the upper decks was a deafening crash on the lower starboard foredeck, as the iceberg ripped open a great gash. Some of them had been thrown out of their bunks. Now they are trying to make their way to safety. They remember how to get up to the dining room from that morning's service, but doors that were open then are now closed and locked, and officers are sticking to the regulations and refusing to let them come any farther. No admission to first class. "Do you want our children to drown?" cries a fiery Irishman. "If you do, then answer me, man!" But the third-class passengers obediently retreat. Altogether, there are more than seven hundred of them. Not until much later that night, cursing, do they begin to make their way through on their own, but by then panic has begun to spread and most of the lifeboats have been lowered. Only a few women get away, and only half the children.

In one intact engine room, engineers and greasers are keeping things going—the ship has to have electricity as long as possible. The voltage must be kept up. Light is needed on deck for the clearing of the lifeboats. The wireless, which has to send distress signals into the night, has to have electricity. The engineers work away, unable to see much. Distant crashes can be heard behind the watertight holds, iron plates crushed by the water, engine parts falling. At regular intervals they have to vacate boiler rooms and engine rooms as the water suddenly gushes in.

Only a handful of them ever see the starry skies again.

⚜

Save Our Souls—the *Titanic* sends out the new international distress signal for the first time at a quarter to one in the morning:

SOS . . . SOS . . . SOS . . . 41°46'N, 50°14'W WE ARE SINKING BOW FIRST COME AS SOON AS POSSIBLE TITANIC

The vast deserted ocean is full of voices, signals calling to each other over great distances. The voices are very close in the headphones of wireless operator Phillips, as close as if they were standing just by him and whispering in his ear.

But they are not close. They are far away.

From the *Olympic*, their sister ship:

WHAT IS THE MATTER OLD MAN? ARE YOU COMING SOUTH TO MEET US?

"Idiot," mumbles Phillips. "I've told him about twenty times already." He taps away like a madman.

WOMEN AND CHILDREN BOARDING LIFEBOATS

Slowly the *Olympic* appears to realize what is happening. Signals flash back and forth between all ships within reach and are passed on by others, finally reaching the Cape Race Station and registered in the newspaper offices in New York, then sent on via transatlantic cable to London. Listen! Listen to the voice of the *Titanic*! She is sinking. A hundred voices answer over the ether:

HEADING FOR YOU FULL STEAM AHEAD . . .

HAVE INFORMED CAPTAIN AND HEADING FOR YOU AT TOP SPEED . . . TELL TITANIC WE ARE COMING TO HER ASSISTANCE . . .

PLEASE TRANSMIT TO TITANIC THAT WE CAN BE THERE IN THREE HOURS . . .

Listen to the voices from the *Titanic*. Toward two o'clock the signals grow fainter.

. . . UP TO THE BOILERS . . . CQD . . .

❧

Listen. Listen in the night. You can hear her, but you can't reach her. She is sliding away, disappearing into the darkness.

Can you hear?

❧

As the lounge emptied of people, the musicians moved into the foyer on the boat deck, wheeling the piano with them, and once there, they played marches and cheerful tunes until almost a quarter past one, keeping to music with lively, cheerful rhythms. The atmosphere among the first-class passengers was still good, but they were paying less attention to the music now as activities on deck increased.

At twenty to two the foyer had also more or less emptied of people. Jason looked around, then signed to the musicians to take a break while he went out on deck to find Purser McElroy for new instructions.

He was soon back, a strange expression on his face.

"It's true. They are getting into the lifeboats. They've nearly all been launched. And . . ."

The others looked at him. Jim frowned, but said nothing.

"I think we'd better go out on deck and play on. We haven't been told to stop."

❧

They take their instruments with them out into the cold on the port side. Luckily it is the little dining-room piano they have to move and not the grand piano from the lounge.

Thomas Andrews comes up to them with a bundle of life belts in his hands.

"Here," he says. "Put them on. Let people see you've got life belts on." He seems very upset. "Put them on."

"Is it really necessary to . . ." Spot begins.

"Yes!" cries Andrews. "These geese think they will float on their own. Hardly anyone wants to put them on. The ladies think they're so unbecoming, and one man said jokingly he would rather go down in evening dress like a gentleman."

The musicians exchange looks.

"Put them on. Set an example."

Spot gets up off the piano stool and goes over to the railing to look down, then whistles quietly.

The water is almost up to the promenade deck.

He turns to his colleagues.

"We're sinking," he says. "No doubt about it."

"What!" cries David. *"Wie! Wie!"*

"Now now," says Jason. "No need to panic. Spot . . ." He signals imperceptibly to Spot. "Come and sit down. We'll go on."

"Go on?" says Spot. "Shouldn't we . . ."

"Put your life belts on," says Jason. "Put them on, all of you. There's sure to be plenty of room for us in the boats. I saw some of them were scarcely half full. There must be more boats on the starboard side."

They tie on their life belts.

Andrews has disappeared into the smoking room, where he sinks down into a winged chair after tying on his own life belt. He stays there.

The band plays quieter music now, the tune "In the Shadows," last year's hit in London, extracts from classic suites, and Godfrey's "Reminiscences of Wales."

At five past two things have become chaotic. Few of the passengers are listening to the music any longer. People are running along the decks, calling, waving their arms about, falling, getting up, and running on. Others are still calm and look on those who are frightened with astonishment.

A shot rings out ahead. Panic has broken out as they are lowering collapsible D to the water. The officers encircle the crowd trying to storm the boat and Second Officer Lightoller fires a warning shot.

The *Titanic* is going down even faster now, her bows under water. Small waves splash against the electric winches on the foredeck and loose objects are floating around her hull. The sea is black, clear, and cold.

The sky is deep that night, the stars brilliant, but on the lighted decks, in the spotlights, no one sees the stars. They see nothing but darkness.

⚜

J. Bruce Ismay, the shipping magnate, is on collapsible C, already on the water, staring at the sinking ship. Ever since the captain informed him of the situation after midnight he has been close to breaking down. He has known the lifeboat capacity all the time. He has frenziedly tried to help, tried to take responsibility, issuing orders. But an officer reprimanded him when he was trying to assist with lowering the boats on the starboard side. Since then he has walked around on deck, giving a helping hand wherever possible. Just as he was passing collapsible C, he leaped into it at the last moment without thinking. It was soon lowered into the water and there was no turning back. Now he is sitting there saying to himself that his testimony will be required at the inquiry.

The ship's angle with the surface of the sea grows steeper, and soon the propellers appear; the rudder is already visible.

Ismay looks on, feeling as if he has splinters of glass in his eyes.

Waves of panic break out on board. The third-class passengers have broken through onto the upper decks. Over fifteen hundred souls are still on the ship.

In the Marconi room, Captain Smith is giving the two wireless operators orders to stop signaling and get away as best they can. One of them pays no attention and, dog-tired, goes on hammering on the keys—he can hear ships out there in the night calling to him, but they obviously can no longer hear what he is saying. There must be something wrong with the voltage, a short circuit perhaps—the electric light is much brighter than usual.

On the aft boat deck a Catholic priest has assembled panic-stricken passengers from second and third class around him.

He is listening to confessions, giving absolution.

It is seven minutes past two.

"Well," says Jason. "I think it's time we stopped. No point in going on. No one's listening."

"No," says Alex, nodding. He puts his violin down.

Spot is sitting at the piano, his eyes half closed. Jim and Georges go over to the railing and look in both directions.

David is pale.

A nearby officer shouts: "It's every man for himself! Every man for himself! Orders."

"Hm," says Jason. He smiles at David and thumps him on the shoulder. "We clearly won't be first ashore in New York. But you'll never get ashore anyway, my boy."

"What? What?"

"I forgot to tell you. You have to be able to produce fifty dollars before you're even allowed to set foot on the quay."

David tries to smile. "I hadn't thought of running away."

"Good," says Jason. A man runs past, almost knocking Petronius and his bass into the water. Petronius looks at him in amazement and seems to wake up.

The other musicians are all deep in thought.

"You heard what the officer said," says Jason. "Every man for himself. We'll have to help each other as best we can and try and get into one of the boats. Thanks a lot, all of you, and best of luck to you . . ."

One voice rings out, loud and clear: "We must not stop playing. Not yet."

They turn to Petronius.

"First," says Petronius, "first let's play one last number. It has to be like that. Something appropriate."

They say nothing, and stare at him in astonishment as he stands there, authoritative and determined, by his great instrument.

"Well, Jason?" Alex says, looking searchingly at his friend. He smiles.

"Well, what's a minute or two either way."

Jim and Georges come back from the railing and pick up their violins.

"What shall we play?"

Jason has to answer. Then something occurs to him.

"Let's play Handel's *Largo*," he says. "Do you all know it?"

They nod.

"My mother taught it to me," says Jason, half aloud.

They play.

⚜

Then everything happens very quickly. A funnel collapses and people scream in anguish, leap overboard, or are carried out into the icy sea by falling debris. Thousands of cups, glasses, and plates crash to the deck, a piano rolls along the railing, a case of champagne explodes. From inside the ship comes another colossal crash as the boilers are wrenched loose and slide forward, smashing everything on their way. No one had a thought for music and no one heard what they were playing. No one knows what the musicians were thinking during those last minutes. They were separated from each other as they ran to save themselves.

What they saw was the lights on board flickering, flickering once, then vanishing altogether. The ship and the sea were in pitch darkness.

Then they could see the stars. They were unusually clear.

❧

Then the ship sank.

POSTSCRIPT

———◆◆◆◆———

IT seems necessary to point out that the musicians described in this novel bear no relation to the actual musicians, who all went down with the ship on April 15, 1912, together with 1,495 other passengers and crew.

The real musicians were:

Wallace Henry Hartley (leader)
George Krins (violin)
Roger Bricoux (cello)
W. Theodore Brailey (piano)
J. Wesley Woodward (cello)
P. C. Taylor (piano)
J.F.C. Clarke (double bass)
John Law Hume (violin)

Stories could also be told about them, about the heartless aftermath of the disaster for the parents of young John Law Hume. They sought compensation for the loss of their only son (he was just twenty-one). Neither the company nor the agent felt called on to pay any kind of compensation or pensions. On the contrary, the Hume family received a demand for five shillings and fourpence to cover the loss of their son's uniform, the property of the agent.

A story could also be told of bandleader Wallace Hartley's monumental funeral in his hometown of Colne after his body was found. Or of the great memorial concert given in aid of the bereaved and held in the Royal Albert Hall, at which five hundred musicians from seven orchestras played, conducted by Sir Edward Elgar. The musicians were so numerous they almost had to be stacked up the walls. It was the largest professional orchestra the world had ever seen at the time, and the concert was one of the great events in London that spring. The organ thundered and stylish hats swayed becomingly in the audience. Stories about that could also be told, and a great deal more about the *Titanic* and the people on board. But all those are other stories which others have told or will tell. I have wanted to tell mine, and my musicians are invented.

Details about the ship and her days at sea are essentially true, taken from the mass of information available on the *Titanic*. The question alone of what the musicians played at the end has given rise to fierce debates among "Titanicologists." According to recent research, it seems fairly evident that the last piece they played was not a hymn but a melancholy waltz in fashion at the time: "Songe d'automne," a tune that may be familiar to older readers.

But this is a novel and not a history book, and I have also invented what happened during the musicians' last hours.

Walter Lord of New York is the author of the books *A Night to Remember* and *The Night Lives On*. I owe him a debt of gratitude for his patient written answers to my questions, including that of the orchestra's last tune. Similarly, I would like to thank John Maxtone-Graham of New York, the author of the wonderful history of trans-atlantic steamers *The Only Way to Cross*, who kindly contributed information and was good enough to encourage me in the writing of this book.

Finally, I would like to thank all those who have otherwise helped me, friends and experts, at home and abroad, as well as my own family.

Erik Fosnes Hansen

FINIS

Leningrad—Stuttgart—Tversted—Vienna—Anguillara—
Rome—Capranica—Oslo
MCMLXXXVI–MCMXC